Elizabeth Murphy was born in Liverpool and has lived in Merseyside all her life. When she was twelve, her father gave her a sixpenny book from a second-hand bookstall, *Liverpool Table Talk One Hundred Years Ago*, which led to her lifelong interest in Liverpool's history.

Throughout her girlhood, she says, there was an endless serial story unfolding in her mind with a constantly changing cast of characters, but it was only in the 1970s that she started to commit the stories to paper. Her first novel, *The Land is Bright*, was shortlisted for the Romantic Novel of the Year Award in 1989 and the continuation of the story of the Ward family, *To Give and to Take*, *There is a Season*, *A Nest of Singing Birds* and *Honour Thy Father*, won even more readers and gathered critical acclaim, as did her novels *A Wise Child* and *When Day is Done* (all available from Headline).

Praise for Elizabeth Murphy's heartwarming Liverpool sagas:

'The whole-heartedness of Liverpool shines through in a refreshing tribute to Merseyside' *Liverpool Daily Post*

'As heartwarming as it's sincere, this is storytelling at its best' *Best*

'A family saga you won't be able to put down' *Prima*

'A rolling domestic drama of many years filled with triumph and tragedy' *Lancashire Evening Post*

Also by Elizabeth Murphy

The Land Is Bright
To Give And To Take
There Is A Season
A Nest Of Singing Birds
A Wise Child
Honour Thy Father
When Day Is Done

Comfort Me With Apples

Elizabeth Murphy

HEADLINE

First published in 1999
by HEADLINE BOOK PUBLISHING

First published in paperback in 2000
by HEADLINE BOOK PUBLISHING

10 9 8 7 6 5 4

ISBN 0 7472 6300 0

Typeset by Avon Dataset Ltd, Bidford-on-Avon, Warks

Printed and bound in Great Britain by
Clays Ltd, St Ives plc

HEADLINE BOOK PUBLISHING
A division of the Hodder Headline Group
338 Euston Road
London NW1 3BH

www.headline.co.uk
www.hodderheadline.com

For my family, with all my love.

Stay me with flagons, comfort me with apples:
For I am sick of love

Song of Solomon, ii:5

Chapter One

The first Sunday in January 1900 was bitterly cold, but the congregation streaming from St Francis Xavier's church in Everton, Liverpool, greeted each other cheerfully with cries of 'a happy new century'.

Anna and Dorrie Furlong moved out with the crowd, greeting and being greeted by their many friends, and Dorrie clutched her sister's arm.

'Isn't it exciting, Anna?' she exclaimed. 'A completely new century!' Her blue eyes were sparkling and her cheeks pink with excitement as she waved and smiled around her.

Anna looked down at her affectionately and squeezed her arm. At nineteen, two years older than Dorrie, she was completely different in looks and temperament. In contrast to Dorrie's fashionably rounded figure and milk-and-roses complexion, Anna was tall and thin, with a pale complexion, brown eyes and smooth dark hair. She was as quiet and reserved as Dorrie was lively and outgoing, and her friendships, though fewer, were deep and lasting. Dorrie had many admirers among the young men of the parish but treated all equally.

One of these was James Hargreaves, a pale and plump young man, the only son of a possessive, widowed mother. He had admired Dorrie from afar for many years, but although he saw her every week when he accompanied his mother to church, he had never spoken to her.

One memorable morning his mother was confined to her bed with sciatica and he went to Mass alone. He sat where he could look at Dorrie throughout the service and when he left Anna and Dorrie were standing in the porch, talking to the local doctor and his wife.

'Good morning, Hargreaves,' Dr O'Brien had greeted him. 'How is your mother?'

James had mumbled a reply and the doctor had introduced him to his wife and the two young ladies. James was scarcely conscious of the others, as Dorrie smiled at him and he fell deeply and irrevocably in love with her.

After that he felt that he only existed from one Sunday to the next, when he could see Dorrie, although he never found an excuse to speak to her again, and he had managed to conceal his love from his mother until this first Sunday of 1900.

Anna and Dorrie had moved away from the crowd streaming towards the gates, and into the courtyard to wait for a friend. As James left the church with his mother, a dumpy woman dressed in black with a jet trimmed bonnet, heavily veiled, he saw Dorrie and eagerly raised his hat and smiled at her.

Dorrie smiled and nodded and Mrs Hargreaves looked at her, then at her son. She immediately let her large prayer book fall to the ground and exclaimed loudly, '*James*! You are so *clumsy*!' The young man, although so stolid in appearance, flushed deeply as he bent to retrieve the book.

His face was still red as he turned away, keeping his face averted from Dorrie, and Anna was disgusted. 'What a hateful woman!' she exclaimed to Dorrie. 'Her son didn't touch the prayer book. She let it fall deliberately.'

Before Dorrie could reply they were joined by the girl they had been waiting for, Isabel Jenson, who lived near them in Westbourne Street, and like them was the daughter of a ship's captain. She greeted them and said she had seen the incident.

'Isn't she a ridiculous old woman? Still wearing widow's

2

weeds and her husband died years ago when the son was a baby,' she said scornfully.

Anna agreed. 'She looks like Queen Victoria with those clothes and that sour expression.'

'I'm so sorry for Mr Hargreaves,' said Dorrie. 'He seemed so embarrassed.' Anna squeezed Dorrie's arm, feeling a rush of affection for her sweet-natured sister and shame at her own sharp tongue.

The girls were joined by Dr and Mrs O'Brien. 'Good morning. A happy new century, young ladies,' the doctor said heartily, as his wife murmured and smiled beside him.

'A happy new century!' they echoed.

'Let's hope it is,' he said. 'The last one finished badly enough, God knows. Nothing but bad news from South Africa all through December. Defeats at Magersfontein and Colenso, and Ladysmith and Mafeking and Kimberley all under siege. And by a bunch of Boer farmers! The disgrace!'

'The girls don't want to talk about the war,' said Mrs O'Brien. She explained to the girls, 'He worries because his nephews are in South Africa with the Army,' and glanced fondly at her husband.

'The Irish regiments have done well though,' he said. 'Even Queen Victoria spoke about "her brave Irish".' O'Brien was a big red-faced Irishman and looked more like a farmer than a doctor, but the girls knew his bluff manner concealed sensitivity and compassion for all his patients.

As he spoke he had been constantly raising his top hat to the many people who greeted him and, still doing this, he said, 'Well, things will be better now that Bobs will be taking charge. We'll soon hear better news.'

'Bobs, doctor?' Dorrie said enquiringly and he replied, 'Lord Roberts, my dear. The best soldier in the British Army.'

'And an Irishman, of course,' his wife teased him.

3

They all laughed and Dr O'Brien said heartily, 'A pity you were not able to attend the Midnight Mass on New Year's Eve, Miss Anna. You'd have enjoyed the music.'

'Yes, I hoped to go with the Deagans from next door, but . . . it wasn't possible,' Anna said quietly.

She said nothing about the scene with her mother, who had declared that her nerves would be unable to stand Anna 'wandering the streets at that hour' and Dr O'Brien said, 'Pity. You'd have appreciated the music.'

'It was wonderful,' said Mrs O'Brien. 'At the stroke of midnight Fr Hayes came on to the high altar to start the Mass and the choir burst into the Gloria.'

'And sang magnificently throughout the Mass,' the doctor said. 'They finished with "The Heavens are Telling" from Haydn's *Creation*. Wonderful! I'll never forget it.'

'We went into church in one century and came out in another. So exciting,' his wife said and the doctor added, 'The moon was shining and I looked up at it and thought how many centuries it had looked down on this old earth, and seen mankind making the same mistakes over and over again. Perhaps this century will be different. With all these new ideas and cures found for illnesses, perhaps at least disease and war and poverty will be banished from the earth.'

'We must pray for that,' said Mrs O'Brien. She shivered suddenly and her husband looked at her with concern. 'Are you cold, my dear?' he asked, but she shook her head. 'No. A goose walked over my grave as my grandmother used to say. She believed in the second sight.' She smiled at him.

'We'd better move anyway,' he said. 'It's too cold to stand about.'

The group moved away, disappointing several young men who were hanging about hoping to walk home with Dorrie. Mrs O'Brien walked ahead with Dorrie and Isabel, asking

4

about Isabel's father, who was due home, and Anna followed with Dr O'Brien.

'I hoped to see your mama at church,' the doctor said. 'The Cullens offered seats in their carriage for your mother and aunt, y'know.'

'I didn't know,' Anna said quietly. 'Mama felt faint this morning and Aunt Clara went to eight o'clock Mass.'

'Well, well, perhaps when your father is home,' the doctor said.

'That won't be for several months,' Anna said. 'They're still trading along the China coast.'

'The weather should be better then anyway,' said Dr O'Brien. 'That will encourage your mama to leave the house.'

They had reached his home and surgery in Shaw Street and the three girls said goodbye and walked up to Westbourne Street, Isabel and Dorrie chattering and laughing, but Anna very silent. It was clear to her that the doctor thought her mother should be trying to live a more normal life.

After the birth of Dorrie, Mrs Furlong had borne five more daughters, all of whom had died at birth or soon afterwards. Captain Furlong's mother died soon after the death of the fifth baby, leaving his only sister alone in the family home in Hull.

He had arranged for the house in Hull to be closed and his sister, Clara, to come to live with them as a help and comfort to his wife while he was at sea. Unfortunately, he had not consulted his wife or his sister and the arrangement had been a disaster.

Under a veneer of sweetness there was a state of war between the two women, and as Anna and Dorrie grew up they were often unwillingly involved in it.

Eventually Mrs Furlong had decided to retire to her sofa to cultivate ill health, leaving her shrewish sister-in-law to take charge of the household.

Now the three girls had reached the Jenson house in Westbourne Street, where a row of little boys in sailor suits stood looking out of the parlour window. Isabel laughed. 'I've told them Papa can't come home yet. Told them about the tides, but they won't leave the window.'

She and Anna and Dorrie smiled and waved at the little boys and Dorrie said wistfully, 'It's so pleasant to see such affection, Isabel. They're lovely little boys.'

'They're all so excited, yet they've been as good as gold, except Wilma. She's so different to the boys. She never stops crying,' said Isabel.

'Better now than when your father arrives,' Dorrie consoled her, and Isabel laughed and ran lightly up the steps of the house. She was the eldest of a family of six boys and a baby girl and she stayed at home to help her mother.

As they stood with Isabel, three of the Deagan family from next to the Furlongs had passed, Jim and Luke raising their hats and Norah smiling at the girls. Anna was relieved that she had not offended them by refusing their invitation on New Year's Eve.

The Deagans were a large family of three sons and three daughters and a widowed mother. The eldest girl, Maggie, was married, but the others, although much older than Anna and Dorrie, were single, living happily at home. They had always been kind to the two small girls next door, and when they discovered that Anna shared their love of music Jim and Norah began taking her to concerts.

Now, as Anna and Dorrie left Isabel and walked along Westbourne Street, Dorrie said gently, 'Is something wrong, Anna? Don't you feel well? You're very quiet.'

Anna smiled bitterly. 'Nothing wrong with my health, Dorrie,' she said. 'In fact nothing wrong with me at all, except I'm ashamed to say I'm envying Isabel her happy home.'

6

Dorrie sighed. 'I know. She's very fortunate,' she said. 'But who knows, Anna? Things might be different at home in the new century.'

Anna laughed, and squeezed Dorrie's arm. 'Always the optimist, Dorrie,' she said. 'But as you say, who knows? Miracles can happen, I suppose.'

Now, as they entered their house, they could hear their aunt scolding the girl who helped in the kitchen and they turned into the parlour where their mother lay on a sofa before a blazing fire. Coming in from the frosty morning, the room seemed unbearably hot to the girls, but Dorrie sat down beside her mother.

'How do you feel, Mama?' she asked gently.

Her mother sighed. 'Dreadful, dearest, dreadful. My poor head aches so and Aunt Clara has been so obnoxious. Bathe my head, Dorrie.'

Dorrie took the eau de Cologne from a side table and Anna stood up. 'I'll go to help Aunt Clara, Mama,' she said. 'It sounds as though I'm needed.'

'She has young Ada,' her mother said peevishly. 'But she makes a difficulty of everything. She doesn't think the girl should do anything for me.'

Anna said nothing, but went upstairs and covered her Sunday dress in a large holland pinafore before going to the kitchen.

She was greeted with a storm of complaints from her aunt, a thin woman with a sour expression and grey hair drawn back tightly in a bun. 'Too much is left to me. I can't do everything. Bad enough that this girl is so slow, but your mother keeps ringing for her to make up the fire or make her a drink. How does she think the dinner will be cooked?' she demanded.

'Tell me what's to be done and I'll do it,' Anna said, managing to smile at the girl behind her aunt's back. Ada,

7

who had seemed tearful, looked more cheerful and Anna followed her muttering aunt into the dining room and began to lay the table.

'My brother would be horrified if he knew how I am put upon. How much is expected of me,' Clara Furlong complained.

'You can tell him when he comes home,' Anna said dryly, but then, fearing the sulks which would result, she added, 'Captain Jenson's ship docks today. The little boys are very excited. They were standing at the parlour window, waiting for him.'

'Let's hope they have some discipline from him. Mrs Jenson spoils them,' Clara said.

Anna made no reply and when she had finished laying the table she returned to the kitchen, but her aunt told her crossly she was only in the way so she went back to the parlour.

Her mother appeared to be sleeping so she joined Dorrie, who was sitting nearby. Any handiwork was forbidden on a Sunday so they whispered together for a few minutes, Anna saying that her aunt had refused help. 'Determined to be a martyr,' she said.

Mrs Furlong opened her eyes. 'Tell Aunt Clara I'll have a tray today, Anna, but you must prepare it. I don't want to cause her any more work.'

Anna gave her mother's message to her aunt, who snorted and said spitefully, 'I know why she wants you to prepare it and so do you. I'm not daft.'

Anna said nothing, but replaced her pinafore and picked up the carving knife and fork. A sirloin of beef had already been taken into the dining room and she went to the sideboard to carve a generous helping for her mother. Then Ada began to carry in tureens of vegetables and Anna filled her mother's plate from them.

'The tray's ready in the 'all,' Ada whispered. 'I done a separate jug of gravy for it.'

'Thanks, Ada,' Anna said, smiling at her, then she took the well-filled plate to the tray and quickly carried it to her mother before her aunt could see it. When she returned to the kitchen her aunt was ordering Ada to take the roast potatoes through and Anna was told to start carving.

Aunt Clara bustled about, closing dampers and moving the kettle, while Anna went to the dining room. She was met at the door by Ada with some roast potatoes on a small plate. 'The missis didn't get no roasts,' she whispered and Anna slipped back to the parlour and handed the plate to Dorrie at the door.

'Better late than never, I suppose,' she heard her mother complain before she returned to the dining room. As she rapidly carved the joint Anna reflected bitterly that even Ada was aware of the charade that revolved around her mother's meals.

When Adelaide Furlong had first taken to her sofa Anna or Dorrie had prepared trays laden with generous meals for their mother. Later, when Clara had taken complete charge, the kitchen had been forbidden to them so their aunt prepared the trays.

She had astounded Adelaide by serving her a tiny portion of steamed fish, a coddled egg or other invalid fare instead of the well-filled plate of meat and vegetables she was accustomed to. 'Much better for you while you are so inactive,' Clara said sweetly.

Clara continued to cook tasty meals for herself and the girls, carefully leaving the kitchen door open so that appetising smells drifted through the house. After a short spell of this Adelaide decided that she would force herself to sit at the table for her meals. She was unwilling to make more work for dear Clara, she said.

9

Now only on Sundays, when the girls were allowed to help in the kitchen, could she indulge her wish to have a tray brought to her sofa, knowing that her daughters would ensure that she received enough to satisfy her hearty appetite.

It's like a war, Anna thought now, and about *food*. It's so degrading. She said so to Dorrie when their mother and aunt were having a nap after dinner and they were able to escape to their bedroom.

'I suppose food becomes very important to an invalid,' Dorrie said doubtfully. 'The days must seem long to Mama.'

'But Dr O'Brien seems to think Mama could do more if she wished, Dorrie,' Anna said.

'Perhaps she would if Aunt Clara wasn't here,' said Dorrie. 'You know how she likes to be in charge in the kitchen.'

'And everywhere else,' Anna said bitterly. 'Oh, I detest her. She can't say a good word about anyone. Even when I spoke about the Jensons she said the children were spoilt.'

'But they're lovely children. Everyone says so,' Dorrie said indignantly.

They were silent for a moment then Anna suddenly burst out, 'Oh, Dorrie, I hope I don't grow into a bitter old maid like her.'

Dorrie put her arm round Anna's shoulders. 'Don't be silly,' she said affectionately. 'You could never be like her and, anyway, you're bound to marry, Anna.'

Anna smiled ruefully. 'I'm not so sure. Not much sign so far, is there?' she said.

'That's because you freeze men off. You don't encourage them. In fact, you're not even friendly with them, as you would be if they were girls,' said Dorrie.

'I don't want them to think I'm chasing them,' Anna muttered. 'I see enough girls doing that.'

'But you don't have to go to the other extreme,' Dorrie retorted.

Anna laughed, but the thought of becoming like her aunt was a real worry to her. She knew she saw faults in people far more easily than Dorrie did, and she tried to curb her sharp tongue, but sometimes remarks would pop out before she could stop them.

She tried to explain this to Dorrie, but her sister only said, 'You're just witty and you think quickly, that's where you're different from me, but you never say anything to hurt people.'

'Not intentionally,' Anna said. 'But perhaps I do without meaning to. And perhaps that's how Aunt Clara started and she gradually got more malicious.'

'*Never*!' Dorrie said emphatically. 'I'm sure she's always been wicked and enjoyed hurting people.'

'I can't remember her being any other way,' Anna admitted. 'I remember when the last little baby was born and Aunt Clara came here. She said to Father, with a horrible smirk, "Another rose for your rosebud garden of girls, Jeremiah." '

'Yes, and you told me it was because Father admired Mr Tennyson's poetry,' Dorrie said. 'It was only years later that we realised it was because Father was hoping for a son, and she was pleased that he and Mama were disappointed.'

'Fancy you remembering that, Dorrie,' said Anna. 'You would only be about nine and I was eleven when the baby was born.'

Dorrie sighed. 'Yes, and poor little Emma died so soon afterwards anyway,' she said. 'But I've noticed that Aunt Clara has that same horrible look on her face whenever she's saying anything very nasty. Never think you could be *anything* like her, Anna. You haven't got that malice in you.'

'I hope not,' Anna said. She changed the subject, unwilling

to tell Dorrie the other reason she thought she might be an old maid. When they were children she had overheard a visitor remark, 'What a pity they're not alike. Dorothea so pretty and the other girl so plain.'

Anna had never forgotten those words and as she and Dorrie grew older she noticed the differences in their looks and characters more and more, especially in the company of young men. They all vied for Dorrie's attention and ignored Anna, or used her as an excuse to draw near to Dorrie, but Anna knew it was not her sister's fault. She did nothing to invite it except be herself.

They heard movement downstairs and went down to make tea for their mother and some scones and fruit pies to follow the cold meat of the evening meal. Ada had Sunday off after she had washed the dinner dishes and Aunt Clara sat in the parlour reading missionary magazines while Anna and Dorrie prepared the meal.

Afterwards, the girls set off to attend Evening Benediction at the church, where they saw many of their friends, sons and daughters of large families in the parish.

James Hargreaves was there alone. He was rarely seen without his mother and never seemed free to join the many clubs and sodalities attached to the church, and Anna whispered to Dorrie, 'Has the worm turned, do you think?' He passed by them as they left the church and gazed hungrily at Dorrie, and because she suspected that his heightened colour meant he was remembering his humiliation of the morning, she smiled warmly at him.

He was soon pushed aside by others claiming Dorrie's attention and was too diffident to fight back, but he walked away thinking only of the warmth of her smile.

Aunt Clara opened the door to Dorrie and Anna when they returned home, and she was obviously in a bad temper. 'Your mother's asleep again,' she snapped. 'I don't know why. She never does anything to make her tired. I'm the one who's worn out.'

The two girls said nothing, but went into the parlour where their mother lay asleep on the sofa. In sleep the peevish lines on her face were smoothed away and there were signs of the beauty she had been, in her small straight nose and soft mouth and the long lashes lying on her cheeks.

'She must have been lovely when she was young,' Dorrie whispered, and Anna smiled and nodded.

They went to the kitchen where their aunt was banging about, and began to prepare supper. Aunt Clara was still grumbling and to divert her Dorrie made an innocent remark about her mother being a Society beauty. It only provoked more fury.

'Society beauty! Is that what she told you? More of her fairytales!' Clara snapped. 'She was a ladies' maid. That was the nearest she got to Society! And where she got her airs and graces. I suppose she told you she married beneath her too! Let me tell you, miss, your mother took a step up in the world when she married my brother. He should have done better for himself.'

Dorrie shrank back and burst into tears, but Anna said furiously, 'That's not your business or ours and you shouldn't be talking to us like this.'

Clara, who had said more than she intended, replied quietly, 'I can't abide lies and you shouldn't be speaking to *me* like that.'

Dorrie had already rushed to the parlour and Anna said briefly, 'Mama doesn't tell lies. Dorrie misunderstood. That's all,' then picked up the tray and followed her sister.

When her mother stirred Dorrie dried her tears and was plumping up cushions behind Mrs Furlong when Anna walked in, followed by Clara. Nothing was said about the scene in the kitchen, and after drinking cups of tea and refusing sandwiches the two girls said goodnight and went to their bedroom.

'I hope it's safe to leave them together while Aunt Clara's in such a temper,' said Dorrie.

'Don't worry. They'll be all sweetness with one another,' Anna said bitterly. 'That's what sickens me.'

'If only Father hadn't brought her here,' Dorrie mourned. 'We could be so happy, just you and I and Mama.'

'He had no right to do it without asking them,' Anna said suddenly. 'Women are *people* with feelings and ideas, not chattels to be moved about to suit men.'

'But he did it for the best, Anna,' Dorrie protested. 'He must have been so worried, going off on a long voyage with Mama so grief-stricken and Aunt Clara alone in Hull. You can see why he did it.'

'I still say he should have consulted them,' Anna said stubbornly, 'and us, although we were only children. He's been home often since then though, and never asked how it was working.'

'But Mama and Aunt Clara never quarrel when he's at home,' Dorrie said innocently, 'and they don't even talk about each other to us.'

Anna smiled at her with affection. Dorrie's like the three wise monkeys, she thought. See no evil, hear no evil, speak no evil.

They had been preparing for bed as they talked and Dorrie was soon asleep, but Anna lay awake, her mind too active for sleep. Eventually she got up and stood looking out of the window. Frost rimed the branches of the trees in the little park opposite the house and further down the hill she could see moonlight glinting cold and blue on the roofs of the houses in Shaw Street. She thought of the doctor's words about the moon shining down on the world and of how little she knew of it.

If only I was a man, she thought, I could be on a battlefield far away like the doctor's nephews, or sail the seven seas like Father. Even if I stayed in Liverpool my life would be different, more free.

Sometimes, when she listened to music, Anna had a sensation of a door opening on a wider world, but she could never pass through it. Disgust at the events of the day, the pettiness of the quarrels, and the narrowness of her existence overwhelmed her.

Is this all there is? she thought. There must be more to life than this. She looked ahead and saw her life as an endless procession of empty days, with interminable Sundays, the same ritual of meals, the same petty quarrels and hidden warfare between her aunt and her mother.

She saw all the paltry restrictions of her narrow life, away from all that was happening in the world. I can't bear it, Anna thought, beating her hands on the windowsill in frustration. Yet what can I do? Nothing.

She realised that she was trembling, not only with anger, but with cold. She crept into bed, moving close to the warmth of her sister's body, but careful not to touch her with her icy feet, and eventually she fell asleep.

The next day was one of Anna's days for helping at the Ragged School and she felt ashamed of her self-pity when she saw the poor hungry children who came for the free dinner which she had helped to prepare.

When Anna left school she had hoped to train as a nurse or a teacher or to work in an office, but her father had dismissed the idea. 'I can support my daughters,' he said, and his word was law.

Jim Deagan, the eldest son next door, had offered to find Anna a place as a clerk in a Friendly Society, and when Anna told him that she would be forbidden to take it, he spoke to her father.

'It's quite usual now for unmarried girls to work, sir,' he said. 'Although not married women, of course.' But Captain Furlong was adamant. He could, however, find no reason for refusing to allow Anna to do charitable work, so another of the Deagan family arranged for her to help with the free dinners two mornings a week.

Dr O'Brien had also asked the captain to allow Dorrie to make regular visits to one of his patients, a Mrs Wendell. She was a widow, alone in the world, so it was almost impossible for the captain or his wife to refuse Dorrie this limited freedom.

Dorrie arrived home from a visit to Mrs Wendell at the same time as Anna so they went into the house together. They found their mother and aunt sitting together, both anxious to be the first to announce an item of news.

'Dr O'Brien has been in,' Mrs Furlong said immediately. 'Mrs Hargreaves died last night!'

'An apoplectic seizure,' Aunt Clara cut in. 'Doctor said he'd expected it for years.'

'But we saw Mr Hargreaves at Benediction,' Dorrie gasped. 'Did she die alone?'

'No. He was there,' said Clara. 'Ran for the doctor, but it was too late.'

'Poor Mrs Hargreaves. Like our dear Queen, she never recovered from the death of her husband,' Mrs Furlong sighed sentimentally. 'Death was a merciful release for her.'

'And for her son,' Anna whispered to Dorrie as they hung their coats in the hall, but Dorrie only said, 'Poor man. I feel so sorry for him.'

Mrs Wendell had heard the news and was agog when Dorrie went to see her again. 'I never liked Amelia Hargreaves, or

Seddon as she was. Our families were neighbours, but we were never friends. She was always taking offence, imagining she was being slighted or insulted, and she was such a man chaser!'

'A man chaser!' Dorrie gasped. 'I can't imagine it.'

'Oh yes. Poor Sam Hargreaves was too nice and too gentle, that's how she caught him, and he had a terrible life with her. Nag, nag, nag, then when he died, the tears! I swear the Mersey rose.'

Dorrie, who enjoyed the old lady's salty comments, smiled at her. 'I don't think her son had a very happy life with her either. He never seemed very free or happy.'

'I don't think there'll be many tears shed for her, except by her brother, because they were two of a kind,' said Mrs Wendell. 'Still, I'd like to attend her Requiem, although I won't be invited to the funeral. Would you be able to come with me, dear?' and when Dorrie agreed she said with a satisfied sigh, 'This is where it makes such a difference to me, having your company, Dorrie. Now I can plan these little outings.'

Dorrie's lips twitched at Mrs Wendell's idea of 'a little outing', but she was fond of the old lady and she also thought it would be comforting for James Hargreaves if the church was full of people, so she readily made the arrangements for them to attend.

There was only a small group of official mourners, but there were many other people in the church to attend the Requiem Mass. People like Mrs Wendell, who had known the family in earlier years, and others who attended every Requiem or Nuptial Mass as ordinary worshippers. Some came to fill empty lives, watching the joys or sorrows of others.

Whatever their reasons for being there, Dorrie was pleased to see the church so full for James's sake. Yet, as James

Hargreaves followed his mother's coffin, it was only Dorrie's face he saw in all the large congregation.

Chapter Two

The chief mourners at the funeral were James and his Uncle James Seddon, his mother's bachelor brother who was general manager in the firm of cotton brokers where James was a clerk.

James felt no grief for his mother. She had never shown him any affection and as a child his main feeling for her had been fear, although he craved her approval. It was soon after his father's death when he was little more than a baby that she began beating him, and the beatings increased in ferocity as he grew older. He knew that she enjoyed them by the way she licked her lips as she reached for the cane.

Amelia Hargreaves knew that James was afraid of the dark, so she often locked him in the cupboard under the stairs or in the coal cellar. It was his job to carry the coal up from the cellar, a room whose only light came from the door at the top of the steps. James always shovelled the coal frantically into the scuttle, knowing that at any moment his mother might shut and lock the door, leaving him terror-stricken in pitch darkness, perhaps for hours. Even when the door was opened and he made a rush for the stairs she sometimes shut it in his face.

James dreaded most the visits from his uncle, who came several times a month and sometimes stayed the night. At first his mother asked her brother to beat James, saying, 'He needs a man's hand, Brother. It's too much for a weak woman.' They always took James to his bedroom and made him strip naked for the beatings.

One night when he was about ten years old he was made to stand before them after the beating and as they examined him his mother wailed that he would never be a proper man. With the same sanctimonious air with which he intoned, 'Spare the rod and spoil the child,' his uncle handled James's genitals and sighed, 'Poor boy. How sad. I'll do what I can, Sister, but . . .' He shook his head.

Torn between fear and humiliation James stammered, 'What is it? Am I going to die?'

Neither answered. His mother only said curtly, 'Get into bed,' and they left the room. A little later, as he lay there trembling, his uncle reappeared in his nightshirt, carrying a candle.

'You are an ignorant boy, James, but I am going to do what I can to help you for the sake of my poor sister.' He blew out the candle and slipped into bed beside James. What followed was so unbelievable and so horrifying that James's mind refused to accept it. He must have passed out at some stage, as he came to with his uncle gone and his mother shaking him.

'Get up,' she said harshly. 'Come to the scullery.' He stumbled after her, scarcely able to walk. There was an earthenware bowl half full of water in the scullery and his mother poured in the contents of a large black kettle, and handed him a bar of soap and a flannel. 'Wash yourself thoroughly,' she said. 'Then go back to bed. There's a clean nightshirt.'

He washed and went back to bed, feeling that it was all a nightmare. Only the pain he felt made it real, but his mother handed him a cup of dark liquid. 'Drink that,' she said, and he drank and fell asleep almost immediately.

His uncle's next visit passed as though nothing had happened, but after that his visits to James's bed were often repeated, always on the pretext of 'helping him'. The physical damage was never as bad after the first time, but the fear and revulsion that James felt increased with every visit.

His mother warned him that nothing must be said about his uncle's efforts to help him. 'We don't want people to know you're a freak,' she said, and she never left him alone with Frances O'Neill, a small woman with a deformed spine who came daily to clean, and who was the only person who ever showed him kindness.

School should have been a respite for James, but his mother's love of food and hatred of waste meant that he was made to eat up the vegetables swimming in butter and the stodgy puddings she enjoyed but was unable to finish and the fatty meat she disliked. As a result, he was not only nervous and timid but fat and spotty, and a natural butt for the school bullies and a sadistic teacher.

The visits from his uncle ceased quite suddenly and as James grew taller than his mother the beatings also ceased, but her verbal and emotional abuse of him increased and destroyed any confidence he might have had in himself.

When he was fourteen school was exchanged for a position as a clerk in the cotton brokers where James's uncle was general manager, but it was only one misery exchanged for another. He made no friends, as the other clerks resented his connection with the general manager, and the office manager, a toady of his uncle, constantly found fault with James.

Lonely and unhappy, James, as usual, hid his feelings behind a dull and stolid appearance and rarely spoke. Each evening, when he returned from the office, he and his mother had the usual heavy meal, after which she slept for an hour while James did various household tasks, then he was required to play cards with her. He was too used to submitting to his domineering mother to resist, but it was a miserable existence, made bearable for James only by the opportunity to see Dorrie on Sunday mornings.

After the scene with the prayer book he and his mother rode home in silence in a cab, but as soon as they were inside the house Mrs Hargreaves began to scream at James.

In spite of his anger and bitter sense of humiliation, long habit made him stand silently while she poured out a torrent of abuse, but when she screeched, 'Don't you know you're only a laughing stock to them? A fat, stupid fool and a laughing stock. Only a harlot like that girl would encourage you,' something seemed to burst in his brain.

'Don't you dare to speak of her like that!' he shouted, stepping towards her threateningly. 'She's so— So—' He felt that if he stayed he would physically attack his mother and turned and rushed out of the house.

His mind was a jumble of emotions as he strode along the quiet Sunday streets – rage at his mother, humiliation when he thought of the scene at the church, love when he thought of Dorrie and even, after a lifetime of being told he was at fault, a feeling of guilt at his behaviour to his mother.

He walked about for hours, unaware of his surroundings and of the people he passed, his mind in turmoil. Gradually he became calmer, and when he heard a church bell he was surprised to find that he had walked full-circle and was once again near St Francis Xavier's church. He felt suddenly exhausted and went to compose his mind, soothed by the familiar ritual of the Benediction, and making vague plans.

He saw Anna and Dorrie as he left and flushed at the memory of his humiliation that morning, but Dorrie smiled at him warmly. The thought of that smile and his musings in church gave him the courage to confront his mother again, determined to ignore any abuse she flung at him.

His mother had been stoking up her anger all the time he

was away and as soon as he appeared she unleashed it. 'How dare you defy me?' she screamed. 'I'm your mother. You owe me respect, but you've always been useless and ungrateful. I wasted my life with your fool of a father and ruined my health when you were born and for what? A half-witted idiot who's been nothing but a curse to me and a disgrace to my dear brother, who deserves better.'

She stopped for breath, and James stood, half turned away, his lips set, letting the abuse wash over him, but when she went on, 'And now making a show of me, you fat, stupid fool, with that common brazen hussy who's only laughing up her sleeve at you,' it was too much.

He bent over her, staring at her with hatred and shouting, 'That's enough! You evil, foul-mouthed old bitch. You're not fit to wipe her shoes.'

The effect on his mother was dramatic. She fell back in her chair, gasping for breath, with her face purple and her eyes protruding. There was no one he could ask for help so he ran to Dr O'Brien's surgery. Fortunately, the doctor was at home and returned with him immediately, but they found Mrs Hargreaves already dead.

'It's my fault,' James said. 'I killed her. I called her an evil, foul-mouthed old bitch.'

'And what had she said to you to cause that, eh?' the doctor said shrewdly. 'Now, listen to me, young man. I don't want to hear any more of that. Your mother died of a bad temper, no matter what I put on the death certificate. She wasn't the first of my patients to die of that and she won't be the last. I've warned her about overeating and allowing herself to fall into these rages, so she was responsible for her own death, nobody else.'

'But it was right after I shouted at her,' James said.

'No matter. She could have controlled her temper, but she

chose to indulge in it. I don't want to hear another word about you blaming yourself, and say nothing to your uncle. I know all about the pair of them. My advice is put this behind you now and get on with your own life.'

He scribbled a note and went to the door to send a boy with it to his wife. 'Now, suppose we have a cup of tea,' he said. 'My wife will make the necessary arrangements and notify your uncle, and I'll stay with you until he arrives.'

They went to the kitchen and Dr O'Brien helped James on to a chair. 'You've had a shock,' he said. 'I'll make the tea.'

After drinking the tea and eating a thick slice of bread and butter James felt that he was back to normal, but when the doctor questioned him gently he spoke more freely than he had ever done, and Dr O'Brien gained an insight into his life and the events of the day, of which James would normally never have spoken.

Shortly afterwards, two women arrived to lay out the body, soon followed by James Seddon. 'My condolences,' the doctor said. 'A great shock for her son, but not unexpected.'

'What do you mean?' James Seddon barked, and Dr O'Brien said smoothly, 'I'm sure your sister has told you that I warned her about the state of her heart. Two inches of fat around it. This could have happened any time in the past few years.'

'She complained of her health, but a lot of that was distress caused by her son. Have you been upsetting her again?' James Seddon said fiercely to his nephew.

Before James could speak Dr O'Brien intervened. 'Mr Hargreaves has been a most devoted son, and he behaved admirably on this occasion. Did all the right things, but nothing could have saved his mother. She died shortly after I arrived.'

James listened with amazement but said nothing and his uncle growled, 'You surprise me. Not what I would have expected.'

Dr O'Brien stared at him and said deliberately, 'A family physician learns a great deal about his patients and their families, but, like a priest, we never divulge what we learn unless it is necessary.'

James Seddon stared back at him for a moment, then his gaze dropped and he said no more.

The doctor picked up his bag and James escorted him to the door and tried to thank him. Dr O'Brien put his hand on his arm. 'That fellow is a bully and a windbag. Stand up to him, James. Windbags are easily pricked.' He smiled. 'Don't forget, call me if you need me. My wife and I will do anything to help.'

'Th-thank you,' James stuttered, but the doctor was already gone.

James closed the door, feeling bemused, not least by the doctor's use of his Christian name, but it gave him a feeling of security, of having a friend.

James Seddon seemed unusually subdued, but he took charge of all the arrangements for the funeral. After the Requiem Mass, followed by the burial at Ford Cemetery, the mourners went to James Seddon's house in Fairfield to be served a meal by his grim housekeeper.

Everyone dispersed after the meal. James knew that his uncle would have liked them both to return to the office, but for form's sake they had the rest of the day off. After the gloom of his uncle's house James was relieved to find Frances O'Neill, at his own house with a bright fire burning and the kettle on for tea.

Although he pretended no grief for his mother he was astounded when Frances said cheerfully, 'You won't know yourself now, will you? You'll be able to have a bit of life for yourself at last.'

James was lost for words, but Frances was only saying what

he had already thought, that now he would be free to go where he would see Dorrie, even speak to her.

'Wasn't no life for a young man,' Frances went on. 'Stuck in the office all day with that Seddon, then coming home to do the housework that I couldn't do and play cards with your ma.'

'It was my duty,' James felt compelled to say, but Frances snorted.

'Aye, I know that's what she drilled into you,' she said. 'The truth is, you were too nice for your own good and she played on it like she done with your father. You take after him. There's nothing of her or your uncle in you.'

James smiled at her. He liked the plucky little woman who worked so hard in spite of her disability and, knowing nothing but bullying and disapproval all his life, her kindness had meant a great deal to him. She was a strong character who could give as good as she got from his mother, and had worked for her for many years despite frequent quarrels.

Mrs Hargreaves knew that no one else would work so hard for long hours and little pay as Frances, and it suited Frances to stay, so these storms always blew over. Frances had once told James that she stayed because without a regular job she would be used by her family.

'I'd just be a handrag for them, called on when any of them were confined or thought I'd be handy. Being as they're family I'd get no thanks and of course never a penny. This way I can do this and my other little job and I'm never there for them.'

James knew that her 'other little job' was cleaning offices very early in the morning and in the evening, before and after working for his mother.

Now she handed James a cup of tea and perched on a kitchen chair to drink her own, gazing at him with bright eyes, her head on one side. James was reminded of a thrush.

'What are you going to do now then?' she asked.

'I'm not going into the office today. My uncle isn't either, so it's all right,' he said, misunderstanding her.

'I don't mean that,' she said. 'I'm talking about what you're going to do with your life now you're on your own. D'you know what I'd do if I was you?'

'No. Go on – tell me,' he said, smiling at her.

'I'd strike out. Find another job. You'll never get nowhere in that office 'cos your uncle's against you. You'd have to carry on for a bit, get yourself sorted out like, but now's your chance to have a life of your own.'

James said nothing for a moment, sipping his tea and thinking, but he said finally, 'I think you're right, Frances, but I don't think I can do it. I mightn't get another place. I only got this job through my uncle and I'm pretty useless, you know.'

He smiled ruefully, but Frances said indignantly, 'No, you're not. That's only what she told you – and him – your uncle. You don't know what you can do without them on your back.'

James shrugged. 'I'd like to do it, Frances, but I need my salary. I mean, what about this house, the bills here? Mother handled all that, but we only just managed on my salary. I couldn't risk being without it.'

'There isn't much to lay out here. Food and coal, and a few shillings for cleaning stuff and lamp oil and that, and my few bob,' Frances said. 'The house is bought and paid for.'

She hesitated, then said, 'Your ma had a long stocking, y'know. She kept it quiet from you, but she had a good pension from your father's job and she saved outa your salary and all.'

'How do you know that?' James said in surprise.

'She had to talk to somebody and I suppose she thought I didn't matter. She had to brag how clever she was. I thought it was funny, a woman handling all the money, but she told me

27

once why she done it. She'd had a bit of money left to her when she was young, but when a woman got married everything she had was her husband's property like.'

'But that was altered in 1882. The Married Women's Property Act,' James said.

'I don't know about that,' said Frances. 'But she'd been married for a while then. As soon as she was married she started saving from her housekeeping money.'

'But why?' said James. 'I'm sure my father wouldn't have touched her money or insisted on his legal rights.'

'I know,' Frances said. 'But she said laws were made by men to suit men and it was up to women to look out for themselves. She was determined to have a nest egg that was just hers.'

'I never knew she felt like that,' James said. 'Or that she would do anything so secretive. She was such a pattern of rectitude.'

'That's the impression she gave,' Frances said dryly. 'She couldn't talk about it to her brother so I suppose that's why she talked to me. She knew I didn't blame her for hoarding the money, and it'll come in handy for you now, won't it?'

'If I can find it,' James said, but Frances said airily, 'I know where she kept it. At the back of her wardrobe. She got me to lift the bag on to her bed once. I think she wanted to count it.' She glanced at the clock, then carried her cup and saucer to the sink. 'I'd better get on,' she said. 'And you can go and look for the money. You'll need the key to her wardrobe.'

'My uncle took the keys,' James said. 'He's the executor of her will.'

Frances sat down again and stared at him in amazement. 'That didn't give him no right to take your keys,' she said. 'What did he say about the house and that?'

'He said the house and contents would be mine, but he'd supervise me,' said James.

'Why? You're over twenty-one, and anyway, it was your father left the house to you, not her. You want to go and see the lawyer fellow and ask him about your father's will. You needn't let on to old Seddon what you're doing.'

James looked stunned. 'I'm sure you're wrong, Frances,' he said. 'How could my father leave it to me? I was only a baby when he died.'

'I don't know. I only know he done it,' Frances said stubbornly. 'And with a lawyer. Your ma was in bed with sciatica and I was looking after her when your father come in and said he'd done what she said. "The house and contents and any money," he said. "It's all quite legal." Years after he died she told me he'd tricked her, left everything to her while she was alive and then to you. Real mad she was, calling him for everything. Said he was making sure your uncle never got nothing.'

James stood up and walked about, too agitated to keep still. 'It's unbelievable,' he said. 'All this and I knew nothing! What a fool I've been, drifting along, never asking any questions. I knew she hated my father although she pretended to grieve for him, but I never dared to question her. That's the truth of it, Frances. I never dared to question anything. I'm just a coward.'

'No, you're not. You was just unlucky, bullied by the pair of them from when you was a little kid. No wonder you was afraid to ask questions. Anyone would've been. And she put on a good act about your father, the wicked mare. Well, maybe she's paying for it now.'

Frances took a flask from the drawer of the table and poured brandy from it into the cap. 'Here, get that down you, lad,' she said, and took a swig from the flask herself. James felt the brandy exploding like fire inside him. 'We both needed that. I found it skied away in her room,' Frances said.

She sat down again. 'That's a facer, him taking the keys, though,' she said. 'Your ma was such a one for locks. I can't even get me cleaning things 'cos the cupboard's locked, and the tea caddy's nearly empty but the store cupboard's locked.'

'And the coal cellar,' James said grimly. 'I must have gone round in a dream, but I've woken up now. I'm going round to my uncle's for the keys *this minute*.'

Frances encouraged him, knowing that his anger, and possibly the unaccustomed brandy, would give him the courage to outface his uncle.

James called a cab to drive to his uncle's house in Fairfield and told the cabby to wait. 'My business won't take long,' he said grimly. The housekeeper was reluctant to admit him, but he insisted and was shown to James Seddon's study. 'I've come for my household keys, Uncle,' he said abruptly.

'The keys! I'll keep those. I intend to go through your mother's papers, but this is not a suitable day,' his uncle said sternly.

'I need them now,' James said. 'Everything in the house is locked up. The coal cellar, the store cupboard, even the cleaning cupboard, so I must have the keys at once.'

His uncle still demurred, but James insisted and finally the keys were produced. 'Make sure you relock everything immediately,' James Seddon said. 'And take care of these keys. Have you still got that hunchback coming in?'

James felt a rush of anger, but he said calmly, 'Frances O'Neill is absolutely honest. Anything is safe with her and not because of locks and keys. She's a good-living woman.'

'All very well,' his uncle grumbled. 'Trust nobody, that's the best policy.'

'I kept the cab,' James said. 'Goodbye, Uncle.'

'Don't be late tomorrow,' his uncle growled.

James drove home. In addition to his usual feelings of revulsion he felt anger at his uncle's words about Frances and was amazed at his own temerity in answering him. He felt that he had taken the first step in his new life.

Frances told him he looked a different man already. 'I feel different,' said James. 'You're right, Frances. This is my chance to change my life and I'm going to start by unlocking every door and cupboard in this house and leaving them unlocked.'

When he opened his mother's wardrobe he was met by an overpowering smell of camphor, but at the back he found two large canvas bags, containing sovereigns and half-sovereigns to the value of over four hundred pounds. He was both hurt and angry at the discovery when he recalled how all his salary had been claimed for the house.

He took ten pounds in sovereigns and ten in half-sovereigns and went down to Frances. 'You were right,' he said abruptly. 'There was over four hundred pounds there. I know you've been underpaid for years, Frances, so I've brought this for you.' At first Frances refused to take anything, but finally they compromised on ten pounds. 'And a fair amount for your work in future,' James said.

'Will you still want me to come in then?' Frances asked. 'I was wondering.'

'Yes, if it suits you,' James assured her. 'It would certainly suit me.'

'Glad to,' said Frances. 'I'd have a chance to give the house a good clean. I don't want to interfere like, but if I was you I'd sell this house and most of the furniture. It's all good stuff, walnut and mahogany. You'd get a good price for it. You might even sell the furniture with the house, they go so well together.'

'But where would I live?' James said, stunned by the suddenness of the suggestion.

Frances had evidently thought it out. 'Plenty of good houses to rent, especially just for one man. The house'll be clean when you come to sell and you could add the money you make from it to that nest egg,' she said. 'Buy a house and furniture to suit your bride like when you come to settle down,' she added with a sidelong smile.

James looked at her in stunned silence, and she looked back at him with twinkling eyes, then took down her shawl and pinned a battered felt hat to her bun of hair. 'I'll go to the butcher's on my way here tomorrow and get something for your tea, and I'll have the fire lit and the tea ready when you get home. Your mother had weekly accounts at the butcher's and the grocer's. I'll carry that on, shall I?'

James smiled at her. 'Yes please, Frances. I can see I'd be lost without you. I'm glad you've decided to stay.'

'Aye, well, I'll do anything I can to help,' she said. She picked up the blue sugar-bag containing her sovereigns. 'Thanks for the baksheesh too. Don't get upset over that money. She couldn't help her nature.'

Frances left and James sat down by the fire, enjoying his solitude and intending to look through his mother's papers later, but the events of the day and the revelations from Frances had exhausted him. He went to bed and fell asleep immediately.

At the office the next day he saw his uncle briefly when they met in a corridor. James Seddon glowered at him without speaking, but James was not intimidated.

His position in the general office was invidious. His connection with his uncle made the other clerks wary of him, yet he and his uncle ignored each other as far as possible. James had closed his mind to the past and refused to explore his feelings of fear and revulsion towards his uncle, although he frequently suffered nightmares, and his uncle rarely spoke to him. Only his mother's insistence, James knew, had resulted in his position in the office.

As the weeks passed, he often thought of Frances's suggestion that he should change his job, but he put off doing it, lacking the confidence to make the move. Frances said no more about it, or about selling the house, content to have planted the seed in his mind. Meanwhile, she was gradually spring-cleaning the house, and there was always a bright fire burning and a savoury meal ready when he returned home.

Frances's meals were more to his taste than those provided by his mother, and after he had eaten he would leave the gloomy house and walk for miles, thinking and planning. He wove fantasies about marrying Dorrie, although he knew that realistically there was little hope for him. So many men with more to offer materially and socially are attracted to her, but no one could possibly love her as much as I do, he told himself. His walks always took him near her home at some stage and he often saw her, but never had the courage to approach her.

After Mass and Benediction he was usually among the group surrounding the girls, and Dorrie was always gentle and sympathetic towards him because of his bereavement.

He was unable to resist talking to Frances about her, and Frances said she knew the family. 'The poor mother. She lost every child she had after Dorrie,' she said. 'But the two girls she has left are always together. The younger one's a lovely-looking girl and a nice nature too. She'll make a fine figure of a woman. Pity the older girl's so thin, but she's nice too. Very classy-looking. Lovely eyes, and with those bones she'll still be lovely when she's an old woman.' But James only wanted to talk about Dorrie.

As usual, Frances offered good advice. 'You can't do anything about other men falling for her,' she said. 'But you could smarten yourself up. You've lost weight these last few months and that suit's hanging off you. It's old-fashioned too. You should go to one of them new tailors in town and try a different barber and all.'

James took her advice and the tailor shook his head over James's old suit. Before he realised it James had ordered two suits, a business one and a lounge one. From there he went to a new barber, and although he was amazed at the luxurious premises and the high prices, he decided that the result was worth it.

As the weeks passed the sisters saw James regularly at church and Dorrie, who felt he must be lonely without his mother, made a point of smiling at him warmly and sometimes speaking to him. In this he was more fortunate than her other admirers. She flirted light-heartedly with all of them, but never made any distinction between them.

Anna, more realistic than Dorrie, believed that James was more relieved to be free of his overbearing mother, and she began to worry that James was being encouraged too much.

'You smiled very sweetly at James Hargreaves this evening, Dorrie,' she said, as they prepared for bed one Sunday night. 'I could see that Jim Halligan noticed it.'

'I can smile at whoever I like,' Dorrie said indignantly. 'It has nothing to do with Jim Halligan.'

'I know, but do you think you might be encouraging James Hargreaves too much?' said Anna. 'He might think he's your Mr Right, as they say in those sugary novelettes you're so fond of. Unless, of course, he *is* your Mr Right,' she added teasingly.

'Of course not,' said Dorrie. She smiled dreamily. 'I *will* meet him one day though, Anna, I'm sure, and when I do I'll know instantly that he's the man I'm going to marry.'

'And he'll know too,' Anna teased her affectionately. 'And you'll both fall in love and live happily ever after.'

'But I believe it, Anna,' Dorrie said earnestly. 'That there's someone in the world for everyone, and if I meet my someone we'll fall in love and marry. If we don't, I'll be an old maid. I could never marry a man I didn't love.'

Anna smiled, but said nothing, and Dorrie went on, 'I know you laugh at my novelettes, but I think the sentiments in them are true – just as true as those in those big books by Mr Dickens and Mr Bennett that you read, Anna. Mrs Wendell reads novelettes and she's very clever.'

Later, in bed, Anna lay awake long after Dorrie was asleep, worrying about this conversation. Dorrie was too trusting, she felt. Often she failed to see the malice behind a jealous remark and smiled at the speaker. In this way her goodness and innocence protected her, but Anna worried that it might also betray her.

All their social life centred round the church and people they had known all their lives, but Anna distrusted some of the young men, whom she classed as 'bad hats'. What if Dorrie fell in love with one of these? she thought.

Ada Cleary, a classmate of Anna's, had married a man who had soon begun to gamble away his wages, and had been seen on a ferryboat with another woman. What if Dorrie's Mr Right behaved like that after they were married? Ada had rather enjoyed the sympathy she received and enjoyed even more the retribution which fell on her husband when his affair became known to her brothers, but she had never truly loved him.

Anna felt that her sister, loyal and obstinate, would never change once her love had been given. She worried that in Ada's situation Dorrie would pretend indifference in public, but in private her heart would be broken. Then, suddenly realising how absurd it was to worry about something that might never happen, she turned over and fell asleep.

Chapter Three

Anna soon had a more real cause for worry. Her mother still refused to leave the house and spent most of her time lying on the sofa, in spite of being urged to take some exercise by Dr O'Brien.

'If your mother doesn't use her legs soon she won't be able to,' he said bluntly to Anna, but any attempt by Anna to persuade her ended in hysterical tears and accusations that Anna was cold-hearted and selfish.

'Wait until you know what it is to lose your health for your children,' her mother sobbed. 'And to think that of all my lovely daughters you had to be the one to survive.'

Bitterly hurt, Anna decided she would do no more to encourage her mother. Her father was due home in a few weeks' time and perhaps she would listen to him.

Mrs Furlong was still angry with Anna when Clara decided one Sunday to visit an old friend who had been prayed for in the list of the sick at Mass. She asked Dorrie to accompany her and Anna was left to prepare the dinner and look after her mother.

Anna had basted the meat and peeled the potatoes and she took a cup of tea to her mother and sat with her to keep her company.

They spoke about the dying woman Clara was visiting and Mrs Furlong said disparagingly, 'She was always a queer creature. Used to say that women were equal to men. She even said it to Father once.'

'I agree with her,' Anna said. 'I think women *are* equal to men.'

'Don't be stupid, Anna. Women's brains are smaller,' her mother said crossly, and the next moment they were involved in a heated argument. Suddenly Mrs Furlong fell back against her pillows, her hand on her heart and her eyes closed.

Nothing that Anna did revived her. She patted her mother's cheek and called her name, but she lay motionless until her arm slipped from across her body and her hand swung limply, brushing the carpet.

I've killed her, Anna thought with horror, and she rushed in panic to their next-door neighbour, Mrs Deagan, for help.

Normally she would have knocked at the door, but in her terror she pushed it open and raced down the hall, then stopped in amazement at the open living-room door. The three sons and two daughters still at home, all responsible adults who either owned their own business or held a respectable position, were standing in silence as their tiny widowed mother stood in the centre of the room, stamping her little foot in a brightly polished button boot, and declared fiercely, 'I'm master and mistress in this house and let no one forget it.'

Her family chorused meekly, 'Yes, Ma,' then Mrs Deagan saw Anna and her angry expression softened.

'What is it, girlie?' she asked gently. 'What's happened?'

'It's Mama. She's fainted. I can't bring her round,' Anna gasped, and the next moment she found herself at home with Mrs Deagan bending over her mother, who still appeared to be unconscious.

'Have you tried smelling salts?' Mrs Deagan asked.

'I couldn't find them. They're usually on that little table,' Anna said anxiously.

'Never mind, I've brought some,' Mrs Deagan said, taking a bottle from her apron pocket and passing it under Mrs Furlong's nose. She wrinkled her nose but her eyes remained closed, and Mrs Deagan said abruptly, 'Fetch me a jug of cold water, child. Cold water in the face often does the trick.'

At these words Mrs Furlong's eyelids fluttered and she moaned and sat up hastily. 'Where am I?' she said in a die-away voice.

'On your sofa, where you spend far too much time,' Mrs Deagan said forthrightly. She thrust her hand down beside Mrs Furlong and turned to Anna. 'Look. The smelling salts were here all the time after all.'

'I'm sorry. I shouldn't have bothered you,' Anna said, but Mrs Deagan replied robustly, 'Nonsense. You were right to come for me, girlie, but your mama'll be all right now.'

'Thanks, Mrs Deagan,' Anna said gratefully, as she escorted her neighbour to the door. 'I was so frightened.'

'Well, you know what to do now, girlie, if it happens again. A jug of cold water,' said Mrs Deagan. 'What brought that on?'

'I was arguing with Mama,' Anna admitted. 'I said men and women were equal.'

'*Equal!*' Mrs Deagan exclaimed. 'The man hasn't yet been born who's *my* equal, girlie, and never will be. Men! They're poor tools, even the best of them, and they'd be lost without us.'

Anna was smiling as she closed the door and went back to the parlour. Her mother had rearranged herself on the sofa with a novelette in her hand, and she scarcely raised her eyes when Anna went in, although she said petulantly, 'There was no need to bring that woman in here. You are useless in an emergency, Anna.'

Anna flushed with anger. 'It was good of Mrs Deagan to come,' she said, and before she could stop herself she added tartly, 'She seemed to know the right remedy anyway.' Then she went back to the kitchen, leaving her mother staring at her, speechless, and resumed her cooking until Dorrie and

Aunt Clara arrived shortly afterwards.

Anna said nothing about the events of the morning to her aunt, unwilling to expose her mother's dramatics to Clara's spiteful tongue.

Mrs Furlong had said nothing either, even to Dorrie, and for once there was harmony in the house. Even Clara seemed contented, pleased that Anna had the preparations for dinner well underway. Anna asked about the sick woman, and her aunt shook her head. 'Not long for this world,' she said mournfully, 'but she'll go to her reward if anyone will.'

Anna was amazed to hear her aunt speak well of someone and couldn't believe her ears when Clara went on, 'She was a good woman, Philomena Boyle, and she did a lot of good. She worried about poor children and she got things done to help them. Not making things for bazaars either. She'd tackle anyone, landlords, businessmen, city councillors. She spoke her mind to everyone, but she got things done.'

'Dr and Mrs O'Brien were there,' Dorrie said. 'They were both really upset, weren't they, Aunt?'

'Yes, they thought the world of her,' Clara replied, then, with a return to her usual manner, she added, 'He must've been upset. Never mentioned the war once, not even the relief of Ladysmith.'

Later, when she and Dorrie were alone, Anna told her sister what had happened earlier, and of her terror when she thought her mother had died.

'I could tell Mrs Deagan knew Mama was play-acting though,' she said. 'She soon recovered when cold water was mentioned, but she fooled me. I was terrified, Dorrie. I really thought she was dying.'

'I wish you hadn't been on your own,' Dorrie said. 'And I'm glad you could go for Mrs Deagan.'

'Yes, and Mama referred to her as "that woman",' Anna

said indignantly. 'I *admire* Mrs Deagan.'

'So do I,' Dorrie agreed and their admiration for their neighbour grew even more when they talked to her daughters the following week.

A group had been formed to make articles for a bazaar planned for 1901, and Anna and Dorrie had been working with Norah and Kate Deagan. Norah was a quiet, artistic woman, twenty-nine years old, and owned a small florist's shop. Kate was two years younger and more extrovert, and was a dress buyer for a shop in the city.

'You must've got a shock on Sunday, Anna,' Kate said, laughing. 'Seeing us all getting the rounds from Ma. I know some people think she's a tartar but she had to be hard when we were young or we'd never have survived.'

'I was too upset about Mama to notice,' said Anna. 'Your ma was so good.'

'Ma's had a hard life,' Norah said in her quiet voice. 'Married at sixteen and widowed when she was twenty-seven.'

'And she had twin boys who died as well as the six of us,' said Kate.

'After Da was buried she only had five penny pieces in her purse and six of us to feed,' Norah went on. 'She just gathered us round her after the funeral and told us if we all pulled together we'd get through.'

'You must have been very young,' Anna said.

'Yes, Kate and Gerald were only babies. Maggie was ten and Jim eight,' said Norah. 'They both got little jobs after school and on Saturdays, and Ma took in washing. She made pea soup and scouse too and sold it for a penny a basin. But we were always clean and well fed, even if it was mostly scouse and pea soup, and we always had good boots.'

'I don't know how Ma did it,' said Kate. 'You know she can't read or write, although nobody'd do her out of a farthing, but she even found the pennies to send us to school. It used to be if you hadn't got the penny it was the Ragged School and she wasn't having that.'

'Yes, she was determined we'd all be scholars,' Norah said quietly.

'She must be very proud you've all done so well,' Dorrie said, and Kate replied, laughing, 'We didn't dare not to.'

Later Dorrie and Anna agreed that it was no wonder the Deagan family submitted so meekly to their mother. It was out of respect, not fear, they felt.

Mrs Furlong still seemed to feel resentment towards Anna, so she spent more time helping her aunt when she was at home and less with her mother. It was easier, because the girls now went out on Sunday afternoons with the Wheelers, a church group, riding into the countryside near Liverpool, or across on a ferryboat to beauty spots on the Wirral.

They usually had a cream tea in a cottage before riding home, and both thoroughly enjoyed the outings with a lively group of young girls and men.

Their mother had objected, saying that cycling was unladylike, but she had been overruled. The fact that she objected meant that their aunt had supported them and had spoken of it to Dr O'Brien when he called.

'Splendid, splendid,' he said. 'Very healthy exercise. There would be less TB if more girls got out in the fresh air.'

Mrs Furlong could only hope that when her husband returned he would forbid it, and also forbid Anna to attend any more concerts with the Deagans.

Both Jim and Norah Deagan were very musical. Jim played the violin and Norah the piano, which was also a Pianola. Anna and Dorrie were sometimes invited to the Deagans' Sunday evening gatherings of family and friends, and when Jim discovered that Anna liked the Pianola rolls which played music by Chopin and Mendelssohn better than the ones which played modern ballads, he and Norah invited Anna and Dorrie to attend concerts with them.

Dorrie was bored by the classical music concerts and soon only Anna accompanied them, but she returned so exalted that her mother became suspicious.

'Jim Deagan's old enough to be your father,' she said to Anna.

'He's just had his thirty-fourth birthday,' Anna replied.

'Exactly, and he's still not married,' her mother snapped. 'He must be desperate to find a bride.'

'Why?' asked Anna. 'Why should he marry unless he really wants to? He has a good home and a full and enjoyable life as he is.'

'There are things you don't understand about men,' Mrs Furlong said. 'Anyway, it's his duty to marry. Someone of his own age. There are so many single girls.'

Anna thought the comment so ridiculous that she said nothing. Typical of her mother's generation, she thought with disgust, their minds always ran in the same rut, and she continued to enjoy the concerts with her neighbours.

Anna looked forward to her father's return but with some apprehension. Dorrie seemed to be eagerly counting the days but even she said one day, 'I wish Father was more like Captain Jenson, Anna.'

Anna nodded. 'I know what you mean,' she said. 'But I suppose people are just true to their natures, or perhaps all Dutchmen are like Captain Jenson.'

When Isabel's father was at home in January he had welcomed them warmly when they called for Isabel. He was a big man with a full golden beard and curly hair and he had hugged Anna and Dorrie. 'So what is this?' he said in his booming voice. 'All more beautiful every time I come home.

Mama and Isabel and now you, all more beautiful. It must be the Liverpool air!'

Several of the little boys were clinging to his legs and he said, 'Like a ship with barnacles I am. I must go in dry dock to be scraped, eh, boys?' He had laughed heartily and they had all laughed with him.

Dorrie and Anna were silent now, thinking of that scene, then Dorrie said loyally, 'Father loves us, though, and worries about us. We know that by his letters, don't we?'

Anna agreed. 'At least there'll be a truce between Mama and Aunt Clara while he's home,' she said, smiling.

Both girls were out when their father actually arrived, but Clara opened the door to them, her face flushed with excitement. 'He's here,' she said. 'My brother's here. We're in the parlour.'

Mrs Furlong lay on the sofa in a pretty tea gown and her husband sat near to her. He rose and came to greet the girls. 'Annabel,' he said as he kissed her, and 'Dorothea,' as he kissed Dorrie. He was the only person who used their full names, and hearing him they felt that he was really home at last.

'You both seem much older than I expected,' he said. 'More grown up.'

'It *is* two years, Father,' Mrs Furlong said in a weak voice, and he returned to sit beside her.

'I know, my dear,' he said gently. 'I'm sorry to see you so frail. Can Dr O'Brien suggest nothing to help?'

By chance, Mrs Furlong's eyes met Anna's and she said hastily, 'Don't let us talk about illness. Tell us about China. Were you in danger there?'

'Only from thieves,' he said. 'I had to keep a watchman posted and keep as much as possible under lock and key. Always bowing and scraping, these Orientals, but you have the feeling that secretly they despise us.'

Anna was surprised by such a perceptive remark from her father and would have liked to ask him more about it, but her mother was darting glances at her, as though she expected her to blurt something out about her illness, so she went with her aunt to the kitchen to help with the meal.

Clara grumbled that *she* would like to stay with her brother, but *someone* had to prepare the meal, but she was interrupted by the arrival of a seaman at the back door with Captain Furlong's chest and bags.

After dinner the gifts the captain had brought were distributed. A length of beautiful sapphire-blue silk for Dorrie, a length of shot silk for Anna, of lavender colour for her mother, and a pale grey for Clara.

After the first excitement her father had become withdrawn and silent, but Anna felt that Dorrie was right. Her father did care for them. The carefully chosen dress lengths were evidence of that, and he had also brought exquisite china ornaments, tortoiseshell combs, and fans and soft leather gloves. Also crystallised fruit and a variety of nuts and strange preserved vegetables.

'You've taken a lot of trouble for us, Brother,' Clara said. 'I hope the girls appreciate it.'

'Of course we do,' Anna said indignantly and Dorrie kissed her father's cheek. 'You know we do, don't you Father?' she said, and he smiled at her.

'I'm glad you're pleased,' he said, but Anna wondered whether he had noted her sharp reply to Aunt Clara. I'm sure he'll hear plenty on that score before he leaves, she thought grimly.

Captain Furlong had been shocked by the change in his wife and consulted Dr O'Brien as soon as possible. 'I wondered about TB,' he said tentatively, but the doctor told him that his wife's heart and lungs were sound.

'But she looks so frail,' the captain said. 'I'm alarmed by the change in her since I was last ashore. Surely there must be *some* reason for it.'

Dr O'Brien hesitated, then said bluntly, 'If you live the life of an invalid you soon become one. All your wife needs is fresh air and exercise, and to be needed. I've tried to persuade her to leave that sofa, but in the present situation I can't.'

Captain Furlong was puzzled. 'What do you mean, the present situation?' he asked sharply, but he listened without speaking as the doctor explained.

'Your sister's a forceful character,' he said. 'When she came here your wife was quite ill and weak and very distressed. Quite unable to manage the house, so Miss Furlong took over. The trouble is that when your wife recovered she found there was no place for her. Your sister had taken complete charge and resented any interference in her regime. Your wife took the line of least resistance by continuing to be an invalid, and this is the result.'

'But my sister came here – What? Seven or eight years ago. When did this happen?'

'No, no,' Dr O'Brien said. 'It didn't happen suddenly. I told you the result and the reason for it, but it was all very gradual. At first your wife did a little light dusting, arranged flowers, that sort of thing, but nothing stands still. As she got stronger she tried to run the house again and that your sister wouldn't allow.'

'Wouldn't allow!' Captain Furlong exclaimed. 'That is my wife's home. In my absence *she* runs it. I brought my sister here to help her, not to usurp her.'

'None of it was planned,' Dr O'Brien said. 'They've simply drifted into this situation, but something must be done. If your wife doesn't leave that sofa soon she won't be able to.'

Captain Furlong had stood up and begun to walk up and down the room in his agitation. 'Do you think my wife is well enough to manage if I move Clara to a place of her own?' he asked.

The doctor said quickly, 'Probably, with help from your daughters, but there's no need to be so drastic. Your wife and sister quarrel but it's the breath of life to them. They need each other. Women!'

He laughed, but the captain still looked worried. 'I'm only home for three weeks. I must take some steps,' he said.

'Do you mind a suggestion?' Dr O'Brien asked.

The captain shook his head. 'You seem to understand the position,' he said.

'Why don't you tell your wife that you're surprised your sister does all the cooking. Remind her of a meal she used to cook and you enjoyed. Ask her to do it again.'

'But would she be well enough?' asked the captain.

'She could sit on a chair and supervise the girls. She's their mother and she should be the one training them to become good wives,' said Dr O'Brien.

He wondered whether he had gone too far when Captain Furlong shook hands with him and thanked him then suddenly departed. He told himself that he had done his best for the family, but it was a relief to him to see Captain Furlong arriving at church in a cab with his wife and sister the following Sunday.

Anna and Dorrie had walked down to church, but when they returned home they all had the usual cup of tea then Captain Furlong saw his wife installed on a chair in the kitchen, with her two daughters in attendance, and went for a walk with his sister.

Mrs Furlong had chosen a leg of pork for the meal. 'Your aunt was against it,' she said, 'because there isn't an R in the month. Nonsense! A fortnight ago she'd have thought it was all right because there's an R in April.'

'I suppose the origin of that is that May, June, July and August are summer months and hot,' Anna said. 'But as you say, Mama, this is the very start of summer.'

At first Mrs Furlong was content to supervise, telling Anna to rub salt into the crackling and not to baste it, but soon she asked for bread and began to make breadcrumbs for the stuffing while Dorrie chopped onions. The girls were surprised to see her suddenly stand up and walk across the kitchen for a rolling pin to crush dried sage.

'Mmm, that smells lovely already,' Dorrie said, bending over the basin, and her mother said complacently, 'It's a family recipe. It was my mother's and probably her mother's too.'

'You'll have to show us, Mama, tell us the quantities so we can teach our daughters,' Dorrie said with a giggle.

'I'll show you how to make proper apple sauce too,' her mother promised. 'Your aunt insists on mixing it with salt, but I always use sugar. You'll taste the difference.'

When their father and aunt returned, the table was laid and the meal almost ready, and although Mrs Furlong was flushed and happy she was obviously tired. Her daughters urged her to rest while they put the finishing touches to the meal.

'You don't want to be too tired to eat, Mama,' Dorrie said, and Anna added, 'No, you want to be able to enjoy seeing Father eat this meal. You've worked so hard.'

Clara declared that she would go to the kitchen and do all that was necessary, but she was stopped by her brother. 'No, sit down, Clara,' he said, 'this is your day of rest. Adelaide will have instructed the girls,' and with a smug smile at her sister-in-law Mrs Furlong willingly lay down on the sofa and fell asleep immediately, but only for a short time.

The nap had refreshed her and she glowed at the

compliments about the meal, although Clara's were grudging. 'These roast potatoes are perfect,' Captain Furlong said. 'Soft and floury inside and crisp outside, just as I like them. I wish you could train my Chinese cook to cook like this, Adelaide.'

Anna had been responsible for the roast potatoes, but she said quickly, 'And the stuffing, Father. Isn't it delicious? It's a family recipe, Mama says, so she's teaching it to Dorrie and me.'

After the meal Clara went out to make some visits and Anna and Dorrie tactfully went for a walk, leaving their parents alone. As they walked along to Brunswick Road they saw James Hargreaves approaching and Anna said, 'Now don't be too encouraging, Dorrie. It's not fair.'

James Hargreaves raised his hat and the girls bowed but continued walking, although Dorrie could not resist smiling at him. James was elated by the meeting, but Anna's caution was unnecessary. Although he constantly wove fantasies about Dorrie he had no real hope that she would ever marry him.

With his healthier lifestyle, his spots and plumpness had gone and he now appeared slim and smartly dressed, but mentally he still saw himself as his mother had described him. Fat, stupid and clumsy. The mental and emotional scars inflicted by his mother would take a long time to heal, and he was still the nervous, diffident person he had always been.

He had done nothing about selling the house or changing his job. He hated the cotton brokers but lacked the confidence to break away. Fortunately he rarely saw his uncle, who as general manager had his own office, but the office manager curried favour with him by constantly criticising James and every mistake was blamed on him, with the eager co-operation of the other clerks.

Protests were useless and James, who knew he was a figure of fun to the younger clerks and that the older men took their cue from the manager, soon adopted an air of stolid indifference to hide his feelings. He had long ago erected a mental barrier against his uncle.

He walked to work as usual on a crisp September morning, wishing he could stay outdoors to breathe the bracing air, and dreading the day in the office. It was as bad as he feared.

The office manager was a smarmy creature. His hair glistened with macassar oil, as did the points of his moustache, which he continually fingered. He began to find fault with James before he even reached his desk, and continued at intervals throughout the day, frequently glancing over his shoulder to the office where James's uncle sat in solitary state.

Mid-afternoon he accused James of making a mistake which had been made before the document in question had even arrived on James's desk. Normally James would have borne this abuse in silence, but after all the other petty humiliations of the day, suddenly it was too much.

A vision of the bags of sovereigns and half-sovereigns rose before him and he thought grimly, I don't have to take this. He seized a piece of paper and while the man was still ranting he rapidly wrote out his resignation and handed it over. 'My resignation. I'm leaving,' he said.

While the manager was still bleating, 'You can't, you can't,' James's uncle appeared.

'What's this?' he demanded angrily.

'I'm leaving,' James said brusquely. For the first time in many years he made eye contact with his uncle and this so unnerved him that he brushed past him roughly without another word. When he reached the street he found he was shaking, and turned into the small café where he had eaten his solitary lunch all his working life.

Chapter Four

James still found it hard to believe that he had found the courage to actually leave the office at last, but he was trembling with reaction. He ordered hot sweet tea and toast and gradually became calmer. I don't know what came over me, he thought, but I don't care. If I can't get an office job I'll turn my hand to anything.

He ordered more tea and when the café owner brought it he said curiously, 'Don't usually see you in at this time. Finished early have you?'

'I've walked out on my job. Had enough,' James said briefly.

The café was empty and the man perched on a chair near him. 'Go 'way!' he said. 'Got you down like, did it?'

Suddenly James found himself telling the man what had happened and the background to it. 'Relations!' the man said with disgust. 'They're always the worst to work for. What'll you do now?'

'I don't know and I don't care,' said James. 'I've only got myself to keep.'

A moment later the man said thoughtfully, 'I know where there's a job going. In a fruit importer's. Young feller going to America and the job come up at the last minute so he's sailing Friday. If you're free to start right away you might have a chance.'

'I won't be able to get a reference,' James said doubtfully.

The café owner shrugged. 'Worth a try,' he said. 'You've lost nothing if you don't get it. It's only five minutes' walk away. Hackins Hey.' He wrote the name of the firm and its

51

manager, and the address on a page from his order pad and handed it to James. 'Good luck, lad,' he said, coming to the door to watch him cross the street and turn into Hackins Hey.

This was the oldest part of the city and Hackins Hey was narrow and dark, unchanged, it seemed, for centuries. James's courage almost failed as he stumbled over the cobbles and up the twisting stairs to the office, but he thought of the café owner's words and went on.

The manager was a quiet middle-aged man and James gave details of his work in the cotton brokers then said nervously, 'The general manager was a relative. We parted on bad terms so I won't be able to get a reference.'

The manager, Mr Morgan, smiled briefly and asked if he was free to start immediately. He gave James details of the hours and salary and said that in view of the lack of reference he would suggest a month's trial, to which James eagerly agreed.

He was introduced to the man whose place he was taking and he rattled off details of figures and documents so rapidly that James was bewildered. I'll never do it, he thought despairingly, but as the clock struck six the man collected the papers together, and departed.

The man at the next desk stood up and held out his hand. 'Henry Mortimer,' he said. 'Don't worry. He tried to make the job seem more difficult than it is to make himself seem important.'

One of the other men laughed. 'Uncle Sam won't know what's hit him when Archie arrives,' he said. 'Mind you, he'll probably meet his match there.'

Henry introduced the man and others in the office and as they left he said quietly to James, 'I'm sure you won't have any difficulty, but if you do at first I'll be on hand to help.'

James felt that he had made a friend and would enjoy

working there. He went back to thank the café owner. 'You'll be all right there,' the man said. 'The feller what's leaving – he wasn't well liked. Big head and big mouth. Probably suit the Yanks.'

Frances was delighted when she heard that he had finally left the brokers and found a new position. 'You done well. I'm made up for you,' she told him.

When Frances had gone James's feeling of euphoria gradually seeped away and he began to worry about whether he would be able to do the work. He spent a sleepless night, remembering all his mother's comments about his stupidity, but he soon realised that his fears were groundless.

The next day Henry Mortimer greeted him pleasantly and introduced him to the clerks he had not met the previous afternoon, and James found the friendly atmosphere a striking contrast to the cotton brokers' office. Quiet and diffident and always grateful for help which was freely given, he was popular, unlike his bumptious predecessor, and he settled in happily.

At the end of the month he was told by the manager, Mr Morgan, that his work was satisfactory and his position was permanent.

James even dared to hope that he might rise in his new position, and one day feel able to approach Dorrie, but his doubts soon returned.

The news of the relief of Mafeking came while Captain Furlong was still at home and even he was swept up in the general rejoicing. Flags appeared everywhere, and small ones were proudly carried by children who had been given a holiday from school, and fluttered from women's shopping baskets.

There were church services of thanksgiving, and firework displays, and patriotic songs were sung in music halls and whistled by errand boys.

No one rejoiced more than Dr O'Brien, and Clara said tartly, 'Anyone would think he'd done it all himself, or his precious nephews. Ridiculous!'

But her brother said sternly, 'This is an occasion when everyone should rejoice. I myself feel proud to be an Englishman this day.'

'He's not even that,' Clara muttered, but Captain Furlong heard her and said, 'He is an Irishman and the Irish regiments fought very bravely, particularly at Ladysmith, with enormous loss of life. Our dear Queen herself has remarked on it.'

Clara said no more, and later Anna said to Dorrie that she thought their father seemed to have turned against their aunt.

Dorrie disagreed. 'I think he's still very fond of her, but perhaps he sees how nasty she can be,' she said. 'Although she's not as bossy as she used to be, is she? Perhaps she doesn't get the chance while Father's home,' she giggled.

'You know, I wonder if Dr O'Brien has talked to Father, Dorrie. I seem to see his fine Irish hand in all these changes,' Anna said thoughtfully. 'Mama cooking and Aunt Clara going visiting.'

'Father might just have thought that Aunt Clara was doing too much,' said Dorrie. 'Heaven knows she does enough moaning about it, and she's probably been complaining to Father too.'

Anna shrugged. 'Whatever,' she said. 'I just hope it will last when he goes away, but I doubt it.'

Her father evidently shared her doubts. On the evening before he left, Mrs Furlong cooked the meal with help from her daughters. Afterwards they had coffee in the parlour and Captain Furlong stood commandingly on the hearth-rug, looking round at his family. 'I'm pleased to see that your health has improved,' he told his wife. 'I've spoken to Dr

O'Brien and he assures me that the improvement should be lasting.'

'I do feel better most of the time,' Mrs Furlong murmured.

'Good, good,' her husband said, then looked severely at his family. 'When I leave tomorrow my wife will take my place as head of this family. She has my authority to make all decisions and plans. Annabel and Dorothea, you must take a greater part in the housework. Your mother intends to train you both to become good wives and mothers when the time comes, and I expect you both to do all you can to help her.'

'We will, Father,' they said meekly and he looked at them approvingly.

He turned to his sister. 'I know you will help too, Clara, and my wife will need your help. You stepped into the breach when Adelaide was so ill, but now you must have time for yourself. I'm pleased that you've joined the Guild and made so many friends.'

Then he asked for more coffee, as a signal that the lecture was over.

As soon as Anna and Dorrie were alone Anna declared that she was now certain that Dr O'Brien had been advising her father. 'Otherwise Father would never have bothered to explain so tactfully. He would simply have announced his decision without giving a button whether we liked it or not,' she said.

'I was amazed,' Dorrie admitted. 'I've never heard Father talk like that before. He's been quite different on this leave, hasn't he? Taking us out on Mafeking night and everything, and spending so much time with Mama. Usually he goes out alone or just sits in his study.'

'Aunt Clara's very meek too,' said Anna. 'I wonder how long it will last when he goes. Unless perhaps Dr O'Brien has put his oar in there too.' They giggled, but quite by chance Anna had hit on the truth. Dr O'Brien had slid in a suggestion that a brief

55

reference to her brother's idea of moving her to her own place might make Clara more amenable, and it had worked. In spite of all her complaints, Clara dreaded living alone.

Later, when he was at sea, Captain Furlong would be amazed that he had allowed the doctor to speak so freely about his family, and to make so many suggestions.

It was because I was afraid that Adelaide had TB, he decided, and as a just man he had to admit that the advice was good. I've left my family shipshape, he thought complacently. They needed a man's hand.

Dr O'Brien was pleased with the result of his scheming when he saw Mrs Furlong so much better and living a normal life, but when he met Anna and Dorrie his conversation was all about his nephews.

Queen Victoria had shown her appreciation of her Irish soldiers by ordering all Irish regiments to wear shamrock in their headdress on 17 March, St Patrick's Day, and the doctor was delighted.

A few days later a proposal that a regiment of Irish Guards should be formed to commemorate the bravery of the Irish soldiers was made and approved by the Queen. The first recruits for the new regiment came from Irishmen serving in other regiments and both of Dr O'Brien's nephews immediately volunteered. The doctor could talk of little else.

Covert hostilities between Clara and Mrs Furlong were resumed soon after Captain Furlong sailed, but they continued to follow his instructions.

Mrs Furlong had been bored and frustrated by her role of invalid for some time, but as Dr O'Brien had shrewdly realised, she had drifted into a situation she was unable to change. Now she enjoyed being in charge of her household again, although she frequently rested on her sofa during the day, and most evenings.

She still refused to allow the girls to do more to help in the house or with the cooking, in spite of her husband's instructions, and instead preferred to rely on Nelly, the middle-aged daily maid. Nelly had been on the point of giving notice to Clara, but she became Mrs Furlong's devoted slave.

'What would I do without you, Nelly?' Mrs Furlong frequently said, and Anna listened in angry disbelief. What about me? she wanted to say. What about my long, empty days? But she knew it was useless. At least Dorrie had her visits to Mrs Wendell, but Anna had been unable to continue her work at the Ragged School.

Clara had been undecided whether to be offended because her work had not been appreciated in the past, or to be pleased that her brother wished her to have more free time. She decided on the second attitude and told her friends that her brother insisted she had time for her own life. 'One can be too unselfish,' she declared, 'and people take advantage.' She spent far more time outside the house now, involved in church activities and with a growing circle of acquaintances.

A bazaar had been planned for 1901, to reduce the debt of the church and the elementary schools. For a while there was a feeling that it must be postponed, because of the death of Queen Victoria on 22 January, but it was decided that as the bazaar was not due to take place for several months the plans should not be changed. A committee had been formed and Clara elected to it, and she was active in making suggestions for raising money, and in criticising any made by anyone else.

As on other occasions, Anna and Isabel were due to help on the needlework stall and Dorrie was on the fancy-goods stall. There were always fretwork pipe-racks and carved cigar boxes on Dorrie's stall, which made a pretext for young men to flock to her, attracted by her smiling face.

An older woman, Miss Gittings, who had a more noticeable

moustache than some of the young men, usually helped Dorrie on the stall and watched her admirers with eagle eyes, ensuring that none left without buying something. She and Dorrie were a formidable team and had raised twice as much as other stalls at previous bazaars.

The morning of the bazaar in 1901 was bright and sunny and Anna, Dorrie and Isabel set out together to walk to the hall in Salisbury Street. Anna and Isabel both wore white blouses and dark skirts, Anna's brown and Isabel's navy, and both wore boaters trimmed with matching ribbon. Dorrie wore her favourite blue, and a small bonnet-shaped blue hat with artificial forget-me-nots under the brim which framed her face. She carried a basket containing their holland pinafores which they would wear while preparing the stalls.

'I'm so excited,' said Isabel. 'I seem to have been looking forward to this for so long.'

'The committee must feel that too. I only hope there aren't any sharp knives or hatchets on any of the stalls,' Anna said, laughing, 'or someone's sure to attack Aunt Clara. Can't you just see the headlines in the *Echo*? Tragedy at bazaar. Enraged stallholder attacks organiser.'

'She's certainly made a few enemies,' Isabel agreed, 'but she's worked very hard.'

The hall in Salisbury Street was already busy with stallholders and their helpers and many young men. When Dorrie began to set up her stall James Hargreaves made sure he was nearest to her when she needed someone to nail up some drapery. He rushed to do it and Dorrie was thanking him warmly when Miss Gittings appeared.

'That's very good, Mr Hargreaves,' she said. 'Thank you. Dorrie, have you seen a parcel of pen wipers?' Dorrie was whisked away, leaving James staring after her, elated that at least he had been able to speak to her.

Soon the doors opened and people flooded in and dispersed to the many stalls, but most of the young men made straight for the fancy-goods stall, where Dorrie stood smiling in welcome. James had been standing nearby, feasting his eyes on her, but the stall was soon surrounded by a large laughing crowd. James pushed through and selected a stud box, but another helper whipped it from his hand and wrapped it.

Anna and Isabel were also busy on the needlework stall, although most of their customers were ladies. The bazaar was going well. Money was rattling into the pudding basins on the stalls and the air was filled with the sound of talk and laughter.

A sudden hush fell near the door when Dr and Mrs O'Brien appeared, accompanied by two tall young soldiers. The doctor seemed ready to burst with pride as he introduced them to people nearby then began a circuit of the stalls, his nephews attracting admiring glances from all the ladies.

One was as dark as the other was fair, but they were both striking in appearance. When they reached the fancy-goods stall the crowd parted to let them through and Dr O'Brien introduced them first to Miss Gittings and the older ladies, then to Dorrie and another young helper.

'My nephew, Eugene D'Arcy,' he said of the fair young man, 'and my other sister's son, Michael Farrell. They're going home to Ireland on leave but they've stopped off for a few days with us. We've just looked in for an hour,' he added proudly.

The tall soldiers bowed and smiled and the dark young man held Dorrie's hand and smiled into her eyes. 'If I'd known you were here, sure I'd have been here when the doors opened,' he said in a low voice and Dorrie blushed and giggled.

His dark hair grew in a widow's peak on his forehead, and his blue eyes were fringed with thick dark lashes. He was clean-shaven, with even white teeth and a cleft chin, and

Dorrie thought she had never before seen such a handsome young man. The red coat and uniform trappings made him seem even more romantic.

She scarcely noticed the other soldier, although he was handsome too, with classical features, a straight nose, and soft, full lips. Fair curls clustered on his brow and as he and the doctor approached their stall Isabel whispered to Anna, 'He's like a Greek god, isn't he?'

Michael Farrell had lingered with Dorrie, much to the chagrin of the other men, particularly James Hargreaves.

Mrs O'Brien touched Michael's arm. 'Your uncle is waiting to introduce you to Dorrie's sister,' she said, so after whispering urgently, 'I'll see you later,' to Dorrie, he followed his aunt to the needlework stall.

'You're not at all alike, are you?' Isabel said when they were introduced, glancing from Michael to Eugene, and Dr O'Brien laughed.

'They're not from the same family, Miss Jenson. Michael is the son of my elder sister, Bridie, and Eugene is the son of my younger sister, Nuala.'

'But sure you're not like your sister,' Michael said to Anna, glancing back at Dorrie, 'and you're true sisters, aren't you?'

'Yes, and very devoted sisters,' Mrs O'Brien said, smiling at Anna. 'It's just a difference in colouring.'

The doctor was impatient to move on to introduce his nephews to others, but he smiled approvingly when D'Arcy bought some tray cloths and a set of egg cosies for his aunt.

He handed them to Anna and watched her as she wrapped them, then, still looking at her, he bowed and smiled before moving away. 'I think he's fallen for you, Anna,' Isabel whispered. 'Aren't they magnificent? So *manly*.'

The two soldiers were so tall that the girls could easily see them as they moved about the hall, and Eugene looked across to their stall several times. One of the older ladies bustled up to Anna and Isabel. 'You have your tea now, young ladies. Mrs Bligh and Miss Doyle have come to help. No need to hurry. You've been working very hard.'

Tea and biscuits were served at the end of the hall and the helpers usually went there for a short break, to sit down to rest and drink a reviving cup of tea. When Anna and Isabel passed Dorrie's stall she joined them, and several young men followed like the tail of a comet.

All in vain. When they reached the tea section the two soldiers were waiting to escort them to a table where Mrs O'Brien was sitting and waving to them. 'How did you manage that?' Isabel said in amazement.

'One advantage of being tall,' Michael said with a smile. 'We could see when you moved.'

'I still don't see how you got here before us,' Isabel said, and Michael replied, laughing, 'We learnt that against the Boers, and now it's come in handy.'

Dr O'Brien arrived puffing. 'I didn't see you go,' he said to his nephews. 'I turned to introduce you. One minute you were there and the next you were gone. Now I see why.' They all laughed but Mrs O'Brien gave him a wifely look and he said no more about it, but told his nephews that it would soon be necessary for them to leave.

Michael paid no attention, engrossed in conversation with Dorrie, his head bent close to hers. Eugene seemed as interested in Anna, although he politely included Isabel and his aunt in the conversation.

Before they left the table the cousins asked if they could meet the girls later, but Anna said firmly that they should spend the evening with their uncle and aunt.

'Ah, sure they'll understand,' Michael said. But Eugene said quietly, 'I think Miss Furlong is right.' They all looked at

Dr and Mrs O'Brien, who were turned away, talking to people who had stopped by their chairs, but the doctor smiled so proudly at his nephews that Michael was forced to agree.

Anna smiled at Eugene, thinking that he had shown consideration for his aunt and uncle, and when Michael said, 'What about tomorrow? Are you free tomorrow?' she recklessly suggested a trip on the ferryboat over to Eastham Woods. The men politely included Isabel, but she said tactfully that she was needed at home.

Dorrie looked doubtful. 'Will Mama allow us?' she said quietly to Anna, who was already regretting her eager acceptance. They'll think I'm forward – or desperate, she thought, but Michael had overheard Dorrie and he immediately turned to his aunt.

'We want to invite the Miss Furlongs out, Aunt Maureen. Would you ever introduce us to their parents and put in the good word for us?' He whispered something which made her laugh then said aloud, 'We have so little time.'

Mrs O'Brien smiled at him. 'I can't introduce you to Captain Furlong, Michael, because he's at sea, but I believe Mrs Furlong and Mrs Jenson are coming to the bazaar. Isn't that so, Miss Furlong?' she said to Anna, who agreed.

'But my uncle is wanting to go,' Michael said.

His aunt smiled and said, 'Don't worry. I'll see we don't go before you have your introduction.'

Michael pressed Dorrie's hand and gazed into her eyes before escorting her back to the fancy-goods stall, while Eugene escorted Anna and Isabel.

'I wish you'd come with us tomorrow, Isabel,' Anna said when he went, but Isabel laughed.

'No, I don't fancy being the unwanted third,' she said. 'I'm so pleased for you, Anna. I'm sure Eugene is smitten.'

Anna smiled. 'I don't know,' she said. 'I'm sure Michael is

with Dorrie, and I think he'll see that we have our trip tomorrow. He can certainly charm his aunt.'

'I think he's a man who can charm anyone, including Dorrie, but she'll have to be careful. He might be *too* much of a charmer,' said Isabel.

Anna looked alarmed. 'You don't think he's sincere?' she said quickly.

'I could be wrong,' said Isabel. 'But with so much charm is he just going to use it on one person? Eugene seems different. More reliable.'

Anna kept glancing at the watch pinned to her blouse. 'I wish Mama would come,' she said. 'I'm so afraid the O'Briens will go before she gets here.'

'Don't worry. Mrs O'Brien won't let them,' Isabel said comfortably. 'Our mamas will be here soon.'

Mrs Jenson had been friendly with Mrs Furlong for some years, because of their shared interests, but it was only now that the friendship had developed, and they shopped locally or in town together.

The girls were busy when their mothers arrived, but as soon as they appeared Mrs O'Brien welcomed them, and the doctor hastened to introduce his nephews. The two ladies gazed admiringly at the handsome young soldiers.

Michael said softly to Mrs Furlong, 'You'll excuse me, ma'am, but I have to say I can see why your daughters are so beautiful.'

Mrs Furlong blushed and preened and she listened attentively when Mrs O'Brien told her that Michael and Eugene were the sons of her husband's sisters, both from very well-respected families in Ireland.

A friend had come to speak to Mrs Jenson and the doctor was now introducing his nephews to a priest, so Mrs O'Brien seized the opportunity to whisper to Mrs Furlong, 'Your daughters have made a conquest. Michael and Eugene want to ask your permission to take the girls on a trip to Eastham tomorrow. It's very sudden, I know, but they have so little time.'

Mrs Furlong looked doubtful. 'It's such a responsibility with my husband away,' she said. She looked over to where Clara was supervising an alteration to one of the stalls. 'I don't know what my sister-in-law would say.'

'Well, of course, she is a spinster,' said Mrs O'Brien. 'You and I, as married women – well, we have our memories, don't we?'

'Indeed,' Mrs Furlong said, smiling smugly, 'and of course *I* make the decisions in my husband's absence.'

Michael, while appearing very attentive to the priest, had been listening to his aunt and as soon as the party reformed he moved beside Mrs Furlong. 'I have to ask you a favour, ma'am,' he said, smiling shyly at her. 'Would you allow my cousin and myself to escort your daughters tomorrow? We'd take very good care of them.'

'I'm sure you will,' Mrs Furlong said graciously. 'Your aunt has already spoken to me about it.' Eugene came to add assurances, and Mrs Furlong gave her permission.

'And now, will you allow us to take you to tea, ladies?' Michael said, and he and D'Arcy escorted Mrs Furlong and Mrs Jenson to the tea area, watched enviously by other matrons.

'You have a large family, I believe,' Michael said to Mrs Jenson. 'And a very devoted daughter to help you to care for them.'

'Yes, I don't know what I'd do without Isabel,' Mrs Jenson said, pleased, and Michael was able to leave Eugene to talk to her and devote himself to Mrs Furlong.

Dr O'Brien watched with amazement as his nephews

escorted the two ladies to the tea place. 'God bless my soul!' he exclaimed to his wife. 'Whatever are they up to now? McDaid will think I've dropped dead on the way with them.'

'Dr McDaid knows what these things are like,' his wife soothed him. 'It's a bit of strategy. They've fallen for the Furlong girls and they want to ask them out.'

'I'm pleased to see it,' he said. 'Particularly Eugene.' His wife looked at him enquiringly, but he said no more.

A little later Michael and Eugene were free to leave with their uncle and aunt. They had escorted Mrs Furlong and Mrs Jenson to the stalls where their daughters were, and Mrs Furlong had given the girls permission for the outing the next day. They saw the soldiers leave with regret, an emotion not shared by Dorrie's admirers, especially James Hargreaves.

Anna found it difficult to concentrate and Isabel seemed almost as excited as she was. 'I'm really sure he's smitten, Anna,' she said. 'The way he looked at you, and asking you out so soon! And he's so handsome. Like a Greek god, or do I mean Roman? Anyway, I can just see him with a laurel wreath on his head.'

Anna smiled at her friend. 'I do hope you're right, Isabel,' she said. 'But it seems almost too good to be true, doesn't it? There must be fashionable women in London who admire him and have a lot more to offer than I do.'

'Don't belittle yourself, Anna,' Isabel said indignantly. 'Whoever marries you will be a *very* lucky man. Anyway, the O'Briens seemed to notice it and be pleased.'

'Michael certainly seemed smitten with Dorrie, didn't he?' Anna said. 'And that I *can* understand.'

'I didn't pay much attention to them,' Isabel admitted. 'I was more interested in the way Eugene behaved to you.'

The rest of the bazaar passed in a happy dream for Dorrie and Anna, although they were careful to conceal their feelings.

Dorrie's eyes were brighter and her cheeks more flushed, but she flirted with her admirers as light-heartedly as usual and they all thought the danger from the soldiers was over.

Only James Hargreaves was not deceived. His own deep love for Dorrie made him realise that her heart had been touched by the gallant soldier, and he spent a miserable night. He compared his fantasies about Dorrie with the reality of Michael holding her hand and looking into her eyes.

If I'd had the courage to try to court her and to ask her out, would she have accepted? he wondered. Even if she had refused, at least she would have known how he felt about her, and perhaps someday she would have turned to him.

In the small hours, though, all his doubts and fears seeped back. Who was he deluding? Dorrie would never look at him. Why should she? A gauche fool without any social graces or achievements, and no fortune to offer. Only what his mother had furtively saved from her housekeeping, nothing from his own efforts. I'll make myself successful, he vowed, even if it means working night and day, and I'll improve myself, try to make myself worthy of her, but his depression returned when he thought it might already be too late.

There was good reason for his fears. The trip to Eastham was a great success and when the young people returned Mrs O'Brien had a supper ready for them. She had created a garden in the large paved area behind the house and after supper the two couples sat out there on seats among the greenery. Eugene put his hand over Anna's as they sat on a stone seat, but Dorrie lay in Michael's arms, well back in a green bower.

Before supper Michael had followed his uncle into his surgery, saying that he must talk to him.

'I'm head over heels in love with Dorrie, Uncle,' he confessed. 'I've never met a girl like her and I know this is the real thing for me. I can't go off and leave her with all those fellows around her like wasps round a honeypot, although she says she loves me too.'

'You've spoken to her!' Dr O'Brien exclaimed. 'After one day and with not a word to her family or your own. You're mad, young man.'

'I'm desperate, Uncle. I'm so afraid I'll lose her. I want to declare myself. Ask her to marry me,' Michael said.

Dr O'Brien sat down and wiped his face with his handkerchief. 'Have sense, man,' he said. 'You know nothing of Dorrie and she knows nothing of you. She's barely eighteen and never been a night away from home.'

'And I'm twenty-seven,' Michael said eagerly. 'So the age difference is right. And I've been about, but it's different for a man.'

'I'll have to get my wife,' Dr O'Brien said abruptly, but nothing that Mrs O'Brien could say would shake Michael's determination to ask Dorrie to marry him.

'Her father won't be home for another six months at least, and you can do nothing without his permission,' Mrs O'Brien said. 'Don't think you can wheedle Mrs Furlong into giving permission. Her husband will deal with anything like this and he's a strict father.'

'I want it settled before I go back,' Michael said stubbornly. 'Even if it's not official, if people know the position I'll feel safer.'

The doctor and his wife looked at each other helplessly. The convention was that a young man might flirt as much as he liked, even declare undying love for a young lady, but until he actually asked her to marry him he was free to move on without reproach. Once the proposal was made the engagement was considered as binding as marriage and the girl could sue for breach of promise if it was broken.

Mrs O'Brien felt that Michael had perhaps not realised this

and tried to explain, but he looked at her as though she was speaking a foreign language. 'We love each other. Why can't we at least be engaged?' he said.

Dr O'Brien suddenly lost his temper. 'You're not an idiot,' he said. 'Don't behave like one. And think of Dorrie. You'll put her in an impossible position. She knows nothing can be done until her father returns, so don't be talking about people knowing because nothing can be said publicly, whatever you might decide between yourselves.'

Michael said nothing for a moment then he smiled and said ruefully, 'You're right entirely, Uncle. I was only thinking that it would be easier for Dorrie to fight off the hordes if they knew she was engaged, not that I think for a minute she'd ever play me false.'

'She'd never do that but, Michael, she could change her mind. She's very young and innocent, never been away from home or seen anything of the world,' said Mrs O'Brien.

'I'll take care of her, Aunt,' said Michael eagerly. 'I promise I'd protect her.'

'Ah, well, she's a lovely girl and nobody would be more pleased than myself to see you with her as your wife, but don't be jumping your fences too close or you'll come a cropper,' said Dr O'Brien. 'Make what promises you like to each other, but say nothing to anybody else. And you'll both need to do a lot of thinking too.' And with that Michael had to be content.

'It's just as well Captain Furlong won't be home for a while,' Mrs O'Brien said later. 'It'll give them time to calm down. I wouldn't like Michael to be hurt, or Dorrie either.'

'He's grown into a fine young man,' the doctor said. 'And young D'Arcy too.' He puffed on his pipe for a while in silence then said suddenly, 'I was glad to see him taking an interest in young Anna. I was afraid he was – not the marrying kind.'

'You worry too much,' his wife said placidly. They followed Michael back out to the garden but soon the doctor took out his watch and looked at it and the young people took the hint and prepared to leave.

Anna was puzzled by Eugene's behaviour. He had been formal and silent while they had been alone in the garden, but seemed almost effusive when the O'Briens appeared.

He became silent again as they walked home and Anna found it hard to make conversation with him, but with Dorrie and Michael, who walked in front of them, it was entirely different.

Michael's head was bent close to Dorrie all the time and Anna could tell that they were talking seriously, although occasionally she heard Dorrie giggle.

The light from a street lamp fell on their house so both young men only shook hands formally as they wished the girls goodnight, and saw them admitted to the house.

'I'm so happy,' Dorrie whispered, as they took off their coats. 'Aren't you?'

Anna smiled and agreed, but she was puzzled too by Eugene's behaviour. I just haven't enough experience of men, she decided.

Dorrie was so excited and happy that she looked as though a lamp had been lit inside her as she told Anna that she and Michael had become engaged, but only privately. 'Dr and Mrs O'Brien know, but they say we must say nothing, not even to Mama, until Father comes home and we have his permission,' she said. 'Of course, they know I'll tell you.'

Anna hugged and kissed her sister. 'I take back all I said about the novelettes,' she said, smiling, and Dorrie said eagerly, 'I knew I'd know immediately when I met my Mr Right, Anna, and I did as soon as I saw Michael. Wasn't it lucky that he felt the same way?'

'It was indeed,' agreed Anna. 'Although it would have been odd if he hadn't.'

'And Eugene is smitten with you. Isn't it wonderful, Anna? We might have a double wedding.'

'Hold on,' Anna protested. 'Eugene has said nothing like that. He hasn't even said he's smitten.'

'Only because he's more reserved than Michael, but it's obvious from the way he looks at you,' said Dorrie. She giggled. 'The O'Briens think Michael's mad. Oh, Anna, aren't we lucky? The two most handsome men we've ever met and they've fallen for us. I'm so happy.'

'And so am I,' said Anna joyfully, wondering why she had ever doubted it, and they hugged each other rapturously.

Chapter Five

Before the two young men boarded the Irish boat the following morning, Dr O'Brien again talked seriously to Michael. 'Remember, not a word must be said until you've spoken to Captain Furlong,' he said. 'I was responsible for introducing you to Miss Dorrie and her father would be justified in blaming me if there was any scandal.'

'Scandal!' Michael exclaimed. 'Sure, I wouldn't hurt a hair of her head.'

'I know, I know,' Dr O'Brien said. 'Everything's above board with you, but it has to be seen to be. Take a leaf out of D'Arcy's book. He tells me he has asked if he can write to Miss Anna, but there's no wild talk about marriage.'

Michael looked angry, but he only said, 'I suppose it's all right if Dorrie and I write to each other about how we feel?'

'Yes, but slow down man, for God's sake. If Captain Furlong approves and you're both of the same mind I'll be delighted, but you're both young and if either of you changes your mind there's no harm done – as long as you haven't been shouting it from the housetops.'

'I'll be sensible,' Michael promised. 'I hadn't realised it could harm Dorrie.' He grinned. 'Mother says I talk first and think later.'

Dr O'Brien looked alarmed. 'Say nothing to your mother, for God's sake. She'd be on the first boat over and come down on me like the wrath of God.'

'I'll be the soul of discretion,' Michael promised, and Dr O'Brien could only hope that he would.

In the excitement of talking over the bazaar and the amount of money raised, there was little gossip about Dr O'Brien's nephews or the trip to Eastham Woods, although of course they had been seen at the Pier Head.

Aunt Clara told Anna sourly that it would not have been allowed when she was young. 'Young girls going off for the day with strange young men would lose their good name,' she said.

'Yes, but times are different now and I'm glad they are,' Anna retorted. 'This is a new century and a new, modern King, and those silly ideas are forgotten.' Aunt Clara sulked for the rest of the day, but Anna and Dorrie were too happy to care.

Little could be said about Michael and Eugene in public, in case it led to a slip of the tongue about the proposed engagement, but in the privacy of their bedroom the girls talked about little else.

Eugene wrote to Anna every week, mostly about his new regiment, the Irish Guards, and events in London, but he always wrote lover-like messages at the end of the letters and always sent messages to Dr and Mrs O'Brien.

Dorrie received letters from Michael every day, sometimes twice a day, but with the help of Nelly she was able to conceal most of them from her mother and aunt, and more importantly from Anna, in case she was hurt by their frequency, compared to Eugene's weekly letter.

When the girls read and reread their letters in their bedroom Anna could not avoid seeing that Michael's were very different from Eugene's neat letters in copperplate handwriting. Michael's were decorated with Cupids and hearts and arrows scattered among his untidy scrawl.

Anna still doubted that Eugene really loved her, partly because she felt that she was plain and uninteresting and wondered how she could possibly have attracted him. He told her that he loved her in his messages at the end of his letters, but in very formal and restrained language.

She hinted at these fears to Dorrie, who dismissed them. 'It's just the type of man he is,' she told Anna. 'Most men are like him. Look at the engaged men in this parish. They know they'll be engaged for years, to give them time to get a home together, so they don't go overboard like Michael.' She smiled fondly. 'He's the exception. The mad Irishman.'

Anna knew that Dorrie, although so trusting and affectionate, was sometimes very shrewd, especially about men, so she believed her, because she wanted to believe her, and was happy.

She was pleased and proud to pass on the messages to Dr O'Brien. 'I had a letter from that scamp Michael,' he said, shaking his head. 'Mad as a March hare. Still raving on about Dorrie and marriage. You're better with a sensible fellow like D'Arcy, my dear.' Anna blushed and smiled. The doctor seemed disproportionately pleased that she was still receiving letters from Eugene, but she was unaware of the nagging doubt that they silenced in him.

At his last port of call Captain Furlong received letters from both his daughters, his wife, and his sister, and also one from Michael and one from Dr O'Brien, so he knew the situation when he arrived home.

He talked of general matters during the meal, but after it he said, 'Dorothea, I would like to speak to you in my study.'

When Dorrie stood before her father at his desk, he had Michael's letter open before him. 'I was surprised to receive this letter from a man I have never met, Dorothea,' he said, and as she blushed and stammered he said more kindly, 'Fortunately, I had a more sensible one from Dr O'Brien who, it seems, is his uncle.'

Captain Furlong questioned Dorrie closely and before she left she ventured to ask nervously, 'Will you allow us to marry, Father?'

'I will give it some thought,' he said dismissively.

Later, he said to Anna, 'I believe you too have an admirer, Annabel, but a more sensible and correct young man than your sister's.' Anna smiled. Sometimes she wished that Eugene was less formal and reserved, but as Jim Deagan often said, 'People are what they are. If you were he you'd do as he would do.'

Perhaps a mixture of Michael and Eugene would produce a happy medium, she thought, but she was happy to be courted by such a handsome gentleman and felt herself more and more in love with him.

The following morning, which was Friday, a telegram arrived from Michael to announce that he had a weekend pass and would be arriving on Saturday morning.

Captain Furlong walked down to Shaw Street to see Dr O'Brien, but the doctor was out on a case when he arrived and Mrs O'Brien talked to him about Michael and Eugene. She expected the doctor back, but a small ragged boy arrived with a note, and she excused herself and took the child to the kitchen fire, where she left him with thick slices of bread and jam and a cup of cocoa.

'My husband might be out all night,' she told Captain Furlong when she returned. 'It's a bad confinement. These poor young things are starving very often. Too weak to bear the child. He wants soup and blankets.'

The captain looked grim. 'Aye, and it happens sometimes with the best of care, ma'am,' he said.

Mrs O'Brien agreed. 'Very true. Heaven knows that was the case with Mrs Furlong, but still, thank God you have two lovely daughters. We were never blessed at all.'

They were silent for a moment then, as the captain rose to leave, she said brightly, 'Still, we have Dr O'Brien's nephews, who are like sons to us. God is good.'

Captain Furlong was thoughtful as he walked home, reflecting that he must tread carefully. He had not realised that Dr O'Brien's nephew was regarded as a son, and a refusal could offend his good friend.

The following morning Dr O'Brien walked up to Westbourne Street with his nephew and went into the captain's study alone at first. 'You had little sleep, I think,' Captain Furlong said. 'How did it go?'

'Lost the child, saved the mother,' said Dr O'Brien briefly. 'Right way round as she has three others, and not enough in the house to feed a sparrow.'

Dorrie and Anna were hovering in the hall and Michael seized the opportunity to draw Dorrie behind the grandfather clock and kiss her, before his uncle called him into the study. The three men were in the study for some time and Michael came out alone, looking downcast.

His face brightened when he saw Dorrie and he whispered to her, 'He's not against us, but we have to stay as we are for another six months. My uncle may talk him round a bit.' He turned to Anna. 'D'Arcy was disappointed not to be able to come with me to see you, but sure there was no way. I had to use bribery and corruption and a parcel of lies to get the pass. I even resurrected my poor grandmother who's dead these twenty years and now I'm burying her again.'

He had brought a photograph of Eugene wearing the red jacket and bearskin of his regiment, taken when he was on guard duty. Eugene had actually given him the photograph for his uncle, but Michael felt so guilty about Anna that he impulsively gave it to her. Anna was delighted. Her only complaint was that too much of Eugene's face was hidden, but she framed the photograph and kept it by her bedside.

Before Michael left on Sunday, Captain Furlong told him that Dorrie must meet Michael's parents before their engagement was announced in six months' time. Dr O'Brien would arrange it. If everything was satisfactory, Michael and Dorrie could become engaged, and marry when Dorrie was twenty-one.

'A two-year engagement!' Dorrie said in dismay when he told her. 'On top of waiting a year.'

But Michael said cheerfully, 'Never fret, darling. I'll talk him round long before that. He says this will only be a short voyage and he'll be home in six months' time, then we can announce the engagement if we are both of the same mind! As if we'd change!' They clung together, kissing each other passionately.

Anna found all her old resentment against her father's autocratic ways returning as she saw how hard it was for Dorrie and Michael to keep their love secret and wait to announce their engagement. 'It's a farce, anyway,' she said one day as she walked home with Dr O'Brien. 'I'm sure everyone in the parish knows we're receiving letters from your nephews. I know Mama's told Mrs Jenson and probably other people too.'

'Your father is only thinking of your sister's good name, Anna,' the doctor said. 'I've seen it happen. A girl nearly suicidal after being let down and humiliated before everyone. Mind you, there's usually more to it.'

It was not possible for him to explain further to an unmarried girl, but Anna was already saying indignantly, 'You don't think that either Dorrie or Michael would ever change, surely, doctor?'

'Not for a minute,' he assured her. 'That's true love if ever I saw it, but your father has only seen them together such a short time.'

But he still thinks he should order their lives, Anna thought mutinously, even though he knows nothing about it. If I was Dorrie I'd elope.

Then she realised. Even if Dorrie wanted to elope, it would be impossible. Even for that she'd need *some* money, and they had none at all. It was so degrading, Anna thought. It hampered them in every way. Their father would not allow them to work, but he refused to give them an allowance. 'You are denied nothing that you need,' he said, and it was true that they had all the clothes and comfort they required.

They chose their clothes and the cost was charged to their mother's account, and their home was more than comfortable. But the girls had no money of their own. The collection money for church was given to them by their mother and any other small expenses had to be applied for. Mrs Furlong enjoyed her power and seemed to enjoy refusing requests, especially by Anna.

Am I unreasonable, Anna thought now, to want to be independent? It doesn't seem to worry Dorrie as much, even having to ask for coppers for stamps.

Her thoughts were interrupted when she realised that the doctor was talking about her father. 'You're fortunate girls that your father cares so much about you,' he was saying. 'And he's a good man, Anna. He came to my house when I was out on a case and heard about the destitution of my patient. When I was at your place with Michael he put a bag of money in my hand for the poor girl he'd heard about. No fuss. Just quietly done when he had a lot more to think about than my patient. I respect him for that, Anna, and indeed for many things.'

Anna felt ashamed of her thoughts about her father, and decided that he honestly believed he had made the best possible arrangements for his daughters.

Before he left, he confirmed that he planned only a short

voyage, which meant he would be home by August 1902. 'And then we can get engaged!' Dorrie said later with delight. 'Has Eugene hinted anything, Anna?' Anna shook her head. 'Perhaps when we get engaged,' Dorrie said. 'They say one wedding makes another. Wouldn't it be lovely if we could have a double wedding?'

Anna managed to smile. 'I think you're going too fast for us, Dorrie,' she said. 'Eugene isn't as impetuous as Michael.'

'But if we have to have a two-year engagement as Father says,' said Dorrie, 'that would be long enough, wouldn't it?' Anna smiled and agreed. In her heart it was what she was hoping for, but to hear it put into words made it seem like an impossible dream. And yet she was still receiving letters regularly, always with a loving message.

Eugene had told her that he saw little of Michael now and in May he came alone to Liverpool en route for his home in Dublin. The girls were both excited, Dorrie more openly than her sister, and they spent hours trying out new hairstyles for Anna. Dorrie offered all her most precious possessions – a coral bracelet and necklace and her favourite shawl.

Eugene arrived on a Friday night and walked to the Furlong house with Dr O'Brien. He greeted Anna tenderly, holding her hand and gazing deeply into her eyes, watched approvingly by his uncle and by Anna's family. The weather was fine and a picnic was arranged at Calderstones Park on Saturday afternoon.

Anna and Eugene, Dorrie and Mrs Furlong, Dr and Mrs O'Brien, and Mrs Jenson and Isabel travelled in a wagonette driven by the doctor through the fresh green of the lanes and avenues leading to the park.

The ladies had brought picnic hampers, and table cloths were spread on the grass and the food laid out on them. There was much laughter as Dr O'Brien declared himself in charge of the spirit kettle and managed to singe his moustache.

Anna and Eugene took no part in the activities, sitting apart on a rug taken from the wagonette, talking in low tones, but no one seemed to mind.

Eugene spoke more freely than he had ever done about his parents and his four sisters in Dublin. 'My father is an Englishman,' he said. 'A member of staff at Vice Regal Lodge.'

'Your mother is Dr O'Brien's sister, isn't she?' Anna said shyly. 'Are they alike?'

'They couldn't be more different,' Eugene said, smiling as he looked at Dr O'Brien's antics with the kettle. 'My mother is . . .' He shrugged. 'Languid, I think would describe her, but she's very beautiful. Very devout too. Insists on morning and evening prayers for the servants.'

He laughed, but Anna listened in dismay. His family seemed to move in very different circles to her own, and it seemed even more incredible that he would want to marry her. Yet he had taken her hand and was smiling at her as a shadow fell over them.

'You must come and get some food,' Dr O'Brien said. 'Food for the gods it is. Can I help you up, Miss Anna?' But Eugene had already lifted her effortlessly to her feet.

Later, they wandered around the shrubberies and flower gardens, Anna holding Eugene's arm. She was in a daze of happiness, feeling she must pinch herself to make sure that she was not dreaming. This tall, handsome soldier was smiling at her lovingly, and talking about the poetry and the music which she loved, and it seemed he loved them too. He said nothing of marriage, but it was early days by the standards of most people. As Dorrie said, Michael was the exception.

The day seemed to end far too soon, but Mrs Furlong issued a general invitation to afternoon tea the following day. Everyone accepted and Dr O'Brien said jovially to Mrs

Furlong, 'I'm thinking you'll have a lot of festive occasions to organise in the near future.' His wife tugged at his arm and he said no more, but he was only saying what most of the party were thinking.

Eugene left for Dublin on the Monday morning boat and was seen off affectionately by his aunt and uncle. 'Tell your mother she has a good son,' Mrs O'Brien whispered as she kissed him goodbye and Dr O'Brien clapped him on the shoulder before leaving him at the boat.

Everyone was pleased with the way things had gone during the weekend, not least Eugene. He smiled secretly as he paced the deck of the boat and thought of his uncle's approval.

He had told Anna something of Michael's family too, most notably that Dorrie would have a formidable mother-in-law. 'She rules the roost there,' he said. 'And Michael is her favourite. I think the other son, Dermot, and his father cling together for protection.'

They had laughed together and Anna was pleased that Eugene had dropped his formality and correctness and gossiped to her. She felt that it was a step forward in their relationship.

Dr and Mrs O'Brien planned to have a holiday in Ireland in June, visiting relatives, and invited the Furlong sisters to go with them, for young company, they told people. Anna wondered whether she should warn Dorrie about Michael's mother, but decided it would be better to let her make her own judgement.

The weather was beautiful when they set off. It was the first time the girls had been away from home, and their delight increased the pleasure the O'Briens felt. By some means best known to himself, Michael had managed a few days' leave and he was waiting by the gangway with his father when the boat arrived.

Mr Farrell was a man of few words, and said only, 'You're very welcome, miss,' when he was introduced to Dorrie, but his smile was warm and welcoming. For the last part of the journey they drove in a trap, with Dr O'Brien up beside Mr Farrell and Anna and Mrs O'Brien sitting together.

Opposite them, Michael sat by Dorrie, his arm around her, and Anna sat blissfully breathing the soft air and reflecting that she was in Eugene's homeland. The farmhouse was larger and grander than she had expected and Michael's mother was waiting at the front door to greet them.

'You're too fat, Paddy,' she said to Dr O'Brien as she kissed him, then to Mrs O'Brien, 'You must cut down on his oats, my dear.'

Before either of them could answer she had taken Dorrie in her arms. 'And this is the little girl who has my son's heart broken,' she said, but Michael said easily, 'Only if her father won't let me marry her, Mammy.'

'Ach, leave him to me,' she said, then turning to Anna, 'You must be Anna. You're very welcome, my dear. Come in, come in.' They were swept into a large hall and Anna could see a well-furnished drawing room through an open door, but their hostess swept them on to the back of the house. 'We'll sit in the kitchen,' she announced. 'It's where we spend all our time anyway. Kathleen! Molly!' she shouted, and two shy young Irish maids took the girls' coats and showed them to their bedroom.

'Don't worry about Bridie,' Dr O'Brien said, seeing their bemused expressions before they left the kitchen. 'She was the talk of Dublin when we were young. The enfant terrible, and she's still the same. It was a relief to the family when she married a farmer and buried herself in the country.'

When they reached their bedroom the two girls collapsed on to the feather bed, trying to stifle their giggles with handkerchiefs.

'I can see why Michael's mad,' Anna gasped at length. 'It runs in the family.'

'I thought Dr O'Brien would be offended,' Dorrie said. 'But he didn't seem to mind. Or Mrs O'Brien. Cut down on his oats!' This started them off again, but eventually they composed themselves and washed their hands and faces before returning to the kitchen.

An enormous meal had been prepared for them and Anna avoided Dorrie's eye when she saw her hostess heaping food on Dr O'Brien's plate. But she needn't have worried, as Michael was sitting by Dorrie and they were engrossed in each other.

Michael's brother, Dermot, arrived in time for the meal. Anna had expected either a replica of Michael or a blond giant like his father, but Dermot was not like either of them. He was smaller and thinner, with gingery hair. He had a narrow face with a narrow beard, and he seemed full of nervous energy. He wore a tweed jacket over an open-necked shirt, with a red scarf knotted around his throat. His mother explained that he had come from working in the fields and would be returning there.

He was polite to the visitors, asking about their journey, but Anna felt that he looked down his sharp nose at Michael. She was sure of it when he looked at Michael, who was wearing civilian clothes, and said to Dorrie, 'I suppose you prefer my little brother in his fancy dress.'

Anna was pleased when Dorrie replied with spirit, 'I'm interested in Michael, not in his clothes.'

Dermot grimaced and said, 'Touché,' then turned to speak to Dr O'Brien. Michael beamed proudly at Dorrie. His mother seemed pleased too, but Anna felt that it was as much to hear Dermot snubbed. Already she could see signs of the division in the family that Eugene had spoken about. Mrs Farrell obviously doted on Michael, but not on Dermot, and at the end of the meal she saw Mr Farrell put his hand on Dermot's shoulder.

He said quietly, 'I'll be with you above in the field soon, son,' and Anna saw the look of affection that passed between them.

After the meal, Michael and the girls went for a stroll round the lanes and Dorrie said indignantly, 'I don't think your brother should have described your uniform as fancy dress, Michael.'

'Ah, he's never forgiven me for taking the Queen's shilling,' Michael said easily.

'Why? Did he think you should work on the farm too?' Dorrie said.

Michael laughed. 'No. He's just a Bold Fenian Man, as the song says.'

Dorrie looked shocked but said no more, and Anna moved ahead, looking in the hedgerows and at the wildlife round a tiny stream, while Dorrie and Michael kissed and cuddled in a secluded corner by a gate.

After the evening meal they had music and Anna listened, entranced, as Dr O'Brien played the *Moonlight Sonata*. 'You haven't lost your touch, Paddy,' his sister said.

He shrugged. 'I'm rusty, I know. I have little time for music now, although I love it still.'

He stood up and said, 'Let the young ones entertain us now,' and Dorrie played the accompaniment, blushing and smiling as Michael sang 'Drink to Me Only with Thine Eyes' in a pleasant baritone voice.

'Dermot now,' Mrs O'Brien said when they had finished. 'I remember you had a fine voice when we were here last, Dermot.'

'No rebel songs. Remember our guests,' Michael said in a

low voice as they passed Anna's chair.

Dermot paused and laughed. 'What about your fine new regiment? I hear the quick march is St Patrick's Day.' He sang in a low voice, 'But join in her cause like the brave and true-hearted, who rise for their rights on St Patrick's Day,' then the slow march, 'Come Back to Erin'.

Before he could say any more, Dr O'Brien called from across the room, 'Come along, Dermot. Don't keep us waiting.'

Dermot said to his father, ' "Roisin Dubh",' and his father accompanied him on his violin as Dermot sang in a true tenor voice, explaining first that Roisin Dubh was Irish for little dark rose.

Anna glanced across to where Michael sat beside Dorrie. He was scowling, but Dorrie was applauding and saying, 'Oh, what a lovely song, and you have a lovely voice too, Dermot. Do sing something else.'

'Thank you. I will,' he said, with a twist of his lips. ' "Kathleen Mavourneen", Dadda.'

Dorrie sat, entranced, listening to him, but although Anna could not help enjoying the music she felt troubled. She knew from the Deagans that the dark rose of the song was Ireland, and so was Kathleen Mavourneen.

These were really rebel songs in disguise, Anna realised. She saw that, although Mrs Farrell seemed to rule her kingdom, it was a bitterly divided one and the seeds of more trouble were evident. Would Dorrie, so innocent and trusting, be hurt by it?

When the entertainment was over, supper was served, and Anna had more cause for worry. On 1 June, shortly before they left for their holiday, the Lord Mayor, Alderman Petrie, had announced from the balcony of the Town Hall in Liverpool that the war in South Africa was over. There was great rejoicing that the Boers had finally been defeated, and Dr O'Brien described some of the scenes to his sister and brother-in-law.

Dermot, who was sitting beside Anna, muttered, 'They'll not rejoice for long. England will reap what she sows there in bitter tears.' Anna looked at him in surprise and he said in the same low, bitter tone, 'They'll drive out decent, good-living Dutch farmers for adventurers without principle who are out to make their fortunes in gold and diamonds and by any means. They'll treat England as England has treated others. She'll reap what she sows.'

'You seem pleased at the prospect,' Anna said coldly.

'I am,' he said. 'England's enemies are my friends.'

There was a slight pause in the conversation and everyone heard him. Michael jumped to his feet, his face congested with anger and his fists clenched, but Dorrie laid a pleading hand on his arm. Mrs O'Brien was restraining her husband too, but Mr Farrell went on eating calmly.

Mrs Farrell beat her clenched fist on the table. 'How dare you, you uncouth, ignorant— I'm ashamed to have reared you. Miss Furlong is English. I don't know how to apologise, my dear.'

'I'm sorry. Will you forgive me?' Dermot said, bending his head to look into Anna's face. 'Sure, I thought you were at least half Irish. I thought everyone in Liverpool had Irish blood in their veins. Is that not so? You've not even a teaspoonful of Irish blood?'

He looked so comical with his eyelids and all the planes of his face drooping in contrition, in contrast to his rakish beard, that Anna could not help smiling. 'Not even a teaspoonful,' she said. 'Many people in Liverpool are Irish or of Irish descent, but there are a lot of Welsh people and Scottish and many Chinese.'

'But you're English?' Dermot said.

'Yes. My father's family are from Hull. That was his home

port until he came to Liverpool when he switched from sail to steam. My mother is a Londoner.'

Anna's face was flushed, but she spoke calmly and Mrs Farrell said approvingly, 'That's very interesting and you're a grand girl to forgive my renegade son.'

'He'd better not attack the Irish Guards, though, because both Miss Anna and Miss Dorrie have an interest in that regiment,' said Dr O'Brien.

'This soda bread is delicious, Bridie,' Mrs O'Brien said smoothly. 'I can never get it like this in Liverpool, although I use the same ingredients.'

'Perhaps it's the Irish water,' Dorrie suggested, and the talk turned to safer topics.

For the rest of the visit harmony prevailed, at least while the O'Briens and the Furlongs were present, but on several occasions saw Dermot and Michael together, away from the house, and they always seemed to be arguing fiercely.

Dermot was out for most of the day, working in the fields, and Michael sometimes went to work with his father for a few hours, but he spent nearly all his time with Dorrie. Anna enjoyed wandering along the sweet-smelling lanes, where she was greeted by everyone she met and invited into every house.

Every night there was music and talk before supper and Anna told Mrs O'Brien that she had been made so welcome that she felt she had known the family for years.

'I know,' Mrs O'Brien said. 'I was nursing in Dublin and Paddy was a medical student here when we met, and I felt the same when I went to his house. Bridie was very kind to me. John Farrell's a fine man too.'

One evening the talk turned to events in Liverpool and London, where celebrations were planned for the coronation of King Edward VII. The O'Briens planned to return to Liverpool on 20 June so as to be home in good time for it.

Anna and Dorrie were amazed at how well informed all the Farrell family seemed to be about affairs in England, better, Anna thought ruefully, than she was herself, and Dorrie agreed with her. 'Some of those politicians they mentioned, I'd never even heard about,' she said. 'I felt so ignorant.'

Michael was due to return to barracks a few days before they were to leave for Dublin, and on his last day Dermot drove Dr and Mrs O'Brien and Anna and Dorrie to spend the day at the Vale of Avoca, leaving Michael and his mother to have a day to themselves.

Dermot was an entertaining host, pointing out places of interest they passed, and talking of Ireland's ancient history. Of Queen Maeve and Malachi and his collar of gold.

Dorrie missed Michael, but she was consoled when Dermot said quietly to her, 'You're a good girl, acushla, to let Mammy have this day with Michael all to herself. It means a lot to her.'

They were all entranced by the peace and beauty of the Vale of Avoca, and went to the point at which the waters met. A few wild flowers grew on a tiny projecting piece of land and Dermot plucked three of them. He gave one to each of the ladies, saying, 'This will remind you of the Vale of Avoca.'

'Even the name is poetic!' Anna exclaimed, and Dermot said immediately, 'Thomas Moore wrote a poem about it.'

He stood resting his arm along the branch of a young tree and in his pure tenor voice sang, 'There is not in the wide world a valley so sweet, as the vale in whose bosom the bright waters meet.' He sang it right through and then, smiling at them, he sang the last verse: 'Sweet Vale of Avoca how calm could I rest, in thy bosom of shade with the friends I love best, Where the storms that we feel in this cold world should cease, and our hearts like thy waters be mingled in peace.'

It was a moment of magic and everyone was silent. The only sounds were the ripple of the water and the cry of a bird, until Dermot walked back to the trap. 'I'll remember this all my life,' Anna said softly, and Dorrie replied quietly, 'So will I.'

The O'Briens were holding hands, but they stood up when Dermot came back with a huge picnic basket. 'We won't starve, anyway,' Dr O'Brien said as he lifted the lid.

As they drove home Dorrie whispered to Anna, 'I think I was quite mistaken about Dermot. He's really nice, isn't he?' She giggled. 'Imagine any of the fellows we know at home standing up and singing like that, yet it was so beautiful and so *right*. He wasn't showing off or anything, just so natural.' Anna nodded, and Dorrie went on, 'But imagine it at home! Imagine James Hargreaves doing it!'

'Poor James,' Anna said. She wondered whether he knew of their holiday and what it meant, but her thoughts were really on Dorrie's words about Dermot. She could not agree. She felt that they had seen the real Dermot when they first arrived, but he was now hiding that side of his nature out of courtesy to the family guests. She liked him and thought him clever, but he could be a dangerous young man, she felt.

They arrived back in time for supper, followed by a musical evening. Mrs Farrell, who was flushed and happy, cried joyously to Michael, 'Come on now, Michael. I'm sure you have a song to sing.'

'I have, Mammy,' he said, smiling at Dorrie. ' "Believe Me If All Those Endearing Young Charms".'

Dermot sat down at the piano and played the accompaniment while Michael sang the words of love, gazing at Dorrie while the older people looked on, smiling. He followed this with 'The Lark in the Clear Air', another love song, then Dr O'Brien exclaimed, 'Something for us older people now.'

Mr Farrell picked up his violin and played 'Love's Old Sweet Song', then at the end of the evening they all sang 'God

Be With You Till We Meet Again', which everyone felt rounded off a most successful visit.

Michael left the following morning, then for the others it was all packing and leave taking before they set off for Dublin to visit Dr O'Brien's younger sister, who was Eugene's mother, and her family.

Chapter Six

When they drew near to Dublin Dorrie leaned close to Anna and whispered, 'Now you'll meet *your* future in-laws, Anna. I hope they're as nice as Michael's family.'

'Be careful, Dorrie,' Anna said in alarm. 'You and I are in different positions altogether. Marriage has never been mentioned. I don't suppose Eugene has said anything about me to his family.'

'I'm sure he has. Perhaps not about marriage, but only because it's early days yet for anyone less madcap than Michael.' Dorrie smiled fondly, then added, 'You'll be able to see what Eugene's family is like in good time anyway.'

'If they're half as nice as Michael's I'll be pleased,' Anna said, but before the visit was over she decided that they were not even that.

The D'Arcys' family home was a beautifully proportioned Georgian house in a quiet Dublin square, but the O'Briens and their young companions were coolly received. There was none of the open-handed comfort of the Ballinane farmhouse, or the warm welcome, and Anna soon decided that everything in the house was for show.

She felt that Eugene's description of his mother as 'languid' fitted her perfectly. Three of the daughters were away on visits and the one remaining at home was only a pale imitation of her mother. They saw little of Mr D'Arcy and were not sorry.

His high, stiff collars held his head at an angle so he seemed to look down his long nose at them, and they all, even Dorrie, found his manner patronising.

Although the fires were small and the food at the formal meals was poor, the house was overrun with servants who solemnly assembled for morning and evening prayers. Dr O'Brien had little patience with the pretensions of his younger sister and treated her robustly, although Mrs O'Brien and the two girls secretly felt intimidated by her.

At dinner the first evening Mrs O'Brien nearly provoked a quarrel between her husband and his brother-in-law. They had been speaking about the beautiful countryside near the Ballinane farmhouse and Mrs O'Brien innocently remarked that Charles Stewart Parnell had been born not far from there.

Mr D'Arcy, who had scarcely spoken until then, said sneeringly, 'Not a fact to be proud of.'

'*I'm* proud of it,' Dr O'Brien said hotly. 'Parnell was a great man. The uncrowned King of Ireland.'

'An adulterer and a fool,' Mr D'Arcy sneered. 'Pressing for Home Rule when it was a lost cause. What would these people do with Home Rule anyway? They're ungovernable as it is.'

'You'll see what they'll do with Home Rule,' Dr O'Brien said, his face red with anger. 'Because it will come, mark my words. Gladstone's Home Rule Bill was thrown out in eighty-six, but he'll get it through eventually. Parnell wasn't the only one working for it.'

'The others have lain very low since Parnell was disgraced, then,' said Mr D'Arcy. 'He was the ringleader.'

'Yes, and that's why he was brought low,' Dr O'Brien said passionately. 'The Home Rule Bill was thrown out in eighty-six. In eighty-seven *The Times* tried to tie him in with the murder of Lord Frederick Cavendish, but they failed, so they used that foolish woman to bring him down. Just shows how much he was feared.'

Nuala gave a tinkling laugh. 'Well, it's all over now. You won't be able to see much of Dublin on this visit, will you?

Perhaps we could have a drive out tomorrow?'

Mrs O'Brien followed her lead and said that although she knew Dublin well she hoped that Anna and Dorrie would be able to return when they had more time for sightseeing.

Dr O'Brien had cooled down, but Anna, who sat next to him, was amused to see that he was served with the best food from the serving dishes by the manservant. She heard the low whisper from the man, 'More power to you, sor. God save Ireland.'

The following day Nuala ordered her landau to drive them round Dublin. 'Unless you would prefer a closed carriage?' she said to Mrs O'Brien.

'Not at all. We'll see more in the open carriage,' she replied, but the fact that the D'Arcys also owned a carriage was not lost on her or the girls.

Soon after leaving the Georgian square, they passed once-imposing houses that were now almost derelict and were evidently home to the gaunt and haggard women and the dozens of barefoot, ragged and hungry children who swarmed there.

'Good God, I've never seen such poverty, even in Liverpool,' Dr O'Brien exclaimed. 'It's much worse than when I was last here. Is nothing being done for them?'

'There are always appeals for charity. Soup kitchens and all that sort of thing,' Nuala said carelessly. 'Really, you grow tired of it. They prefer to live like animals, shiftless and dirty, drinking any money they get. Cleanliness costs nothing.'

'Of course it does!' Dr O'Brien exclaimed. 'And water is hard enough to come by for cooking and drinking in these places, never mind washing.'

'Look at that,' Nuala said scornfully as they passed a group of poor children with mops of unruly hair. One redhead was scratching her head vigorously. 'They could at least cut and comb their hair.'

'Yes, if they had scissors or a comb,' Dr O'Brien said. 'I can't believe you don't feel compassion for them, Nuala. You're not the girl I knew.'

Dr O'Brien's back was to the coachman so he was unable to see that the man was flicking his whip at the children who were running alongside the horses, but from her seat Anna could see that a child was often caught with the whip and left crying in pain.

She grew steadily more indignant, especially as Nuala, sitting beside her, could also see what was happening but chose to remain oblivious. Probably told the man to do it, Anna thought savagely.

They soon left the district, but the beauty of the rest of the drive was lost on them and they were glad when it was over. 'We'll come again to Dublin, girls,' Mrs O'Brien whispered to Anna and Dorrie, 'but we'll give this crowd a wide berth. *I'll* show you the city.'

Later, as they prepared for dinner, Anna said suddenly, 'I wish we could go home now, this minute, Dorrie.'

'Yes, I feel the same,' Dorrie said. 'And I'm sure the O'Briens do too. It seems an awful thing to say when we're accepting the D'Arcys' hospitality, but I'll be glad to leave.'

'I dread this dinner,' Anna said, and Dorrie agreed. So they were all the more surprised by the warmth of the welcome they received when they went downstairs and the effort that all the D'Arcys put into being pleasant and hospitable.

They would have been less surprised if they had heard a conversation between Mr D'Arcy and his wife as they dressed for dinner.

Nuala had been complaining about the drive. 'Really, my brother has grown quite uncouth,' she said. 'And so contentious. He really annoyed me.'

She was sitting at her dressing table and her husband

stood behind her, putting studs in his shirt. Their eyes met in the mirror and he said meaningly, 'I hope you didn't show it, my dear. It appears that the red carpet was rolled out for them at Ballinane.' She said nothing and he went on, 'As the eldest nephew, Eugene is your brother's natural heir, but young Farrell seems to have made himself a favourite with the O'Briens.'

'There is an understanding between young Farrell and the younger girl, Dorothea, I believe,' said Nuala. 'Patrick and his wife approve, apparently.'

Her husband stared into the mirror, pursing his lips. 'We must be careful, my dear, and do our best to promote Eugene's claim. You know how important it is for him – how little we can do for him. Your brother could easily decide to make them joint heirs.'

'Or even worse,' Nuala said, looking alarmed, 'it could all go to Michael Farrell.'

Her husband said smoothly, 'Yes, so you must hide any irritation you feel and try to charm them.'

'You were the one who argued with him at the table last night,' Nuala said in a sulky voice, but he replied dismissively, 'Politics. Men's talk. Not an argument.'

Nothing controversial was mentioned at the dinner table that evening, and Nuala and Mr D'Arcy talked only about Dublin and some of the literary figures they had met. Dr O'Brien, who had been dismayed by the change in his sister, was only too happy to see her 'more like herself' and to charm and be charmed. Mrs O'Brien decided that perhaps their hosts had only been stiff and shy the previous night and willingly responded to the warmer atmosphere.

Even the daughter, Maeve, talked to Anna and Dorrie about the dances which took place in Dublin in winter. When they moved to the drawing room for coffee Mrs D'Arcy began to sing the praises of Eugene and asked Mrs O'Brien what she thought of her son.

'He's a fine young man. Very classy-looking,' Mrs O'Brien said. 'And very polite and pleasant with us. We really enjoy his visits. Did he tell you about the grand picnic we had in Calderstones Park when he was in Liverpool for the weekend?'

Anna dreaded a remark about his attentions to her, as she was sure he had said nothing about her at home, but Mrs O'Brien was far too diplomatic to speak in any but the most general terms. Dr O'Brien, fortunately, was being shown a folio of paintings of the Mansion House and missed the conversation.

'I do love a picnic, don't you? If the weather's good, of course,' Mrs O'Brien went on.

'Yes, you must have the weather,' Mrs D'Arcy agreed. 'Eugene does love Liverpool. He says he always leaves it very reluctantly because you are so kind and make him feel so much at home.'

Not much of a compliment with a home like this, a small voice in Anna's head remarked, but she ignored it and smiled blandly.

Nuala raised her voice. 'I'm just saying, Patrick, that Eugene loves Liverpool and he admires the work you do there among the poor. He thinks you're very heroic.'

'Nothing heroic about it,' Dr O'Brien growled, his face red. 'I prefer treating the real illnesses of the poor, rather than rich women with imaginary ailments, that's all.'

Mr D'Arcy suggested some music and a manservant was called to set up a harp for Maeve to play. Anna was sitting near Mrs D'Arcy and heard her husband drawl as he passed by them, 'Discard the trowel, my dear.' She saw the venomous glance he received from his wife too, and decided that it was a strange and uncomfortable house, in spite of all the suddenly effusive treatment they were receiving.

But she soon forgot these thoughts when Maeve began to play. Anna was not qualified to judge how well she played, but Miss D'Arcy was wearing a flowing dress and flowers in her hair and she struck such an attitude, drooping against the harp with her eyes upturned soulfully to the ceiling.

Anna was seized with a desire to giggle and was afraid to look at Dorrie in case she was in the same state, so for the length of the music she suffered, swallowing madly and pressing her handkerchief against her lips, as though to prevent a cough.

Anna dreaded an encore, but Dorrie was being politely pressed to sing. She glanced at Anna, who rose and went to the piano. Dorrie's face was flushed and her eyes brighter than usual, but otherwise she was composed and her example helped Anna to sit sedately at the piano and accompany her as she sang 'The Last Rose of Summer' and 'The Little Toy Soldier'.

Afterwards, more coffee and sandwiches were brought in and Nuala pressed Dr O'Brien for his opinion of Eugene and whether he had been wise to join the Irish Guards.

'Yes, indeed,' he said heartily. 'It was a good move for both of them. The discipline is very strict but that's good for them, and they've both grown into fine young men. We enjoy their company and, as I said to Eugene the last time we saw him, it's very good of yourself and Bridie to let them spend time with us when you must be desperate to see your sons.'

'I am, but you have a claim to him too. Eugene is your eldest nephew and very fond of both of you,' Nuala said.

'As we are of him,' said Mrs O'Brien. 'We really enjoy his company, and he's well liked by our friends.'

'Yes, they're fine young men, both of them, and we're very proud of them, although the credit is yours for the way they've been reared. Eugene is quieter and more reserved than Michael, but sure that's no bad thing,' Dr O'Brien said, looking with twinkling eyes at Dorrie. But Mr D'Arcy and his wife were too busy looking at each other with complacent smiles to notice.

The farewells the next day were effusive, with invitations to return at any time. Dr O'Brien had insisted on hiring a cab to take them to the boat, so they were able to speak freely as they drove away.

'That was a strange visit altogether,' Mrs O'Brien said. 'I wonder had there been some trouble just before we arrived. They seemed so stiff and unwelcoming, but perhaps we came at a bad time. They were different altogether last night.'

'Yes, I'm glad we didn't leave before dinner last night,' said Dr O'Brien. 'I'd have gone away thinking I'd lost my little Nuala, but she was her old self last night, thank God.'

'We'll have happier memories of the visit now,' his wife agreed.

'I know I've eaten his bread and salt and I shouldn't say this, but I can't stand that fellow D'Arcy,' said Dr O'Brien. He began to look out of the window and comment on places they passed and Dorrie pressed Anna's arm.

'Never mind,' she whispered. 'The family were hard to understand, but it is Eugene you'll be marrying, not his family.'

Anna said nothing. She wondered if indeed she would be marrying Eugene. It was obvious to her that his family knew nothing about her. He had not even mentioned her as a special friend.

She felt depressed, but thought about his behaviour at the picnic and at the tea party, and the words of love in his letters, and felt more cheerful and hopeful. If it wasn't for Michael being so impetuous it wouldn't occur to me to think of marriage so soon, she thought, and she decided that Dorrie was right. Michael was the exception!

It was a difference in temperament, perhaps even in upbringing, that made the two men so different in their courtship. Anna could understand this better after meeting both families, and she pushed away her fears and looked forward to the future.

The crossing of the Irish Sea was not as smooth as on their journey to Ireland, and Mrs O'Brien and Dorrie soon took refuge in their bunks. Anna stayed on deck with Dr O'Brien. She felt that the holiday had led her to know and like him even more than before.

'I *have* enjoyed these last weeks,' she said gratefully as they paced the deck arm-in-arm. 'But I felt so ignorant. I know so little of Irish history, or of English for that matter. At school we only did the Black Prince and King Alfred burning the cakes.'

'It's an interesting subject, right enough,' the doctor said. 'Jim and Luke Deagan are very well informed. You should talk to them.'

'Jim often talks to me about things,' Anna said. 'You know what Dermot was saying about the Boer War? Jim agrees with him. He was angry about the concentration camps that Kitchener set up for the women and children, especially when we heard of all the deaths among them. He said if it was just good farming land they'd have been able to live in peace. The war was only because gold and diamonds were found there.'

Dr O'Brien nodded, then chuckled. 'I wonder what that stick D'Arcy would have said if I'd told him that Dermot agreed with him about Home Rule?'

'Does he?' Anna exclaimed in surprise.

'Aye. His father said, "Half a loaf is better than no bread, and if Home Rule comes independence will come in time," but me bold Dermot erupted like Vesuvious. "To hell with

Home Rule. We want independence and we want it *now*!" he shouted. "It's the curse of Ireland, letting ourselves be fobbed off." I can just see D'Arcy's face if he knew he was on the same side as Dermot,' the doctor laughed.

'I thought they seemed hard to understand,' Anna said. 'But the Farrells are lovely, aren't they?'

'Aye. John Farrell is true as steel, but D'Arcy! I'm very fond of Nuala, though she's a foolish girl in many ways, but she's worth better than that chancer. He deceived her – deceived us all. Made out he was in a high position in Vice Regal Lodge when he was nothing but a pen pusher.'

'But he seems so superior – and that lovely house!' Anna exclaimed.

'Bought with Nuala's money. I felt like reminding him where it came from. My father's uncle, an old bachelor farmer in Carlow. Never spent a penny when a ha'penny would do. Mean as dirt.' He laughed. 'When I think of the airs and graces of D'Arcy and those girls and the state of the old clod farmer who provided the money for them, I could die laughing.'

'I don't suppose they ever think of that,' Anna said.

'No. I don't suppose they do. Old Jeremiah, who used string for everything. To tie up his glasses, his pipe, his furniture, and without string half his farm tools would have fallen to pieces. We went there twice a year and the basket of food Mammy took him was all he had apart from scraps all year.'

'I'll bet he never visualised Mr D'Arcy spending his money,' Anna said.

The doctor squeezed her arm. 'You see the joke anyhow, Anna,' he said. 'Jeremiah left his fortune to my parents, and it *was* a fortune, believe me.'

'Sad that he denied himself any comfort, though,' Anna said.

'I'd think that too, except he told Mammy when she was urging him to buy food and coal that it gave him more pleasure to save a penny than to spend it. My father was a careful man too, but not mean, so he left the five of us well provided for. Myself and Bridie and Nuala and the sister and brother in America. Bridie and John invested some in more stock, which has reaped rewards for them, and I've looked after mine, but I think Nuala's has been wasted on show.'

They leaned on the rails in companionable silence for a while, then Dr O'Brien mused, 'It seems a love match right enough between Michael and Dorrie. Bridie and John are delighted with her. They think she's a lovely girl, and you too, Anna. Bridie said she loves the bones of you.' He laughed. 'You wouldn't think of taking on Dermot now just to please her?'

'No thanks,' Anna laughed. 'Not even to please her, although I liked him, you know, doctor.'

'Aye, he's a good lad and a talented one, but he keeps queer company. I'd be sorry to see you mixed up with him. Anyhow, you have at least one young man – what's the latest word – smitten with you already.'

'You're very well up on slang!' Anna exclaimed to hide her confusion.

'Right up to the minute,' the doctor said, smiling, then he added, 'But you've plenty of time to look around. Don't do anything in a hurry.'

He said nothing of Bridie's reaction when he spoke about Anna and Eugene. 'Tell her to look nearer home, Paddy. Have nothing to do with that fellow. Find a decent lad from her own parish.'

As though she read his thoughts, Anna said thoughtfully, 'There'll be a few broken hearts in the parish when Dorrie marries. James Hargreaves for one.'

'Poor lad,' the doctor said with a sigh. 'He deserves some happiness, Anna. God knows he's had little enough so far.'

'I didn't like his mother,' Anna said, but she was surprised when the doctor said vehemently, 'May she roast in hell and I hope her brother joins her there.'

She turned her head to look at him in surprise and he said, 'I've shocked you, Anna, but our Lord Himself said, "Whatever you do to the least of My little ones, you do it to Me," and He spoke of being cast into the nether darkness. You know, I long, Anna, yes *long* to see that young man happy.'

'I think he looks better since his mother died,' Anna said timidly.

'Yes, he does,' the doctor said, more calmly. 'D'you know Frances O'Neill?' he asked, then without waiting for an answer he went on, 'She cleans and cooks for him. Proper meals, instead of his mother's greasy leftovers, and she got him to go to a different tailor and barber. He looks better, but I'd like to see him happy too.'

'Dorrie was very sorry for him. She thought he was lonely without his mother, as they were always together, so she was friendly to him. She didn't mean to encourage him,' Anna said, looking troubled, but the doctor patted her hand.

'Of course not. She was just being kind. I wasn't thinking of Dorrie. His won't be the only broken heart when she marries, but he'll get over it. You'll miss Dorrie yourself if you're still at home; you've always been so close, but remember our door is always open for you, Anna. You know having the company of you and Dorrie, especially you, made a big difference to this holiday for both of us.'

The boat was in smoother water, now that they had passed the bar, and they were joined by Mrs O'Brien and Dorrie.

The happy group arrived home to the news that the coronation had been postponed as the King was seriously ill.

He recovered, and it eventually took place in August, but by that time both girls were more interested in their father's arrival home.

On his return, Captain Furlong said nothing about the engagement, but after the usual celebratory meal and distribution of gifts he walked down to Shaw Street to see Dr O'Brien.

Michael had again wangled some leave and was due at Lime Street Station at eight o'clock. Dorrie hoped that her father would still be at the surgery when Michael arrived. She was sure that he could charm her father into announcing the engagement.

Michael walked back to Westbourne Street with Captain Furlong, so he was there, holding Dorrie's hand, when her father called the family together and told them that he had decided to announce the engagement between Dorothea and Guardsman Farrell before he returned to sea.

No firm date was set for the wedding, but Michael told Dorrie later that although her father wanted a two-year engagement they had compromised on eighteen months, bringing the wedding to February 1904.

Dorrie said doubtfully, 'February! I don't think that's a very good month for a wedding. We usually have the worst weather then.'

'I wonder, would he agree to September or October instead,' Michael said hopefully, but Dorrie thought it unlikely.

'He didn't think it was at all surprising that Father agreed to eighteen months,' she said later to Anna, 'but you know as well as I do, Anna, Father never changes his mind.'

'No. Compromise isn't a word he knows,' her sister agreed. 'But you're engaged anyway. No more secrecy,' and Dorrie said joyfully, 'No, I can't wait to tell everybody.'

Anna wrote immediately to Eugene to tell him, wondering

how he would react to the news. It was only when she received the usual cool reply, dwelling more on the fact that the regiment had acquired an Irish wolfhound named Brian Boru as a mascot than on the engagement, that she realised how much she had been hoping for a different response.

On Sunday morning Michael and Dr and Mrs O'Brien joined the Furlong family at ten o'clock Mass. Captain and Mrs Furlong led the way down the aisle, followed by Dorrie, proudly walking beside Michael, then Anna and Aunt Clara, followed by Dr and Mrs O'Brien.

A ripple of interest ran round the church, but Anna was looking at James Hargreaves, sitting by the wall of the side aisle, staring at Dorrie with a stricken look on his face. A thought went through her mind. I suppose he's been hoping against hope, like me. It was a shock to her to realise that this was the way she felt about Eugene. She had never acknowledged it before and the service passed in a blur as she tried to discover her true feelings.

The two families came out of the church to be greeted and congratulated on all sides. Captain Furlong seemed proud to introduce Michael to friends and it was hard to decide who was the more pleased between he and Dr O'Brien. It was a revelation to his daughters to see the captain in such a jovial mood.

Dorrie's eyes were like stars and Anna thought she had never looked lovelier. She had looked for James Hargreaves as they left the church, but he had slipped away, and she was glad that he had been spared the sight of this happy scene.

Chapter Seven

Before Captain Furlong sailed on his next voyage, he told Dorrie that he had left a sum of money with her mother, to buy her trousseau.

'So he still doesn't think you can be trusted, even to buy your own trousseau,' Anna said bitterly. 'You'll still have to ask for anything you want, like a child.'

Dorrie looked surprised. 'I don't see it like that, Anna,' she said. 'I think Mama will enjoy shopping for it with me, and she's told me that Father has been very generous.'

Anna hugged her. 'I'm sure she will,' she said contritely. 'Ignore me. I'm just a misery.'

It was true that Mrs Furlong was as anxious as Dorrie that she should have everything a bride needed, and she seemed to acquire the strength for marathon shopping days. Mrs Wendell shared in the excitement and she took Dorrie into her linen cupboard, where she presented her with several pairs of beautiful linen sheets, carefully laid away in blue tissue paper to prevent yellowing, a dozen pairs of matching linen pillowcases, and a dozen pairs of pillowcases edged with handmade lace. She also gave Dorrie five sovereigns to buy 'pretty knick-knacks'.

Dorrie wanted to share this good fortune with Anna, but her sister refused. 'But if you got any money you'd share with me,' Dorrie protested. 'We've both felt the need for money of our own.'

'I know, but this is different,' Anna said. 'This was given to you for a special reason. Honestly, money doesn't worry me now. What you never have you never miss!'

She convinced Dorrie, but it was not really true. Now, more than ever, she longed for money of her own to buy things for Dorrie. She did beautiful embroidery on nightdresses and underwear for her sister, and on the household linen with which Dorrie was filling her bottom drawer, but the materials had all been provided by her father.

Anna delivered the parish magazine, the *Xaverian*, and one day she took Mrs Deagan her copy and stayed to talk. They discussed the amount of money raised by the bazaar and Mrs Deagan said the needlework stall had done well. Her arms going like pistons as she kneaded the bread dough in the panmug, she said, 'It was those lovely embroidered sideboard runners you did, and the antimacassars. They sold like hot cakes, Norah said. Our lads bought a set for me.'

'Yes, we thought the antimacassars would be a change from the crocheted ones. Isabel made them and I embroidered them,' Anna said.

'It's a gift you've got, girlie, that lovely embroidery,' said Mrs Deagan. 'I suppose you're doing plenty for Dorrie now she's building her nest.'

She laughed, but Anna said impulsively, 'It's all I *can* do. I can't *buy* anything to make gifts for her.'

She had never intended to speak of her lack of money, feeling ashamed of it although she knew this was irrational, but Mrs Deagan was very easy to talk to. Anna stressed that it was just that her father failed to understand her need for independence, not that he ever denied anything to any of the family.

'But he likes to keep things in his own hands,' Mrs Deagan said, nodding. 'It's the way with many men, girlie.' She had turned the dough on to a floured board and kneaded it again and now she was forming it into loaves for the tins that stood ready. When she had finished she covered them with a white cloth and kept them to prove. The kitchen was filled with the fragrant smell of the loaves she had just taken from the oven, which were cooling on a side table.

'We'll have a cup of tea,' she said, moving the black kettle closer to the fire. She had rubbed the dough from her hands and rinsed them in the scullery and now, while Anna made the tea, she took a flat round loaf from the oven, then cut it and spread butter on the steaming slices. 'Our Jim calls this food for the gods,' she said. 'He'd rather have this than the richest cake.'

'I agree with him,' Anna said. The butter had melted into the hot bread and she closed her eyes in bliss as she ate. 'No wonder your Jim doesn't want to leave home,' she said when she had finished.

'Well, if he found the right girl I'd be glad to see him happily married,' said Mrs Deagan, 'but he says he hasn't, and there's no sense in marrying for the sake of it. He has a full and happy life as it is, and there's nothing worse than a bad marriage. Be very careful when your time comes, girlie.'

'I will,' Anna promised. She smiled. 'I used to laugh at Dorrie when she said that she'd know when she met her Mr Right, but it's happened.'

'Yes, that's a good lad she's got,' said Mrs Deagan. 'He'll look after her. You'll miss her when she's gone though, child.'

'I can't bear to think about it,' Anna said. 'I'm so happy for Dorrie, but I dread the future without her.'

'You were always good friends as well as sisters, from when you were little,' Mrs Deagan said. 'And closer maybe because there was only the two of you.'

'I wish I was needed at home like Isabel is,' Anna said. 'Aunt Clara objected when we tried to help, but even now, with Mama in charge, I have to be careful not to offend Nelly.

When I suggested doing more charity work Aunt Clara talked about getting rid of Nelly and me doing all the work, but Mama wouldn't hear of it.'

'I should think not indeed,' Mrs Deagan said indignantly. 'Nelly Maguire needs that job, and you should be making use of the talent God has given you. Do you think your father might let you work at a clerical tailor's – embroidering vestments and such like, Anna?'

'I don't think so,' Anna said. 'He thinks it would disgrace him if we worked for our living, you see. Says he can support his family. I envy your family being free to work.'

'Not from choice, girlie,' said Mrs Deagan. 'They'd have been glad to change places with you many a time, but now, thank God, they're all doing work they like and doing well at it. God has been very good to us.' She stood up and began to rap her knuckles on the bottom of the cooked loaves.

Anna stared wistfully into the fire and Mrs Deagan looked at her and said, 'Y'know, child, I've been turning over in me mind what you said before and I've thought of something.'

Anna looked up, smiling, and Mrs Deagan crossed to the sideboard. 'Now this can't upset your da because there's only the two of us will know, well, three with Norah,' she said. She picked up a black leather purse and sat down opposite Anna. The purse was stamped with the word 'Mother' and opened out like a concertina with many compartments. From one of them Mrs Deagan took two half-crowns.

'Now, this five shillings, girlie, is an investment. With it you can buy the linen and silks you need to make embroidered runners, and table mats and handkerchief cases. Norah can sell them in her shop and with the money you make you can buy the stuff to make more. With some of the money anyway.'

'Oh, I couldn't. I couldn't take your money, Mrs Deagan,'

Anna cried, her face red with embarrassment. 'I feel as though I've come begging.'

'Now if you talk like that you're going to annoy me,' said Mrs Deagan. She drew herself up to her full five feet, and Anna was suddenly reminded of the day her mother fainted. In a cutting voice Mrs Deagan went on, 'I thought we were friends. I thought I had a good idea for you and Norah to help each other as friends, but you seem to think it's beneath you.'

'I don't. It's not that,' Anna said. 'You know how I feel about you and your family. You've always been so good to us.' She burst into tears, horrified that she had offended her old neighbour.

Mrs Deagan patted her arm and poured her another cup of tea. 'There now, child, don't upset yourself,' she said. 'I spoke harsh words for your own good.'

'I'm sorry,' Anna said, mopping her eyes.

Mrs Deagan said soothingly, 'Drink your tea and we'll say no more. I think you'd be better starting with the small things first, then you could try the antimacassars later.'

She seemed so certain that the matter was settled that Anna meekly picked up the half-crowns and put them in her pocket. Mrs Deagan opened her purse again to show Anna the central section, which was closed with a steel clasp. She opened it to show Anna a sovereign.

'I had five penny pieces in this purse when I was left a widow with six children, and for a few years afterwards it was often empty. Our Maggie was ten and Jim eight when their father died, but as soon as Jim managed to save enough for a sovereign he put it in my purse. It took him a few years, of course.'

' "It's there as a standby, Ma," he said. "If you spend it I'll put another in its place. Your purse will never be empty again while I live." A knife went through me when he said that. If I

109

lost him I wouldn't care if I never saw another penny. If I starved to death.'

'It's not likely,' Anna comforted her. 'He's a fine, healthy man.'

'And I'm a fool to be talking like that,' Mrs Deagan said. 'Now don't worry about deceiving your da. It's for his own good. What he doesn't know can't hurt him.'

The dough in the tins had risen and was ready for the oven, so Anna left. There were questions about repayment she would have liked to ask but she was afraid to provoke Mrs Deagan.

She confided in Dorrie about the arrangement, which proved a great success. Norah's shop was in Scotland Road and was very busy. She always said that people from the poorer parts of the city spent most on flowers, as the burial-club money was often the largest sum of cash they ever had, and they liked to give their relations a good send-off.

She had carriage trade too, as the shop was on a main road, and there was great competition for Anna's work. Dorrie was unable to help her as she was not good at sewing, but she covered Anna's long spells in their bedroom by pretending that she was working on her trousseau.

'When I've gone you can tell them you are working on your own,' she said, giggling, then more seriously, 'It will probably be true, Anna. I was hoping for a double wedding, but Michael says that would be too hasty for Eugene. Perhaps when we're married he'll feel it's time to speak.'

Anna picked up Eugene's photograph and looked at it. 'You know how I feel, Dorrie,' she said in a low voice. 'You and Michael were lucky. You both felt the same and there were no doubts with either of you, but with Eugene – I don't know.'

'But to me he behaves like a man in love,' Dorrie said. 'Just in a quieter, more reserved way than Michael.'

'I want to believe that, Dorrie,' Anna said. 'I know he's

fond of me and he speaks of love in his letters, but it's as though something holds him back. I wonder sometimes if he's had an unhappy love affair and is trying to get over it. There's something missing, Dorrie.'

Dorrie had come to sit beside Anna and now she hugged her. 'I'm sure you're worrying for nothing,' she said. 'I think it's just a difference in character between him and Michael. And your own character might have something to do with it. The fact that you are both so reserved. Couldn't you be a bit warmer, Anna? More encouraging?'

'I'll try,' Anna promised. 'Oh, Dorrie, I'll miss you so. I couldn't talk like this to anybody but you.' She felt Dorrie's tears wet on her cheeks as she hugged her, and decided that she must put all these fears behind her. This should be such a happy time for Dorrie and she mustn't spoil it, just take each day as it came and enjoy her last months with her darling sister.

Meanwhile, it was a pleasure to Anna to feel that she was earning money and a delight to surprise Dorrie with small gifts. She had repaid the original five shillings to Mrs Deagan, but Norah refused to accept any recompense for selling the items.

'It's the boot on the other foot,' she laughed. 'Your embroidery is bringing me trade. They come for a tray cloth and buy flowers too.'

A date had still not been set for the wedding, but Captain Furlong had only signed for a short voyage which would bring him home in the summer of 1903.

Michael and Eugene had both written that the Irish Guards were to visit Dublin for the first time in July. There was to be a Royal Review in Fifteen Acres in Phoenix Park, with ten thousand troops and three field marshals.

When Dr O'Brien heard that his hero, Lord Roberts, was to

head the Irish Guards, he was determined to be there. It was arranged that he would stay in Dublin with an old friend, then visit the Farrell family, but Bridie was also in Dublin for the event and she travelled back to Liverpool with her brother.

'The opportunity for you to meet was too good to miss,' Dr O'Brien told Captain and Mrs Furlong.

'And glad I am to meet you,' Bridie told them. 'You have two daughters to be proud of. Beautiful, well-behaved girls. My John would say the same if he was with me, but he can't leave the farm at this time of the year.'

She charmed all of them, even Aunt Clara, and the girls were not surprised that before she left the wedding had been fixed for March 1904.

Michael, predictably, had hoped for an earlier date, but Dorrie was quite happy to spend the winter months in preparation. For Anna, the time seemed to be flashing past too quickly and she knew that James Hargreaves felt the same. She saw him in church, gazing hungrily at Dorrie, as though trying to imprint her features on his mind for when she would be gone.

The letters still came regularly from Eugene, but the loving messages at the end never became any warmer. In spite of Anna's constant references to the forthcoming marriage in her letters to Eugene, he never commented on it or spoke of a possible future for himself and Anna. He puzzled her, but she tried to crush her doubts.

She thought of the lovely weekend of the picnic and the tea party, and recalled every loving glance, every pressure on her fingers, and the poetic words of love that Eugene had quoted to her. She looked at the photograph that stood beside her bed, at his wide-set eyes and straight nose and the full lips above his cleft chin, and felt weak with love for him.

She was struck by a sudden thought. When Eugene sent her

the photograph he might have expected her to send one in return! Dorrie was always telling her she froze men off. Could she have unwittingly hurt Eugene?

She spoke about it to Dorrie. 'When Michael brought this photo for me it never occurred to me to send one of myself to Eugene. Do you think he might be hurt that I didn't?'

'Has he said anything about it?' asked Dorrie.

'No, but if he expected one and I didn't send it he might be too proud to ask,' Anna said.

'I'll ask Michael about it,' Dorrie promised.

But the thought that she might have disappointed Eugene in some obscure way comforted Anna. It could be a reason why the courtship seemed to be making little progress.

She looked out the most flattering photograph of herself, but Dorrie told her that Michael advised against sending it by post. 'He said it might fall into the wrong hands, but he'll collect it when he comes here the weekend after next,' she said.

Anna wondered why Eugene seemed unable to get weekend leave, when Michael could get it so frequently, but she said nothing. Aunt Clara, however, often wondered aloud about it.

'Michael says it's because Eugene has a more important job than he has,' Dorrie said loyally, but Clara grumbled, 'They were both free to go to Dublin, I notice. Dr O'Brien was bragging about them. Everyone's tired of hearing about that parade from him.'

'Dear Dr O'Brien,' Mrs Furlong said sweetly. 'He enjoyed himself so much. He said the Irish Guards had a wonderful reception. The route was lined by the Royal Irish Constabulary, but the crowds were so enthusiastic they broke through to cheer the soldiers. He said the best moment was when Lord Roberts came galloping up to head the Irish Guards, led by the regimental band and the mascot.'

'It would be for him,' Clara said sourly, 'He's ridiculous about Lord Roberts for a grown man.'

Anna could not resist adding fuel to the fire. 'Eugene says the mascot is an Irish wolfhound named Brian Boru,' she said. It was too much for Clara, who jumped to her feet and flounced out.

'Oh, dear, I'm afraid we've annoyed Aunt Clara, Anna,' Mrs Furlong said with mock regret.

The next day Anna was delighted to receive a letter from Eugene, in which he said that he had obtained some leave and would be staying in Liverpool with his aunt and uncle for the following weekend. Fortunately, she was unaware that this was in response to a letter to Eugene from his mother, in which she complained that he was not making enough effort to secure his rightful position as Dr O'Brien's heir. Her brother lived so simply, Mrs D'Arcy said, and earned a respectable sum of money from his profession, so his inheritance from his father must be virtually untouched.

'It is your only hope,' she wrote. 'Your father can do nothing for you and you can hope for nothing from his poverty-stricken relations, so you must exert yourself. The Farrells are working at it. Michael, it appears, is constantly travelling to Liverpool and Aunt Bridie even met your uncle in Dublin and travelled back to Liverpool with him. We did not receive the courtesy of a visit, which I feel might be because you are so dilatory.'

Dr and Mrs O'Brien were also unaware of the scheming and were pleased to welcome Eugene. 'It'll be nice for him to have a weekend without Michael,' Mrs O'Brien said. 'Eugene's such a quiet lad and I think sometimes he's very much in Michael's shadow.'

'It'll be nice for Anna, too,' Dr O'Brien said. 'I know he writes regularly, but they're both shy people. Perhaps I'll hurry things along.'

Mrs O'Brien looked alarmed. 'Don't, Paddy,' she exclaimed. 'Keep out of it. Leave it to the young ones. Dorrie and Anna must have talked things over, because they're very close, and Michael and Eugene are good friends, so they all know the situation. They'll sort it out.'

'But Eugene couldn't do better for himself, and the girls could still be together,' the doctor said, but his wife said firmly, 'Eugene might be waiting for a promotion or something before he speaks. You complained that Michael was too hasty, and now Eugene isn't hasty enough. Don't go clattering in with hobnailed boots.'

'Me! I'm always the soul of discretion,' he said, offended, but he was never angry for long.

It was a happy time for Anna. Because the days with Dorrie were passing so quickly she consciously savoured every one, and she and Dorrie had never been closer. She enjoyed doing the embroidery and making money by it, and now she had the added joy of the prospect of a weekend with Eugene.

Michael, however, was in a dilemma about his best man. He had intended to have his brother, but Dermot wrote that he would only agree if Michael was married in civilian clothes. 'I'd feel ridiculous standing up with you in your fancy dress,' he wrote.

Dorrie had taken it for granted that Michael would be married in uniform, and that Eugene would be his best man. She had said innocently how nice it would be for Anna, who was to be her bridesmaid. But Michael was reluctant to ask Eugene, for several reasons, and in the end he consulted his aunt.

'Dermot is entitled to his views,' Mrs O'Brien said. 'But it's your wedding. You must do what suits you and Dorrie. I'm sure Eugene will be pleased to be asked, and your mother will understand about Dermot.'

He still hesitated and she said quietly, 'I know Anna is the bridesmaid, but it wouldn't commit her or Eugene any more than they are now. It would be convenient if they made a match of it, but it doesn't have to follow just because of you and Dorrie.'

'I wouldn't like Anna to be hurt,' he muttered, looking down at his boots, but his aunt said briskly, 'She won't be. She likes Eugene, but she's not head over heels like Dorrie with you, and she's a sensible girl.'

Michael hugged her. 'Thanks, Aunt Maureen,' he said. 'I'm glad I thought of asking your advice.'

'Write to your mother and Dermot right away,' she advised. 'Tell Dermot you respect his views, but you and Dorrie want you to be married in uniform, so you'll ask Eugene. Then fix it up with Eugene.'

He took her advice, but he spoke more frankly to Eugene than he had to his aunt. 'I don't want to be any part of whatever game you're playing,' he said. 'But remember, Anna will be my sister and I won't stand to see her hurt.'

Eugene was angry, but his mother's letter decided him to apply for weekend leave and to agree to be Michael's best man.

He wrote to Anna twice that week, once about his leave and once to give her the news about the wedding. 'Apparently, the Fenian won't be involved if Michael is in uniform, so he has asked me,' he wrote.

So that's why he never mentioned the wedding, Anna thought. Because Michael hadn't asked him! Men! They're like little boys.

She showed the letter to Dorrie, who by now had heard the full story of Dermot's refusal from Michael. 'I never even thought of Dermot,' she confessed. 'I'd just assumed it would be Eugene, although I hope Dermot will come to the wedding. I like him.'

116

The weekend with Eugene passed quietly. The weather was now too bad for picnics, and Mrs Furlong said nothing about a tea party. Nowadays, she often said that she felt exhausted, and spent more and more time on the sofa.

Anna had hoped that this would be an opportunity for her to establish her place in running the house, but Clara had quarrelled with many of her new friends and seized the chance to take over once again. Anna was unwilling to spoil Dorrie's happiness with any discord, but she had talked to Isabel about the continuing power struggle.

'I wouldn't worry about it now,' Isabel had advised. 'There's plenty for everyone to do before the wedding, but as soon as it's over, Anna, you must be very firm about your place in the house.' Anna thought it was good advice from her sensible friend.

Eugene was charming and attentive to Anna during the weekend and bought her a copy of *Sonnets from the Portuguese* by Elizabeth Barrett Browning. He read some of the love poems aloud to her, but never spoke actual words of love. On Saturday night he took tickets for the theatre, but also invited Dr and Mrs O'Brien. Then during the play he put his hand on Anna's and cast soulful glances at her throughout the evening. By the time he went on Sunday he had charmed his aunt and uncle, but left Anna feeling even more confused and uncertain.

A talk with Mrs O'Brien made her feel better. 'Poor Eugene,' Mrs O'Brien sighed. 'It was so easy for Michael, with that good family behind him, but Eugene has nothing but his Army pay. Those stuck-up D'Arcys wanted him to be an officer, but they couldn't even afford the commission, let alone the mess bills.'

'I thought they were wealthy, with that lovely house and all those servants,' said Anna, 'but Dr O'Brien told me it was all his sister's money.'

'Yes, and a good lump of money they were all left,' said Mrs O'Brien. 'Enough to provide for a family, but those D'Arcys have squandered it on empty show. Poor Eugene will have to rely on getting a promotion before he can afford to marry. Still, he tells me he is hoping to be made up to lance-corporal shortly, so that's a start. I think he talked to me in confidence, but I know you won't speak about this to anyone, Anna.'

'Of course not,' Anna assured her, but she felt light as air as she walked home, thinking that the mystery had been solved for her.

Chapter Eight

The preparations for the wedding were now racing ahead. Captain Furlong had brought home a bolt of white silk and another of pale blue silk, and a friend of Kate Deagan's, who was a cutter in an exclusive dress shop in Bold Street, had cut out the bridal dress from the white silk, and Anna's bridesmaid's dress from the blue silk. The dresses were now being made up and the girls had already been for fittings.

Mrs Furlong could always summon up enough energy for a shopping trip for Dorrie's trousseau, sometimes with Anna, at Dorrie's insistence, but she preferred to have only Dorrie present.

One day she called both girls into her bedroom. 'I have so much beautiful underwear, given to me by Lady Dorothy,' she said. 'It's too old-fashioned for you to wear as it is, Dorrie, but I'm sure Anna could make it over for you. The material is so beautiful it's a shame to waste it.'

She directed them to open the long drawers under her wardrobe and lift out the contents, which had been carefully wrapped in tissue paper. The sisters gasped in amazement at the voluminous chemises in the finest silk, the bust bodices, cruelly boned, and the underskirts in lawn and silk. There was a nightdress in silk so fine that Mrs Furlong said proudly, 'My lady could draw that through her wedding ring. She always had the very best of everything.'

Anna had lifted out the contents of the next drawer and held up a strange garment. 'Whatever is this, Mama?' she asked. It seemed like a pair of drawers made of very fine linen, with a drawstring round the waist and a very large open vent between the legs.

'Trust you to find those,' Mrs Furlong snapped. 'Put them back. They'll be no use for altering.'

'But what are they, Mama?' Dorrie asked. 'They seem like drawers, but why are they made like that?'

'It was for a purpose,' her mother said. 'Ladies were out all day at places like Hurlingham or Ascot, and no provision was made for their natural needs.' The girls looked at her uncomprehendingly and she said crossly, 'What else could they do? Their stockings were held up by garters and their skirts were very full, so they simply – well, watered the grass.'

Anna looked at Dorrie and they both began to laugh, but their mother was offended. 'I don't see why you think it's funny,' she said. 'It was very difficult for them. At a garden party they might be able to go into the house, but public places were difficult.'

There was a magazine in the drawer, with photographs of ladies with S-bend figures leaning forward with their hands clasped over the handles of their parasols, and large hats balanced on their heads.

'You mean that ladies like that were, er, "watering the grass", Mama?' asked Anna, remaining serious with difficulty.

'Yes. It was very clever of someone to think of a way round the difficulty,' Mrs Furlong said.

'I can see that it would work on grass,' Dorrie said, 'but what if they were standing on hard ground or paving stones?'

'There was always dust if the weather was dry. Their dresses would sweep the dust over where they had been standing as they moved away.'

Their mother seemed to accept it so easily that neither Dorrie nor Anna dared to laugh, but later, in their own room, they collapsed in giggles as they thought of the stately ladies smiling sweetly as they leaned on their parasols and solved their difficulty.

Anna was able to make some beautiful underwear for Dorrie from the lawn and silk garments, and the nightgown which would go through a wedding ring she left untouched.

Michael was dismayed by the amount of linen that Dorrie had collected, and told her that only a small amount could be taken to London. 'We'll be living in married quarters at Caterham at first,' he told her. 'Not much room for storage.' So it was suggested that the rest should be left in Liverpool until needed.

Dorrie readily agreed and Michael smiled fondly at her, obviously thinking what a complaisant wife she would be. Anna smiled at his smug expression. He had a lot to learn about Dorrie, she thought. Although she was usually so placid, Dorrie's rare rages were spectacular, and when she felt deeply about something nothing could change her mind. Still, love could work wonders, Anna reflected.

Norah Deagan was providing the bridal flowers as her wedding present. There was to be a bouquet of hothouse-raised pink and white roses and carnations for Dorrie, and a bouquet of spring flowers for Anna. She was also providing buttonholes for the men, corsages for the mothers, and the flowers for the church.

Bridie had made several visits to Liverpool during the winter, inundating them with offers of practical and financial help with the wedding, and on one occasion her husband came with her. 'He wouldn't want to come to the wedding as a stranger to you,' she told them, and everyone liked John Farrell. Bridie also told them that Dermot would be present at the wedding, but had promised to behave himself and keep his mouth shut. Nuala and two of her daughters would travel to Liverpool with them, but Oscar D'Arcy

121

would be unable to leave Dublin.

'No loss,' Bridie said frankly to Mrs Furlong. 'He'd only put a damper on a happy day.'

'I hope it will be,' Mrs Furlong said. 'I have this awful feeling my husband won't be here for it.'

'Oh, Mama, that's only because of Miss Cook!' Anna exclaimed. 'Take no notice of her.' There had been some collisions between ships in the Mersey because of fogs, and every time Miss Cook, a friend of Clara's, called she talked of these and disasters at sea.

Mrs Furlong became convinced her husband would be lost at sea before the wedding, but he arrived home safely in the second week of March as planned, a week before the wedding. He seemed bemused by all the activity in the house, and either took refuge with Dr O'Brien or in his study.

The wedding morning was bright and sunny, with a boisterous March wind which lifted Dorrie's long veil in the air as they arrived at the church, but it was securely fastened to her hair. Anna thought she had never looked lovelier as they stood in the church porch with Captain Furlong, in uniform, standing proudly beside Dorrie.

The cleverly cut white silk dress emphasised her figure and fell in soft folds from the tiny waist, and her long veil was secured to her fair curls by a headdress of pearls and tiny fresh rosebuds. Her blue eyes were like stars and her cheeks pink with excitement, and as Anna kissed her she could only murmur, 'Oh, Dorrie, Dorrie.'

She rearranged the ribbons hanging from Dorrie's bouquet as Luke and Gerald Deagan, who were acting as ushers, looked to see if they were ready, then signalled to Jim, who was playing the organ. The music swelled and all the guests rose to their feet.

The guests behind Mrs Furlong and Clara were Mrs

Wendell, sitting with Isabel and her mother, who had brought her, Mrs Deagan, Norah, Maggie and Kate Deagan, family friends, and the captain's crew and some seafaring friends. On Michael's side of the church sat Dr and Mrs O'Brien and the Irish contingent.

Many people had come to see the wedding and were at the back and sides of the church. Anna looked for James Hargreaves, but was not surprised that he was unable to bear seeing Dorrie married.

Poor man, she thought briefly, but then, as she saw the tall figure of Eugene standing beside Michael at the altar steps, she forgot James Hargreaves.

The priest who married Dorrie had known her all her life. He spoke affectionately of her and admiringly of Michael who, he said, had fought bravely for his country.

Of Dorrie he said, 'Another Jesuit said, "Give me a child until he is seven and I will give you the man." Dorothea is now three times seven and she is the same good, sweet-natured and happy person she was as a very young child. Her character, formed in infancy and nurtured in a good home, is the best basis for a happy marriage. Her husband will be blessed with her as a wife, and let us hope that in God's good time she will also be a good mother.'

Anna had been wrong about James Hargreaves. He had been unable to resist seeing Dorrie, but had slipped in a side door and concealed himself behind a large stone pillar to see her entering the church on her father's arm. She looked so beautiful that he felt his eyes fill with tears, and it was only when the music died away that he realised she had reached the altar.

He stood as though in a dream as the ceremony proceeded, but when the priest began to speak of Dorrie he felt that the words pierced him to the heart. 'Give me the child and I will give you the man,' he heard, and stumbled out of the church, digging his nails into the palms of his clenched fists and gritting his teeth in pain.

Where does that leave me? What kind of monster am I after the childhood I had? he thought. How could I have ever thought of courting any ordinary girl, let alone one as far above me as Dorrie?

Since his mother's death he had tried to block out all memory of what had happened before that, particularly scenes from his childhood, not always successfully. The episodes when his uncle had visited his bedroom he never thought of, because his mind had refused to accept what was happening at the time, and the shutter he had drawn over it had never lifted.

Now, memories of his mother's physical and emotional cruelty flashed across his mind, and he thought of the priest's words – 'Give me the child and I will give you the man' – and of Dorrie's character – formed in childhood and nurtured in a good home. James groaned aloud and a passing man stared curiously at him, so he turned into a public house nearby and ordered a pint of stout.

But he was too restless to stay and, leaving his drink almost untouched, walked rapidly, not knowing or caring where he went, but unable to escape his thoughts. He had seen Frances at the church and was reluctant to go home, lest she should want to tell him about the wedding.

Meanwhile, at the church the wedding ceremony was over and Michael and Dorrie had become man and wife. Eugene had smiled at Anna, but not spoken to her as they performed their duties as best man and bridesmaid, but as they followed Dorrie and Michael into the sacristy to sign the register, he whispered, 'You look beautiful, Anna.'

Anna received many compliments that day, as the dress of pale blue silk and the wreath of flowers on her dark hair suited her, and happiness for her beloved sister melted her usual reserve and made her sparkle, but the one from Eugene meant most to her.

A lavish meal had been prepared at the Furlong house and the wedding party were to visit a photographic studio later, but outside the church Gerald Deagan took a photograph of Dorrie and Michael, Anna and Eugene. Eugene seemed to be looking down at Anna almost as fondly as Michael was looking at Dorrie, and Anna treasured the photograph for many years.

The photographs taken at the studio were very formal, with the wedding party stiffly posed and all staring unsmilingly at the camera, but they were fashionable and Mrs Furlong had several framed. Anna kept the one that Gerald had taken hidden away in her room.

Everybody was happy as they gathered for the wedding breakfast, but Dr O'Brien was the life and soul of the party. He had been warned by his wife not to make any reference to Anna and Eugene and she stayed close to him as speeches were made after large quantities of food and drink had been consumed.

'Remember now, Paddy,' she hissed as he rose to his feet, but the nearest he came to indiscretion was when he raised his glass to Anna.

'To the other beauty in the family. I suppose we'll soon be losing you, Miss Anna. They say one wedding makes another.'

'Now you know, doctor, why people say that,' Mrs Deagan said. 'It's wishful thinking. They're enjoying themselves at one wedding, so they think they'd like another.' Amid the laughter Dr O'Brien sank back into his seat, much to his wife's relief.

Later, Dorrie and Michael left to spend a week's honeymoon in Coniston in the Lake District, and shortly afterwards Dr O'Brien was called away to a difficult confinement. Anna had been kept busy attending to the guests so she had seen little of Eugene. She had expected him to help her to carry drinks to people and he had done so briefly, but after Dr O'Brien left he seemed to spend his time talking to the crewmen of her father's ship.

Mrs O'Brien was sitting with the relatives from Ireland, and the party was still going well, when Anna saw Eugene go to Mrs O'Brien, then both of them go to her parents and speak to them. All sorts of wild surmises whizzed through her mind. Outwardly calm, she took a tray of sandwiches from Kate Deagan, who was helping her, but her hand trembled as Eugene and Mrs O'Brien approached her.

'Oh, Anna, isn't it a shame that Eugene has to go?' said Mrs O'Brien. 'We thought he would be here overnight, but he has to return to London.'

'Yes, my pass expires at midnight, unfortunately,' Eugene said. 'I had great difficulty getting one at all.'

Kate Deagan had taken the tray back from Anna and moved away, and as Eugene took Anna's hand and bent over it she blurted out, 'But when did you find out? About the pass, I mean.'

'I knew about it, of course,' Eugene said easily. 'I thought that everyone else understood the position too. I'm sure Michael and I had spoken about it.'

'Not to me,' Mrs O'Brien said. 'I was thunderstruck when you told me just now, and Anna hadn't realised, had you, my dear?'

'I'm so sorry. I just took it for granted—' Eugene began, but pride had come to Anna's aid.

'Oh, well, if duty calls,' she said lightly, managing to smile at them. 'The important thing is that Michael got his leave.'

'Indeed,' Mrs O'Brien said. 'But I still think it's a shame you have to go in the middle of the party. Wait until Dr O'Brien

126

hears. He'll be writing to Lord Roberts.' Eugene looked so alarmed that she added quickly, 'Only joking,' but Anna thought Eugene seemed only slightly less alarmed when his aunt suggested that she and Anna should accompany him to the station to see him off.

'I'm going back to barracks, Aunt, not to war,' he said.

Anna cut in quickly, 'I'm afraid I couldn't leave anyway. Mama needs me here to look after the guests.'

Eugene bent over her hand, squeezing it and looking into her eyes as he murmured, 'A lovely wedding and a delightful reception. I've enjoyed myself so much.'

Several of the other guests, who were very old or had travelled a long way, were also leaving, and some of Captain Furlong's crew. Anna had seen Gerald Deagan speaking angrily to one of them and wondered if that was why, although she thought the men had behaved very correctly under their captain's eagle eyes.

When everyone had gone, except the family and the Irish relations, and the Deagans, who had helped to restore order to the rooms, they all gathered round the piano for a sing-song. Dr O'Brien had returned, happy at the outcome of his emergency call.

'They wanted a boy,' he said. 'But by the time it was all over they were so thankful to have the mother alive and a healthy little girl they thought that was what they'd always wanted.' He was too happy to care that Eugene had left, and his singing and his loud, infectious laugh kept them all in high spirits, even Anna.

When at last she went to bed, to sleep alone for the first time she could remember, her mind was a jumble of memories and emotions, but she was too tired to sort them out and fell asleep instantly.

When Dorrie and Michael arrived at the hotel in Coniston

Dorrie knew nothing of the facts of life, and had only the vaguest idea of what to expect on her wedding night, but Michael initiated her very gently. She proved a willing pupil, loving and trusting Michael absolutely, then swept along on a tide of passion to respond to him.

When they were returning to Liverpool at the end of the week she said innocently to Michael, 'It's been lovely, hasn't it? I feel quite a different person to when I left Liverpool,' and she was surprised when Michael crushed her in his arms and said in a muffled voice, 'Oh, Dorrie, never, never change, will you?'

Anna had been kept too busy during that week to feel the loss of Dorrie. Her father was still at home, which always made more work, and there seemed to be almost as much work to do putting everything back to normal after the wedding as there had been preparing for it.

Everyone agreed that it had been a great success and a very happy occasion. From the wedding ceremony and Nuptial Mass to the reception which followed.

Captain Furlong had gone down to his ship the morning after the celebrations and been annoyed to find that his cabin boy was missing, but the boy had turned up later, looking sheepish, and said he'd 'slept it off' in an alleyway.

Another of the crew had apparently annoyed Gerald Deagan, but that had a happy outcome. Gerald had been courting Winifred Parsons for many years. She was a quiet, shy girl, apparently devoted to happy-go-lucky Gerald, but although they were always invited out as a couple the affair seemed to make no progress. At the wedding one of Captain Furlong's crew showed an interest in Winnie, which annoyed Gerald and led to a quarrel between them.

A few days later they announced their engagement, and their intention to marry in September. There was general approval, as both were popular. Winnie lived in Margaret Street with her elder sister and widower father, and worked in a shop in Brunswick Road; Gerald owned a ships' supply business.

'It should have happened years ago,' Aunt Clara said. 'I don't know why that girl's father didn't do something.'

The Deagan family seemed to agree with her. 'About time,' Kate said to Anna. 'Winnie's a lovely girl, and she'd have married him anytime this last five years, but it was him! Dozy article! It's not that he doesn't love Winnie, you know, but he's just so dilatory and Winnie could hardly pop the question, could she?'

'No, but some hardfaced girls would have done something,' Anna said. 'Anyway, it's a good thing that sailor gave Gerald a fright, isn't it?'

Kate agreed, but she said thoughtfully, 'I wonder if Ma put him up to it, Anna? I saw her talking to those sailors. I wouldn't put it past her.'

'Neither would I,' said Anna, laughing. 'Her or Dr O'Brien. He would say the end justifies the means.'

Dorrie and Michael could only stay in Liverpool for one day before travelling to Caterham, so Anna had little opportunity to speak to Dorrie alone. She often thought of Eugene's abrupt departure, and wondered why Dorrie had not warned her he would be leaving if she had known. She was sure that Dorrie, like herself, had expected that she and Eugene would have some time alone after the guests had left, no matter how late, but there was no chance to ask her about it.

By the time the wedding and the reception had been discussed in detail, and Dorrie and Michael had told of their honeymoon hotel and the other guests there and the beauty of the scenery, it was time for bed.

The next morning was dominated by Mrs Furlong's lamentations at losing her favourite daughter. She seemed to resent anyone but herself being upset about Dorrie leaving, and her husband could do nothing to console her.

'Oh, why did it have to be Dorrie!' she cried. They were all standing in the hall, as only Anna and Captain Furlong were to accompany the young couple to the railway station, and everyone heard her. Dorrie pulled herself from her mother's grasp and flung her arms round Anna. At the same time, Michael bent over his sister-in-law, smiling and winking.

'Sure isn't the grass always greener on the other side?' he murmured, and Dorrie whispered, 'Mama doesn't mean that. She's just hysterical.' Anna was grateful for their loving concern for her, but knew that her mother would make her pay for it after they had gone.

Captain Furlong cut short any further lamentations by taking his watch from his pocket and declaring that they must go or miss the train.

Lime Street Station was full of steam, but when it cleared Anna saw a familiar figure in the distance. James Hargreaves, she thought. He must have been unable to resist a last look at Dorrie.

She was feeling so wretched herself at the parting that she almost wished she could talk to him. He would understand, as no one else seemed able to do. Dr O'Brien, who had met them at the train, and her father seemed quite cheerful and Mama, she thought viciously, was enjoying her dramatics.

Porters were banging doors and it was time for a last frantic hug and kiss from Dorrie before she and Michael stepped aboard the train and were borne away to their new life.

Chapter Nine

It had been a mistake to go to Lime Street Station for a last glimpse of Dorrie, James Hargreaves realised as he walked away. The growing feeling that a glass barrier stood between himself and ordinary people had intensified as he watched the farewell group, their brave smiles, and loving hugs and kisses.

It comes naturally to them, to know how to behave, he thought. If I was there I'd stand like a log, not knowing how to feel or act because I'm different to other people.

When he returned to the office, one of the older men said pleasantly, 'Did your friend get away all right?'

James growled, 'Yes,' then felt ashamed.

The man only said, 'Good, good,' and returned to his ledgers and James immersed himself in work. Since the day of the wedding he had felt himself set apart, and he was sleeping badly, with memories of his childhood and his mother coming back to haunt him. He was consequently tired and irritable, with Frances and with colleagues in the office, snapping at them in a way completely unlike himself.

The men knew that he kept a photograph of a pretty girl in his desk, and the older men smiled knowingly at his ill temper and forgave him. 'In the spring a young man's fancy,' one of them murmured tolerantly, and the others agreed.

Frances also showed no resentment, but only concern for him. She prepared tasty meals, but he left most of them uneaten and went out walking or sometimes cycling. Where his mind had been full of images of Dorrie, now he could think of nothing but his mother.

131

He occasionally saw his uncle, as their offices were so close, but they never spoke and passed with heads averted. He did glimpse enough to know that his uncle looked suddenly shrunken and old, but it was still a shock to hear that he had died.

James expected to feel a sense of release, but instead, the following night, the door he had so firmly closed against his experiences with his uncle seemed to be coming open. James leapt up from his bed, remembering what had happened there, and went to try to sleep in another room, but the images pursued him.

It was the start of a period when James believed he was going mad, and Frances became seriously worried about him. Eating and sleeping badly, he was rapidly losing weight, and he seemed unable to sit still. He scarcely spoke or seemed to hear what was said to him.

Frances wondered if he was the same at the office, and told him he should consult Dr O'Brien. 'You can't go on like this, lad. You're wasting away. He could give you something to settle your stomach,' she told him. James mumbled something, but he knew that Dr O'Brien could do nothing to help him. It was his mind, not his body, that was destroying him. He was beginning to see and hear his mother everywhere, even now in the kitchen which had been his refuge.

He had been avoiding the other rooms for some time, particularly the small parlour where he had spent so many evenings with her, and the dining room. There, he could always see her, the beady eyes, the small, bitter mouth, and the malevolent sneer as poison dripped from her lips. 'Stupid, fat, clumsy idiot. No use to yourself or anyone else. A laughing stock. Why was I cursed with you?'

Since his uncle's death, James had been afraid to go to bed, afraid of the nightmares which came to him, so he had stayed in the kitchen all night, dozing on the old sofa. Now, even that refuge was denied him. His work in the office was suffering, as he often heard his mother's voice in his head, mocking him, and he made many mistakes. The other men were kind and helpful, but his fragile self-confidence was shattered.

I'd do away with myself, he often thought, if I had the courage. But the idea of hell was very real to him, and for him hell would mean being reunited with his mother and uncle. And for all eternity, he thought with horror. But he feared that someday his life would be too unbearable for him to go on.

Frances was well aware that his bed had not been slept in, and that his mind was troubled, and she wondered if he spent the nights roaming the streets. She knew that the kitchen fire was kept going all night and that he spent some, possibly short, time on the horsehair sofa. No matter how carefully she probed he never told her the reasons, only looked at her wildly, once even saying, 'I'm sorry, Frances, I can't help it. I don't know why you put up with me.'

For the first time in all their years together she burst into tears. Lifting the corner of her white apron to wipe her eyes, she sobbed, 'Oh, lad, lad. I'm worried to death about you. The flesh is falling off you. You're nothing but skin and bone.' She tried to recover herself but James was shocked out of his self-absorption and made an effort to eat some food to comfort her.

A few nights later, after Frances had gone, there was a knock on the door, and he opened it to find Dr O'Brien on the doorstep.

'Good evening, James,' he said cheerfully. 'As the mountain wouldn't come to Mahomet, Mahomet has come to the mountain. In the kitchen, are we?' He led the way and James followed, too surprised to speak, but he recovered enough to offer tea.

'No, sit down,' the doctor said. 'Never mind the tea for now. I met Frances O'Neill and she said she was worried about you. I can see why. The flesh has fallen off you, to quote her words. She says you're not eating or sleeping. Why?'

'I don't know,' James mumbled.

The doctor leaned forward to take James's wrist, and pulled out his watch to monitor his pulse, then lifted his eyelid. In a gentler tone he said, 'The sleeping? Are you unable to fall asleep, or do you sleep and wake up?'

'Both,' James said. 'I don't fall asleep quickly, but when I do I wake up again.'

'Nightmares?' the doctor asked in the same conversational tone.

James nodded and Dr O'Brien said, 'I think we'll have that tea now, James. I want to talk to you.' He asked a few innocuous questions while James made the tea, then as he sipped it he said quietly, 'Did you see Dorrie Furlong married?'

'Er – no, not married,' James stuttered. 'I heard the priest but – but I left.'

'Lovely wedding. Very happy occasion for us. She married my nephew, you know,' said Dr O'Brien. 'A good lad and I'm sure they'll be happy. They've gone to live in London.'

'I saw them leave,' James blurted out.

He wished he could recall his words when the doctor said, 'Did you? I didn't see you at the station.'

'No, I was hiding behind a pillar,' James said bitterly. 'That's when—'

'That's when this all started,' Dr O'Brien finished calmly. James's cup was rattling on the saucer and he took it from him.

James said, 'No, no. Before that. The priest said, "Give me the child and I will give you the man." What hope for me to be sane and ordinary?'

The doctor went on quietly sipping his tea, and James found himself telling him how he had felt that day on Lime Street Station.

'You were all so ordinary and happy and all so at ease with one another, and I was where I would always be, looking on. I felt I didn't belong with ordinary people. How could I, after the life I'd had? I felt as though there was a sort of barrier between me and other people. I'd never been happy and I didn't know how. It all sounds melodramatic, I know.'

'Not to me,' the doctor said gently. 'I know more of what went on here than you realise. I didn't know at the time, of course, although I suspected it, but you were always such a stoic, James.' He patted James's hands as the young man twisted them together in his lap. 'You hid your feelings so well, pretended to be stupid. I blame myself for not doing more.'

'It was the only way I could get through,' James said huskily. 'But I should be happy now. They're both dead. But it is worse since my uncle died. The nightmares.'

'May he rot in hell,' Dr O'Brien said suddenly and viciously. 'Tell me, James. I know you had bad beatings as a child—'

'How do you know?' James interrupted.

'Your headmaster spoke to me about it. One of the teachers saw your back when you changed for games. He said he had spoken to you, but you wouldn't say anything, so he concluded the beating was deserved. He said it was difficult for a widow with a growing boy and you were very sullen.'

'I didn't realise anyone knew,' James said. 'But it wasn't the beatings I minded so much.'

'This is what I want to talk to you about,' the doctor said. 'But I don't want you to remember things you'd rather forget.'

'I can't help it.' James exclaimed. 'I thought I had shut it all away, but since he died . . . I can't talk about it. Not to anyone. No one would understand or believe me. I can hardly believe it myself, but I'm so ashamed.' He jumped to his feet and began to pace about the kitchen.

'Sit down, James,' Dr O'Brien said quietly, 'and *I'll* talk.' James sat down again and the doctor began, 'I know your uncle visited here regularly, but do you remember a time when he stopped coming for a while?'

'Yes, very clearly,' James said. 'I was twelve at the time, and when he came again after eighteen months I was never alone with him. Mother was always with us. He never spoke to me and I didn't speak to him, but when I left school Mother said I had to work in his office. I hardly saw him there, either.'

'And you never wondered why he stopped coming?' the doctor asked.

'I was just thankful,' James said bitterly. 'I never wondered about anything, though. Just kept my head down and . . . and . . .'

'And endured,' the doctor finished for him. 'The reason he stopped coming was because there were rumours about him. There was a good man living at his end of the city, who worried about the street Arabs. He opened a soup kitchen with his own money, for these lads who lived rough, sold newspapers and such to survive. He took his soup handcart round for them at night and he was horrified to see how they slept in odd corners. He wanted to build a night refuge for them, so he asked businessmen to help.'

'Hasselton!' James exclaimed. 'I remember his name.'

'Yes, and your uncle responded. It was fashionable to support charities and he'd put his name to several. Very well respected in the district, he was,' the doctor said grimly.

'But what—' James began.

The doctor continued, 'I'm coming to that. Your uncle got very involved with the street-Arab scheme, but under cover of

136

it he was using some of the boys for sex.' James started, and the doctor nodded his head as though he had confirmed a suspicion.

'You can understand what I mean, James, I see. This happened to you.'

Few people would have recognised the bluff, hearty Irishman in the gentle man who sensitively drew from James the details of the horrors of his childhood. At the end of it James sat back feeling purged, with a great sense of relief.

'Thank you, doctor,' he said. 'I didn't think I could ever speak about it to anyone, even admit it all to myself.'

'You needed to,' the doctor said. 'Ever heard of a man named Sigmund Freud?' James shook his head and the doctor said, 'I've just been reading his book, *The Interpretation of Dreams*. Heavy going, but very interesting. Clever man. Understands the mind.'

'But why now, doctor? Why am I like this now?' said James.

In the same quiet tones Dr O'Brien explained that he had met Dorrie just as he was growing up and leaving his hated childhood behind him. His infatuation with her had filled his mind with happy dreams and hopes, and crowded out unhappy memories.

'You met her just at the right time,' the doctor said. 'But, unfortunately, when she married it was a bad time for you to relinquish your dreams. Because you were vulnerable, your uncle's death opened Pandora's box and you began to remember what you had shut away.'

They were both silent for a while, James thinking over the doctor's words, and Dr O'Brien waiting patiently. Finally, James said, 'But the street Arabs? What happened about that?'

'He was guilty all right. It had been going on for some time, but he made the mistake of using the younger brother of a lad who had refused him. When the older boy found out he went to the police first, but they chased him away. A street Arab's word against a rich man like your uncle! Then the lad went to a clergyman, who wouldn't believe him. Finally, he went to Mr Hasselton.'

'He should have gone there first,' James said.

'Yes, but he was a sick man by now. Apparently, he had instinctively distrusted your uncle from the first. He started enquiries – it was all hushed up, of course – and your uncle left the charity. Supposed to be because of unfounded rumours, but people close to it knew the truth. They came to see your mother, because of you, but you said nothing and she had hysterics at the very idea. I was sent for.'

'That was the worst of it,' James said in a low voice. 'She knew. Even helped him.'

'Yes, and now you've spoken about all that and confronted it, James,' the doctor said gently. 'You've laid your demons to rest. Now we've got to get you right physically so you can start enjoying life.'

'I'm so grateful to you, doctor,' James said with deep feeling. 'I thought I was going mad. I'd have done away with myself if I'd had the courage.'

'You should have come to me,' the doctor said sternly. 'No need ever to keep feelings like that to yourself when I'm here. Still,' he said more cheerfully, 'I think we've sorted that out now.' He took a small bottle from his bag. 'There are two teaspoonsful in this. Take one tonight in hot milk and you'll have a good night's sleep, and the other one tomorrow night. Come to the surgery tomorrow and I'll make up a proper bottle for you. When you're sleeping again you'll want to eat.'

'I must, for Frances's sake,' James said. 'She's been so good and so patient with me.'

'Aye, she's a good woman, and very fond of you,' the doctor said. 'The first thing you must do when you feel better is get rid of this house. Put all this behind you now and start afresh. Why not move into a boarding house for a while, like that one where Hugh Manly and the other bank clerks live? You'd be looked after and have young company.'

'But what about Frances?' James said.

The doctor had looked at his watch and was collecting his hat and stick. 'Talk to her about it,' he said. 'But *do* something to change your life without delay. Don't forget to come for that bottle.'

As James saw him out he tried again to stammer his thanks, but the doctor waved them away, smiling. 'Only trying to do what I should have done years ago,' he said, walking away with a wave of his stick.

James went back to the kitchen and sat thinking over the whole amazing evening. The feeling of a burden being lifted from him was still strong and he bent his head and gave thanks to God for a good friend in Dr O'Brien.

He took half of the contents of the small bottle in hot milk and went to bed, conscious of no presence in the house but his own, and slept dreamlessly until morning.

When he arrived home from work the next day there was a savoury smell coming from the oven, but Frances had not yet returned from her office cleaning. James left a note asking her to stay later, as he wanted her advice, and went to the surgery.

The maid admitted him and Mrs O'Brien came from a room with a counter across the door, where medicines were dispensed, holding a bottle wrapped in white paper.

'Good evening, Mr Hargreaves. You've come for your bottle,' she said cheerfully.

At the same moment a gaunt, shabbily dressed man came out of a room, holding a slip of paper which he held out to Mrs O'Brien. 'I'm the last, ma'am,' he said.

'Thanks, Mr Brady,' she said. 'Go and have a cup of tea while I get this made up.' She opened a door, through which James could see a large kitchen, and said, 'Mary, pour Mr Brady a cup of tea.'

James heard the maid say, ''Ee are, lad, sit here. How's your Alice?'

It's not only bottles of physic that are dispensed here, James thought, as he took the white-wrapped bottle from Mrs O'Brien.

Just then, Dr O'Brien came into the hall, wearing his coat and hat. 'I'll just have a look at that confinement in Great Homer Street, and a couple of others, my dear. I won't be long,' he said to his wife, and to James, 'I'll walk along with you. It's on my way.' They left the house together and he asked if James had slept well.

'Yes, I took the medicine and slept all night,' James said. 'I'm very grateful for your help, doctor. I feel so different.' He hesitated, then said diffidently, 'One thing worries me. I think I should have fought back against my uncle.'

'Nonsense,' the doctor said. 'You were a young child, bullied and cowed by him and your mother all your life. How could you? Your uncle had laid his plans, as he did with those street boys. He went after those who were vulnerable. That's what made him so dangerous and so despicable. No, forget it now. Look forward, not back.'

'I've asked Frances to stay late tonight, to advise me about selling the house, and all the furniture and clutter in it,' said James.

Dr O'Brien laughed heartily. 'She'll have the time of her life,' he said. 'Sure, you won't know whether you're coming or going from now on. She'll be made up. Still, God knows it's time she had some pleasure, the life she has.' He paused. 'I leave you here,' he said, turning down one of the steep streets leading down to the river. 'Goodnight.'

'Goodnight,' James echoed, and walked on slowly, realising how little interest he had shown in other people while he was sunk in his own troubles. Even Frances, who had been so good to him. *She never talks about herself and I've never asked,* he thought, conscience-stricken.

He knew she cleaned offices early in the morning, then spent the day cleaning his house and cooking a meal for him. Afterwards, she cleaned another set of offices. But he knew nothing of her private life, only that she still lived in the house in Queens Road where she had been born.

When he reached the house, Frances was waiting for him. 'It's hotpot, so it hasn't spoiled,' she said, lifting a dish from the oven.

'It looks good,' James said. 'You haven't had your meal, have you? There's enough for two of us there.' She hesitated, and he said persuasively, 'I'll eat more if I have company.'

'Go away with you,' she said, laughing, but she sat down.

As they ate companionably James told her an edited version of the doctor's visit the previous night. 'He says I should get rid of this house and I know he's right, but I don't know where to start. I thought you could help me, Frances.'

'I'll be glad to,' she said. 'I've said all along you'd be better out of here.'

'Yes, but there's so much stuff. Fifteen little tables I counted in the front parlour alone, and every one full of knick-knacks.'

'That's no problem. There's a jumble sale at the church in a few weeks and the rest can go to Con Doolan, you know, the secondhand dealer. You won't have any trouble. They'll be fighting to get their hands on them,' said Frances.

'And the furniture?' James said. 'There's so much. You know we talked about selling this house once before, and you thought I should put the money for it with that – that nest egg, and rent a house . . .'

'Yes, I thought you could rent a house and keep the money for when you was getting married and settling down,' Frances said.

James smiled. 'I don't know when that will be,' he said. 'But the point is, this furniture is too big for a smaller house, and anyway, I'd rather get rid of it.'

'I wouldn't be rushing to sell it,' Frances said. 'As I said before, this house might suit someone that would want to take the furniture and all. It'd cost a lot to furnish it if it was empty.'

James shook his head and smiled ruefully. 'You can see why I need your help,' he said, then he picked up a fork and began to draw patterns on the table cloth, unable to look at Frances. 'Er, I don't know how to say this, Frances,' he said.

'You don't want me in the new house.'

His head jerked up. '*No!*' he almost shouted. 'Just the opposite. Frances, I don't know your circumstances, how badly you are needed at home, but I wanted to ask if you could . . . Have you ever thought of living in?'

She sat looking at him, for once unable to speak, and James went on, 'You see, I want to take a house that would suit you as well as me. I've heard there's some being built on Kensington Fields, but they might be too far for you. I don't mind where I go really, as long as you're willing to keep looking after me. I'd be lost without you, Frances, but I don't want to be selfish if your family need you.'

The fact that she had even considered that she would be unwelcome made him able to speak freely and honestly, but he was shocked to see that Frances was struggling with tears. In the end, she wept openly and he went to sit beside her to try to comfort her.

Finally, she wiped her eyes and said shakily, 'I only give the offices a lick and a promise and rushed back here, I was that worried about what you wanted to talk about when you left that note. I thought maybe you'd found out you had something terrible wrong with you, and you was going to die. And I thought perhaps you were fed up with me. You've been a bit funny with me lately.'

'Oh, Frances, you make me feel ashamed,' James exclaimed. 'I've been like that in the office too, but I'll be different from now on, I promise. What do you think of that idea – is it possible or, more to the point, would you want to?'

' "Living in", you mean,' said Frances, then she smiled and said simply, 'I'd be glad to.'

'And your family won't mind?' James said.

'My family,' Frances said bitterly, 'will be glad to see the back of me. My brother's wife has wished me dead for years.'

'Surely not!' James exclaimed, horrified.

She went on, 'I heard her say to him she thought my sort died young, but I was hanging on to spite her.'

James was too dumbfounded to speak and she explained. 'I've got four brothers, see, and I was the last and the only girl. "The runt of the litter", my father called me. He was a horrible man, a selfish bully. Everything had to be done to suit him. My poor mother was a sick woman for years, but he still expected her to wait on him. We were all glad when he died, but then my eldest brother and his wife moved in.'

'But when was this?' James asked.

'Thirteen years ago my father died and they moved in. Me brother thought he'd be the new master of the house, but it's his wife that wears the trousers. My mother hardly left her bed after that and I nursed her, but gradually we got moved further and further up the house when my brother had children. Ma died not long before your Ma and I got moved to the attic.

That's when I heard my sister-in-law say that about me.'

'Good God,' was all James could say.

Frances immediately began to talk about possible houses. 'You won't want to leave the parish, will you?' she said. 'But there's plenty of good houses to rent round about. I'll keep my eyes and ears open.'

The clearance of the house was quickly organised. The ladies of the parish who were running the jumble sale were invited to select anything useful to them, and Frances watched cynically as they flitted about, avidly examining the silver or plush photograph frames, the ornaments and tall vases.

There was a quantity of jade and some ivory, but Frances had prudently moved items that she thought James should keep into the kitchen.

'They brought a man with a handcart, but they finished up with a horse and cart, they took that much,' she told James later. 'Things like them small tables and whatnots and the fish kettle and preserving pans you won't have room for. That Miss Furlong, y'know, the auntie, she was one of the worst. She got into the kitchen while my back was turned and I found her with her head in a cupboard, looking at the china.'

'I thought you made the kitchen out of bounds,' James said.

Frances said grimly, 'I did, and so I told her. I said I thought they had so much already they wouldn't need jumble from anywhere else and I didn't know how it would fit on the stalls. She went as red as fire.'

'She was just enthusiastic, I suppose,' James said, unwilling to criticise anyone connected with Dorrie.

Frances snorted. 'If a quarter of that stuff reaches the stalls I'll be surprised,' she said. 'I just hope they watch each other and make each other pay a fair price.'

'I think you're too hard on them, Frances,' James said. 'I'm sure they're all good women. Anyhow, I'm glad to get rid of the stuff.'

James had suggested that Frances moved into one of the empty rooms immediately, to be on hand for the business of moving. He also suggested that she gave up her office jobs, as she was now a housekeeper and must be paid accordingly. It was quickly arranged and Frances furnished the room with pieces she liked from the house, chosen with a view to fitting them in a smaller home.

The next day the secondhand dealer came and with the walls bare and the floors uncluttered it already seemed like an empty house to James when he returned from the office.

Frances found a house to rent in Cresswell Street, off Everton Road, with a small front garden and a bay window, and a flagged path running from the gate to where three steps rose to the front door.

James was pleased with it until he saw a circular metal plate set midway up the path. 'Is there a cellar?' he asked.

'Yes, a coal cellar. The coal can be tipped in there, but some people store coal in the backyard instead,' the landlord's agent said.

'But the cellar's still there. I don't want a house with a cellar,' said James. But the man insisted on showing him the inside of the house and James agreed that it was nice. There was a long hall with stairs rising at the end, a bright parlour with the bay window to the front, and a kitchen-cum-living room with a blackleaded grate. There was also a flagged back-kitchen with a sink and a tap, and a clothes boiler. In the large yard was a WC and a coalplace.

'There you are,' the agent said, and as they went through the back kitchen he opened the door to a space under the stairs. 'That's the entrance to the cellar,' he said. 'If you store things there it'll be covered over.' But James was adamant.

'I don't want a house with a cellar,' he said, and eventually a house was found in Eastbourne Street. It was a solid house with large rooms. There were three good-sized bedrooms and a boxroom which had been converted to a bathroom. There were attics, but no cellars.

The man who showed James round seemed surprised that he had asked Frances to accompany them, and he said gloomily, 'The people who had it before were very arty, like. All this white paint and that puts people off, but I suppose they never thought about it showing the dirt.'

'What do you think, Frances?' James said, and she replied chirpily, 'If the dirt's there, I'd rather see it and get rid of it.'

'It's the brightness of the house that I like,' James said. 'Can we decide now? I'm willing to pay six months' rent in advance.'

'And key money,' Frances put in.

The man shook his head. 'My guv'nor never asks for key money,' he said proudly. 'I'll have to ask you to come to the office, sir. He likes to meet his tenants and there's paperwork, rent book and that to be done. Could you come now, sir? It's not far.'

James agreed and the transaction was soon completed. The landlord told James that he had known his father as a young man, and added, 'You've got a look of him.' This pleased James greatly and they parted very cordially. The men in the office were surprised that the landlord had not required references, especially from a young single man, but James had a warm feeling that the landlord's regard for his father had made them superfluous.

He sold his own house without difficulty to a woman who wanted to open a boarding house and was pleased to obtain the large, heavy furniture cheaply. Frances took the furniture she had earmarked for her bedroom, but James took only a writing desk, which had belonged to his father, and some china and kitchen utensils.

He gradually filled his new house with furniture and fittings of his own choice, suited to the bright rooms with their light walls and paintwork.

It seemed like a fresh start and he felt that he had left many burdens behind in the old house, but although he understood the reasons for his malady it was too deep-seated for him to recover easily.

'Your body has healed, but it'll take longer for your mind,' Dr O'Brien told him. 'You'll still have these morbid feelings at times, but they'll grow fewer. The thing is to keep busy.'

James felt that it was easier to be cheerful in the new house, where there was still much to do, and Frances was so happy that it raised his own spirits.

She had promoted her Sunday shawl and hat to be her everyday wear, in honour of her new status, and as often as possible she shopped where she could see and be seen by friends and neighbours of her sister-in-law. She told James with glee that her brother's wife had said, 'Good riddance to bad rubbish,' when Frances had told her she was leaving. 'But then she had second thoughts. She realised she'll miss my rent money, and although I'm not as useful to them now as when the children were little, I'm still useful sometimes.'

'But you're not sorry to leave?' James said.

'What! That's a joke,' Frances laughed. 'You know, she even said I recommended strangers for my office jobs and never thought about the family. I just looked at her and I said, "How was I to know you wanted the job? You told me once your girls were ashamed of me cleaning offices. You think they wouldn't be ashamed of you doing it?" I was made up to get that dig in, and she didn't know where to look.'

James listened, smiling. Although it sounded out of

character for Frances, he felt she was entitled to be a bit catty and to crow over her brother's wife after all she had suffered at her hands.

During the worst of his depression, James had often gone into the church to try to find comfort and strength, and several times he had seen Anna Furlong there, kneeling alone, with her hands covering her face. Sunk in his own misery, he had felt no curiosity about her, but soon after the move to the new house he went into church one day to give thanks.

A few people were dotted about, a man making the Stations of the Cross, several women with shawls drawn over their heads, kneeling in prayer, and others flitting about the altar with flowers. James went into a side chapel and knelt down, then realised that Anna Furlong was kneeling a few rows in front of him.

With her shoulders bowed and her hands covering her face, she could have been deep in prayer, but with his new awareness of people James was sure that she was weeping bitterly. She had obviously chosen this secluded corner for privacy, and James rose and silently moved away.

For the first time, he realised that, deep and bitter though his own pain had been when Dorrie married, others were suffering too, and he began to think about what it must have meant to Anna. He felt ashamed of his self-absorption.

Chapter Ten

It was true that the summer following Dorrie's wedding had been a most miserable time for Anna. She had expected to miss Dorrie, but not nearly as much as she did. Loyalty to her family meant that there was now no one with whom she could discuss the situation in the Furlong household, the daily bickering between her mother and her aunt, and the petty manoeuvring to gain an advantage.

Even in letters to Dorrie she had to be circumspect, because the letters would probably be shown to Michael. It had all been so much easier to bear, she thought, when she could talk things over with her sister, even make a joke about them. She missed Dorrie in every way, from when she woke each morning to the fresh pain of remembering that her sister had gone and would never again be there when she woke, to when she went to bed alone, with no one with whom to discuss the day.

Most of all, she missed being able to discuss her worries about Eugene. She had hoped for so much from the wedding day, and at first she had been very happy, but later he had made little effort to be with her. She had been kept busy attending to the guests, but he could have helped her, or at least stayed by her side, yet he had spent the time with the crew of her father's ship. Then he had made his sudden departure, saying that he had to return to Caterham, surprising the O'Briens as well as herself.

She had been reassured by Mrs O'Brien's words about Eugene's financial position, and her hint that he would be unable to propose until he had established himself by his own efforts, but now doubts crept in.

Surely, if that was the reason, he would discuss it with her and ask her if she was willing to wait for him, not blow hot and cold without any explanation. There must be some other reason, some secret in Eugene's past to account for his changes of mood, she thought. It seems he wants to love me, but something holds him back.

If only she could discuss it with Dorrie. Lying in bed with her sister in the friendly darkness, it had been possible to speak of all her secret fears and worries, knowing that Dorrie would understand and would find a comforting explanation for Eugene's behaviour, but she could only hint at her troubles in a letter.

She hoped that Dorrie might have learned something which would explain Eugene's strange mood swings, but Dorrie only wrote that they saw very little of Eugene. She gave very little information in her letters, and this was a fresh worry for Anna, because she feared that her beloved sister was unhappy in her new life.

Anna had become closer to Isabel Jenson since the wedding, and she told her her fears about Dorrie, but Isabel dismissed them. 'Dorrie's just settling in,' she said. 'You know what she's like, Anna. Shy with people until she gets to know them, then they're always the best of friends.'

'That's true,' Anna agreed. 'You know, she's very tactful. She sends letters to Mama, Aunt Clara and myself, all to arrive by the same post. I suppose she says the same to them as to me, that the married quarters are nice, the other soldiers' wives are nice, and the Commanding Officer's wife is very nice. Then I suppose she adds the personal bit about Mama's health or Aunt Clara's church work.'

'Does she say much about Eugene?' Isabel asked.

Anna's face clouded. 'No. She says they see very little of

him,' she admitted. 'I think he's in a different company or something.'

They were walking down to the sodality meeting, arm in arm, and Anna said impulsively, 'I don't know what to make of him, Isabel. Since the wedding his letters have been very formal, but suddenly one came last week that was quite different. He quoted poetry, love poetry, and asked me to give his regards to Dr and Mrs O'Brien.'

'Doesn't he write to them himself?' Isabel asked.

'Yes, but he often sends messages to them through me. I wish he wouldn't, really, because you know what Dr O'Brien's like. Makes me feel really embarrassed.'

Isabel laughed. 'He doesn't mean any harm,' she said. 'I think he'd love to see you and Eugene married. But I wouldn't worry too much about the letters, Anna. I don't suppose there's much privacy in Army barracks. I think he may write loving letters if he's alone, but more formal ones if other men are nearby.'

Anna squeezed her arm gratefully. 'You're a great comfort to me, Isabel. Sorry to be such a miz. I promise I'll look on the bright side in future.'

'I think you worry too much about Eugene,' Isabel said. 'Don't forget, Anna, I was there when you met, and he was definitely smitten. The way he looked at you. And he's never stopped writing to you, has he? In all this time.'

'No, that's true,' Anna said, and she enjoyed the sodality meeting so much that several people asked if she was getting over missing her sister.

It was not so easy to maintain her high spirits at home, where she could do nothing right. She tried to help Nelly by taking over some of her many tasks, but Nelly was offended, and Mrs Furlong told Anna to stop upsetting her.

'She can do everything twice as well as you, and in half the time, so don't interfere,' she said.

Anna was so stung by the injustice of this remark that she was unwise enough to retort, 'You said last week it was wrong that Nelly had so much to do while there was an idle, useless girl like me wasting her time. Now, when I try to help, you tell me not to interfere.'

The predictable hysterics from her mother followed, and reproaches from her aunt and Nelly, but Anna escaped into the Deagans' kitchen. 'If I go out, it doesn't suit, and if I stay in, I'm in the way, so I may as well do what I want,' she told Mrs Deagan. 'The result's the same.'

'Well, it means one person's satisfied, anyhow,' Mrs Deagan said equably. 'And you're always welcome here, girlie.'

Mammoth baking sessions were taking place in preparation for Gerald's wedding, and Anna knew her help was always welcome. She also embroidered the underwear that Winifred was collecting for her trousseau, and her household linen.

'Winnie's sister's going to miss her when she marries, isn't she?' Anna said, thinking of herself and Dorrie.

'Yes, she'll miss her coming in from work, and I suppose they'll miss her wages,' Mrs Deagan said. 'But Peggy and her father are made up for Winnie. He's a lovely old man, you know, Anna. A bit deaf, but hale and hearty otherwise, and he does a lot of good turns for people.'

'I've seen him with the girls,' Anna said. 'He looks a good man. Such a pleasant face and that thick white hair.'

'Peggy and him do a lot to help a poor man called Jimmy O'Dowd who lives two doors away from them,' said Mrs Deagan. 'His wife's out of her mind. The doctor calls it premature senile dementia. Doesn't know who she is or where she is, poor soul, but it's terrible for her husband. She can't be left alone for a minute, day or night.'

'But how does he manage?' Anna asked.

'God knows, girlie. I think he's a living saint, but Winnie tells me he says he has to keep to his marriage vows. There's not many would. Even the doctor thinks he should have her put away, but he won't hear of it.'

'If she's so confused, though, would she know?' asked Anna, as she eased a large fruit cake from its tin.

'If she was in a lunatic asylum? She'd realise soon enough, girlie, the way they get treated there, after the care she gets from him. And he says there's sometimes a few minutes when she seems normal again, then the shutter comes down on her. I can see why he can't do it,' said Mrs Deagan.

'But what about his work?' Anna said.

'He's had to give up his job to look after her, and they're living on his savings. He was a master printer, earning good money, and they had no family so he saved a good bit, but it won't last for ever. Olive could live a long time like this, the doctor says.'

'What a tragedy,' Anna said soberly, feeling ashamed of her own misery.

'Aye, for more than one,' said Mrs Deagan. 'Olive was never a proper wife to him. The house mattered more than he did. Fanatically houseproud she was, made him take off his shoes at the door and all that. When she started to go funny she wouldn't even cook a meal – wouldn't use the pans, so he used to sneak fish and chips in, but then she wouldn't allow even that. He'd have a meal out in the day and take pies home for her to eat out of the bag so she didn't dirty a plate. But she put them right in the bin for fear of the crumbs. I don't know how she survived.'

'It's a wonder she didn't starve to death,' said Anna.

'Well, that didn't last long. She got worse and started eating like an animal. Poor Jimmy tried to hide it for a while, but she used to rush to the door when the breadman came, and snatch the loaf off him. Tear it up and stuff it in her mouth. Even the butcher's lad. She used to snatch the raw meat off him and stuff *that* into her mouth. Jimmy had to stop deliveries, but of course they talked.'

'That's true love, isn't it?' Anna said. 'To stay with someone even when something like that happens.'

Mrs Deagan snorted. 'Don't make me laugh, girlie,' she said. 'Love never came into it, except with him and Peggy. He and Peggy were always in and out of each other's houses when they were young. Everybody expected them to marry when they were old enough, but then Jimmy's mother died when he was sixteen. That Olive worked near him in the printer's as a taker off. She took him off all right, poor lad. I don't know how she done it, but she tricked him some way and married him on his seventeenth birthday, and moved into the house. That's all she was after, and now he's landed with this.'

Mrs Deagan and Anna worked in silence for a while, then Anna sighed. 'Poor Peggy,' she said. 'But she still stayed friends with him?'

'Yes, she's done his shopping and cooking for years, and old Mr Parsons is very good. Jimmy can leave Olive with him for hours at a time. It's the only break he gets. Mr Parsons says she's always saying, "What've I got to do?" over and over, and he tells her she has to mind him. He gets out the dolls' teasets that the girls had and plays tea parties with her and things like that. I think Jimmy'd be as mad as her by now otherwise,' said Mrs Deagan.

Anna caught sight of the kitchen clock. 'Heavens! I'll have to go!' she exclaimed. 'I don't know what they'll say about this.'

'Take no notice, girlie. Let it all wash over you,' Mrs Deagan said. 'Don't answer back or you'll only make things worse and anyway, you have to show respect to your mother.'

It was better than Anna had expected when she returned home. A neighbour from a few doors away had called to see Mrs Furlong and Clara and had asked too many questions about Dorrie's wedding and her life in London.

'Such impertinence,' Mrs Furlong said. 'The type of questions she asked. Clara and I soon put her in her place, though, didn't we, Clara?'

'We did indeed,' Clara said, with a self-satisfied smirk. 'She won't be back in a hurry asking *you* questions, Adelaide.'

Anna gave them a few details about the preparations for Winnie and Gerald's wedding, enough to give them something to talk about, without betraying any confidences, and the unusual air of harmony lasted throughout the evening.

Anna had hoped for a letter from Eugene, but none had arrived. At bedtime she lay awake thinking over the day and the sad story of Peggy and Jimmy. It seemed there was a tragedy behind so many of the doors she passed, but Anna reflected that, although her own worries might seem trivial by comparison, nothing she heard made them any easier to bear.

The next morning letters from Dorrie arrived for her mother, aunt and sister, all making the same joyful announcement. Michael had ten days' leave. They would spend the first weekend in Liverpool, then travel to Ballinane to see Michael's parents and Dermot, then return to Liverpool for Friday, Saturday and Sunday, before returning to Caterham.

'Two long weekends,' Anna said, her eyes shining. 'Doesn't it seem a long time since we saw Dorrie?'

'It *is* a long time,' her mother said. She looked at her letter. 'Two weeks today they'll be here. It'll give us time to get ready for them.'

Anna was about to say that preparations didn't matter. She just wanted to see Dorrie as soon as possible, but she was learning to think carefully before making any remark to her mother.

Gerald Deagan's wedding took place on the Saturday. Winnie had planned to have a quiet wedding early in the morning, with just a few friends and relatives present, but Gerald had persuaded her to have what he called a 'proper wedding'.

Winnie wore a traditional white dress, wreath and veil, and Peggy a pink dress, and Norah provided all the flowers. Winnie drove to the church in a carriage with her father and Peggy, and it would have been hard to say who was the happiest of the three.

The wedding breakfast took place at the Deagans' house and was an hilarious occasion. Even Mrs Furlong said afterwards, 'A nice wedding. Not as stylish as Dorrie's, but very happy.'

Clara couldn't resist adding, 'I suppose they were relieved to get the knot safely tied after all this time.'

Anna had watched Peggy with more interest now that she knew her story, and was surprised to see how happy she seemed. She spoke of it to Mrs Deagan, who told her that, when all the arrangements had been made, Peggy had said she had always been afraid someone like Olive might move in and trick Gerald into marriage, leaving Winnie broken-hearted.

'You can see why she worried,' Anna said thoughtfully.

'Yes, but I told her, "Over my dead body would he have married anyone else," ' declared Mrs Deagan.

Anna laughed. 'I'm sure you'd have seen off more determined women than Olive,' she said.

'I've given our Gerald a talking to, now,' said Mrs Deagan. 'Told him he's got to pull up his socks and look after Winnie. "The wedding's not the end," I told him, "it's only the beginning, so you'd better stop drifting along".' She laughed.

'He was real indignant. Said Winnie thinks he's done wonders with the house they've taken, and the business, so I said no more.'

The following weekend, when the excitement of the wedding had died down, Norah announced her engagement to Frank Sutton, the man from the Town Hall who had been so frequently in the florist's shop when Anna called there. 'I thought it would be a surprise to everyone,' Norah told Anna, 'but they were all expecting it. I might have known. You can't keep anything quiet in this family.'

'I guessed, Norah, but I didn't say anything, honestly,' Anna said.

Norah smiled. 'I know you didn't, Anna. I suppose I've given myself away, talking about him, but I couldn't resist it.'

'I know what you mean,' Anna said, thinking of how much she longed to talk about Eugene, but there were now so few people she could talk to about him. Letters still came from him, but at more infrequent intervals, and she wondered whether he still corresponded with the O'Briens, as he sent messages to them in most of his letters.

Dr O'Brien always appeared very pleased to receive the messages and seemed to take it for granted that she and Eugene were in love. Yet Anna discovered he received regular letters himself from Eugene, as he did from Michael and Dorrie. It all seemed odd to her and part of the mystery of Eugene.

The present weekend was the last run of the Wheelers before the winter and Anna had been determined to go with Isabel, even though her mother complained that there was too much still to do before Dorrie came.

Twin brothers, Albert and Alfred Reid, always known as Bert and Fred, had attached themselves to Anna and Isabel, riding with them, and insisting on buying their cream teas when they stopped at a café. They had escorted them home and wanted to take them out at night, but the girls had made excuses.

After Mass on Sunday the two young men joined Anna and Isabel as soon as they emerged from church, and they were standing together talking when Anna looked up to receive an outraged glare from Dr O'Brien. Immediately, her temper rose. Am I supposed to refuse to speak to any young men, just sit about waiting for Eugene to make up his mind, she thought furiously, and began to laugh and talk animatedly to Fred.

Others from the Wheelers joined them, and the girls also greeted families such as the O'Briens. Three of her small brothers were with Isabel and soon she and Anna used them as an excuse to leave, without committing themselves to going out with the Reid brothers.

'I don't want to encourage them, do you?' Anna said.

Isabel shook her head. 'No, they're nice, polite boys, but awful bores, and they've both got clammy handshakes.' They laughed and Isabel added, 'I thought you'd suddenly been sprinkled with love dust, though, the way you were flirting with Fred.'

'Was I! Is that what it looked like!' Anna exclaimed. 'Oh Lord, Isabel, what have I done? I was just mad because Dr O'Brien gave me such a dirty look, as though I was cheating Eugene.'

'Never mind, you've made Fred very happy,' Isabel said, laughing, then when she saw Anna's face she said, 'I'm only joking. Don't take things to heart so much, Anna. I wonder why they have suddenly tacked on to us? How many times have we been out with the Wheelers this summer?'

'Perhaps they suddenly realised the summer was over and it was their last chance of getting off,' Anna said.

'Certainly not our fatal charms, so don't worry about them,' Isabel said as they parted outside her home.

How clear-sighted and sensible Isabel was, Anna thought as she walked away. I'm so lucky to have her for a friend.

Dorrie and Michael arrived on Friday and were met at Lime Street Station by Anna and Dr O'Brien. Anna and Dorrie sat together as they drove home, and Dr O'Brien and Michael sat opposite, talking, so Anna was able to ask Dorrie quietly to tell her truthfully if she was happy.

'I am now,' Dorrie said. 'I was always happy when Michael was there, but when I was on my own, I wasn't. I've made a friend, though, and she's explained things to me.'

'What's her name?' asked Anna.

'Mrs Rafferty. She's – sort of rough, but very kind. She's been an Army wife for many years. At first it was like living in a strange tribe with all different customs, and I kept doing the wrong thing without realising it.'

Anna hugged her. 'Poor Dorrie, it must have been dreadful. Really frightening.'

'It was,' said Dorrie. 'Mrs Rafferty helped me understand. She said it was almost like India, where her husband served for seven years. A caste system, each lot turning their noses up at one of the others.'

'But it's like that in civilian life too, Dorrie, with the class system,' Anna said.

'Yes, but worse in the Army because there are so many grades and they have more power over you, Mrs Rafferty said. She said we were the lowest grade of all. Untouchables.'

'But why?' Anna said indignantly.

'Because we are the wives of the lower ranks. Mary Froggatt's husband is a batman and he heard them talking, the officers I mean,' said Dorrie. 'They said they must devise something to keep us out of mischief, and they decided to tell us to do the laundry.'

'The impudence!' Anna exclaimed.

'I know. I said I would refuse, but Mrs Rafferty said that's not the way. You don't argue, but you do the laundry so badly that they have to give up the idea.'

They were driving along Shaw Street by now and Dr O'Brien said he would get off there. 'I hope you'll come in and see my wife for a few minutes,' he said. 'She won't detain you, but she's longing to see you.'

They agreed, and spent a pleasant ten minutes with Mrs O'Brien, but as they drove away Anna said, 'We won't mention this unless we are asked.'

Dorrie added, 'Indeed, and I'm sure the O'Briens will be too tactful to say anything. Remember, Michael.'

He smiled and agreed, although he looked puzzled, but Anna reflected that he would soon learn to negotiate the quicksands of the Furlong ménage.

Dorrie's mother and aunt were waiting in the hall and Mrs Furlong clung to Dorrie, weeping copiously. 'I've missed you so much,' she wept. 'No one knows. Only a mother would understand.'

'I'm here now, Mama,' Dorrie said. 'And I'm sure we're going to have a lovely time for the next few days.' But her mother still wept and had to be assisted to her sofa.

Dorrie looked helplessly at Michael and he said cheerfully, 'We thought you'd be happy to see us. We've been looking forward to coming back to Liverpool, haven't we, Dorrie?'

Mrs Furlong sat up and dried her eyes. 'Oh, I am,' she said. 'I was just overcome for a moment. I'll be all right now.'

Now you've had enough attention, Anna thought cynically, but she said nothing.

Later, after their meal, Dorrie played the piano and Michael sang, then Michael sat with Dorrie's mother and aunt, charming them with anecdotes about the Army and London, freeing Dorrie to slip away with Anna.

'I'll pretend I'm helping you to unpack,' Anna said, but the two girls sat close together on Anna's bed and Anna at last was able to ask Dorrie about Eugene and to pour out all her doubts.

Dorrie looked troubled. 'It's true, Anna, that we hardly ever see him. He's in another company, but Michael's worried about you and him.'

Their mother's careful training in grammar was forgotten, as Anna said eagerly, 'Why? What way? I know there's something, Dorrie.'

'I don't know exactly, but Michael was worried one night, saying he had a duty to you as you were his sister now, but he might be wrong about Eugene,' said Dorrie. 'But he said he thought he was devious and if you could meet someone else he'd be happy.'

'Eugene would?' Anna exclaimed.

'No, Michael,' Dorrie said.

'But why, Dorrie? He must have a reason for saying that. Is Eugene in love with someone else? Could he even – even be married?' said Anna.

Dorrie said emphatically, 'Oh no, no, Anna. Not that. There are always rumours and gossip flying round the camp and one of the wives would have told me. I've told Mrs Rafferty he fell in love with you when he and Michael came to Liverpool.'

'I told you Mrs O'Brien said he was waiting to be promoted before he could afford to marry, and that's why he's said nothing. I was made up, Dorrie, but the more I think of it the less likely it seems. Surely he should ask me to wait for him. I wouldn't care how long, if I only *knew*,' Anna cried in frustration.

'Do you still love him, Anna?' Dorrie asked gently.

Anna nodded. 'I should have more pride, I suppose,' she said. 'But I can't help it. I think about him all the time, day and night, and remember when we first met and the way he looked and I'm fathoms deep in love again.' She burst into tears and Dorrie put her arms round her and wept with her.

'If only I could tell you something that would help,' Dorrie said. 'But even Michael doesn't really know anything, or understand Eugene.'

Anna still wept and clung to Dorrie. 'It helps so much, Dorrie, to be able to talk to you. I couldn't say any of this to anyone else. I'd be ashamed,' she said.

Dorrie said indignantly, 'Ashamed! You've got nothing to be ashamed of!'

'I'm ashamed of clinging on to a man who can't decide whether he wants me or not,' Anna said bravely. 'If it was anyone else I'd say they should cut their losses and finish with him, but I can't. I love him too much.' Her voice trembled as she added the last few words.

Dorrie hugged Anna closer and wiped her eyes. 'I'm sure he loves you, Anna. The way he looks at you. It could be just because of the headlong way Michael and I rushed into getting married that Eugene seems slow. How many couples do we know who were courting for years? Gerald and Winnie for one.'

'Yes, but they had an understanding. You know I wouldn't mind how long I waited, if I only *knew* where I stood,' said Anna. 'But don't compare it with you and Michael, Dorrie. You both fell truly and deeply in love at the same time, and you both wanted to be married as soon as possible.'

Dorrie smiled fondly, and Anna went on, 'Michael was ready to move heaven and earth for a quick wedding, and he succeeded. It was all lovely, like a fairy story that came true, and I'm so happy for you, so don't talk about rushing headlong and spoil that just to make Eugene's tardiness seem better.'

'That sounds more like you,' Dorrie said, smiling and hugging her sister. 'I'm quite sure that Eugene loves you.

Look how he was when he was here, and then the letters all this time. Why else would he write? But that might be the trouble – that you have to rely on letters. They might not say what he means them to, or you might read something different into them. It's not like seeing someone every day.'

Anna agreed. 'Isabel has suggested that he writes formal letters when other men are about, and loving ones when he is alone,' she said.

'She could be right,' said Dorrie. 'And then there's his family. Michael says he doesn't understand Eugene. He's got strange ideas, but he thinks it's because of his family. They're all very devious. Michael hears rumours, but he knows they can't be true because of you, and Eugene seems truly fond of Dr and Mrs O'Brien, yet he doesn't give a button for his immediate family.'

'I wouldn't blame him for that, from what I saw of them,' said Anna dryly. 'But what rumours, Dorrie?'

'Army stuff, I think,' Dorrie said vaguely. They could hear movement downstairs and Dorrie hurriedly gave Anna some powder leaves to press round her eyes, while she did the same.

As they went downstairs Anna squeezed Dorrie's arm. 'This is typical of Michael's kindness, keeping them occupied while we had a talk, Dorrie. Tell him how grateful I am, won't you?'

They were relieved to find that they had not been missed by their mother and aunt, who had been completely charmed by Michael.

The weekend seemed to pass in a flash and there were no other opportunities for long confidential talks between the two girls, but Anna felt much happier about Eugene.

Mrs Furlong was proud to be joined at Mass on Sunday morning by her married daughter and handsome son-in-law, but Anna was sorry that their party came face-to-face with James Hargreaves as they left the church.

He raised his hat and wished them good morning and they all responded, but Dorrie whispered to Anna, 'Who was that?' She was amazed when Anna told her, and said she had not recognised him. 'He's so thin,' she said. 'And his face! Positively lantern-jawed. Poor man. He must have grieved more than we realised.' Anna said nothing.

There was the predictable scene from Mrs Furlong when Dorrie and Michael left for Ireland, but five days later they were back for the second weekend before returning to London.

This time the sisters did manage some more time alone, when Dorrie crept into Anna's bed early one morning, but there was little new to be said about Eugene.

Michael had admitted to Dorrie that he had a feeling his cousin was not to be trusted. 'He doesn't ring true. I think he's playing a crafty game,' he said. 'Try to warn Anna.'

Dorrie had been deeply upset to realise that Anna still loved Eugene so much. She had always behaved with such coolness and dignity towards him, and even when she and Anna had exchanged confidences after the bazaar, and Anna had admitted that she loved him, Dorrie had no idea that it was as deep and passionate a love as her own for Michael.

How could I have been so blind? she mourned. So wrapped up in my own affairs. To see her proud and reserved sister weeping bitterly and admitting that the thought of Eugene was always with her, night and day, and to know that she had been suffering in silence with no one to confide in, made Dorrie feel quite frantic.

She pestered Michael with questions about Eugene all the time they were in Ireland, but realised that he had truly told her all he knew. How could she add to Anna's fears with just 'a feeling' that Michael had? Yet how could she warn her as he suggested?

It was as they lay in bed talking about Dorrie's life in

London that an idea came to her. She had just told Anna that she hated married quarters. 'If I had my own place you could come and stay with me,' she told her sister. 'That's what you need. To get away from this house for a while.'

'And perhaps to see Eugene?' Anna said with a smile.

'That too,' Dorrie said, although her idea had been that Anna might meet other men. The household was stirring so she slipped back to her own room, but all day she turned the idea over in her mind.

In the evening, Dr and Mrs O'Brien had been invited, and at the first opportunity Dorrie spoke privately to Mrs O'Brien. She had absolute faith in her discretion, so she told the older woman that she felt Anna needed to have a break from home and an opportunity to meet other men.

'There doesn't seem to be anyone among the few people she sees,' Dorrie said. 'And Michael's worried. He thinks she might waste her life waiting for Eugene and nothing come of it in the end.'

'Why does he think that?' asked Mrs O'Brien.

'He can't tell me,' said Dorrie. 'He can only say it's a feeling he had that Eugene won't marry her. You won't mention this to Michael, will you?'

Mrs O'Brien patted her hand. 'No, my dear, nor to anyone else, even Dr O'Brien, but I'll think of something. I've great confidence in Michael's judgement. There's a lot of Bridie in him, and you're a good girl to be so concerned. I'm glad Anna has you both to look out for her, but don't worry any more.'

Dorrie took her advice and left for London feeling that she had done all she could for her beloved sister, but determined to find out more about Eugene.

Chapter Eleven

Anna felt happier now that she had been able to talk to Dorrie about Eugene, although admitting her love made it even stronger, she felt. She had been able to talk freely too about the situation in the family. Dorrie had been shocked when Anna said she thought her mother hated her, and treated her like a cat with a mouse.

'You must be mistaken, Anna!' she had exclaimed.

Anna insisted she was not. 'She doesn't want me here because she knows I see through her play-acting, but she won't let me go because she wants to torment me,' she declared.

'What about Aunt Clara?' Dorrie had asked, and Anna told her that although her aunt constantly criticised her, it was only in her usual way, quite different from her mother's malice.

Dorrie had been horrified and hoped that if she could arrange for Anna to be away from the family for a while matters might improve.

Norah Deagan had told Anna that she and Frank planned an early wedding, but she would keep on her shop and still sell Anna's embroidery. Anna had little opportunity during the day to work at it, being at her mother's beck and call, but she bought herself some candles, and worked while the household was asleep.

After talking to Dorrie she was more determined to stand up for herself and refused to be upset by the scenes she faced if she went out without permission.

'I'm not a child,' she had told her mother once. 'I'm nearly twenty-three years old,' but her mother had replied cuttingly, 'While you are living under this roof you are a child, a dependent child. Living under my roof and being kept by me, so under my jurisdiction.'

Anna had fled to her room. If only she could have run from the house, but where would she go? There were no relatives she could turn to, and no other possibility. At her age, and with no training, no one would employ her, even as a servant. Strong young girls of thirteen or fourteen were taken to be trained in housework, and at her age she would be expected to have years of training as a parlourmaid or housemaid.

Even the Deagans, with all their contacts, would be unable to find a job for her, although they could have done when she was younger. Why didn't I go then? Defy Father? Anna thought, but she knew she could not have done it.

She had taken her troubles to a priest in the confessional, but he could only advise her to accept her lot. 'God has a plan for everyone, my child,' he said. 'And this is His plan for you. Don't fight against it. Trust in God and offer up your sufferings for the souls in purgatory. Take your sorrows and bitterness to Our Lady, the Mother of us all, and she will help you to bear them. Go in peace, my child. I will pray for you.'

That was the day that James Hargreaves saw Anna weeping in church, as she realised how hard it would be for her stubborn nature to accept the priest's advice.

Now she made a neat parcel of some embroidered collars and cuffs, and an embroidered bell pull and matching table runner, which had been a special order. Concealing it under her cape, she went downstairs. She looked into the drawing room where her mother was reading and said briefly, 'I'm taking a message to Norah Deagan from the sacristan about the flowers. Goodbye,' and closed the door before her mother could reply.

She walked out of the front door with her head held high, although her legs were trembling. I've done it, she thought exultantly. No more slipping out of the back door for me, or leaving a message with Nelly.

She found Norah alone in the shop and delighted to receive the parcel. 'Will you let me set the price for these, Anna?' she asked. 'You don't charge half enough for your work. I know how anxious Mrs Drew is for these and how much work has gone into them, and I want to see you get fair recompense.'

'You're very good, Norah, with so much else to think about,' Anna said gratefully. 'How are the wedding plans going?'

'Very smoothly. We only want a very quiet wedding. Frank has very few relations and I only want our own close family, no second cousins once removed,' Norah laughed. 'Of course, Ma would like to go out into the highways and byways to bring them in, but she had everyone for Winnie and Gerald's wedding, so they can't grumble if they're not asked to mine, coming so soon after.'

'You've fixed a date, then?' Anna said.

'Yes, only last night we went to see Fr Kavanagh. It's the second Saturday in January, nine o'clock Mass on the side altar. Kate will be my bridesmaid and Frank's brother, John, his best man. I hope you'll be there, Anna. And afterwards it's back to our house for the wedding breakfast. We'll go right off to York for a week after that.'

'But you're only having family,' Anna protested.

'We think of you as family, you and Dorrie,' Norah said. 'You stayed with us when you were little girls and your poor Mama was having such troubles, losing all those babies.'

Anna was silent, not wanting to think of her mother, but feeling a warm glow that the Deagans regarded her and Dorrie as family. 'I nearly forgot,' she said suddenly, 'Brother Shaw gave me a message for you about the church flowers.'

Norah took the slip of paper and put it on the corner of the counter, weighting it with a pebble. 'He told me,' she said. 'But he always confirms everything. A real perfectionist.'

'And it shows,' Anna said. 'The altar is lovely.'

There was a sudden influx of customers and she got up to go, but first Norah took a tin from beneath the counter and took a sovereign and a florin from it. 'Your embroidery money,' she said.

'Twenty-two shillings!' Anna gasped. 'It's more than many a man's wages, Norah.'

'And hard earned,' Norah said. 'I saw the candle burning in your room when I got up in the night. You've brought me extra trade too.'

Anna walked home, delighted with her payment. It was the result of several weeks' work and she knew she would be unable to live independently on what she earned, but it gave her a wonderful feeling of confidence to have the coins in her pocket.

She looked in the drawing room, where her mother still sat and said, 'I'm home, Mama.'

'And about time,' her mother said. 'Nelly needed help with the curtains, but as usual you were not here when you were wanted.' She sighed heavily. 'To think of the children I lost and the one spared to me had to be you.'

'What about Dorrie?' Anna said.

'Don't mention my darling Dorrie in the same breath as yourself,' her mother said angrily. 'You wicked, ungrateful girl.'

Anna withdrew before the hysterics started. Why did I have to mention Dorrie? If only I could curb my tongue, she thought. Still, I've taken a step forward today.

She found Nelly and apologised for leaving her to hang the curtains without help. Nelly tossed her head. 'The day I can't hang a pair of curtains on my own I'll be finished,' she declared. She said there was nothing else Anna could help her with, so she went to the kitchen where her aunt told her to wash some dishes, but refused to let her help to prepare the vegetables.

'Go and keep your mother company,' she said.

'But I've looked in the drawing room and she's reading,' Anna protested. 'Can't I do something here, Aunt?'

'Drawing room!' her aunt snorted. 'Every other house in this road has a parlour, but hers has to be a drawing room. Your mother's a fool.'

Anna said nothing, but could see there was no work for her in the kitchen. She took her writing box into the drawing room and settled down at a side table to write letters.

Her mother ignored her for a while, then said, 'Who are you writing to?'

'To Father,' Anna said. 'Do you want to send a message, or will you be writing yourself?'

Her mother made no reply, only held out her hand imperiously for the letter. Anna took it to her and she read it through, then handed it back, saying, 'I don't want you grumbling to Father and upsetting him.'

A dozen replies rose to Anna's lips, but she firmly repressed them and said nothing. She wrote Dorrie a brief letter, saying little except that she had enjoyed her and Michael's visit, because she knew her mother was quite likely to demand to read it. When she had finished she asked her mother for stamps.

If she knew about the money I have hidden she'd have a fit, Anna thought, but it means I can write letters privately and buy my own stamps. As far as her mother knew she was still completely penniless and dependent on her, even for stamps or collection money.

The next batch of letters from Captain Furlong came as much of a bombshell to Anna as to her mother.

Mrs O'Brien had understood Dorrie's worry and agreed with her that something must be done to help Anna. She had been thinking of possible solutions ever since and had taken Dr O'Brien into her confidence.

'Anna's in an impossible position there,' she told him. 'Dorrie told me more than she knew. I can see that she believed her mother's fantasies and made the right response, but Anna sees through her and can't avoid showing it.'

Dr O'Brien nodded. 'So her mother's behaving like the vicious little shrew I always knew she was,' he said forthrightly. 'She fools that good man, but she doesn't fool me.'

'Yes, and to make it worse, Clara and Nelly don't want Anna to help in the house. Whatever she does her mother says it's wrong and upsetting Nelly, so how can she fill her day? Her mother objects to her going out.'

'There's already a battle on with Clara fighting to keep her position there, and Nelly, of course, is clinging to her job,' said Dr O'Brien. 'It's not that they are against Anna personally.'

Mrs O'Brien was amazed. 'I'd no idea you knew so much about them,' she said.

He tapped his nose. 'Not much I miss, my dear,' he replied. 'I promised Captain Furlong I'd keep an eye on them. I think the best thing is for me to have a word with Eugene. Marriage would be the best solution for Anna,' he said, but Mrs O'Brien was so adamantly opposed to any interference that he reluctantly abandoned the idea.

Instead, he and his wife decided that she would have a holiday in Dublin before Christmas, and ask Anna to accompany her, as the doctor would be unable to get away. 'I'll write to ask her father's permission,' the doctor said. 'Take the wind out of her mother's sails if she wants to say no.'

172

'Good idea,' said his wife approvingly. 'And we'll say nothing until we hear from him.'

Consequently, when the bundle of letters was delivered, Anna and her mother learnt at the same time about the proposed holiday.

'You knew about this and said nothing!' her mother accused Anna furiously. 'You knew I wouldn't let you go. You put them up to this.'

'I knew nothing,' Anna protested. 'You should know. You read all my letters,' she added bitterly, but her mother had snatched Anna's letter from her hand.

Captain Furlong had written, 'My dear Annabel, Among my letters when we put into port was one from Dr O'Brien, asking my permission for you to accompany his wife on a short holiday in Dublin, as he is unable to leave his patients at that time. This I have gladly given. I am only too happy to oblige my good friend and I know you will do all you can to assist Mrs O'Brien, Annabel. I have asked your mama to entrust a sum of money to you so that you may pay your share of the expenses, although Dr O'Brien stressed that you will be his guest and will be doing him a favour. I am writing these letters in haste, so that they may go by return as time is short, but will write longer letters next time.'

Mrs Furlong hurled the letter to the floor. 'I don't believe it. I don't believe you knew nothing about it. When are you going?'

'I don't know, Mama, honestly!' Anna exclaimed. 'I think I'll go and see Mrs O'Brien.'

She jumped to her feet, but her mother said immediately, 'You'll do no such thing. Let them have the courtesy to come to me and ask *my* permission.'

Anna sat down again. Both of them knew her mother's permission was unnecessary now, but Anna was too excited and happy to argue. She picked up her letter and went up to her room.

Later in the afternoon, Mrs O'Brien called and was frostily received by Mrs Furlong, but she appeared to notice nothing. 'I see your letters have arrived,' she said cheerfully. 'We received one from Captain Furlong and we were so happy to have his permission to invite Anna to travel with me.' She turned to Anna. 'I do hope you are willing, Anna. I'd be so grateful for your company. The doctor and I so looked forward to a short holiday in Dublin, but he can't get away, so he thought of asking if you could come with me.'

'I'd be glad to,' Anna said eagerly. 'When is it?'

'From the seventh to the fourteenth of December. It will be lovely in Dublin then and we'll be back in good time for Christmas. I know it's November now, but all you have to do is pack your clothes. All the arrangements have been made.'

'Have they indeed? So you were quite sure of getting your own way?' Mrs Furlong said angrily.

Mrs O'Brien replied coolly, 'The arrangements that were made for my husband are simply being transferred to Anna.'

Mrs Furlong couldn't resist saying, 'You should have consulted me. In my husband's absence I am in charge of this household and I make the decisions.'

'On household matters, but this is different, surely. It never occurred to my husband to do anything but apply to the head of the family, and Captain Furlong appeared to think he was correct,' said Mrs O'Brien.

'But to say nothing to me. So deceitful!' cried Mrs Furlong.

'I'm sorry you see it like that. We thought it would be quite wrong to mention it until we had Captain Furlong's permission,' said Mrs O'Brien.

Frustrated and angry, Mrs Furlong said viciously, 'I wish you joy of your travelling companion. You'll find her very

174

different to my darling Dorrie. Moody and selfish, totally different to Dorrie. Oh, how I miss her, but it's always the way. The best are taken from you.' She began to weep.

'Dorrie's not dead,' Mrs O'Brien said crisply, 'simply very happily married. The doctor and I are delighted about it and I'm surprised you're not. After all, that's what every mother wants for her children, surely.'

'Yes, but if only she had married and settled near me, where I could see her every day, or it had been . . .' Even she was unable to complete the sentence, with Mrs O'Brien and Anna looking at her, but they all knew the next word would have been 'Anna'.

Mrs O'Brien stood up. 'I'm sure there are things you want to ask me about the holiday, Anna. Our door is always open. Take plenty of warm clothes. We have a stateroom for the crossing, so you won't have to worry about the journey.' She said goodbye and left, reflecting that if someone murdered Mrs Furlong she would not be in the least surprised.

Realising that she had been outwitted, Mrs Furlong declared that she washed her hands of the whole affair, and took no interest in the holiday. She only gave Anna the two guineas her father had stipulated at the last possible moment before the holiday, and offered no help with the expense of the preparations.

It could have been difficult for Anna, but Winnie Deagan, née Parsons, lent Anna a suitcase and various small travelling necessities, and Anna was able to supplement her wardrobe from her own nest egg, unknown to her mother. Isabel knitted a warm jacket for her and Mrs Jenson crocheted a pretty warm shawl. The little boys offered her all their treasures, from a double-bladed penknife to a thrush's egg.

All the Deagans did something to help. Jim gave her a book on Dublin's architecture, and Luke a set of maps of the city. Maggie knitted her some bedsocks for the journey and Norah gave her a nightdress.

'But isn't this from your own trousseau?' Anna protested, but Norah laughed and said it would never fit her.

'I had some lawn left so I just guessed your measurements, or rather our Kate did,' she said.

They were all in the Deagans' kitchen and Kate said, 'I didn't guess, Anna. I had your measurements from your bridesmaid's dress.' She produced a parcel. 'When this order was uncollected I grabbed it, because I knew the measurements were so nearly yours.' She opened the large box and from swathes of tissue paper took out a beautiful dark blue evening gown, cut on classical lines.

'My gift, Anna, and if there's any alteration needed I'll do it.'

'But no, no. I couldn't,' Anna stammered, then, as there was a chorus of protest, she burst into tears. 'You're all too good,' she sobbed. 'I can't – I can't.'

Mrs Deagan, sitting near Anna at the kitchen table, tut-tutted loudly. 'It looks as if my present is going to come in handy,' she said, opening the drawer in the table and taking out a large flat bottle of brandy, wrapped in tissue paper, and a small leather flask.

'The flask is full of brandy,' she said. 'And it's small enough to go in your pocket, so you can take a nip when you need it. You can fill it up from the bottle.'

Laughing and crying at the same time, Anna tried to wipe her eyes and compose herself.

'Here, try the flask,' Norah said. 'That was a good idea of Ma's.' She held the flask to Anna's lips.

Anna took a sip then, as the spirit seemed to explode inside her, her eyes widened. 'That's powerful,' she gasped and everyone laughed.

Anna was easily persuaded to accept the dress from Kate, who told her that the staff were allowed to buy uncollected orders at a discount. Mrs O'Brien had told her that they would be going to several evening parties, as she intended to look up old friends, and now Anna felt she could be suitably dressed.

When she went to say goodbye to Isabel and her mother the day before she left, Anna found another ship's captain and his wife there. 'They have come to tell us they've seen Papa,' Isabel said excitedly as she admitted Anna. 'They passed at sea. Isn't that wonderful?'

Captain Olafson and his wife greeted Anna and told their tale more fully. 'The sky and the sea were so blue and so calm and sunny,' Mrs Olafson said. 'A beautiful day.'

'We wouldn't have thought so if we had still been under sail,' her husband said with a rumbling laugh. 'We would both have been lying becalmed, but steam is different. We drew near Captain Jenson's ship when we were off Kinsale. He was outward bound and we were homeward, but we managed to get close. So close that as we passed we saw him on his bridge.'

'Did he look well?' Mrs Jenson asked eagerly.

'Yes, and in good voice,' said Captain Olafson. 'He shouted as we passed, "Give my love to my wife and children. Tell my boys to look after Mama and Isabel and little Wilma." There was something else, but we were too far past.'

'And you thought he seemed well?' Mrs Jenson said, her thoughts obviously on the message from her husband.

'Wonderfully well. So solid as he stood there, with the sunlight making his beard and his hair look like gold,' said Mrs Olafson.

Her husband made an impatient movement. 'The last time I met him he told me he was doing well with these runs. That's the sort of gold we should be interested in,' Captain Olafson said.

'Yes. It's a good shipping line. Willie will be fifteen when his father comes home again, and he will arrange for him to be apprenticed with them.'

'So, you'll be going for your ticket,' the captain said to Willie. 'Means a lot of book learning, now. You'll have to work hard.'

'I will, sir,' said Willie. 'It's what I've always wanted.'

'And his father wants him in apprentice quarters, rather than the fo'castle,' Mrs Jenson said.

Isabel and Anna slipped away to say goodbye to the little boys, but before they went back downstairs Isabel said seriously, 'You'll meet a lot of new people in Dublin, Anna. Remember you're still free. Not bound to Eugene.'

'Not legally,' Anna said with a wry smile. 'But in other ways . . .' She shrugged.

'But think,' Isabel urged. 'Do you want to go on with your life as it is now? I know you have your dreams of Eugene to sustain you, but is it enough? Hope deferred maketh the heart sick, they say.' She slipped her arm round Anna's waist. 'I don't want to interfere, but I care about you, Anna. I'd hate you to lose this chance of meeting someone who could make you happy.'

'I don't think I could be happy with anyone but Eugene,' Anna admitted.

'But how do you know?' Isabel persisted. 'I can't betray a confidence, but someone I've known as happily married for many years told me that she carried a torch for someone else for years. Another man wanted to marry her, but she wouldn't even consider it. Felt she would be unfaithful to the first man, although he never declared himself. Then one day she was very unhappy and she decided if she couldn't have what she wanted she'd settle for what was possible.'

'I could never do that,' Anna said decidedly.

'She said she was ashamed of thinking that now. She said the first man hurt her very much. She liked and respected the second man, although she didn't love him, so she married him. She said over the years her love for him grew and she couldn't imagine being married to anyone else, particularly the first man, who turned out a real bad hat.'

Anna squeezed her waist. 'You're a good friend, Isabel, and I know you're right. I promise I'll encourage anyone who shows any interest, even if they don't look at all like Eugene,' and they went back to the parlour smiling, for Anna to say her final goodbyes before she went to Ireland.

Mrs O'Brien had kept in touch with many friends in Dublin from her nursing days and she had many relatives there so invitations poured in. Every minute of the day was occupied and it was difficult to find time for the carriage drive through Dublin that Mrs O'Brien had promised, but they managed it.

'I'm determined you'll see *my* Dublin and forget that horrible drive with Mrs D'Arcy,' she told Anna, but unfortunately wherever they went Anna could only think that this was Eugene's home city and he might have walked these streets.

They were staying with a nursing friend of Mrs O'Brien's, whom she had known as Deirdre Quinn, but was now Mrs Duffy, the wife of a Dublin surgeon. Only two of their large family were still at home, Eileen, who was a few years younger than Anna, and Dominic, a doctor a few years older. The three young people became friends instantly and Eileen accused her brother of neglecting his patients to be so constantly at Anna's side.

Before an evening party, when Anna wore her new dress for the first time, Eileen had exclaimed in delight at it and offered to dress her hair. She combed it out from its usual severe style and drew it up on Anna's head, producing gold-coloured narrow ribbon to bind it in the style of a Greek goddess, with soft curls framing her face. Mrs O'Brien and the family were amazed at the transformation and told Anna she should always wear her hair like that, and Dominic told her ardently that she was more beautiful than a Greek goddess and he was sure there were fires burning under her cool appearance.

At all the lunches and dinners, and particularly at the evening parties, Anna was introduced to charming young Irishmen and was an instant success. There was no jealousy from the girls and Anna and Mrs O'Brien were charmed by the warm welcome they received from everyone they met.

Anna was thoroughly enjoying the attentions of the young men and she told herself that she was truly trying to keep an open mind. If I met someone I thought I could love as much as Eugene I would encourage him, she told herself. They are so nice and charming and handsome, but none of them have made my heart turn over the way he does. I wish they did. It would solve everything and I'm sure Mrs O'Brien would be pleased.

More and more, as the week went on, she suspected that Mrs O'Brien was deliberately introducing her to eligible young men. I thought she was as anxious as Dr O'Brien for us to marry, but it seems she has doubts about Eugene too. Just because he doesn't want to rush into matrimony now, they seem to think he never will.

She put these thoughts out of her mind and determined to enjoy the holiday to the full. It was not hard. She especially enjoyed the lunches with Mrs O'Brien's friends from her youth.

'Ah God, we were all half in love with Paddy O'Brien,' one matron sighed. 'Then Maureen here married him and carried him off over the sea where we couldn't get at him.'

'I like that. It was him!' Mrs O'Brien protested. 'I never wanted to leave Dublin.'

'What a card he was,' said another. 'Do you remember the

night he said he knew the colour of the bloomers of half the nurses in Dublin? Then before he was lynched he said it was from giving them a leg up to go head first through the pantry window at three o'clock in the morning.'

'The chances we took! Those wild parties and being locked out of the nurses' home. We must have been mad,' said Mrs O'Brien. 'Very often we were on the wards for five-thirty and working for twelve hours. How did we do it?'

'We were young,' said another woman. 'And it was the first taste of freedom, if you could call it that with the dragons we had for sisters.' They all laughed.

'It was still better than living in the country with every move watched,' said another. 'The young ones now, they don't know they're born, or the meaning of hard work.'

Dominic, who had accompanied his mother to the lunch, winked at Anna. 'Do you think we'll say this when we're old?' he asked. Anna shrugged and smiled and he whispered, 'I hope I'm with you to find out. I'm quite sure about those hidden fires.'

Before they left Dublin Anna promised to correspond with him and two other men. 'Just as friends,' she stipulated, and they agreed, but smiled as they did. All three were dark-haired, and unlike Eugene, and she liked them all, as friends. She even admitted to herself that if she had met Dominic before Eugene she could have fallen in love with him.

'I'm so grateful,' she told Mrs O'Brien on the boat. 'I've enjoyed every minute. I've never met so many nice people in such a short time, and they were all so kind. I'll never be able to thank you and Dr O'Brien enough.'

'If you've enjoyed it, Anna, that's thanks enough for us,' Mrs O'Brien said. 'We know you must be sad, missing Dorrie and the way things are at home. Perhaps the little break will make you better able to bear them.'

'It will,' Anna said eagerly. 'I have so many happy memories now.'

'And some nice young men to write to,' Mrs O'Brien teased her. 'My friend Deirdre says her son and daughter will be corresponding with you too. Dominic is a grand young man and a good doctor. He's very good to his mother and, as they say Anna, a good son makes a good husband.'

Anna smiled. 'I liked him very much,' she admitted, 'and I think Eileen is a lovely girl. I'll enjoy corresponding with her. I'll have plenty of letters to write. I feel it is the start of happier times for me.'

In these hopes Anna was cruelly deceived, but her increased confidence as a result of her popularity in Dublin helped her to deal with her mother, and all went well over Christmas and for the January wedding of Norah and Frank.

In the February of 1905 two tragedies occurred in quick succession. On a Monday morning the breadman was delivering to Jimmy O'Dowd and as they stood at the door Olive suddenly appeared with some carrots clutched in her hand. Before either man could stop her she had rushed past them and thrust one of the carrots at the breadman's pony.

An empty coal cart was approaching from the opposite direction, returning to the depot with only empty coal sacks on the flat wagon.

The wagoner was sitting with his legs dangling, smoking his pipe, the reins slack in his hands, when Olive suddenly rushed across the road towards the horse, waving the carrots and shouting unintelligibly.

The horse reared and its front hoof caught Olive on the head, knocking her to the ground.

Suddenly Margaret Street seemed full of people. Some rushed to steady the horses' heads and others to stand round Jimmy as he knelt beside Olive. Blood was running from her head and trickling from the corner of her mouth, but she looked quite peaceful. An off-duty nurse from Mill Road Hospital pushed through the crowd and held Olive's wrist. She stood up.

'Take her into her house,' she said, and she put her hand on Jimmy's shoulder. 'Not you. Let these lads.'

She and Jimmy led the way to the bedroom and as they went she said quietly, 'There's no pulse, Jimmy.' He looked at her blankly and turned back the bedclothes for Olive to be laid in the bed.

Even when the doctor arrived and pronounced Olive dead, Jimmy seemed unable to accept it and sat silently in the chair beside the bed, oblivious to everyone around him. It was only when Peggy and her father arrived that he was persuaded to move.

'Come downstairs, Jimmy,' Peggy said gently. 'There are people you must see.' She took his arm and old Mr Parsons said quietly, 'I'll stay with her, Jimmy.' Jimmy stood up and Mr Parsons took his place, sitting placidly beside Olive in death as he had sat so often in life.

Downstairs, the local policeman waited with the breadman and the coalman who had left others in charge of their horses. 'Sorry for your loss, sir,' the policeman said to Jimmy. 'Seems this man was not fully in control of his horse.'

'I was,' the coalman protested. 'She just come out of nowhere and frightened him.'

'No one was to blame,' Jimmy said. 'Except me. I never let her go out of the gate on her own.'

There was a chorus of dissent. 'You couldn't of stopped her, Jimmy, no more than what I could,' the breadman said. 'One minute we was just standing there with the bread and the next she knocked both of us flying and dashed out.'

The policeman and the nurse said kindly, 'You can't blame

yourself,' and the nurse added, 'I've had patients like Olive. They have unnatural strength. You've done wonders, Jimmy.'

Jimmy was still gripping Peggy's hand as he sat by her and she said quietly, 'We only got back when it was all over. We didn't see what happened.'

The breadman explained, 'She pushed me and Jimmy to one side and run out with some carrots. She nearly threw one at my Dulcie then she seen this chap's horse coming and run across the road to it. She'd have been all right if she'd stopped to give the carrot to Dulcie proper. Nothing upsets Dulcie though. She just picked the carrot off of the floor and ate it.'

'Never mind all that,' the policeman said. 'You'd better get off on your round before your bread gets stale. No talking about this, mind, and come to the station after work. My sergeant will want to see you.' He turned to the coalman. 'I'm not satisfied there was no negligence on your part. I'm taking statements from witnesses, but for now you can go.'

The coalman touched his cap to Jimmy. 'Very sorry about your missis. My old Trojan is the quietest hoss you could find, but he was frightened, see. I'm sorry.'

'No, I'm sorry. If there was any negligence, as he calls it, it was mine. I'm sorry you and your horse have had this fright and trouble.'

'I think the witnesses are going,' the nurse said meaningfully as she looked out of the window, and the policeman hastily departed.

Peggy made tea and took a cup to her father while the nurse told Jimmy the doctor would soon return and would advise him on what needed to be done. She left soon after and Jimmy was left with the two people who could help him most.

Chapter Twelve

Anna wrote to Dorrie about the tragedy and her sister replied that, although it was a shocking way to die, she thought it was a merciful release for Olive. 'You couldn't really say she had a life, nor did Jimmy,' she wrote. 'I think he will come to see that it was all for the best.'

Anna smiled when she read the letter, but Isabel agreed with Dorrie. 'I know poor Jimmy's upset now,' she said, 'and blaming himself, but really, Anna, it's a blessing in disguise. Olive could have lived for years, if you could call it living.'

Anna reflected that her sensible friend and Dorrie both held the same opinion. Dorrie was changing, becoming wiser and losing some of her girlish, romantic ideas. I wish I could lose mine where Eugene is concerned, Anna thought ruefully.

The weather had been very bad since Christmas and there were reports of fierce gales at sea. Both Captain Furlong and Captain Jenson were homeward bound and their families worried about them, so Anna and Isabel went to the shipping offices to make enquiries, but they learned nothing.

'No news is good news,' a fatherly clerk told them. 'Both ships are well found and with experienced captains. They've ridden out storms like this before,' he said, and they felt reassured.

The following Sunday, Anna joined Isabel and Willie and three of the little boys to walk to church. Now that James Hargreaves lived in Eastbourne Street he often met the girls at the corner of Westbourne Street as they walked to ten o'clock Mass, and on this morning they all arrived at the same time.

James hung back diffidently, but Willie hailed him. 'Hello, Mr Hargreaves,' he said. 'I won't meet you here much longer. I'll be off to sea in a few weeks. Have you ever been to sea?'

James looked startled. 'Er, no,' he said, and Willie said cheerfully, 'Most fellows in Liverpool have been to sea at sometime or other.'

'Mr Hargreaves doesn't belong to a seafaring family,' Isabel said as they walked along together.

James left them at the church entrance and Isabel whispered to Anna, 'Isn't he thin! Is he ill, do you think?'

Anna shrugged as they entered the church, wondering whether he was merely unhappy. He can't have many happy memories, she thought.

Anna had made a shirt for Willie's outfitting for sea and he thanked her as they parted at the Jensons' house after church. 'It's splendid, really well made,' he said. 'Thank you, Anna. If I had to depend on Isabel's sewing I'd have to be dressed from the slop chest. She can't sew for toffee.'

'She has other gifts you've been glad of,' Anna said. 'A light hand with pastry for one.'

'And a heavy hand with a smack,' he said, as Isabel cuffed him, and they all parted laughing.

Later in the day, Clara, who had been visiting, came into the house saying that she had seen two men at the Jensons' door. 'They looked like Holt Line men to me,' she said. 'I hope there's nothing wrong.'

'They could be Mrs Jenson's brothers,' Mrs Furlong said, unwilling to allow Clara to be first with any news, but Anna was worried. What of those storms? she thought. Restless and uneasy, she slipped away and went to the Jenson house.

The front door was open and before she could knock one of the boys ran down the hall and flung himself at her. 'Anna, Anna, Papa's ship is lost!' he cried, burrowing into her shoulder. Carrying him, she went timidly into the parlour, where Isabel and her mother were locked in each other's arms on the sofa and Willie stood stiff and white-faced behind them.

The two men from the shipping line stood up in evident relief. 'It's true?' Anna croaked, unable to control her voice.

'Nothing certain, miss,' one of the men said. 'But wreckage has been picked up from Captain Jenson's ship. A ship's lifebelt, some planking and other things. There may be survivors but none have been sighted yet.'

The men began to move towards the door and one of them bent over the sofa. 'Goodbye, madam,' he said. 'As soon as we have more news you shall have it. Don't give up hope.'

Anna had gently set the little boy down and she followed them to the hall. 'Is there really any hope?' she whispered and they glanced at each other and shook their heads.

'Survivors may be picked up, but the ship has gone. We think we've lost two,' one man said, and Anna thanked them.

'This must be a hard task for you,' she said.

'Yes, but it must be done, and the sooner the better,' one said. 'That's our experience.'

Anna went back and knelt before Isabel and her mother, putting her arms around them. 'I'm so sorry, so very sorry,' she whispered, tears pouring down her face, and they both drew her close. Willie still stood like a ramrod behind them, and Mrs Jenson looked up at him and stretched out her hand to her son.

'Willie, my poor little lad,' she said, and he came round the sofa and fell on his knees before her.

'I'll look after you, Mama,' he cried, and Anna left the three older Jensons clinging together and weeping and went to the young boys.

They were huddled together, white-faced, and Wilma, as

187

usual, was wailing in her cot. Anna picked her up and led the boys into the kitchen. She put the biscuit barrel on the table and said, 'I think we all need something to eat and a nice drink of cocoa. Pass the biscuits round, Jonathan, while I make the cocoa.'

She gave Wilma a rusk and soon the boys were sitting round the table with biscuits and cocoa, still quiet and subdued, but looking more like themselves. Anna made tea and took it into the parlour, judging that when the first storm of grief was over they would welcome a restoring drink.

'The children? Where are they?' Mrs Jenson said, looking about her wildly.

'They're in the kitchen. I've made them cocoa and given them the biscuit barrel,' Anna said. 'Wilma's got a rusk, so she's quiet too.'

'Thanks, love. What a good friend you are,' said Mrs Jenson. She began to sip the tea, but tears were running down her face and her hand shook so much that Isabel took the cup and gently held it to her mother's lips.

'We're not giving up hope, Mama,' she said. 'Those men had to tell us about the wreckage in case anyone else did, but there are bound to be survivors.'

Mrs Jenson wiped her eyes. 'Yes, Papa always tested the ship's boats and he had a good crew. All the boats would be lowered.'

There was a knock at the door and Anna was not surprised to see Dr and Mrs O'Brien. They went into the parlour and Anna went back to the children. They were still sitting quietly, although the cocoa cups and biscuit barrel were empty. Wilma, in her high chair, was grizzling but ignored.

Anna gave her a drink of milk, then took a book down from a shelf. 'Should I read about the buried treasure?' she asked, and they nodded eagerly.

She had finished the story when Dr O'Brien came into the kitchen. 'Does your mother know about this?' he asked, after giving the boys a large bag of sweets to keep them busy.

'I don't think so,' Anna said. 'Although Aunt Clara saw the shipping men at the Jensons' door. That's why I came.'

He drew Anna into the hall. 'Go home now and tell her, but don't let her come here, Anna. Not on any account. Did you see the men?'

'Yes, they told me the ship had definitely gone, but there might be survivors. I don't think they had much hope.'

'God help them all,' Dr O'Brien said fervently. 'Go now, Anna.'

She looked into the parlour to say she would be back later, then walked home rapidly.

As soon as her mother was told she began to scream hysterically, 'I'll be the next. They'll come to tell me about Father, I know it. I know it. I've thought of nothing else since those storms.' She began to rock backward and forward, moaning, 'How shall I live without him? What shall I do?'

'Don't be ridiculous, Adelaide,' Clara said. 'You've heard nothing. No news is good news, the clerk told Anna.'

'But I will, I will, I know it. I feel it here!' she cried dramatically, placing her hand where she thought her heart was.

Anna looked at her with contempt. 'Dr and Mrs O'Brien are with the family now,' she said.

'I must go to her!' cried Mrs Furlong. 'Only I can understand. Even though my own heart is breaking.'

'Dr O'Brien said Mrs Jenson must have no visitors,' Anna said.

'He doesn't mean me,' said her mother, but Anna said firmly, 'He mentioned you specifically. He said you would want to condole, but Mrs Jenson can see no one. She is

189

completely prostrated. I thought we might have the little boys here.'

'Here!' her mother exclaimed. 'Why here, pray?'

'Because we are their friends,' said Anna. 'I could look after them.'

'It seems to have escaped your notice that you are supposed to look after *me*,' her mother said tartly. 'You know my nerves wouldn't stand those rough boys here, especially now. Don't you dare suggest it.'

She had been temporarily diverted from visiting the Jenson house, but she began to gather her wraps again and rose to her feet.

'I think Dr O'Brien might suggest it if you go there,' Anna said hastily, and her mother sank back onto the sofa.

'Better not,' she murmured. 'At least until I know for sure.'

Anna turned and walked out of the room, feeling unable to stand her mother any longer. She's almost hoping for bad news about Father, she thought, so that she can be the centre of attention. Anna thought of the genuine grief at the Jensons' and of the loving husband and father, the jolly, happy man lost to them, and her tears flowed.

Isabel and her mother might cling for a while to the hope that he was a survivor, but Anna felt sure that he was dead. She remembered the message brought by the Olafsons and wondered if on that sunny blue-and-white day Captain Jenson had felt a premonition of death. Why had he called, 'Tell my boys to look after Mama and Isabel and little Wilma'?

He had always taken care of his family, making short voyages and attending to all the family affairs, seeing the boys as part of his responsibility, not as substitutes for him.

No survivors were found, although driftwood gave evidence that the ship's boats had been launched but destroyed in the mountainous seas. Mrs Jenson's brothers, who were businessmen in and around Manchester, were notified and rallied round their sister.

With such a large family, there had been little opportunity to save. Willie wanted to start work immediately either ashore or afloat, so that he could provide some money for his mother, but his uncles told him his father's wishes should be carried out and he was duly indentured to become a ship's officer.

Two of her sisters-in-law offered to adopt some of the boys, but Mrs Jenson, who had been very calm until now, became hysterical at the idea of the family being split up and the idea was hastily dropped.

One of her brothers, who owned a jam factory, lived in a large house near a village on the outskirts of Manchester. There was a coachman's cottage in the grounds and he offered to have this made into a comfortable home for the family. The three younger boys could attend the village school, and Jonathan and David could travel daily to a school in Manchester as there was a good train service.

Everything was quickly arranged, too quickly for Anna, and it was a sad day for her when the family left for Manchester.

Mrs Jenson wept as she said goodbye to her. 'We'll all miss you so,' she said. 'You've been a good friend, not just to Isabel, but to all of us. I'll never forget how you helped on that dreadful day. My poor little boys are broken-hearted at losing you. As soon as we're settled you must come and stay with us. Promise, Anna.'

The two girls were too upset to speak as they clung together, but finally Isabel said, 'I don't know how I shall bear not having you near. We've been friends for so long.'

Holding back her tears, Anna said, 'I can't talk to anyone as I do to you. Oh God, I'll miss you so much.'

'Anna will come and stay very soon,' Mrs Jenson said.

'And you can write often to each other.'

The girls felt they might be adding to her distress and tried to put a brave face on things, as she was doing.

'That's true, Mama,' Isabel said. 'We'll have a lot to write about, won't we, Anna?' and Anna managed to smile and agree.

When they had gone she felt the full force of the blow that had fallen on her. How was she going to manage without Isabel? Since Dorrie had gone they had become so close that Anna felt she could talk to Isabel almost as freely as she did to her sister, except about her mother.

When she found her home unbearable there was always a warm welcome for her at the Jensons' and she never needed to explain, but would return home fortified against her mother's spite.

Captain Furlong returned safely from his voyage shortly after the Jensons left. There were no hysterics from his wife, although she talked dramatically about the Jenson tragedy and said how much it had upset her because she feared her husband had met the same fate.

'You'd have been informed,' Captain Furlong said briefly, then he added, 'I hope if that does happen you will show the same dignity and care for your family Mrs Jenson showed. O'Brien tells me she was admirable.' He turned to Anna. 'He also said you showed great commonsense and kindness and helped the family when they needed it most, Annabel. I was pleased to hear that.'

'Thank you, Father,' Anna said meekly, aware of her mother fuming beside her.

'I thought you might have brought the young children here while so much had to be done,' he said.

Before anyone else could speak, Mrs Furlong said quickly, 'Mrs Deagan was first in the field as usual. She had the boys whipped away before anyone else could act.' She glared at Anna, daring her to contradict her, but Anna had no intention of speaking and Captain Furlong shook out his newspaper dismissively.

On that tragic day Anna had returned to the Jensons' to find that Wilma and the boys were with the Deagans. They would come home to sleep and be collected early the following morning. She had seen them in the Deagans' kitchen the next day, sitting round the kitchen table with lumps of pastry.

'They're all going to be ships' cooks,' Maggie said, her face rosy and smiling. She had tied Wilma into a chair with a scarf and she was happily banging a tin with a spoon.

'Maggie's in her element,' Mrs Deagan told Anna later, and Anna said she had never seen her so happy.

'Not that she's ever miserable,' she added hastily, 'but she has a sort of sad look sometimes.'

It was then that Mrs Deagan told Anna Maggie's story. 'Her and Andrew Hanlon were together from when they were in the infants',' she said. 'Never anyone else. They were going to get married, but Andrew had to go for a soldier. He was due home and the wedding was arranged, but there was what they called a skirmish. It was a desert, like, and he got lost in a sandstorm. When they found him he'd walked round and round in a circle, driven mad with thirst.'

'And was he alive?' Anna gasped.

'No girl, he was dead when they found him. God only knows what he suffered. That's why Maggie can't bear a dripping tap or water being wasted.'

'And she married Walter?' Anna said.

'Aye, he'd hung after her for years and I think she didn't care what she did. Thought she might as well make him happy, anyhow.' Mrs Deagan looked at Anna. 'She kept her side of it and Walter's never had to regret it. He said to me once, "I knew where her heart was, Ma, but if she liked me enough to marry me that was enough for me. Half a loaf is better than no bread." He's a good lad, Anna.'

Anna went home marvelling at the story, and most of all at Walter. I'll never look at him again as a dull, pompous man, she thought. How interesting people were and how different sometimes to their outward appearance. Some people, anyway, although her mother was as peevish and spiteful as she looked.

Mrs Furlong suspected that her husband had been discussing her with Dr O'Brien, and her dislike of the doctor increased. Captain Furlong ensured that she took a walk with him every day and on Sunday he assumed that all the family would walk to church together.

As they reached Eastbourne Street Anna saw James Hargreaves, but he carefully kept to the opposite pavement. That mother did a good job of destroying his confidence, Anna thought, determined that her own mother would not succeed with her.

After Mass they were joined by some of the Deagan family, and Jim and Kate spoke to Captain Furlong.

'Kate and I are attending an orchestral concert on Wednesday night, sir, and we'd like to ask Anna to come with us, if you will allow it,' Jim said.

'We feel it would cheer her up,' Kate said. 'She must be feeling the loss of her friend Isabel so soon after losing Dorrie's company.'

'Yes, indeed,' her father said. 'That's a kind thought. I'm sure she'll enjoy it.'

'She's always liked good music,' Jim said. 'I remember when she was a child she liked the classical rolls we played on the Pianola better than the music-hall songs.'

Captain Furlong looked thoughtful. Kate had gone to speak to Anna, but he said to Jim, 'I begin to see the drawbacks of a seafaring life. I missed much of their childhood. I hadn't realised Annabel appreciated music.'

'On the other hand, I imagine the joy of being at home is more concentrated when it only comes at intervals,' Jim said with a smile, and Captain Furlong smiled too, but still seemed thoughtful. He looked about for his wife and saw her sitting on a chair in the porch, sipping a glass of water, with several ladies fluttering about her.

'Are you ready, my dear?' he said, extending his arm, and she looked pathetically at the ladies.

'Thank you all so much,' she said in a die-away voice, then rose to her feet and tottered to the door, holding her husband's arm.

'Dr O'Brien is right. You do need more fresh air and exercise, my dear,' Captain Furlong said. 'The weather has not been conducive to it, but it should improve now.'

Later, he studied Anna, then spoke to her about the concert. 'Kate told me they had asked you,' Anna said. 'I *will* enjoy it. I used to go with Norah and Jim before Norah married.'

'You seem to have lost all your companions in a short time,' her father said kindly, and Anna's eyes filled with tears.

She blinked them away. 'I still see Norah at her shop. She does the church flowers and Brother Shaw gives me messages for her.'

She felt guilty about deceiving her father when he was being so kind, but she was afraid he would ask why she went to the shop. She told Jim Deagan later and he laughed and said, ' "The guilty flee when no man pursueth." Your father probably never gave it a thought, Anna. He'd think you went to see Norah if he did. You worry too much.'

Norah had obtained a good price for the bell pull and other items for Mrs Drew, but soon the demand for Anna's work began to fall away. 'They're a fickle crowd, the women who were your customers,' Norah told Anna. 'Too much money and not enough to do and always on the lookout for something new. I believe hand-painted scarves and runners are the rage now. I'll still be able to sell some of your work, Anna, but the demand will gradually die away.'

Anna hid her dismay. 'It was good while it lasted,' she said cheerfully, 'I'm very grateful to you and your mother.'

'No need to be grateful to me. You brought me trade,' Norah said. 'And Ma was pleased with herself for thinking of it.'

She laughed, but Anna said, 'She helped me when I needed it and in such a tactful way. Sometimes, you know, Norah, I feel sorry for myself, but then I think how lucky I am to live next door to your ma and your family.'

'Did you enjoy the concert?' Norah asked, and Anna told her about it enthusiastically. 'Frank doesn't like orchestral concerts,' Norah said. 'That's why we didn't go. He says he's had to sit through too many because of his job to go to one willingly.'

She laughed, but Anna thought privately that Frank could have endured the concert for Norah's sake, or at least suggested that she went with her family as she enjoyed them so much.

She walked home feeling low in spirits, partly because of Norah and partly because her source of income was closed. She still had a few shillings saved and Dorrie had sent her a sheet of stamps so she was able to send letters without her mother's knowledge. I'll have to make that money last and try to think of something else, she thought.

Her mother greeted her as soon as she arrived home with demands to know where she had been. 'I went to see Norah Deagan,' Anna said wearily.

'Without my permission!' her mother snapped. 'While you

are under this roof you'll ask my permission. You were needed here.'

'For what?' Anna asked, but her mother ignored the question.

Instead she sneered, 'Did you go to ask for tips on catching a man? *She* managed it late in the day, but you don't seem able to. All the fuss about that soldier and now – one thin letter a week.' She laughed maliciously. 'You thought you'd ride on Dorrie's coat tails, didn't you, but he couldn't stomach you.'

Anna turned and fled, pursued by her mother's malicious sniggers. In her room she flung herself on the bed and burst into tears. It was the last straw. All week she had worried about a comment Mrs O'Brien had innocently made about letters from Eugene.

The doctor's wife had spoken to Anna about missing Isabel and said that the doctor sometimes went to London for medical conferences. 'Perhaps the next time you and I can accompany him, Anna, for a little holiday,' she said. 'Eugene writes such wonderful descriptions of the scenes in London when his duties take him there, I feel quite frantic to see them, don't you?'

Anna had smiled and agreed, but worried that Mrs O'Brien evidently received much longer and more informative letters from Eugene than she did. The doctor's wife had gone on to say, 'As Eugene says, London is the hub of the Empire, so no wonder there are all these glittering occasions. Of course the King loves pageantry, they say. So different to his mother.' Mrs O'Brien seemed to notice Anna's silence and said with a smile, 'I'm sure your letters are *quite* different,' and changed the subject.

Now her mother's comment about the thin letters had brought this worry to the forefront of her mind and she wept bitterly.

Anna had been there for some time, gradually becoming

calmer, when she became conscious of hysterical screams from her mother, and her aunt's voice raised in anger. She stood up and saw her reflection in the mirror, her eyes swollen and her skin blotched with crying, so she poured water into the basin and began to splash her face, ignoring the sounds from below.

She had finished and was tidying her hair when there was a knock at the door and Nelly said quietly, 'I've brung you a cup of tea, miss.' Anna opened the door and Nelly came in, her eyes like saucers. 'Did you hear that carry-on?' she said. 'Your ma having yisterics and Miss Clara shouting?'

'Are they all right?' Anna asked. 'Had I better go down?'

Nelly shook her head vigorously. 'No, you stay here and drink that tea,' she said. 'This has been brewing for days. It's better out.'

Anna sipped the tea gratefully. 'This is lovely, Nelly,' she said, and the maid sat beside her on the edge of the bed.

'I don't know what the missus said to you, but Miss Clara went in and tackled her about it. That's what started all this,' she said.

'I didn't know Aunt Clara was in when I came home,' Anna said.

'Well, she went in and she was saying sumpn about you didn't need to go out o' the house to learn how to catch a man. You could ask the missus. She was an expert, after the way she trapped her poor brother. The missus started screaming and Miss Clara said she'd fooled the Captain for years with her lies, but now he'd seen through her.'

'Oh God, Nelly, this is serious,' Anna said. 'How can they live together after this?'

'But there's worse, miss,' Nelly said with relish. 'The missus said sumpn about a Mr Somebody and Miss Clara shouted at her that she was a wicked, evil woman who couldn't bear to see anyone happy and God knew what He was doing when He made her lose them other babies. She wasn't fit to live, never mind be a wife or a mother. I peeped in and Miss Clara was standing with her hands on her hips and I think she was crying, and the missus was lying on the sofa, screeching and kicking her legs in the air.'

'I'll have to go down,' Anna said agitatedly. 'Someone will have to see to them.'

'No, Miss Anna, not on no account,' Nelly said firmly, laying a detaining hand on Anna. 'Pretend you don't know nothing and so will I. If they think there's only them know they'll have a better chance to sort it out some way to save their faces.'

'That makes sense, Nelly,' Anna admitted. 'But they've never had a scene like this. I know they hate each other, but it's always been so – so *civilised*!'

'I know what you mean,' Nelly said. She stood up. 'What you wanna do now is stay up here outa the way. I'll bring you sumpn to eat in a minute and tell you where they are.'

The house was quiet now, but Anna sat uneasily, straining her ears to hear any sounds of distress. She knew Nelly's advice was good, but she wondered if her mother and aunt would have physically attacked each other. The barriers of speech seemed to have come down with a vengeance.

Within a very short time Nelly returned with a plate of sandwiches, a piece of fruit cake and another cup of tea. 'All quiet,' she said cheerfully. 'No sign of either of them. They must be in their rooms. And no blood or hair in the parlour.'

'Thanks, Nelly,' Anna said gratefully. 'What about you?'

'Don't worry, I won't starve,' Nelly said, showing her broken teeth in a grin. 'I'll just clatter about in the kitchen so they know where I am if they want me.' She came closer to Anna.

'And don't you worry. Nobody won't hear nothing from me about all this. I'm not like some.'

'I know, Nelly,' Anna sighed. 'I don't know how you put up with us in this house.'

Nelly laughed. 'I often think the same about you,' she said.

'I'd go this minute if I could,' Anna said bitterly, 'but I've no choice.'

'Never mind. "Always darkest before the dawn," my ma used to say,' Nelly replied. She jerked her head towards the door. 'This row might clear the air. Make things better.'

'Thanks, Nelly, I don't know what I'd have done without you,' Anna said, as Nelly moved to the door.

Nelly looked back and winked. 'Just lay low. That's best,' she said, and went out, closing the door quietly behind her.

A little later, Mrs Furlong rang for milk and aspirins in her bedroom, and Nelly reported to Anna that when she took them up Mrs Furlong had ordered her to bring a plate of cold chicken and cold roast beef and some bread and butter, saying she must keep up her strength. She had also had coffee and three pieces of fruit cake.

'She'll live, then,' Anna said dryly, and she and Nelly giggled together.

Clara stayed in her room, but the following morning she was in the kitchen as usual and the row was never mentioned, although Clara and her sister-in-law only spoke to each other when absolutely necessary.

Mrs Furlong seemed subdued and, for the moment, to have tired of her persecution of Anna, who found life much easier. Her aunt allowed her to help more in the house, although she spoke little, and Anna felt she had found a friend in Nelly, who had often seemed hostile to her until the night of the quarrel.

Nelly had not yet discovered the real cause of the argument, but declared that she would, sooner or later.

The weather was pleasant now and every day Mrs Furlong took the walk she had promised her husband she would take, to the little park opposite their house, where she sat on a seat and gossiped with other idle ladies.

Nelly declared that the row had something to do with these sessions. 'She come back one day like the cat that'd got at the cream,' she said. 'An' she kep' looking at Miss Clara. I'll find out, never fear,' she told Anna.

Anna had found another friend in James Hargreaves. She went alone now to ten o'clock Mass every Sunday, but always, as though by chance, James met her at the junction of Eastbourne and Westbourne Streets. They walked together along Shaw Street and down Langsdale Street, and James, who was now a collector, left her at the entrance to the church.

'I was very sorry to hear about Captain Jenson,' he said to her the first morning. 'It was a tragedy for you, as well as for the Jenson family. You were friends with all of them, I know, not just Miss Jenson.'

'Yes, indeed,' Anna said in a muffled voice. He was the first person who had understood that, or at least the first who had spoken to her of it, and when he added, 'It was very hard to lose Miss Jenson's company so soon after that of your sister,' her tears overflowed.

James was aghast. 'I'm sorry, I'm sorry,' he stammered. 'I'm so clumsy. I don't know what to say to people.'

Anna quickly mopped her eyes and swallowed. 'No, I'm sorry,' she said, worried that she had made him feel bad. 'It was just . . . you were so kind.' She managed to smile at him. 'No one else has understood. You said the right thing. You see, I didn't feel I should grieve about that when they had such real sorrow to bear.'

'I know I'm not good with people,' he muttered. 'I say the wrong thing.'

'Not to me, anyway, Mr Hargreaves,' Anna said. 'You were very kind and understanding. I'm sorry it had that watery effect on me.' She felt able to speak with less of her usual reserve because he seemed so vulnerable, and they parted with a smile at the church door.

Because of that early misunderstanding, they found that as time went on they were able to speak freely to each other about things that troubled them. Although neither of them attended the organised groups now, they walked to church services together and, walking home afterwards, often stood talking for a long time before going their separate ways.

Anna felt that in Nelly and James she had found two new friends in unexpected places.

Chapter Thirteen

James Hargreaves valued the meetings with Anna too. He had expected to start a happy life when he moved to the new house, but although he managed to rid himself of the nightmares about his mother and uncle, other baggage from his past was not so easily cast aside.

He still found it very difficult to mix with people and often felt that he had said something to offend them, although this was not always the case. Dr O'Brien had advised him to join some of the many guilds and societies attached to the church, but when it came to walking into the room his courage failed him.

If the men had realised that he needed help, they would have done more to welcome him, but to them he merely seemed taciturn and unwilling to join in the activities.

He was the only single man in the office, apart from a lively young commodore of a local sailing club, who often regaled them with stories of his exploits at the weekend and his conquests among the lady members. One of the older men turned to James one day and said kindly, 'I'm sure you have just as good a social life, Mr Hargreaves, although quieter.'

James smiled and agreed and it was assumed that he had a busy social life centred round his church. He was popular in the office, a reliable worker, and a ready listener to fishing stories or tales of the marvels of children.

He should have been completely happy, but for no reason a black cloud of misery seemed to settle on his mind and nothing he could do would move it. Frances cooked delicious meals which he enjoyed, and he should have gained weight, but he remained thin because this canker seemed to be eating away inside him.

Dr O'Brien told him that he was physically fit, but he also told him that he would need patience to rid himself of 'the black dog'. 'You've recovered physically from the years with your mother, but mentally takes longer,' he said bluntly. 'Enjoy your good days and wait for the bad days to get fewer.'

The bright house and the fact that Frances was completely happy made James feel better. Frances had control of a generous housekeeping allowance and she enjoyed going into the shops near her home, and being greeted by the butcher or the fishmonger saying deferentially, 'Good morning, Miss O'Neill,' then showing her luxury cuts of meat or fish.

If her sister-in-law or one of her cronies was in the shop, Frances enjoyed herself even more. One day her brother's wife came in when the butcher was showing her some Scotch beef. 'Beautiful. The very best,' he was saying. 'A bit dearer, of course, but I know you don't mind that, Miss O'Neill.'

'No, indeed,' Frances said grandly. 'But I think you need a large joint to get the full flavour for a roast. What does that weigh?'

'This!' the butcher said in amazement. He placed it on the scales. 'Twelve pounds, three ounces, Miss O'Neill.'

Frances was conscious of the silent shoppers and her brother's wife breathing heavily near her shoulder. 'I'll take it,' she said recklessly.

A hum of conversation broke out, but Frances spoke to no one. A tray of lamb cutlets was reverently held before her and she chose what she needed, then paid the butcher's wife in gold. She was ushered to the door by the butcher, who was assuring her that her meat would be delivered whenever it suited her, and she left, greeting a few friends, but ignoring her sister-in-law.

Her joy and triumph lasted until after the meat was delivered and she saw the size of the joint on the kitchen table. 'I've been a fool,' she told James later. 'I've bought a joint of meat weighing twelve pounds! We'll never finish it in a month of Sundays. All to show off in front of my brother's wife.'

'The meat's not off, is it?' asked James.

'Oh, no, it's beautiful,' Frances assured him.

'Then why are you worrying?' he replied.

'The waste, we'll never eat it. I should never have bought it. If we have the roast, then cold meat on Sunday night, then again on Monday we won't be half through it.'

James was about to make a joke about feeding the neighbourhood cats, but he saw that Frances was really upset. He drew her down beside him.

'Look, Frances,' he said gently, 'the housekeeping money is yours to do what you like with. I've got a warm clean and comfortable home, and the very best food. I'm very happy with the way you spend the money. If you need more, you know it's there, but I don't like to see you upsetting yourself over a bit of meat. If you're worried about waste there must be someone who can help us out with it.'

'There is,' Frances said. 'My Aunt Polly was the only one who was ever kind to me when I was a kid. She's bedridden now, living with her daughter, May, and May's already got an invalid husband and a tribe of kids. They're very near starving and this'd be a lifeline for them, but I'm not robbing you to feed my relations.'

'For God's sake,' James said, 'there's the solution. If you're worried about waste, pass the meat and anything else on, if they don't mind, but don't let's talk any more about it or the flaming beef will choke me.'

The meat was as delicious as the butcher had promised and James and Frances enjoyed it roasted with Yorkshire puddings, roast and boiled potatoes, several varieties of vegetables, and rich gravy.

After Sunday night's high tea of cold roast beef and pickles, James told Frances that he had enjoyed the meat, but would prefer not to see it again the next day. 'Why don't you take it to your cousin now?' he said.

Frances had great pleasure in taking the food to her relations, where it was so badly needed and gratefully received. James had made it clear that any money left from the housekeeping allowance belonged to her to use as she wished, so she was able to help her aunt and cousin in many ways.

'I've never been so happy in my life,' she told James, and he said it did him good to see her, but he still found it impossible to escape the bouts of depression.

Anna was still very unhappy too. She still corresponded with her friends in Dublin, but she felt that her life was so dull in comparison with theirs that her letters must be dull too.

Dorrie still sent letters to Anna, her mother and her aunt by the same post every week, but she also wrote extra letters to Anna, which Nelly ensured were hidden from their mother.

In these letters, Dorrie spoke more freely about her life in the Army quarters. 'The officers' wives are very patronising,' she wrote, 'but Mrs Rafferty says they mean well. They organise knitting and crocheting classes, and social evenings for us, to keep us out of mischief! One, Mrs Adair, is mad about anything Irish and she says she wants the social evenings to be like meetings at the crossroads in Ireland! We have singers and violin players and even Irish dances. The husbands are invited to the evenings too, which is causing me a problem.

'Several men show an interest in me. I don't encourage

them, honestly, but their wives are really nasty to me. As if I would want any of them when I have my darling Michael. Many of them would love to be in my shoes, but Michael is not interested.

'We had a ladies' excuse me dance, a waltz during which any lady!! can ask a man to dance. I had about one minute with my husband, then he must have had a dozen partners. I was furious and so was Michael. Hc said he'll never be there for another.

'A lot of the women don't like me because of the way I speak. They think I'm stuck up because I don't speak like the other Liverpool wives, but Mrs Rafferty says I'm getting more like them. I don't know what I'd do without her, Anna.'

The letter worried Anna, but at least, she thought, Dorrie had one good friend and Michael seemed as devoted as ever, but Dorrie had never faced hostility before.

When her mother went to the park she slipped in to see Mrs Deagan, and after some general talk about the parish Anna told her about Dorrie's letter.

'Sounds as if she's got a sensible friend in that Mrs Rafferty,' said Mrs Deagan. 'And one that can stand up for her if there's any trouble.'

'I thought that,' Anna said eagerly. 'But I hate the thought of anyone being nasty to Dorrie. She doesn't deserve it. She can't help being pretty or the way she speaks.'

Mrs Deagan laughed. 'You're feeling the drawbacks to that yourself, girlie, aren't you?' she said. 'You'd be better able to mix with the girls in the sodality if they didn't think you were standoffish because of your posh voice.'

Anna looked bewildered and Mrs Deagan said, 'Your ma has a lot to answer for. She wanted you to be ladies, so she wouldn't let you play with other children. When Clara came here she'd say to me, "Those poor children are afraid to eat or speak, the way their mother nags them about table manners and their speech." '

'I remember being scolded,' Anna said. 'But I thought it happened in all families.'

'No. You were kept apart. Your ma persuaded your father to send you to the select school. Told him she was afraid you'd pick up diseases in the elementary school.' She laughed. 'The first thing you done at the select school was come home with measles, the both of you.'

Anna smiled. 'I feel quite self-conscious about my voice now,' she said.

'It isn't just that. The girls in the sodalities and confraternities, they know each other from school or from playing out in the street, but your ma would never allow that. Are things no better at home? Still not speaking?'

'No, you could cut it with a knife, Nelly says.' Anna sighed. 'It's better for me, though, now Nelly and I are friends.'

Anna became increasingly glad of her new ally in the Furlong house. Nothing more had been said by Mrs O'Brien about a trip to London, and Dorrie could tell her nothing about Eugene. His slim letters continued to arrive and every week Anna tried to nerve herself to write ending the correspondence, or simply not reply and see what happened, but while there was any hope at all she clung to it. She had only to look at Eugene's photograph or to think of his beloved face to feel weak with love for him.

I'm a fool, she thought, and I've no pride, but I can't help it. I know the wisest thing is to forget him, and admit that he's not worth loving, but nothing can cure me of loving him.

Because of the way she felt, she understood that James's love for Dorrie was as constant and as hopeless, and she told him little titbits of news about her to cheer him.

Anna was particularly lonely at this time because the

General Election of 1906 meant she saw little of the Deagans and there were no invitations to concerts.

Jim and Luke were campaigning for the Liberal cause, because they thought the best hope of relief for the poor lay with them, and Kate told Anna that she supported the fledgling Labour Party for the same reason, but it would be some time before they were strong enough to make themselves effective.

'Trouble is, they're mostly poor themselves. John Wood, from Stoke-on-Trent, has a brilliant mind and could do so much in Parliament to cure poverty, but he only earns two pounds, ten shillings a week and has a wife and four children and a mother to support. How can he afford to be an MP? Sooner or later MPs will have to be paid so that men like that will be able to stand.'

Anna longed to be able to campaign with them, but hampered as she was by her mother's moods and demands she could never be sure of being free for anything.

She talked to James about the election and he was surprised to hear that she was interested in politics. 'I'm not really,' she said, 'but I *am* interested in the awful poverty in Liverpool. I used to go with Kate to help with the free dinners and I couldn't believe that there could be so many starving children in a rich country like this.'

'I know, it's a disgrace,' he said, 'but it's such an enormous problem.'

'Jim Deagan says all these soup kitchens and refuges help, but they only scratch at the surface. The only way is to attack the root cause of poverty through laws.'

'I'm sure he's right,' James said.

When the election results were published he met Anna with a folded newspaper in his hand. 'Did you see the figures?' he asked, and read out, 'Liberals three hundred and ninety-nine seats, Irish Nationalists eighty-two, Labour twenty-nine and Tory one hundred and fifty-six.'

'Labour twenty-nine!' Anna exclaimed. 'Kate will be delighted.'

James slipped the newspaper in his pocket and offered Anna his arm. 'Yes, they were led by Keir Hardie and Ramsay MacDonald, and the man you mentioned, John Wood, was mentioned as MP for Stoke-on-Trent.'

Anna's face was flushed with excitement and he said diffidently, 'Would you care to walk down to the Pier Head after Benediction? Should be interesting down there among the speakers.'

'Yes, I would,' said Anna. 'It seems a bit tame to just go home, doesn't it?' She knew she would be made to suffer for staying out longer, but she also realised that it had been an effort for James to make the suggestion and she was unwilling to hurt him by a refusal.

After this first outing, whenever Anna could get away to attend the evening Benediction, she and James would go for a walk before returning home, and found that they thought alike on many matters.

Theirs was a very comfortable relationship. Both knew that their hearts lay elsewhere, and Anna felt that he was a good friend, who through his own experiences could understand her problems with her mother.

She was still very troubled about Eugene. The weekly letters arrived, containing mostly details of events in the regiment, but in the middle of one letter he had written, 'Sometimes I wonder if life is worth living. So many worries and decisions.'

The letter had continued normally, but Anna sat for a long time with it in her hand. It was as though he suddenly spoke from his heart, she thought, but without realising that he had done so, and it changed her feelings towards him.

Latterly, she had been growing more and more angry with

him, although she was still as deeply in love with him. Why was there no mention of leave? If she could only see him, something was bound to change, she felt. But now she was filled with love and compassion for him.

That had been a cry from the heart. If only she could help him or comfort him, but was he even aware that he had written it? She read it again. 'Sometimes I wonder if life is worth living. So many worries and decisions.' Was it his private life he was talking about or Army matters?

Whatever it was, he was deeply troubled and she longed to hold him and comfort him. A dozen times she tried to write to him, but she knew so little that it was very difficult. She burned her efforts and went downstairs where her mother sneered, 'Where have you been? Can't have taken more than a few minutes to read the letter from your swain.'

Anna knew some reply had to be made, or else her mother would find more and more wounding things to say and she felt too sick at heart to bear them, so she said she had been tidying her room. She wondered if Dorrie would be able to advise her if she told her of the letter, but then was it fair to Eugene to do that?

That problem was solved when by the second post letters arrived from Dorrie giving the welcome news that Michael was due for ten days' leave and they would do as they had done the last time. Spend both weekends in Liverpool and a few days midweek with Michael's family in Ireland. They would be arriving in a week's time.

Anna spent a sleepless night wondering why Eugene could not get leave as easily, but the following morning a letter arrived from him.

'I have a weekend pass and will arrive tomorrow, Saturday,' he wrote. 'Sorry about the short notice, but this came up suddenly.'

Anna tried to be calm, but she wondered whether Eugene wanted to say something to her face-to-face.

Could he be going to solve the mystery of his strange courtship and the despairing message in his last letter? Although she tried to crush the feeling, she was unable to stop a tiny seed of hope forming. Had some obstacle been removed and he was coming to speak of love? At least if I see him I will be able to judge better how he feels, she thought.

Her mother had not seen the letter and Anna told her nothing, but at the first opportunity she slipped away to see Mrs O'Brien. They had also received a letter and Mrs O'Brien said immediately, 'A pity it's such a brief visit and such short notice, but it shows how important the work he's been doing is. Let's hope it's rewarded with a good promotion, Anna.'

'Let's hope so,' Anna said, too proud to admit what she was really thinking.

'Perhaps that's what he's coming to tell us. It would make such a difference to both your lives, make so much possible,' said Mrs O'Brien. She smiled meaningfully and Anna felt confused. Even down-to-earth Mrs O'Brien was expecting something wonderful from this weekend, it seemed.

She smiled and was relieved when they were joined by Dr O'Brien. 'Good news, eh, Anna?' he said cheerfully.

Anna smiled and nodded. 'I haven't said anything to Mama,' she said.

'Very wise, until we have something to tell her, eh?' Dr O'Brien said. 'Tell you what. I'll send you a note when Eugene arrives and you come down here. Save a lot of argy-bargy, and you won't have much time together, you and Eugene, otherwise.'

'Thanks, doctor. I'd better get back now. There's the usual big clean planned, ready for Dorrie and Michael next week, so I'll be missed.'

She hastened home, glad to be fully occupied in changing curtains and turning out cupboards for the rest of the day.

Even though she was exhausted, she was unable to sleep, with hopes and plans and surmises rushing through her brain. Should she have confided in the O'Briens about the despairing words in Eugene's letter? No, better not, she thought. She would be seeing Eugene himself in a few hours and perhaps be able to help him. At the thought, she trembled with a mixture of delight and fear.

Anna decided that she would go as soon as she received word of Eugene's arrival, whether her mother objected or not, but in the event Mrs Furlong retired to bed with a sick headache before the note arrived. When it did, Anna was able to dress suitably and hasten to Shaw Street immediately.

She thought both the O'Briens seemed ill at ease, and after a brief greeting Mrs O'Brien showed her into the small back parlour where Eugene was waiting. She felt as though her heart would rise and choke her at the sight of his beloved face, and he took her hand, bent over it, and kissed it.

He stood holding her hand and looking into her eyes, then he turned away with a sound that was almost a sob and stood looking out of the window.

'What is it, Eugene? What's wrong?' Anna asked in alarm. Forgetting her pride and her reserve, she went to him and as he turned to her she put her arms around him.

For a moment he held her, then he gently withdrew and led her to a sofa. He drew her down beside him, still holding her hand.

'I've tried, Anna, I've tried so hard,' he said. 'If I could have loved anyone properly it would have been you. But I can't.'

Anna sat up straight and withdrew her hand. She was unable to speak, but she was deeply hurt and it showed.

Eugene said quickly, 'You don't understand.'

'No, I don't understand,' she said. 'I don't understand anything.'

He groaned. 'And I can't explain,' he said. 'Not to a girl like you. My mind is in turmoil, Anna.' He put his hands over his face and Anna sat as though turned to stone as he began to mutter, 'I tried. I tried. God knows I tried, but everything was against me. And then it all turned so sordid. Money, always money or the lack of it.'

He was silent for a while and Anna said timidly, 'Is that the trouble? Are you in debt?'

He turned away from her and laughed bitterly. 'If only,' he said. But he bent his head and murmured, 'If I'd had money I might have been a good man. Taken the hard road but no – I would have failed, I know, and pulled you down with me.'

Anna was bewildered. None of this made sense, but she said bravely, 'How? How do I come into it?'

He stood up and went again to the window, and with his back to her he said bitterly, 'My uncle. I thought his mind would be broadened, but beneath it all he's just a mean, grasping, small Irish farmer. The money he hoards is more than his life's blood to him.'

He swung round. 'I'm leaving, Anna. I don't think we'll ever meet again, but thank you for the happy days when I thought I could . . .' He swallowed, then took her unresisting hand and kissed it. 'Goodbye. I wish you every good fortune.'

He went out of the room, but Anna sat there, literally unable to move or speak. There were sounds outside, but she was too stunned to hear or to interpret them.

Anna was not aware that Mrs O'Brien had come into the room until the older woman sat down and put her arm around her.

'My dear, I'm so very sorry,' she said gently. 'We have all

been cruelly deceived, but you most of all. I blame myself for the part I've played in this.'

She had brought a cup of tea into the room and she urged Anna to try to drink it. 'You've had a bad shock, I know,' she said. 'I don't know how much he told you.'

Anna roused herself. 'Very little,' she said. 'He was – incoherent. I just don't understand any of it.'

She tried to drink the tea, but her hand shook too much and Dr O'Brien, who had joined them, told her to leave it. He poured some brandy into a glass. 'This will do you more good,' he said, and Anna found that it did.

The fiery liquid seemed to clear her head, and she said slowly, 'Do you know why Eugene came today?'

Dr O'Brien snorted. 'Yes, I know why he came. To sniff out his prospects. To make sure where he stood before he made up his mind about something.'

'Now, Paddy,' his wife protested. 'You don't know that.'

Anna said thoughtfully, 'I think he's a very troubled man.'

The O'Briens looked at each other and asked why she thought that, and she told them something of his behaviour before he left, omitting his ranting against his uncle.

She also told them of his outburst in her letter, which she was sure was a cry for help.

'Maybe he was more sinned against than sinning,' Mrs O'Brien said. 'It sounds as though he was very troubled in his mind, like Anna says.'

Dr O'Brien had been pacing up and down and he said suddenly, 'I'm going out. Any calls, send Hogan. I don't know how long I'll be.'

They heard him shouting for his hat and the next moment the front door slammed.

'He's very angry,' Mrs O'Brien said. 'He thinks we've all been deceived.' She put her hand over Anna's. 'The only thing

215

that consoles me is the thought that you were not in love with him. I know you were fond of him, but you won't have the pain of a broken heart to bear, although no thanks to him, the way he courted you. Your own dignity and coolness has kept you from worse harm, Anna.'

Anna sat stiff and silent, feeling that if she moved she would fall apart, attack Mrs O'Brien or scream at the top of her voice. Anything to relieve the searing pain at the thought that she would never see Eugene again.

Mrs O'Brien looked at Anna, at her rigidity and her white face, and realised from long experience and nursing training that she must act swiftly. Anna was quite unfit to face her family, especially her mother, so she rose and said gently, 'Come with me, Anna. You've had a shock and you need to be alone. My guest room is ready and I'll send a note to your mother.'

Anna allowed herself to be led from the room, still moving with the same rigidity, and up to the guest bedroom, where Mrs O'Brien handed her one of her own nightdresses.

Mrs O'Brien had ordered a hot water bottle in the bed and it was only when Anna was tucked up that she finally spoke to say, 'Mama?'

'Don't worry,' Mrs O'Brien said. 'I've sent a note to your Mama. Told her that you had a dizzy spell and the doctor has ordered you to bed and given you a draught. You'll stay here overnight, but can't have visitors. I said I'd keep her informed.'

'Thank you,' Anna said weakly, closing her eyes.

'There's a little handbell beside your bed to ring if you need anything, otherwise you'll be left alone. God bless,' said Mrs O'Brien, leaving and closing the door softly behind her.

Anna lay for a while, puzzling about Eugene's remarks and his behaviour over the years, until to her own surprise she fell asleep.

She woke at about eight o'clock, feeling again the searing pain of loss and rejection, but shortly afterwards Mrs O'Brien came up with a tray of chicken soup and sandwiches. She was closely followed by the doctor, who handed Anna a small glass containing black liquid.

'It's horrible, but it'll mean a good night's sleep,' he said briefly.

Anna drank it and slept heavily until the next morning, when she insisted on rising in time for Mass.

'You've been very kind,' she told the O'Briens, 'but I'm not ill. I must get on. Dorrie and Michael arrive on Friday.'

'You're a brave girl,' Dr O'Brien said. 'And you'll do a lot better than that blackguard.'

'Yes, well, if you want to go to ten o'clock Mass, Anna, we must look sharp,' Mrs O'Brien said quickly.

James Hargreaves was at the Mass and came beside Anna as they left. 'I missed you at the corner,' he said quietly.

'I stayed at the O'Briens' last night,' Anna said. She managed a smile. 'I'll tell you about it later.'

He asked no more but hastened away, and Anna walked back with the O'Briens. She refused an offer of tea at their house and they accompanied her.

'I thought you were at death's door,' her mother greeted her, but Dr O'Brien said immediately, 'You'll all be at death's door if you don't show some sense about this cleaning. Do you think that's what Dorrie and Michael want? Anna with a dizzy spell and you, madam, in bed with a sick headache, I understand.'

He bent over Mrs Furlong and took her wrist. 'Where's Miss Furlong?' he asked.

'Out visiting, as usual,' Mrs Furlong said with a martyred air. 'Everything is left to me.'

'Nelly,' the doctor called, and when she came, wiping her

hands on a cloth and smiling at Anna, he said solemnly, 'Nelly, Mrs Furlong has been doing too much. She must rest in bed to be strong for when her family come. No more housework. Health is more important.'

'Yes, doctor,' Nelly said meekly, suppressing a grin.

He turned to Mrs Furlong. 'Remember, rest in bed. No exertion. Anna has recovered and she and Nelly will do what is necessary.'

'I'll help you to bed now,' Mrs O'Brien said solicitously, and with a pleased smile Mrs Furlong allowed herself to be assisted from the room.

The doctor turned to Anna and gave her a broad wink. 'That should keep her out of your way for a while,' he said, and in spite of her misery Anna laughed.

'You should have been an actor,' she said. 'You were so convincing.'

Shortly afterwards the O'Briens left and Anna thanked them again and said quietly to Mrs O'Brien, 'I'm still in a fog. If you can explain anything you will, won't you?'

Mrs O'Brien promised but said, 'We're still in the dark about so much ourselves, and there wasn't time to ask. Why, he was in civilian clothes, as if he's left the Army.'

'Perhaps Michael will be able to help,' Anna said hopefully as they parted.

Mrs Furlong kept to her bed, telling Clara smugly that it was doctor's orders, so had little opportunity for sniping at Anna and was still unaware that Eugene had been in Liverpool.

Anna was relieved to keep herself too busy to have time to dwell on her trouble, and thrust any thoughts of Eugene away with the determination that she would have some answers from Dorrie and Michael.

On Wednesday she was walking down into town with a list of shopping. As she turned into Shaw Street the door of the surgery opened and Dr O'Brien and Mr D'Arcy emerged and stepped into a cab.

Anna stood rooted to the spot as the cab drove away, wondering if her eyes deceived her, but she knew that it was Mr D'Arcy. What was he doing in Liverpool and driving away with Dr O'Brien? She stood hesitating, wondering whether she could call on Mrs O'Brien, but her courage failed her and she went on into town.

She shopped automatically and took her purchases home, but she left again immediately and hurried to Shaw Street. She was sure that something must have happened to Eugene, and she felt she must know.

Mrs O'Brien drew her into the small back parlour, telling Mary that she must not be disturbed.

'My dear, I don't know how to tell you this,' Mrs O'Brien began, placing her hand over Anna's.

'Eugene? He's hurt?' Anna faltered.

'No, no. He's perfectly well – physically. Well, I don't know. Doctor says he suspected, but then when he fell in love with you he thought he must be wrong. I know about these things as a nurse, Anna. I'll have to try to explain to you. Have you heard of a man named Oscar Wilde?'

'Yes. The poet who went to gaol,' Anna said, puzzled.

'But you don't know why he went to gaol?'

'No, but what has this to do with Eugene? Is he in gaol?' Anna asked.

Mrs O'Brien sighed. 'No, but some men, you see, they're born different. They can hide it for years, because it's against the law, but they are drawn to people of their own sex instead of girls.'

'But Eugene. He couldn't be,' Anna said, thinking of the loving glances, the words of love which she had treasured.

'I think he's tried to fight it for years, Anna,' Mrs O'Brien said gently. 'I think he is one who has two sides to his nature. Some of these men even marry and have children, but sooner or later the dark side takes over.'

Anna was silent, thinking of Eugene's anguished words at their last meeting. Was this what he meant when he spoke of failing and pulling her down with him?

Mrs O'Brien said nothing, to give Anna time to understand her words.

After a while Anna asked, 'But why have Dr O'Brien and Mr D'Arcy gone away together? Is it about Eugene?'

'Yes, they've gone to London. You remember I spoke of Oscar Wilde?' Mrs O'Brien said. Anna nodded. 'He went to gaol because he was thought to have corrupted a young man, Lord Alfred Douglas, whose father was determined Oscar Wilde would be punished.'

'Eugene hasn't done that?' Anna cried in alarm.

'No, no. Just the reverse. It's an older man who has been pestering Eugene.'

'And Dr O'Brien and Mr D'Arcy have gone to stop him?' Anna said eagerly.

'I don't know,' Mrs O'Brien said. 'Mr D'Arcy came to ask for his help, so Paddy went with him. They're family, after all. Before he went he said, "I don't know what we'll find there, what the situation is, but one thing for sure, Maureen, I'll find out the truth. No more lies and deceits." And he will, Anna. He should be home tomorrow and everything will be explained.'

'And we can do nothing,' Anna said sadly.

'Only wait and pray. Try not to guess at what might be happening, Anna. We'll soon know,' said Mrs O'Brien, and Anna could only agree.

Chapter Fourteen

Anna and her aunt spent most of Thursday baking in preparation for Dorrie and Michael's visit, but they were constantly interrupted by demands and complaints from the pseudo-invalid upstairs.

'Even your young legs must be aching with all this running up and downstairs,' Clara said finally, and at the next fretful cry of 'Anna' she stumped upstairs.

'What do you want now?' she demanded.

'I want Anna,' Mrs Furlong said sulkily.

'She's in the middle of some very tricky baking. You want us to be ready for Dorrie, don't you?' Clara said bluntly. When her sister-in-law nodded she said, 'Then stop calling Anna every five minutes. We've got work to do. And another thing, the doctor said to rest so you'd be ready for Dorrie, not be lying in bed when she comes home.'

'I exhausted myself. The doctor said so,' Mrs Furlong wailed.

Clara said roughly, 'And you want Dorrie to think that and feel guilty?'

'No, no, I wouldn't upset my darling girl for the world. She loves me so,' she said, dabbing her eyes, 'but I still feel weak.'

Clara made an impatient gesture, but she said, 'Stay here until tomorrow morning, then. Anna can bring up a tray shortly, but you must stop bothering us,' and Mrs Furlong meekly agreed.

Later, Anna took up a tray containing a pot of tea, a large jug of herb tea and a wine glass, and a generous helping of ham, bread and butter, and fruit cake. She was in a fever of impatience for a call from Mrs O'Brien and thought this should stop her mother asking for her.

It was seven o'clock before a small boy delivered a note. Anna told her aunt she was going to see Mrs O'Brien, and left immediately. She worried that she might have to see Mr D'Arcy, but it seemed he had already left.

Anna and Mrs O'Brien sat together on a sofa at one side of the fire, and Dr O'Brien sat facing them.

'I don't like to talk about such things to a girl with your upbringing, Anna,' he began, 'but Maureen tells me she's prepared you. I'll tell you straight out. When we got there he was gone. Gone with this wealthy old blackguard. An MP and pillar of society, so at least they'll try to hush it up.'

'God forgive him. Poor Eugene,' Mrs O'Brien murmured, taking Anna's hand.

'Poor Eugene!' Dr O'Brien exploded, jumping to his feet. 'He's a grown man. He knew what he was doing.'

'But the temptation, Paddy. Being pulled two ways. You have to pity him.'

'I *don't*!' shouted Dr O'Brien. 'I don't have to pity him or forgive him either for the deceit. Pretending to be in love with this poor girl to pull the wool over our eyes. I had my doubts about him, but when I thought he was in love, planning marriage . . .' He picked up the poker and rattled it furiously against the bars of the grate.

'It was all a plot, a scheme to get at my money,' he went on. 'D'Arcy let out more than he realised on the way to London, and I got more out of him. It seems they were afraid we were getting too fond of Michael and they thought Bridie was as bad as themselves, trying to get at my money. Bridie! The last thought in her head!'

'But sure they couldn't expect to get it until you were dead. They were never wishing you dead, Paddy?' said Mrs O'Brien.

Anna sat as if turned to stone, the words like hammer blows in her head.

'He had the impudence to say Eugene was my elder nephew and my natural heir. It seems they were at him all the time to come here and butter us up. I told him: I've no natural heir. I decide where my money goes, no one else.'

'But, Paddy, what happened in London?' Mrs O'Brien asked.

Dr O'Brien glanced at Anna, then looked down at his boots. 'We saw the officer who had written to D'Arcy. He was very good,' he muttered. 'Eugene has been out of the regiment for ten days, so he really had no responsibility for him, but he thought his father might be able to influence him. He said he appreciated that Eugene got his discharge, so if he goes ahead and he's charged it'll be as a private citizen. He won't bring disgrace on the Army.'

He seemed to realise suddenly that his wife and Anna were staring at him in horror and he said quickly, 'It won't come to that, I'm sure. We went to the lodgings he'd taken, but he had been gone a couple of days. They're probably well on their way to the Continent by now.'

'But if they're stopped, Paddy?' Mrs O'Brien said fearfully. 'You're sure he's with this older man?'

'Quite sure,' Dr O'Brien said, but he added cynically, 'Don't worry, he's not only rolling in money, but extremely well connected. It'd be a very foolhardy man who dared to make any of this public. No, it'll all be swept under the carpet and for the sake of the family I'm relieved it will be.'

'Will they be safe on the Continent?' Mrs O'Brien asked.

'Yes,' he said briefly. 'Foreigners have a different view of such things.'

'I know it's all disgusting, Paddy, but I only care about Eugene,' Mrs O'Brien wept. 'Poor boy. Being pulled every way. His disgraceful family, that horrible man, and his own better nature. His mind must have been in turmoil.'

Dr O'Brien stood up and went to a cupboard, where he poured three glasses of brandy. 'He'll get no sympathy from me,' he said. 'Liars and cheats I can't abide. Why do you think he came here last Saturday?'

Anna sipped at her brandy, hoping to fortify herself for what she was about to hear. She knew by the doctor's grim expression it was not good.

'He had to decide. He wanted to know his chances here before they burned their boats, so he came sniffing round to see what he could get out of me.'

'Oh, Paddy,' Mrs O'Brien said faintly.

'It's true. He said that if – *if* mind you – he left the Army he had an opportunity to set up in business and he asked me to advance him the necessary money. "It can't fail," he said, but he could tell me very little about it.'

'But he'd already left the Army,' Mrs O'Brien said.

'Exactly. He named the sum he needed. I won't tell you what it was, but it knocked me sideways, I can tell you, as much because it showed he'd worked out what I was worth. That was it. I told him he should stay in the Army where he seemed to be doing well. If his promotion was coming too slowly for marriage, I was willing to settle a sum on Anna on their wedding day, but of course it was nothing like the sum he asked for.'

Mrs O'Brien took Anna's hand and squeezed it, looking reproachfully at her husband, and he said hurriedly, 'Of course, when we got to London he was in a worse mess than I thought. Been gambling, living like an officer on a private's pay, and up to his eyes in debt.'

'He must have got in with the wrong people,' Mrs O'Brien said. 'Been led astray by others as well as that wicked old man. I think he came here hoping that if you lent him the money he could make a fresh start. Marry Anna and settle down to live a decent life away from the temptations in London.'

Anna looked at her gratefully. It was what she wanted to believe, but Dr O'Brien snorted. 'Didn't take him long to make his choice when he knew there was nothing doing with me. The old man, of course, has seen to everything. Eugene's debts are paid, bills settled, whatever was necessary with the Army. He can sit back and be taken care of for the rest of his life,' he said bitterly. 'For being what he is. I don't want to hear his name mentioned again, Maureen.'

He pressed Anna's hand, shaking his head and murmuring, 'Forgive us, my poor child.'

Anna could see that his eyes were full of tears and he turned abruptly and left the room.

Left alone, she and Mrs O'Brien clung together and wept, Mrs O'Brien saying, 'It's broken his heart. You mustn't mind him, Anna. Everything is black and white to Paddy. Poor Eugene.'

Anna was the first to sit up and wipe her eyes. 'Do you truly believe what you said about Saturday? That Eugene came here hoping to make a fresh start?'

'I do,' Mrs O'Brien said eagerly. 'Don't you, Anna?'

'Yes. Some of the things he said make sense to me now. He said he tried so hard. If he could have loved anyone properly it would have been me. I was hurt, but I understand now. He said he was being pulled every way.'

'Yes, and those who should have helped him could only think of money. His father, for one. He should have guided him when he was a young boy and perhaps Eugene would have grown up a normal young man. And then this man in London, taking advantage of his trouble. I still say he is more sinned against than sinning. Do you feel bitter towards him, Anna?'

Anna shook her head. 'No, but I feel so confused. All this going on and I've been so unaware of it.'

'There was no reason for you to know of this seamy side of life, Anna, and you were better kept in innocence. Now you've seen it very close to, and you know the heartache that goes with it, you'll understand people more and be more tolerant,' Mrs O'Brien said gently.

'I thought I *was* tolerant,' Anna said in surprise.

Mrs O'Brien smiled. 'I didn't say you weren't. I was only trying to console you by saying no experience is wasted.'

Anna said thoughtfully, 'Of course, I've had hardly any occasion to be tolerant, except about girls who had babies, but I would never condemn them or listen to gossip.'

'I was thinking more of your mother,' Mrs O'Brien said.

Anna looked surprised at first, then shamefaced. 'I know what you mean,' she said, 'but it's my unruly tongue. Things pop out before I can stop them.'

'I know it's hard, but try to understand, Anna. She needs her fantasies. Her life has made her what she is, like all of us.' She sighed, but just then the door opened and Mary looked in.

'The doctor says you have got to have something to eat,' she announced.

'Where is he?' Mrs O'Brien said. She excused herself and left the room and Anna felt free to think over the astounding things she had heard. She could understand Dr O'Brien's anger, but she could only feel love and pity for Eugene, and regret that she had not done more to help him turn to what she saw as the better side of his nature.

Yet how could I? she thought. I didn't even know such things happened. She tried to remember the Oscar Wilde case, but she had known few details at the time. Newspapers were only delivered to the house when Captain Furlong was at home, and although she knew the Deagan family discussed the case Jim had only said to her that it was like caging a bird to gaol Oscar Wilde.

'But why was he sent to prison?' Anna had asked.

Jim had replied, 'To satisfy the venom of a father who couldn't accept his son for what he was, and had to find a scapegoat.'

'But they know the risks when they choose to live like that,' Gerald had said, and Anna remembered Jim saying, 'It's easy for us to talk. Some choose to live like that, others can't help themselves. Nature has played a cruel trick on them.'

Perhaps I'll talk to Jim about this, Anna thought, and with a lift of her spirits she remembered, Dorrie and Michael will be home tomorrow, and Dorrie will be such a comfort to me.

Mrs O'Brien bustled in and put a small table in front of the sofa and laid a cloth on it. Mary followed her with plates of savoury hotpot and Anna was surprised to find that she was hungry.

'The doctor says food is the best cure in trouble, or a glass of brandy. At least, thank God, it's not needed to cure a broken heart in your case, Anna, although I know you were very fond of Eugene.'

Anna agreed, but wondered what Mrs O'Brien would say if she knew how she really felt. At least her pride was intact, and as though on cue Mrs O'Brien said, 'At least no explanations are necessary to other people, Anna. If anyone asks you about him you can just say he's left the Army and gone abroad and you won't bother corresponding any more.'

'I see so few people now anyway,' Anna said. 'Father will be home in four months' time. I won't say anything in my letters and perhaps Dr O'Brien will explain to him.'

'Of course,' Mrs O'Brien said warmly. 'He's cooled down now, Anna. He didn't mean that about never speaking of Eugene. He was just so angry, as much on your behalf as anything, but he just said to me that you were a brave girl.'

'I got most of the shock over on Saturday,' Anna said. 'Since then I've just been waiting for something to happen, and it's a relief to know the worst. I think I should go home soon if you don't mind, Mrs O'Brien.'

When they went into the hall, a shabby young man stood there twisting his cap in his hands, and the doctor was just coming out of the surgery with his bag.

'Is it Lizzie?' Mrs O'Brien asked, and the young man nodded miserably, while the doctor gripped Anna's arm.

'You're a good, brave girl,' he whispered. 'Worth better than that fellow. It will all be for the best. God bless you.'

Anna bent forward and kissed his cheek, unable to speak, and the doctor hurried out with the young man. As she walked home she tried to organise her thoughts. She must have some explanation prepared for her mother, but fortunately only three people knew how she really felt about Eugene – Dorrie, Isabel and James Hargreaves. With other people she could assume indifference.

She tried to concentrate on details to keep at bay the pain of loss and rejected love which she knew was waiting to overwhelm her. She would write a carefully worded letter to Isabel and tell her the details when she saw her in a few weeks' time. She would be able to talk of it to James too, knowing that he would understand and comfort her.

Best of all, tomorrow Dorrie would be home. At the thought, she quickened her steps and when she arrived home her aunt welcomed her. 'I'm glad to see you. Your mother's been asking for you every five minutes.'

'But I left her with plenty—' Anna began, but her aunt interrupted.

'She's got a bee in her bonnet about her clothes. Wants you to look something out for her.' Clara suddenly looked searchingly at Anna. 'Are you all right?' she asked. 'No more dizzy spells?' When Anna shook her head she said, 'You look pale. Don't do too much running up and down.'

Anna blundered up the stairs, blinded by tears. Kindness from her aunt was so unexpected that she was nearly undone, but her mother soon redressed the balance. Anna was kept so busy that the evening went quickly and she had no time to think of what had happened, or even to think of Dorrie's arrival the next day.

Alone in her bedroom, she resolutely crushed any thought of Eugene. She was determined that she would not greet her sister with her face blotched and swollen by crying, but continue to put a brave face on things until she was alone with Dorrie. On Friday, delays on the railway meant that Dorrie and Michael arrived so late, with Dorrie so exhausted that they retired to bed almost immediately.

The next morning, Dorrie's welcome was as warm and affectionate as ever, but as she hugged and kissed Anna she gave no hint that she knew about Eugene. Perhaps she knew nothing of it, Anna thought, but later, when they were alone, Dorrie said petulantly, 'We're very annoyed about this business with Eugene. It's very embarrassing for us because everybody knows Michael is related to him, even though only as a cousin.'

'You know, then?' Anna gasped.

'Of course we know. *Everybody* knows, the whole camp. But of course Eugene didn't think about us. He did what suited himself, without a thought for anyone else. I must say, Anna, I don't understand why you didn't realise what he was.' She looked at herself in the mirror and turned a curl round her finger.

'I know his courtship was very lukewarm compared to Michael's, but surely you must have realised that there was something wrong, Anna.'

'You may be very worldly-wise now, Dorrie,' Anna said with dignity, 'but when we met them you knew as little as I did about these – these problems some men have.'

They were sitting on the side of Anna's bed and their eyes met in the mirror. Dorrie turned and flung her arms around her sister.

'Oh, Anna, it must be so hard for you,' she said. 'But at least nobody knows about it here, do they? In London it's terrible. The jokes! I don't understand most of them, but I know they're nasty. Michael says ignore them, but I can't. I can't bear people to laugh at me.'

She wept and Anna said gently, 'It will only be a nine-day wonder. Something else will take its place.'

'That's what Michael says. He's being so brave, Anna, because I know people are looking at him and wondering, especially as we haven't started a family yet.' She sat up and wiped her eyes, then said angrily, 'I'm determined not to have a family until we have a better place to live and I'm not going to be pushed into it just to prove them wrong.'

Anna said nothing, chiefly because she could think of nothing to say. She felt completely out of her depth. Dorrie's confident and knowledgeable attitude seemed totally different to that of the few girls she knew when they married, and to Dorrie's own attitude before she married.

She could recall Dorrie saying one night as they discussed the wedding, 'I wonder if we'll have any babies? I'd love a little boy just like Michael, but, Anna, I couldn't bear it if I was like poor Mama, losing my babies.' She remembered comforting Dorrie, telling her she was young and healthy, not like Mama. How she had changed!

She managed to stifle her disappointment at being unable to discuss her feelings with Dorrie, as Dorrie went on to ask why her mama and aunt had quarrelled.

'I don't know,' Anna said. 'Nelly has tried hard to find out, but she hasn't been able to.'

'It's not Nelly's place to pry into the family affairs. Perhaps Mama will tell *me*,' Dorrie said confidently.

'Perhaps,' Anna said dryly. She stood up. Her desire to be alone with Dorrie had gone, or at least with this stranger who seemed to have taken the place of the Dorrie she knew and loved.

'I need to check on things in the kitchen,' she said. 'What are you going to do?'

'Michael wants to go to see the O'Briens,' Dorrie said, 'but I had quite enough of them driving from the station. He can go alone and I'll go and make Mama happy.'

With a final complacent look in the mirror, she walked out of the room with Anna.

Anna was surprised to find Michael sitting by the kitchen table. He stood up when she came in.

'I thought you'd gone to see your aunt and uncle,' Anna said.

He replied quietly, 'I wanted to see you alone, Anna. To say how sorry I am about the way things have turned out. I should have warned you, but I honestly didn't know, Anna. I feel I've failed you.'

'You mustn't feel that, Michael. I'm sorry that you and Dorrie are having so much trouble through no fault of your own.'

'She told you then?' Michael said. 'There's always jangle and gossip flying round, but sure she imagines half of it or her and the Rafferty woman build it up between them.'

Anna was surprised by the bitterness in his voice and she said quietly, 'You think Mrs Rafferty's a bad influence on Dorrie then?'

Michael shrugged. 'I think Dorrie needed her at first. I was

231

glad she took her under her wing, told her what to do, and warned off some of the other women, but now! Every notion in her head is secondhand from Mrs Rafferty.'

'I think she's changed,' Anna said. 'Of course, she's only been home such a short time. Perhaps it's too soon to judge.'

'No, you're right. Dorrie has changed,' Michael said sadly.

'What's she like, Mrs Rafferty?' Anna said curiously.

Michael shrugged. 'Typical Army wife, I suppose. She's been around, seen the world, but I don't like some of her views, or the way Dorrie just swallows them. I think she's learning a lot she'd be better off not knowing, but I don't know what I can do about it.'

'I wouldn't worry too much,' Anna comforted him. 'It's all new and strange to her, but underneath she's still Dorrie. This will pass.'

She was moving around, preparing the meal, and Michael said, 'Thanks, Anna. I won't get in your way any longer. I just wanted you to know that I wasn't a part of any of Eugene's tricks. He fooled me too, but I shouldn't have let him. I should have protected you.'

Anna stretched up and kissed his cheek. 'Don't blame yourself,' she said, 'and don't worry any more about me. I'm all right, but thanks, Michael.'

He smiled at her and picked up his cap. 'I'll go to see my aunt and uncle then,' he said, and went out.

Anna reflected that Michael had changed too. His happy-go-lucky exuberance had gone, but he was still an affectionate and cheerful man, with good principles and a warm heart.

Dorrie was still with her mother, and remained with her until Michael returned and the meal was ready. Anna hoped that they were not discussing Eugene. If her mother discovered what had happened her life would not be worth living, she thought. The possibilities for cruel comments from her mother would be endless, and the fact that she knew nothing of the situation had been the one bright spot so far for Anna.

Nothing was said about it during the meal, however, or later when they sat in the drawing room with coffee. Michael asked about the Jensons and Dorrie chattered about the social life among the Army wives, with plentiful references to Mrs Rafferty.

Anna felt that the day from which she had hoped for so much would never end, but at last she was able to escape to her own room. She was wearily taking pins from her hair when the door opened and Dorrie looked in. 'I just came to say goodnight. Michael hasn't come up yet,' she said, and Anna eagerly moved to sit on the bed, her heart lifting.

They kissed and hugged each other and Dorrie began to talk about the Jenson tragedy. 'I know how you must miss Isabel,' she said, 'and the little boys too. Captain Jenson was such a lovely man. It has really upset Mama.' For a while she seemed like the old Dorrie, but soon she returned to the subject of Eugene, and not in the way that Anna wished.

Anna longed to tell her of the love and pity she felt for Eugene and of his struggles, expecting Dorrie to be sympathetic to him, but all that her sister felt, it seemed, was curiosity. 'Did you never suspect what he was, Anna, truly?' she asked.

'How could I? I knew nothing of that, and neither did you, Dorrie. Remember how we used to wonder if he had an unhappy love affair in his past? Poor Eugene.'

'Poor Eugene!' Dorrie exclaimed, her voice rising. 'I don't know how you can say that, Anna. He's just a pervert, Mrs Rafferty says, and your woman's instinct should have warned you. Ugh! To be—'

Before she could say any more the door was flung open and Michael rushed in and roughly pulled Dorrie to her feet.

He bent over her, his face red with temper. 'Don't you dare

use that word to Anna,' he said, quietly but ferociously. 'I don't want to hear it on your lips again. Do you hear me?'

'I was only saying—' Dorrie began, but he interrupted.

'I heard what you were saying. Anybody who passed the door could have heard. I thought you were supposed to love your sister?'

'I do, I do,' Dorrie wailed. 'I do, Anna.'

'Then you've got a damn queer way of showing it,' he said. 'You'd better say goodnight and come away before you do any more damage.' He turned to Anna. 'I'm sorry, Anna, you've been subjected to Mrs Rafferty's peculiar ideas. Try to ignore them. She's just an ignorant woman.'

He had released his grip on Dorrie and he said goodnight to Anna and went to the door, but he turned back to say to his wife, 'I hope you remembered what I said about saying nothing to your mother or your aunt.'

'I didn't mention him,' she said sulkily, then sat down by Anna again as he went out.

'I didn't know Michael had such a temper,' Anna said, smiling to make light of the incident, but Dorrie said angrily, 'Neither did I, but he's been showing it lately. He doesn't like Mrs Rafferty. Says she encourages me to flirt.'

'And does she?' Anna said bluntly.

Dorrie shrugged. 'I can't help it if men find me attractive,' she said. 'Especially if you saw some of their dowdy old wives. I can still twist Michael round my little finger, though.'

'I'll say goodnight, Dorrie,' Anna said. 'It's been a long day.'

She felt that she could stand no more, and Dorrie kissed her goodnight and left. Anna crawled into bed feeling that her head would burst, but exhaustion took over and she fell asleep.

The next morning, Sunday, Anna was up early, but there was no sign of the previous night's quarrel when Dorrie and Michael came downstairs. The November morning was dry but cold and when they all set off for ten o'clock Mass Dorrie carried a large white muff with white fur framing her face.

When they reached the end of Westbourne Street Anna saw James Hargreaves approaching as usual down Eastbourne Street. He bowed and raised his hat before hurrying ahead of them and Dorrie turned to Anna with a complacent smile.

'You told him I was coming home,' she said. 'How cleverly he timed that meeting.'

She gave a trill of laughter, looking up at Michael, and he said, 'An admirer, I suppose.'

'One of them,' Dorrie said airily.

Anna was tempted to tell her that she met James every Sunday, but she thought bitterly, Why bother? For the first time she saw an affinity between Dorrie and their mother. They had always been alike in appearance, but now she saw in Dorrie the same capacity for self-delusion. These thoughts made her feel better, but not really in a suitable mood for church.

James was at the back of the church with the other collectors and Dorrie smiled radiantly at him as she passed him, but he was not too dazzled to smile at Anna behind her.

After Mass they were greeted by various friends and neighbours, but to Dorrie's disappointment they were not surrounded by the usual group of young men and girls.

'Many of them are married or courting now,' Anna told her.

They spoke to Kate and Jim Deagan, and Dr and Mrs O'Brien. Before they approached the doctor and his wife, Michael bent down to Dorrie and Anna heard him say quietly but forcefully, 'Remember. Watch your tongue.'

Dorrie was on her best behaviour, smiling sweetly and speaking about Lord Roberts to the doctor, which pleased him.

Mrs O'Brien greeted Anna warmly and looked searchingly at her. 'How do you feel, my dear?' she asked. 'Are you enjoying the visit? I'm sure you are.'

'She's cooking grand meals for us and working very hard,' Michael said. 'We're very lucky.' He smiled down at Anna and Mrs O'Brien said, 'I'm glad you're appreciated, Anna.'

Dorrie turned to them. 'Oh, she is,' she said, linking her arm through Anna's, but Anna felt unable to respond as they all walked home together, leaving the doctor and his wife in Shaw Street.

Dorrie announced that she and Michael must visit Mrs Wendell and Anna asked her to slip in to see Mrs Deagan. Her mother had been in favour of the visit to Mrs Wendell, but she said pettishly, 'I don't see why you have to waste time at the Deagans', Dorrie. I'm seeing little enough of you.'

Anna looked on in disgust, thinking cynically that Mrs Deagan had no fortune to leave.

For the first time, Anna was pleased when the visit ended and she waved Dorrie and Michael off with relief when they set off for Ireland on Monday. She felt that she needed time and space to sort out in her mind all that had happened with Dorrie, quite apart from the need to come to terms with the event concerning Eugene.

At the end of all the thinking and remembering and musing she was left with one inescapable fact. She still loved Eugene and she always would. She also decided that from now on she would use her own judgement and not rely for comfort or advice on anyone else, although she still appreciated the kindness shown to her by Dr and Mrs O'Brien.

This experience had made her feel older and wiser, and better able to deal with whatever happened in the future, so it was not wasted, she decided.

Chapter Fifteen

During the week that Dorrie and Michael were in Ireland and Anna was arranging her thoughts, James Hargreaves was also facing the fact that his unrequited love was as strong as ever. He thought he had resigned himself to the fact that as a married woman she was lost to him, and he could keep her memory enshrined without feeling any pain, but he realised he had been deluding himself.

He had only to see her beautiful face and to receive such a warm and encouraging smile to feel all the old pain coming flooding back. He decided to go to a different Mass when she returned the following weekend, but he was drawn to her like a moth to a flame.

Knowing it was foolish, he still walked down to see her at the end of Westbourne Street and was rewarded with another dazzling smile. He raised his hat and bowed, then hurried ahead and Dorrie said disparagingly, 'He's still a stick, isn't he? No more lively than when he was under his mother's thumb.'

Anna said nothing. She had decided that this was the best policy with the new Dorrie. It was evident that Dorrie had enjoyed discussing Eugene with Michael's mother and gaining sympathy for all she was suffering from the gossip.

Michael told Anna that he had talked to his parents and received good advice. 'Mammy's a rock of sense,' he said. 'She offered to keep Dorrie there for a few weeks until the gossip died down, but sure Dorrie wouldn't miss all the Christmas junketings at the depot.'

Dorrie had a different version. 'She wanted to keep me there, but I told her I couldn't be apart from Michael for so long. She said it would be good for my health, but what she really meant was she wanted to know why there were no grandchildren appearing on the scene,' she told Anna.

'She may have wanted you to stay to avoid the gossip,' Anna said stiffly.

Dorrie laughed. 'They'll be having a scandal of their own before long. The mad Dermot belongs to the Irish Republican Brotherhood and I'm sure it's against the law. I'm not jumping out of the frying pan into the fire.'

'What is it? I've never heard of it,' Anna said.

'Oh, Gaelic Leaguers and Fenians and all sorts of people. Some poets. Anyway, I didn't want to know about it. He was off recruiting or something so I didn't see him,' Dorrie said carelessly.

When they returned to London Anna felt that she missed Michael more than Dorrie, but her mother made enough fuss about the parting for half-a-dozen people. She declared that her heart was broken and lay on her sofa, sobbing theatrically and demanding smelling salts, brandy and water or her head bathed in eau de Cologne.

Anna found this even harder to bear because of the contrast with what was happening next door. Mrs Deagan had suffered from a varicose ulcer for many years, but it had suddenly become much worse. Maggie dressed it every morning, but now her mother was unable to bear to stand, and had to sit with her leg up on a stool.

She never complained, although her suffering showed in her face, and for a while she tried to do small household tasks, like peeling potatoes, while sitting down. But it was evident that her strength was unequal to it, and the family persuaded her to rest.

Maggie stayed on to cook the evening meal every day and her husband, Walter, came uncomplainingly to eat with the family. Anna went in often to see her old friend, in spite of her mother's objections. Mrs Deagan was bedridden now, looking like a tiny shrunken bird, but she always greeted Anna with a smile.

She told her about Walter. 'He's one in a thousand, girlie,' she said. 'That's what you should look for in a husband, kindness, and I'm praying to God that you'll find it.'

Her face contorted and Anna said gently, 'Is the pain very bad? Should I get Maggie?'

'No, no, just a bit of indigestion. I don't mind the old pain, but I'm worried about my poor Norah. She made a bad choice with that fellow, Anna.'

'But he seemed so nice,' Anna said, 'and so fond of Norah.'

'Aye, well that didn't last,' Mrs Deagan said grimly. 'He couldn't think he was more important if he was Lord Mayor. Thinks she should wait on him hand and foot. They came to see me and he was giving out about when her husband comes home a woman should be waiting with a good fire and his slippers warming and his meal on the table. It's her duty.'

'But he knew she was keeping on the shop,' Anna said. 'I mean, it's a goldmine, isn't it and Norah told me it would make it possible to buy furniture for that big house and all sorts of things.'

'I know, but he wants her to sell it, and I think she's going to. Her shop that she loves and built up from nothing.' A tear trickled down Mrs Deagan's cheek and Anna gently wiped it away.

'Don't upset yourself, Mrs Deagan. I think she'll let him go so far, then tell him that's enough. Norah's nobody's fool.'

'But she seems to be completely under his thumb, girlie.

Our Jim tried to warn her to keep the shop money in her own name, but she fired up.'

'She probably has her own plans made,' Anna soothed her. 'I always think Norah is a lot like you. *You* wouldn't let anyone put on you for long, would you?'

Mrs Deagan smiled, but her eyes were closing and Anna waited a moment then went back to the kitchen to see Maggie.

Maggie had her back to the door and was pouring two cups of tea. When she turned round Anna was dismayed to see that her eyes were swollen with crying.

'Your mum's asleep,' she said, as Maggie put the tea before her and they sat down.

'She won't sleep long,' Maggie said. 'The damn pain will waken her.'

'She had some pain, but she said it was indigestion,' Anna said.

'Oh God, if only it was!' Maggie exclaimed, tears pouring from her eyes.

Anna knelt down and put her arms round her. 'Is it the varicose ulcer?' she asked, but Maggie shook her head, trying to mop up her tears.

'Doctor's just gone,' she said in a muffled voice. 'He said it's a growth in her stomach. As if she hasn't had enough to bear.'

She cried again and Anna cried with her. 'Can't he do anything?' Anna asked finally, but Maggie shook her head.

'He's given me morphine to give her, but we can't give her enough to stop the pain properly in case she gets used to it. He said her heart's strong and she's got a strong will, so she could live a long time, with the pain getting gradually worse, so she can't get too used to the morphine. She'll need it badly at the end.'

They clung together, weeping, then Anna said indignantly,

'You shouldn't have been told this when you were on your own. I'm surprised at Dr O'Brien.'

'It was the other fellow, Dr Hogan,' Maggie said. 'Dr O'Brien seems to be forever dashing off to London or somewhere lately.'

Anna was immediately reminded of Eugene and thought how little the distress over him seemed to matter in the face of this sorrow.

She told Maggie what her mother had said about Walter to comfort her, and Maggie said quietly, 'Aye, God's ways are not our ways, but sometimes things work out well in the end. I hope you find that, Anna. The first choice is not always right, and sometimes there's someone better nearer than you think.'

So the Deagans know about Eugene, Anna thought, but how kind and tactful they were. She hugged Maggie and went home to face her mother.

She was lying on the sofa and greeted Anna with a storm of abuse. 'You've got low tastes,' she shrieked. 'You'd rather be with those creatures next door than your own mother. I *needed* you to bathe my head. Your duty is to *me*.'

'*Shut up!*' Anna suddenly shouted. 'There's a woman dying in agony next door and you – you . . .'

Her mother's mouth fell open, then she flung herself back on the sofa, screaming hysterically and drumming her heels, but Anna turned and ran sobbing from the room.

Clara could hear the screams where she stood in the kitchen, but she firmly closed the door into the hall, and Nelly was out of earshot, scrubbing the back steps. For want of an audience the hysterics soon died away, and Mrs Furlong became frustrated by the silence.

Eventually she went into the hall, but the door to the kitchen was closed and there was no sound from upstairs. She went back to her sofa and rang her bell loudly.

Nelly came in and she said angrily, 'Where have you been? The fire's very low and I could do with a cup of tea.'

Nelly said cheerfully, 'I've just taken one to Anna, so there'll be one in the pot.'

'I want a fresh cup of tea!' Mrs Furlong snapped. She would have liked to add, Not Anna's leavings, but she felt that Nelly was not on her side these days. *No one* was on her side, she thought, tears of self pity rising in her eyes, but Nelly was making up the fire and ignored them.

Anna came down to help her aunt with the meal, but it was an uncomfortable one. Anna usually made small talk to bridge the silences since the quarrel between her aunt and her mother, but tonight she felt unable to speak or to swallow.

Her mother and aunt made a hearty meal and Anna collected their plates and her own, which she had barely touched, and went to bring in an apple pie and a jug of cream before seeking sanctuary in the kitchen, where Nelly was sitting with a cup of tea.

'The only bit of peace,' she said. 'When your ma's busy with her knife and fork.' Then she looked more closely at Anna. 'What's up, girl?' she asked. 'Has she upset you?'

Anna shook her head. 'No. It's Mrs Deagan. Oh, Nelly, she's dying.'

She burst into tears and Nelly stood up and put her arms round her. She was smaller than Anna, but she patted her back as if she was a baby, saying, 'There, there,' then quietly, 'I know, girl, I seen her the other day.'

'But Dr Hogan's told Maggie she's got a growth. She can't give her much morphine for the pain in case she gets used to it. He said she had a strong heart and a strong spirit and she could live a long time, with the pain getting worse, so she'll need the morphine then.'

'She won't,' Nelly said positively. 'Won't live a long time.'

'But the doctor said . . .' Anna began.

'He doesn't know her like I do. She's got the spirit to fight it, but she won't. Not if it's upsetting her family. All her life they've come first. You'll see, girl. When the time's right she'll just let go and die peaceful.'

'Oh, I hope you're right, Nelly,' Anna said, drying her eyes.

'I am, you'll see. Susan Deagan's been in charge all her life. She won't change now.'

In spite of herself, Anna smiled, then she said slowly, 'It's awful to be wishing her dead, isn't it?'

'No, it isn't,' Nelly said sturdily. 'We're just wishing for a peaceful death for her, that's all.'

Anna hugged her. 'You've made me feel much better. Thanks, Nelly. I think I'll go and tell Maggie what you said. Neither of us thought of that.'

'You were too close to it. Yiz couldn't see the wood for the trees.'

Anna had prepared the tea tray and Nelly said, 'I'll take that in, in case your ma nabs you. I'll tell her you're laying down with a headache.'

Jim and Luke were sitting with their mother, and Maggie and Kate were in the kitchen when Anna slipped in to see them. She told them what Nelly had said, and Kate said wonderingly, 'She's right, Anna.'

Maggie agreed. 'I'm surprised we never thought of it,' she said. 'But, like Nelly said – the wood for the trees.'

'Perhaps Ma can have more morphine now,' said Kate eagerly.

'I hope so,' said Maggie thoughtfully, 'but we'll have to ask the doctor. If only we knew.'

Kate suddenly put her hands over her face, weeping. 'I can't believe this is Ma we're talking about,' she wept. 'Oh, Ma!'

243

The two sisters clung together and Anna slipped quietly away.

She found Walter smoking his pipe near the back gate and he came to meet her. 'I'm glad Maggie had you to talk to after that news. Thanks, Anna,' he said.

'I'm glad I was there,' Anna said. She told him that she had just popped in to tell them of Nelly's views, and repeated them to Walter before she slipped through the gate and into her own house. She managed to reach her room unobserved and undressed thankfully and went to bed.

She met James Hargreaves as usual on Sunday morning and apologised for not warning him that Dorrie would be home. 'I had rather a lot on my mind,' she excused herself, but he told her not to worry.

'She looked very well,' he was unable to resist saying, and Anna agreed.

They met again in the evening when they walked down for Benediction. It was also the confraternity night for Anna, and after Benediction ended she moved to the side chapel with the other girls for the confraternity prayers. Afterwards, the others went through for the social side of the evening, but Anna slipped back into the church, where she found James waiting for her.

'I thought you'd be gone,' she said in surprise.

'I remembered you saying you don't go to the socials now, so I waited just in case,' he said.

'I feel lost there on my own,' she said. 'Without either Dorrie or Isabel I feel like a fish out of water.'

'I know exactly how you feel,' James replied, and Anna squeezed his arm sympathetically. She was relaxed and easy with James, and felt that he was the only person she could talk to quite freely now and that he would understand and sympathise.

As they drew near Westbourne Street he said diffidently, 'Do you have to go straight home? Could they think you'd gone to the confraternity social if you came up to my house instead? Frances would like to see you.'

Anna stopped walking and gave a deep sigh of relief. 'I was just dreading the thought of going home,' she admitted, 'but it's not a night for walking about, is it?'

'Not unless you're a glutton for punishment,' James said, as a gust of wind, laden with sleet, drove into their faces. Without another word they continued past Westbourne Street and straight up the hill to Eastbourne Street, Anna thinking how neatly James had indicated that the proprieties would be observed, with Frances present.

'How is Frances?' she asked.

James said quietly, 'I'm worried about her. She's crippled with the rheumatism now and in a lot of pain, but she insists on carrying on working. I persuaded her to get a young girl to help her, but I don't think she accepts much help. The girl has a dog's life, I think.'

'If Frances is in pain, it'll make her short-tempered,' Anna said.

They had reached the house and James said as he opened the door, 'You don't mind the kitchen? It's the warmest room,' and led the way there.

Frances was hunched in an armchair beside a bright fire, with a crocheted blanket over her knees. Her face lit up in welcome when she saw Anna. She tried to rise, but James said firmly, 'Frances, don't move. You know Miss Anna Furlong, don't you?'

'Yes. I seen you first when you were in your bassinet,' Frances said to Anna with a smile.

Anna, usually so formal and reserved, surprised herself as much as James and Frances by bending down and kissing

Frances on the cheek, and the older woman patted her hand.

'Get them wet clothes off as quick as you can,' she said. 'It's enough to give you your death going out in this weather.'

James took Anna's coat and hat, and set another chair near to the fire.

'Haven't you got a cup of tea?' he said to Frances. 'Where's Nonnie?'

'I sent her home,' said Frances. 'I couldn't do with her mooching round with a face like a wet weekend. She made up the fire before she went.'

James shook his head at her, but only said, 'I don't suppose you sent her up to do your fire, did you?'

'Didn't think of it,' Frances replied.

James pushed the black kettle on to the fire, then made and poured tea and put out cake near to the two women. Before he sat down he said, 'Excuse me,' and they heard him running upstairs.

'He's gone to see to my fire. He's insisted on a fire in my bedroom ever since the rheumatics started, and a hot water bottle in my bed. He's one in a thousand and here's me neither use nor ornament to him.' Frances sighed deeply.

'I'm sure he doesn't think that,' Anna comforted her.

She was surprised at how easy and comfortable she had felt as soon as she arrived in the house, and wondered whether it was because pity for Frances stopped her thinking about herself, or because James was so relaxed in his own home.

'I worry about it, though,' Frances said. 'I can still manage the cooking if the girl brings me what I need. It's just my legs so far, but if it gets to my arms I'll be useless altogether.'

'I wouldn't cross that bridge until you come to it,' Anna said. 'My Aunt Clara's had it in her shoulders for years, every winter, but her legs aren't affected and her shoulders are all right in the summer.'

Frances looked more cheerful. 'Aye, I'm all right in the summer,' she said.

'My aunt says she can be lying in a warm bed, but knows the weather's turned bad because her shoulders stiffen up. It's strange that, isn't it?'

James heard the murmur of voices as he came into the room with a stone hot-water bottle and smiled at the two women.

'You're a case, Frances,' he said. 'Your fire was almost out, but it's all right again now.' He took the black kettle into the scullery to fill the hot water bottle, then refilled the kettle from the tap there and brought it back into the kitchen.

'Are you all right?' he asked Anna anxiously. 'Warm enough?' and when she smiled and nodded he said, 'I won't be a moment,' and went out again.

Frances wiped tears from her eyes. 'He's gone to put the hot water bottle in my bed. When I think of the childhood he had and the way he's turned out so kind and thoughtful I can't believe it. That bitch of a mother and that evil old misbegotten swine of an uncle! I hope they're both roasting in hell. They deserve to be, for what they did to that poor child.'

Before she could say any more James came back and sat on a kitchen chair between Anna and Frances. 'Did you tell Frances about Mrs Deagan?' he asked Anna.

'Nonnie told me she's real bad,' Frances said. 'Is it her ulcer, Anna?'

'No, I wish it was only that, although that's bad enough,' Anna said. She had no hesitation in telling Frances about Mrs Deagan, knowing that her questions sprang from concern, not curiosity, and that she and Susan Deagan had been friends for many years. 'Dr Hogan told Maggie she has a growth, and the pain will get worse.'

Frances crossed herself. 'God be merciful to her and grant

her ease,' she said fervently, and James and Anna said, 'Amen.'

Anna told Frances what the doctor had told Maggie and what Nelly had said about Mrs Deagan choosing her own time, and Frances agreed with Nelly.

'She lived for them children from the day she was left a widow and she'll die when it's best for them,' she said.

'She'll be sadly missed,' James said. 'And not only by her own family.'

'I can't bear to think of it,' Anna said with a sigh. 'She's been such a good friend to me. All the Deagans have, but Mrs Deagan's been like a rock and always given me such good advice. I don't know what I'd have done without her, especially since Dorrie went.'

She glanced quickly at James, wondering how her sudden mention of Dorrie would affect him, but he seemed unperturbed.

'You're missing your other friends, too, aren't you?' Frances said. 'The Dutch sea captain's family?'

'Yes, but they've settled down very well in their new lives,' Anna said. 'Mrs Jenson's brother has a big house in the country near Manchester and he's fixed up a cottage there for them. The eldest lad has gone to sea, but the others all live with their mother. The big boys go by train to school in Manchester and the little ones to the village school.'

'It's a big change for them,' Frances said. 'Especially Mrs Jenson and Isabel.'

'They like it,' Anna said. 'Isabel and her mother love gardening. They grow their own vegetables and they keep hens. The boys like living in the country and I think the uncles are very good to them, but Isabel says none of them can really believe that her father isn't just away on a voyage, even when they pray for his soul.'

'Well, that's a mercy,' Frances said. 'By the time they have to face it they'll be over the worst.'

'They've all been very brave,' Anna said quietly.

'What about something to eat?' Frances said. 'I've boiled a ham and made pea soup. You need something to stick to your ribs in this weather.'

'I can recommend the pea soup,' James said, smiling at Anna, 'followed by ham sandwiches, or ham and potatoes and vegetables? What do you think?'

'It all sounds lovely, but I had a meal before I left home,' Anna said. 'Perhaps ham sandwiches?'

'You can try the pea soup another time,' Frances said. 'Will you bring me the makings and I'll do the sandwiches, James?'

'Could I?' Anna suggested diffidently. She had noticed lines of pain in Frances's face as she moved in her chair, but Frances brushed the suggestion aside and James placed a sturdy small table before her and spread it with a white cloth.

He went to the scullery and Frances swiftly plunged her hand into a bag hanging on the side of her chair and brought out a medicine bottle and a spoon. She swiftly swallowed three spoonfuls then recorked the bottle, before thrusting it back in the bag and dropping the spoon in a glass of water beside her.

Anna was amazed by the swiftness and furtiveness of the movements, but she said nothing and James returned, bringing a breadboard and breadknife, a loaf, and a cooked ham.

'Do you prefer mustard or pickles on ham, Anna?' Frances said calmly.

'I like either,' Anna replied.

She was still feeling bemused, but Frances said, 'Right. We'll have mustard then, because James prefers mustard, and I like either,' then winked at Anna as James returned to the scullery.

When he returned he suggested that Anna might like to see over the house while Frances prepared the sandwiches, and they set off. There was gaslight in the hall, and in every room downstairs James went ahead to light the central gaslight.

'I think it's lovely,' Anna said. 'Such a feeling of lightness and space.'

'It looks much better in the daytime, and especially when the sun shines,' James said eagerly. 'The previous people were artistic and had everything, walls and curtains and paintwork, in light colours. I liked it so much I kept it like that. I'm glad you like it too.'

They went back to the kitchen, where Frances was moving much more freely and had managed to lay a cloth on the kitchen table and put out plates of sandwiches, and had moved the kettle on to the fire. She sat down again while Anna made tea and James dashed upstairs to replenish her bedroom fire, then she stood again to drink her tea and asked James to help her to bed.

'I'll go now, before I stiffen up again,' she said, and while James opened the door she looked at Anna and put her finger to her lips, indicating the bag on her chair. Anna nodded, and James tucked Frances's arm inside his own and helped her to walk out into the hall and up the stairs.

'Will she manage?' Anna asked anxiously when he came back.

'Yes, she'll sit by her fire for a while, then she'll manage to get undressed and into bed,' he said.

Anna wondered whether Frances had a bottle of the magic potion upstairs, but felt she should choose her own way of managing her disability.

They ate their supper quickly, alarmed to hear the clock striking ten, and set off for Westbourne Street.

'I hope this won't mean trouble for you,' James said, but Anna laughed bitterly.

'If I'd gone straight home from the confraternity there

would have been something I'd done or left undone to give cause for complaint,' she said. 'At least now I've had an enjoyable night, so anything that's said will be worth it.'

'Have you? Enjoyed tonight?' James said eagerly, and when Anna nodded he said, 'I was just thinking how easy we all were together tonight. Not many girls would have sat in the kitchen and been so kind to Frances.'

'I was impressed by the way you looked after her,' Anna said, but James said quickly, 'Nothing I could do would repay Frances for all she's done for me. She's been a lifeline for me. That's why I feel awful not being able to help her when she's in such pain.'

'You do all you can and she appreciates it,' Anna said. 'She told me so.'

A light sprang up in the hall of her house and they parted hurriedly, but Anna went in feeling that she was armoured against any jibe her mother chose to hurl at her.

Clara had opened the door, but only said, 'You're late,' before going through to the kitchen, but as soon as Anna looked into the parlour her mother began to sceam, 'So you've been walking the streets, looking to pick up a man, have you? You could still behave with dignity even though you've been jilted and everyone is laughing at you.'

'I think you're losing your mind,' Anna said coldly, and walked away. Her mother screamed for her to come back, but she went on into the scullery and drew a cup of water to drink.

Nelly was there and said reproachfully, 'She was real worked up about you, with all this talk about Spring Heeled Jack,' but Anna only said, 'Any more news about Mrs Deagan?'

'She was laughing and joking with Dr O'Brien and she had a good sleep after he'd gone and said she felt better, according to Maggie,' said Nelly.

Lying in bed that night, Anna wondered how she would

feel when she met James next Sunday morning, but the sense of easy companionship remained with both of them. After Mass James asked if she could come to tea, as Frances was anxious to see her, and she accepted.

'I'll simply say I've been invited by a friend from the church,' she said. 'I realise I've been a fool, allowing myself to be dominated.'

Brave words, but they provoked such a scene that Anna wondered whether it was worth being defiant. She had to bathe her face with cold water and press powder leaves round her eyes to hide the traces of her tears, and she was still shaking when she reached Eastbourne Street.

'Was it a battle to get away?' James asked as he took her coat, and she turned away and nodded, not trusting herself to speak. They looked into the kitchen and she said hello to Frances, who was sitting by the fire reading a missionary magazine, then went into the parlour.

The day was dry and frosty with thin sunlight and Anna could see to the full the beauty of the bright pleasant room. A wood fire burned in the grate and was reflected back from mirrors and glass-covered woodland scenes on the walls, and a smell of burning wood and spicy chrysanthemums filled the air.

Suddenly it was all too much for Anna and she bent her head and wept bitterly. James, his face full of concern, moved swiftly to sit beside her and try to comfort her. 'What is it, Anna? Has someone upset you?' he asked.

Anna shook her head. 'It was that before,' she said in a muffled voice, 'but now . . .' She was unable to explain that the contrast between the beautiful room and the sordid scenes she had left at home was suddenly too much to bear.

'The trouble is,' James said gently, 'people who know us well know best how to hurt us.'

Anna swallowed and tried to control herself. 'That's very true,' she said. 'How well you understand. That's why I was upset before, but now – it's just that this room is so beautiful. I can't explain.'

'You don't have to,' James said comfortingly.

Her tears still flowed and he handed her his large white handkerchief and quietly left the room. While he was away Anna tried to compose herself and he returned carrying a tray with a cup of tea and a bowl of sugar.

'I think you should make your tea quite sweet,' he said. 'Dr O'Brien says freshly brewed sweet tea is the best cure for a broken heart.' He stopped, appalled, flushing and stammering, 'I'm – I'm sorry. I didn't mean . . .' but Anna said gently, 'He's got other remedies too. Hotpot and brandy and probably others.'

They both smiled, although James's face was still red, and he said with more dignity, 'I'm sorry. I have a knack of saying the wrong thing.'

'So do I,' Anna said ruefully. 'My aunt says things come into my head and out of my mouth without pause for reflection and I know she's right. I try to hold my tongue with Mama, but before I can stop them sarcastic remarks pop out.'

'I can't imagine that,' he said.

They smiled at each other, feeling at ease in each other's company.

'I should go and see Frances,' Anna said, but James said, 'No need. She'll call us when she's ready and then you can have a talk with her after tea, while I clear away and wash up. We can have a talk now while she's happy with her magazine.'

'Hard to believe that it will be Christmas in a few weeks,' Anna said. 'Even though there are all the Advent ceremonies in church.'

'Do your family do much to celebrate it?' James asked.

'No. Very little, especially since Dorrie went. We used to enjoy joining in the Jensons' merrymaking and tried some of their ideas in our own house, but there'll be nothing at home this year. I love the church celebrations though.'

'I suppose the Jensons will still have some merrymaking for the sake of the children,' James said. 'You'll be going to stay with Isabel early in the year, won't you?'

Anna looked embarrassed. 'Er . . . I may have to wait until Father comes home. He's due in March.'

'The weather should be better then, anyway,' James said, sensing her discomfort, but not knowing the cause. Anna agreed and he changed the subject.

Anna would have been ashamed to tell anyone of the scene with her mother when she mentioned the visit.

'And where do you think you'll get the money?' her mother sneered. 'Not from me, madam. You don't earn your keep *here*, never mind gallivanting off all over the country.'

Anna had felt too shocked and humiliated to reply, because the visit had been arranged and sanctioned for so long, but Nelly had been furious.

'She hadn't got no right to say that,' she said. 'This house is run as if we had a flock of servants and there's only me and you for all the donkey work. Neither of them soil their hands, except for a bit of cooking, so you more than earn your keep and plenty over.'

Anna was comforted by Nelly's support and knew that she spoke the truth, but it made no difference to her mother's decision about the visit. Mrs Furlong now turned a blind eye to Anna's work in the house as she preferred Nelly to wait on her. Anna did the housework Nelly had to neglect to answer the constant ringing of Mrs Furlong's bell.

Each morning Anna and Nelly were downstairs before seven o'clock, and Anna cleaned and aired the drawing room and lit the fire so that it was ready for when her mother chose to appear.

Meanwhile, Nelly made up the kitchen fire, which had been banked down overnight, then went out to scrub the steps and clean the front of the house.

Anna took morning tea to her mother and her aunt, then she and Nelly had their breakfasts. Anna ironed for an hour, then at nine-thirty she took breakfast trays to her mother and aunt. At ten o'clock she took hot water to her aunt who then dressed and came downstairs before going out shopping while Anna and Nelly continued to work without a break.

They had cleaned the hall and all the downstairs rooms before Mrs Furlong rang for hot water at eleven o'clock, and after a lengthy toilette she floated down to settle herself in the drawing room.

After lunch, Anna and Nelly cleaned the bedrooms and Anna helped her aunt in the kitchen, so she felt she was entitled to a few hours to visit next door, or go to church or even go out to tea.

All these thoughts were going rapidly through her mind as she listened to James talking about the men in his office, but she said nothing of them. Gradually, the peaceful surroundings calmed her spirit and she relaxed and began to enjoy herself.

Chapter Sixteen

A lavish tea had been laid in the dining room and Frances sat with them, but ate very little. She chivvied the little girl, Nonnie, to keep their tea cups filled, and pressed food upon Anna until she confessed she was unable to eat another crumb.

'Did you do the baking?' she asked.

'Yes. My legs are better in this weather, better than that mizzly stuff. I cooked the joints yesterday and baked this morning, and the pickles and chutney and that are from before my legs got bad. I've learnt Nonnie how to make a good trifle, anyhow.'

'Yes, it was lovely,' Anna said, smiling at the little girl.

When the meal was over, Anna and Frances stayed at the table while James and Nonnie cleared away and washed the dishes.

'I'd rather talk in the kitchen,' Frances whispered to Anna. 'So we'll wait till they're finished.'

A short time later Nonnie was sent home with a large basket of food and James went to read the newspapers in the parlour, while Frances settled in her usual chair in the kitchen with Anna sitting nearby.

'I wanted to ask you if Maggie Deagan could come and see me,' she said immediately, but Anna looked doubtful.

'I'm sure she wouldn't hesitate usually,' she said, 'but Mrs Deagan could go at any time and Maggie won't leave her, even to go to church.'

Frances sighed. 'There's no way I can get to her,' she said, 'but I can't stand the idea of Susan suffering if I can ease her pain. I didn't want to draw you into it, Anna, but I'll have to.'

'I don't mind, whatever it is,' Anna said.

'It might even be against the law, I don't know. You remember the stuff I took when you was here before?'

'From the medicine bottle,' Anna said.

'Yes, but it's not from no doctor. I'll tell you what started it. After old Mrs Hargreaves died and I was really running the house, like, for James, this gypsy woman come to the kitchen door one day. She wouldn't have dared while the old one was alive, but I think she was desperate. She was starving and in rags and she had three children with her. To cut a long story short, I brought them in to the fire. I had a pan of barley broth on, so I gave three of them bowls of that and did bread and milk for the baby. I knew James wouldn't shout at me.'

'I should think not,' Anna said indignantly.

'Plenty would,' said Frances, 'but it was terrible, Anna, to see the change in them in a few minutes, just with the fire and the hot broth. The baby was blue with cold, like a poor little skeleton with great big eyes, but the way he gobbled that bread and milk and seemed to fill out before my eyes. I done jam butties and cocoa for the others, then I went and rooted through the old one's clothes. Woollen underclothes and skirts that'd go round them twice, but at least they'd cover them and keep them warm. Her boots fitted them too.'

'I'll bet she was turning in her grave,' Anna said with pleasure.

Frances said, 'I hope so,' and they laughed together before she went on, 'The awful thing is, though, I'd have passed that woman in the street and not worried. It was seeing them on the doorstep when my own luck had just changed and I had the run of the house to do what I liked. Anyhow, I gave her the bag of clothes and a ham shank and a couple of loaves and a jar of jam. I gave her a breadknife too, and five shillings out of my savings, so she went off a happy woman.'

'Did you ever see her again?' Anna asked.

'Often,' said Frances. 'I don't mean she was always here begging. She was a true gypsy and she travelled round with a fair. She married an Englishman and when he died they said, "Let the gorgios keep you," but the English family ignored her because she was a gypsy. She trailed after her own family, hoping they'd take her back, so she was only here odd times. The next time she came she brought her two boys, who'd been trying to earn coppers when she came the first time, and the baby. That baby I thought was about nine months old was two and a half, Anna!'

'What was he like the second time?' Anna asked.

'Still frail. Not walking, but much better. Anyhow, as usual, I've gone rambling on. What I wanted to tell you was, the second time she came she sent the boys to wait outside and she said to me, "You have pain, I know." I did, but not nearly as much as when I was doing a lot of scrubbing, but she brought out a black bottle. "This will ease your pain," she said, "but tell no one. It is a Romany secret."

'I did use it now and again and the pain went in minutes, but I was afraid to use too much. I still had some when the rheumatics started and then I *did* need it. Over the years, whenever I've seen her, she's brought some for me, but I didn't want to let on to James. I used to pour some into a medicine bottle and hide the black bottle, but then I got so I couldn't move round to do it.'

'Why didn't you want James to know?' asked Anna.

'Because I don't know what's in it and I don't want him to get mixed up with the law. That's why I didn't want you to be involved, but if it would ease Susan Deagan I want her to have a bottle.'

'Should I ask Maggie, or should I take the bottle for her to decide?' asked Anna. 'I think the morphine is still helping Mrs Deagan.'

'I don't know what to do,' Frances said. 'I want to help Susan, but I don't want to get Rosa into trouble. She's been so good to me. When I told her I couldn't manage to pour the stuff into a medicine bottle, I don't know how she did it, but the next time she brought it in a dozen medicine bottles.'

She looked so worried that Anna impulsively squeezed her hand and said gently, 'Don't worry any more. I'll have a word with Maggie. I'll just find out if the morphine is still working and if it is there's no need to mention the medicine. I can always come to you for some if it's needed.'

Frances sighed with relief. 'That's a weight off my mind. I've been worried about it ever since I heard about Susan Deagan,' she said.

'She's sleeping most of the time now,' Anna said, 'but when she's awake and the family are there she's always bright and cheerful. Still managing their arrangements too.' She laughed. 'She's arranged for Maggie and Walter to move in permanently and for Norah and her husband to have Maggie's house. I didn't think it would be grand enough for Frank Sutton, but I think that big house is too expensive for him, now that Norah's shop has been sold. It'll keep Norah closer to the family too.'

Frances smiled at Anna. 'I'd love to talk to you all night,' she said, 'but it's not fair to James, I suppose. You'd better go and talk to him, because he won't come and interrupt us. You've made a big difference in him, Anna. He's so much happier since he got friendly with you.'

Anna blushed and stood up. 'I've enjoyed our talk, Frances,' she said. 'I'd like to talk longer, but I'll do as you say.'

She went to the parlour and James sprang to his feet. He had already folded up the newspapers and had been idly staring into the fire and he seemed delighted to see her. It was balm to Anna's spirit to be so warmly welcomed by James and parted with so reluctantly by Frances, but she realised that she would soon have to return home.

She sighed. 'I'll have to go home soon,' she said. 'Time passes so quickly here.'

Darkness had fallen and the curtains had been drawn and the central gaslight lit. The fire burned brightly and the room looked cosy and welcoming and she sighed again.

'But not immediately,' James said, looking so dismayed that she said recklessly, 'I might as well be hung for a sheep as a lamb,' and sat down smiling.

'Is there anything I can do to help, anything at all?' James asked, but Anna said, 'No,' very firmly.

She was ashamed to tell anyone of the sordid scenes about money and was determined that when her father came home she was going to tell him what was happening, no matter what trouble it caused. The refusal of money for the visit to the Jensons' was the last straw, but before that her correspondence with friends in Dublin had almost ceased because she was unable to obtain stamps from her mother, and Dorrie had given up sending them, and there had been numerous other humiliations.

She realised her refusal had been too abrupt, and to soften it she said smiling, 'My main offence is not being Dorrie. My mother misses her so much,' then felt she had been tactless in saying that to James and added, 'I'm sorry to keep talking about her.'

He was putting wood on the fire and with his head bent he said gruffly, 'I suppose you think I'm a fool or worse, still thinking like this about a married woman.'

'Why should I?' Anna said. 'I'm the last person entitled to think that. If people knew...' She sat twisting her hands together in agitation and James gently put his hand on them. 'I can't just forget Eugene!' she burst out. 'Whatever he is, I can't stop loving him just like that.' Tears ran down her face and splashed on their hands and James silently handed her his folded handkerchief.

She wiped her eyes and they sat drawing comfort from each other for a moment, then Anna said, 'You don't know what I'm talking about.'

'I know something has gone wrong between you and Eugene and you've been very unhappy,' James said. 'I felt that was why you were so understanding about me and Dorrie.' Anna was shaking and he very tentatively put his arm around her. She leaned against him, twisting the handkerchief between her fingers.

'I don't know how to explain to you. I suppose you know about such things, but I didn't. Mrs O'Brien explained it by saying that he had two sides to his nature, one was attracted to girls and the other to men. Dorrie thinks he never loved me. He just used me to convince Dr O'Brien, because he wanted to inherit the doctor's money.'

'I don't believe that,' James said firmly. 'I saw how Eugene was with you at the bazaar, and other times when he was home on leave. He wasn't like that madman Dorrie married, but he was a man in love, truly in love.'

'Thank you, James,' Anna said gratefully. 'It means so much to me to believe that. You see, I just can't forget him or stop loving him. I'm sorry for him, because he's tried so hard, but other people have made it difficult for him.'

'That weekend when Dorrie was home – had you just been told this?' James asked. Anna nodded and he said, 'I feel very selfish. You apologised to me for not warning me Dorrie was home and just said you had things on your mind. I wish you'd told me, Anna, or that I'd asked why you were upset.'

'I couldn't have told you then,' Anna said. 'It seems easy now.'

'And what's the position now? Are you still writing to Eugene?' asked James.

'No, it's all over. He's left the Army and he's travelling in Europe with an older man, an MP. It was hard for Dorrie and Michael, because there was a lot of gossip. Michael's mother wanted Dorrie to stay with her in Ireland until it died down, but Michael said she wouldn't miss the Christmas festivities at the depot.'

'That was very disloyal of him,' James said indignantly, but Anna assured him it was not intended as criticism.

'He's worried about Dorrie settling down in married quarters,' she explained.

Soon she decided that she must go, but she felt a sense of release in being able to talk about Eugene and it seemed that James appreciated that she understood his feelings for Dorrie.

They walked back to Westbourne Street in companionable silence and Anna felt fortified against the scene she expected, but the house was peaceful.

'Winnie Deagan has had a daughter,' Nelly announced. 'Two o'clock this afternoon, and Gerald was up here at three like a dog with two tails. You just missed Jim and Kate. They come in for you and your ma decided she'd go instead.'

'Isn't that lovely? And Mrs Deagan will see it!' Anna exclaimed. 'Is Mama still in there?'

'No. They gave her a glass of champagne and she's gone to lay down,' Nelly said with a wink. 'Kate said you was to go in when you came home.'

Anna went immediately, and found Jim, Luke and Walter in the kitchen with beaming smiles. Jim poured her a glass of champagne and Luke told her that Maggie was with her mother and Kate had gone home with Gerald to see Winnie and the baby.

'Bring your glass with you to see Ma,' Jim said, leading the way to his mother's big front bedroom, where she lay propped up in bed.

Anna kissed her and raised her glass. 'A toast to Grandma Deagan,' she said, and Mrs Deagan smiled.

'I never thought I'd live to see the day,' she said. 'A granddaughter!'

Even her voice seemed stronger, Anna thought, and there was some colour in her pale cheeks, but there was a warning glance from Maggie and Anna kissed Mrs Deagan again. 'I'm made up,' she said. 'The best news I've heard for ages,' and she and Jim left the room.

In the kitchen, Kate had just arrived and was talking excitedly about the baby. 'She's beautiful,' she said. 'Quite a lot of dark hair and blue eyes and she seems to be looking about her. She closed her fingers round Gerald's finger and we thought he was going to take off like a balloon. Winnie looked wonderful too, tired, but so happy and pretty.'

'It seems to have done wonders for your mother too,' Anna said.

Kate said eagerly, 'It's made her so happy. Do you know, Anna, the first thing Winnie said when the nurse said it was a girl, was, "She's brought her name with her. Susan." Ma cried when Gerald told her and you know she never cries.'

Anna found her own house still peaceful when she returned. Her aunt was out and her mother still slept as Anna told Nelly about Mrs Deagan and about the new baby and her name.

'Did you have champagne?' Nelly asked.

'Yes. It was nice. I liked it,' Anna said.

'They must've give your ma more than one glass, or else put sumpn in it to get rid of her,' Nelly said. 'She could hardly walk up the stairs and she's slept like the dead ever since.'

'I'll have to get a few bottles in,' Anna said dryly.

The baby was christened a week later. Winnie's sister, Peggy Parsons, was godmother and Jim Deagan godfather to the baby, who was baptised Susan Winifred. Winnie was churched in a ceremony before the baptism, then taken to lie down in the Deagan house. All the family had assembled there and only the godparents were present at the baptism.

Gerald was plainly worried about Winnie. 'The nurse went mad at the idea of her getting up and going out so soon,' he said. 'She said all her patients lie flat on the ninth day, but Winnie was determined.'

'Winnie knows what she's doing,' Maggie said placidly. 'Don't worry.'

Anna was invited in next door and went with the family to Mrs Deagan's bedroom. The old lady lay propped up on snowy pillows, as though on a throne, and the baby, in her christening gown, was laid gently against her thin arm while the family gathered round the bed. Luke had set up a camera and took a photograph of his mother with the baby, then one with Gerald and Winnie at either side of them.

'Two Susan Deagans,' he said with a smile.

'Yes. Not for long, but at least we've seen each other,' his mother said, stroking the baby's soft cheek. 'God has been very good to me.' The baby turned her head and seemed to look up at her grandmother and Gerald lifted her so that his mother could kiss her. 'Susan,' she said. 'I hope she has as happy a life as I've had and as good a family. God bless her.'

Gerald gently lifted the baby away and kissed his mother and when Winnie bent to kiss her Mrs Deagan reached up and put her thin arm around her neck. 'Thank you, girl,' she said. 'I'll die a happy woman.'

Winnie left the room in tears. The others had already quietly moved away and she joined them for a few minutes in the parlour, while the baby was passed round and admired, then Gerald took them both home.

Before she left she said to her sister, 'Tell everyone your news, Peg,' but when Peggy hung her head shyly Winnie announced, 'Peg is going to marry Jimmy O'Dowd at the end of January.'

There were exclamations of pleasure from all the Deagans and Kate said emphatically, 'Good. He's entitled to some happiness and I'm sure you'll both be very happy, Peggy.'

The cab was waiting, so Winnie and Gerald left, but Luke found some champagne and they all drank a toast, first to Peggy and Jimmy, then to Susan Winifred Deagan.

'Will Jimmy move into your house?' asked Luke.

'Yes. He's there most of the time anyway. He has all his meals with us,' Peggy said. 'He'll sell his own house.'

'It depends which house would get the better price,' Norah's husband, Frank, said.

Nobody answered and the conversation went on. It was Frank's only contribution all day and Anna felt sadly that Mrs Deagan was right. Norah had made a bad mistake in marrying him.

The group soon dispersed, as Mrs Deagan was asleep. She slept for most of the time, until Christmas Day, when she rallied and entertained all the family in her bedroom.

Anna saw her briefly and felt that when she kissed her goodnight it was for the last time. The dying woman held her hand and whispered, 'You're a good girl, Anna, and you'll soon have the happiness you deserve. God's ways are not ours, but He has a plan for all of us. God bless you girl.'

At two o'clock in the morning, as Maggie, as always, watched at her mother's bedside, she saw a slight change and called the others, and with her family around her, Susan Deagan gently slipped from life to death.

Afterwards, Maggie collapsed completely, but the others made all the arrangements. These were many and complex because, added to the high regard for Mrs Deagan herself, the numerous members of her family were well known and well liked and many people wished to show their respect and sympathy for them in what they knew was a time of grievous loss.

Mrs Furlong spent most of her time at the parlour window, fuming as she watched the numerous callers and the quantity of wreaths being delivered next door. 'Ridiculous,' she seethed. 'There's more fuss being made than for our dear Queen when she died in 1901.'

Anna had been sitting with her and working on the household mending, but she stood up and walked out.

She was more courageous now in dealing with her mother, partly because of her increasing disgust with her, and partly because her friendship with James and his support made her feel stronger. She had been to his house again once after a confraternity meeting and once for Sunday tea.

She felt increasingly at home there and comfortable in talking to James. Frances always welcomed her warmly and was delighted to hear of Susan's grandchild and the happiness she had brought, and she was interested to hear of the proposed marriage between Peggy Parsons and Jimmy O'Dowd.

'Poor Jimmy. He was tricked into that marriage with Olive, but he did the honourable thing and wasted half his life on it. Him and Peggy'll be happy and her old dad'll be made up to have Jimmy living there. This is what I miss, Anna, now I can't get out. All the bits of news. I ask James and he tells me what the Archbishop's been doing! Men!'

Anna was invited to Sunday tea again on the last Sunday in January, but her mother objected. 'No, I need you here,' she said. 'I have two friends coming to tea and I need you to hand round cakes and sandwiches and make fresh tea when we need it.'

Before Anna could speak, her Aunt Clara, who was sitting on a sofa reading, raised her head. She never spoke directly to her sister-in-law now and she said calmly to Anna, 'I should go if I were you, Anna. Your mother is quite capable of handing round a cake basket and Nelly can make fresh tea for them. You should accept the invitation.'

It was ludicrous, Anna thought, to see her mother trying to decide how to react. Whether with hysterics, or the injured little woman with the world against her, or the matriarch demanding obedience, while she was being watched sardonically by Anna and Clara.

Her moment passed and she could only say weakly, 'Wait until my husband hears of this. My own daughter encouraged to defy me in my own home.' She stood up and marched out, pausing in the hall to demand tea and aspirins from Nelly, and went upstairs.

Clara said abruptly, 'I don't know where you go, Anna, and I don't want to know, but if you have a chance of happiness, take it. Don't let your mother spoil it. You've never asked me why I don't speak to her, but I'll tell you. I was friendly with a widower and he asked me to marry him. I was undecided. I was set in my ways, I thought, and so was he, but then we would be company for each other in our old age.'

Anna said nothing and Clara sat looking into the fire. 'He had a very jealous married daughter. He said nothing to her and I said nothing here until we decided, but one of your mother's gossips ferreted it out. Your mother took it on herself to go and see the daughter and cause trouble. I might not have married him anyway, Anna, but it was our decision, nothing to do with your mother. Don't let her do the same thing to you.'

'I'm so sorry, Aunt Clara,' Anna stammered.

Clara shrugged. 'These things happen,' she said, then in the same unemotional tone, 'but hell will freeze over before I speak to her again.' Then she too left the room.

There were many things Anna would have liked to ask her aunt, but she had a lot to think about with what she had already been told. What an evil woman her mother was. Anna wondered whether she had inherited any of her mother's traits and decided to ask Dr O'Brien about heredity. This reminded her that she had been remiss lately in visiting the O'Briens, although she still saw them at church.

The last time she had seen Dr O'Brien he said heartily, 'I'm glad to see that you and young Hargreaves are friendly, Anna. He doesn't find it easy to mix.'

'Neither do I, doctor,' Anna said ruefully, 'although I didn't realise it while Dorrie and Isabel were there to break the ice for me.'

'Aye, well, we're all different,' the doctor said vaguely, before darting off to scold a woman whom he had told to stay in bed.

I wonder if anyone else has noticed? Anna thought now. She had written to Dorrie to tell her all the news about the Deagans and about Peggy Parsons' wedding, but she had never mentioned James or her visits to his house.

Dorrie seemed to have settled down and been very popular at the Christmas festivities and she said nothing about any gossip about Eugene. She did, however, enclose a newspaper cutting which read 'Mr Robert Norton Carpenter MP has been enjoying the sunshine of Saint Tropez with his companion, Mr Eugene D'Arcy, formerly of the Brigade of Guards. Mr Norton Carpenter has resigned his seat.'

Anna was alone when she opened the letter and simply threw the cutting in the fire and said nothing about it when she replied to her sister.

Anna said no more to her mother about her invitation, but

set off on Sunday the twenty-seventh of January. It was bitterly cold and wet and she was glad to see James waiting at the corner of Westbourne Street with a large umbrella. They fought their way up Eastbourne Street in the teeth of a gale and fell thankfully into the warmth and peace of James's house.

James took their wet outer clothes and hung them up and Frances welcomed Anna. 'Come and sit by the kitchen fire and get your breath back and get warm,' she said. 'The tea's ready. I thought it was a day for pea soup.'

'Sounds just right,' Anna said.

She was surprised to see Frances moving about, although with difficulty, and said so, but Frances winked at her. 'I'm keeping moving 'cos once I sit down I'll stiffen up,' she said. 'It's all ready, James.'

They went into the dining room, where there was a large tureen of pea soup on the table and an enormous meat plate filled with slices of home-cooked ham.

'This pea soup is wonderful, heavenly,' Anna said. 'No wonder you're proud of it. I could live on it.' They all laughed and suddenly Anna had a strange feeling. Could this really be her, Anna Furlong, always so stiff and reserved, finding it impossible to respond to people? It must be this house, she decided.

After the meal was cleared away, she and James went into the parlour, where a wood fire burned brightly, the curtains were drawn and the gaslight lit. James sat beside her on a sofa drawn up near to the fire.

Anna had already thanked Frances, but she thanked James quietly for his invitation and for the delicious meal.

'No, I'm in your debt for coming,' he said. 'I've looked forward to this all week, Anna.'

'So have I,' she said.

He coughed and stirred the fire, then said nervously, 'I've

been thinking, Anna. Since we talked about our feelings . . . we both – er – Dorrie and Eugene . . .' He was rubbing his thumb against his forefinger and blushing and stammering, but with a visible effort he spoke more coherently.

'You know about Dorrie, but I admire and respect you, Anna, and feel deep affection for you. We get on so well and I enjoy your company. I don't expect you to feel the same about me and I know how you feel about Eugene, but, well, would you consider marrying me?'

Astonishment kept Anna silent for a moment and James went on, 'When I came back here after walking you home the last time you visited, the house seemed so empty without you, and I thought of you going to where you were not happy and this idea seemed so sensible. Now you must think I'm mad.'

'You're not asking me out of pity, I hope,' Anna said, drawing back. 'I'm not happy at home, but I can manage that situation.'

'Anything but that!' he exclaimed. 'I'm sorry. I'm doing this very badly. It's presumptuous of me to ask any girl to marry me, let alone a lovely girl like you, but we seem to have become friends. I'm a dull dog, though. I'll never get very far in my job or do anything very interesting, but I'd do my best to make you happy, Anna.'

'You have a very low opinion of yourself,' Anna said gently.

He went on quietly, 'I think I should tell you honestly what you'd be taking on. I've had fits of melancholia for years, although I think I'm over them now. Dr O'Brien has helped me a lot. I'm a poor mixer. Never know what to say to people, but somehow, Anna, I'm different when I'm with you.' He smiled. 'You unlock my tongue.'

'That's strange!' Anna exclaimed. 'It was only today, sitting at the table, when I was enthusing about the pea soup, that I suddenly thought, Could it really be me talking like that? I'm

271

usually so stiff and I find it hard to say pleasant things. Although I say sarcastic ones easily enough,' she added ruefully. 'I decided the house cast a spell on me, but now I realise it's you. We must be good for each other.'

'So will you marry me?' James said anxiously, and when she blushed and whispered, 'Yes,' he put his arms around her and kissed her.

She said quietly but firmly, 'I know that there are practical reasons for this marriage, but I wouldn't marry you, James, if I didn't have a genuine liking and respect for you.'

'I know, Anna,' he said, 'and I'm very grateful that you feel that way. I've told you how I feel about you, and I think it's a good basis for a companionable marriage.'

He stood up and poured two glassfuls of sherry and brought one to her. 'I think we should pledge our troth,' he said with a grin, and they clinked glasses and drank.

They spent the rest of the evening discussing details, deciding to tell nobody until Captain Furlong returned in about six weeks' time, when James would go to see him.

'What about Frances?' James said.

Anna replied, 'I'd love to tell her, and she has a right to know, but she has visitors and it might be very hard for her to keep it to herself.'

She told James about her aunt's warning and the reason for it, because she was determined to keep no secrets from him. Although he said nothing he was shocked at this insight into her mother's character and determined to have Anna away from her as soon as possible.

Frances was in bed when Anna left and she whispered, 'Just as well. She'd guess right away if she saw us.' For the sober, companionable marriage they were planning, they both seemed remarkably happy.

As they walked to Westbourne Street James said, 'I keep

thinking there'll be no more of these snatched meetings. You going to where you're not appreciated and me going back to a house that seems so empty without you. I'm looking forward to you being there when I come home from the office and being able to be with you all the time, except at night, of course, when you'll have your own room.'

Anna smiled to herself, thinking that he had worked this reassurance in very neatly, after a long preamble. 'I love your house,' she said. 'I look forward to living there, although you know I wouldn't marry you just for that, James.'

'I know,' he said. 'We understand each other, Anna, and that is the best thing of all.'

When they drew near her home he put his arms around her and kissed her. 'I'll do my best to make you happy, Anna,' he said. 'I know it won't be the romantic marriage that girls like, but we *can* have a *good* marriage.'

'And I'll try to make you happy, James,' she whispered. 'I know how you feel about Dorrie and you know about Eugene, but we *can* have a good marriage, I'm sure, because we like and respect each other.'

He kissed her again and she went into the house, wondering whether they were both trying too hard to reassure each other.

Nelly had opened the door to her and indicated that her mother and aunt were still in the parlour, but Anna followed her to the kitchen. 'How has it been?' she whispered.

'She's had two of her cronies here and she was carrying on sumpn shockin'. Calling you for everything to them. She's dying to know where you go, so watch out,' warned Nelly.

'I'll have to go in and face it,' Anna said and, summoning up her courage, she went and greeted her mother and aunt. Her mother immediately began a tirade about how ashamed she had been for her friends to know the selfish and ungrateful daughter she was burdened with. How sad and unfair it was that the daughter she really cared for and who cared for her was far away in London, and how unlikely it was that a girl as gauche and plain as Anna would ever be taken off her hands.

Anna stood meekly, letting the abuse wash over her, trying to hold fast to the thought that she would soon be married and away, but already doubts had begun to creep in.

At last she was free to go to her room and think about the events of the day. Was it wise, she wondered, for her and James to marry, knowing that both their hearts had been given elsewhere? She took the photograph of Eugene from her drawer and looked at his beloved face. I'll always love him, she thought, no matter what he is or what he's done, but I do feel affection for James.

She thought of his kindness and his humility, and how bravely he had overcome his terrible childhood. He was sensitive to other people's feelings too, she thought, remembering how he had carefully made it clear that they would have separate bedrooms. I hadn't even thought of that side of things, but it might have been worrying me.

I'll be safe with him, she decided, and I'll be happy in that lovely house with people who seem to like me. Not like here, where I've always been crushed, and disliked even more since Dorrie went.

Dorrie! What would Dorrie say? She still thought of James as one of her admirers. What would she say when she heard that Anna was to marry him? The old Dorrie would have been happy for her, but her sister was so different now. I can't tell her until James has spoken to Father, Anna thought.

And Dr and Mrs O'Brien, what would they think? Probably that she was very fickle to forget Eugene so easily, but then she remembered that they were unaware of how deeply she loved Eugene. If only the next few months were over and she was married and safe with James.

Chapter Seventeen

Although Anna and James had decided to say nothing until James had asked Captain Furlong for permission to marry Anna, it was a matter of courtesy, not a legal necessity. They knew that they were free to marry at any time and went ahead with their plans, James even making enquiries about a special licence.

Anna and Dorrie had had accounts at the same exclusive shop as their mother, arranged by Captain Furlong, but his wife had cancelled Anna's at the same time as Dorrie's and said that in future Anna's purchases would go on her bills. This meant it was impossible for her to make a trousseau, no matter how modest, but she reflected ruefully that only she would know how plain and unbridelike her underclothes and nightdresses would be. They would be hidden in the decent obscurity of her own bedroom.

In the week following their engagement, she saw James only once, at church, and only briefly as they were joined by Kate Deagan. She told them of the changes that were taking place in the Deagan house.

'You knew Walter and Maggie were coming to live in our house, didn't you?' she said. 'And Norah and Frank are taking over their little house. Norah'll be nearer the family and it's as much as they can afford, really.'

'It's a good plan,' Anna agreed. 'Walter's very easygoing, isn't he?'

'Yes. He's one of the best. Ma thought the world of him,' Kate said with a sigh. 'I'll be leaving soon, to work in London.'

'In London!' Anna exclaimed.

'Yes, for the same firm. They've asked me before, but I wouldn't go while Ma was here. I'll carry on with my Suffragist work there, nearer the heart of things. I wish you'd take it up, Anna. I thought I'd convinced you.'

'You had,' Anna said emphatically. 'It was just, er, practical difficulties. I might be able to do it now.' She glanced at James and he smiled at her.

'What about Luke and Jim?' he said. 'They'll still live at home, I suppose.'

'Yes, but they're thinking of setting up their own printing business. They've both been at Worrall's for years, since they were apprenticed, and it's a good solid old firm, but they'd like to try out some new ideas.'

'Why not?' said James. 'As master printers they'll never be out of work.'

'You must think we've only been waiting for Ma to go to do all these things, Mr Hargreaves!' Kate exclaimed.

'Oh no, but doing things must help you to bear losing her,' he said kindly.

'Yes, indeed,' said Kate. She linked her arm through Anna's and turned away and Anna had to turn with her. 'Goodbye, Mr Hargreaves,' Kate said, and Anna looked back smiling as James raised his hat and walked away.

'What a nice, understanding man he is!' Kate exclaimed, and Anna was tempted to confide in her, but Kate spoke of the new baby and the moment passed.

Mrs Furlong was now even more unpleasant to Anna and frustrated any attempt she made to leave the house, and Anna's longing to confide in someone grew. She could think of nothing but James's proposal. Finally she decided to write to Isabel, whom she knew would be discreet.

'Dear Isabel,' she wrote, 'You will find this a surprising

letter. In some ways I can't believe myself that this has happened. You know that for some time James Hargreaves and I have walked to and from church together, because he was coming down from his house as I reached the corner of Eastbourne and Westbourne Street.

'I went back to his house after a confraternity meeting. Frances O'Neill, his housekeeper, was there and I've been to tea several times and been made very welcome by James and Frances. Last Sunday he asked me to marry him. I know that Dorrie is his real love and he knows about Eugene, but they are both impossible dreams, so we have decided to marry for companionship.

'He says he feels respect and deep affection for me, and I feel the same for him. You know, Isabel, we wouldn't consider marriage otherwise. We have not told anyone. We are waiting until Father comes home in a month's time and James can ask his permission, but I know you will keep our secret.

'I miss you so much, Isabel, and wish I could see you. I miss your mother and the boys too, and little Wilma, and hope you are all happy. With much love, Anna.'

As a postscript she wrote, 'I haven't yet told Dorrie. Wonder what she will think?'

Mrs Furlong handed over the stamp for Isabel's letter with a sly smile which made Anna uneasy, but she posted the letter herself and knew her mother had no opportunity to read it.

Two days later a letter arrived from Isabel and Nelly, warned by Anna, hid it under her apron before putting the letters by Mrs Furlong's sofa.

Isabel had written warmly but discreetly, telling Anna that her letter had made her very happy and thanking her for her good wishes. 'I send mine to you also, dearest Anna,' she wrote, 'and wish you every happiness. We are happy, but I miss good friends in Liverpool. There are very few young men here and none as good as those we knew, the Deagans and James Hargreaves, men of integrity that we could respect and admire. The village men are hobbledehoys by comparison. My uncle has offered to take me to Liverpool when he goes on business and I am quite desperate to see you again so something will be arranged soon. Fondest love and good wishes, dearest Anna, Isabel.'

Have I ever told Isabel about Mama reading my letters, or has she just guessed? Anna wondered. How carefully she had written, but with warmth and approval to be read between the lines which Anna found gave her comfort and strength.

Her mother had not invited any visitors the following Sunday, so Anna expected no opposition when she said that she was going out. She was quite unprepared for her mother's reaction when, subduing her happiness, she said in a colourless voice, 'I'm going now, Mama. I won't be late.'

Her mother was, as usual, reclining on her sofa, but she sat bolt upright and her head came forward like a cobra about to strike. With all the venom of the deadly snake she hissed, 'Going to chase after your sister's leavings, are you?' When Anna jerked back, as though from a blow, she went on, 'Don't think I don't know where you go. No wonder you're ashamed. A fool that Dorrie wouldn't have wiped her feet on, but I suppose he thinks he'll hear about her through you. He wouldn't want to see you for your own sake, not even a gawk like that. No man has ever looked twice at you, plain, gawky—' but Anna had fled from the room and the house.

She was rushing along Westbourne Street, blinded by tears, when she realised that James, who had come to meet her, had taken her arm. 'What's happened, Anna? What's upset you?' he asked anxiously.

'Mama knows,' she gasped. 'She knows I go to your house.'

'Does she know about our plans to marry?' he asked.

'I don't think so,' Anna said, weeping afresh as she thought of the words 'chasing her sister's leavings'.

He handed her a large white handkerchief and said firmly, 'We won't talk any more about it until we get home. Frances seems a bit better today and she's looking forward to the summer. It's like a spring day today, isn't it, although it's only February?'

Anna agreed and managed to compose herself before they went in to Frances, but after greeting her they went immediately to the parlour to talk.

Anna gave James an edited version of her mother's remarks and told him that someone must have spied on her to find out where she went.

'But you are sure they don't know about our plans to marry?' James said.

Anna shook her head. 'Not yet,' she said.

'I don't see any point in keeping them secret any longer though,' James said. 'Will your father get a letter if it's written now?'

'Yes, I think so,' said Anna. 'But what about Frances?'

'Yes. I think we should tell Frances right away,' said James. 'Then we can both write to your father. I intend to suggest Dr O'Brien and Fr Kavanagh or Fr Ratcliffe to vouch for me, so suppose we go and see the O'Briens later?'

'Yes, I'm sure they'll give us good advice,' Anna said.

Frances was pleased, but not surprised by their news and told them she had been praying for it. After their tea they both wrote to Anna's father then walked down to see the O'Briens, who were both delighted to hear of their plan to marry.

'Excellent! Excellent!' Dr O'Brien exclaimed. 'Couldn't have planned better myself. You'll do perfectly together.'

James glanced at Anna, then said awkwardly, 'We don't want to deceive you. We both know we've er – committed our

– our hearts elsewhere, but I respect and admire Anna and she says she feels the same, so we're marrying for companionship. But we wouldn't marry unless we felt sincere affection for each other.' He turned to Anna. 'I haven't explained that well, have I?' he said.

'Yes you have. Very clearly,' she said gently.

'You've convinced me even more that you're doing the right thing!' Dr O'Brien said delightedly. 'And as for these dream people, you'll probably forget them when you're both leading happier lives. Won't need them.'

'You're on your hobby-horse, Paddy,' Mrs O'Brien said, laughing. 'He's always delving into people's minds. Asking about their dreams.'

'Now don't mock, my dear,' Dr O'Brien protested. 'It's a very interesting subject. The coming thing.'

'I've seen the book you spoke of mentioned in newspapers, doctor,' James said. 'By Dr Freud, wasn't it?'

'*Have* you indeed?' the doctor said eagerly, and Mrs O'Brien said to Anna, 'We'll get no sense out of them now. Let's go and have a cup of tea in my room, Anna, and a good talk.'

They went to the small parlour and Anna told Mrs O'Brien everything that had happened, from first walking home from church with James. 'He's still in love with Dorrie, but of course it's hopeless and I know you'll think this strange, but I can't forget Eugene,' she said.

'So it's Dorrie and Eugene, these dream people, as Paddy calls them,' said Mrs O'Brien. 'Well, you and James are much better off with each other. Dorrie's a sweet-natured girl, but you know we both always cared much more for you, Anna. She was lightweight and you were always much better value.'

'Oh, no. Dorrie was always popular with everyone and she could have married anyone, but she was lucky that she and Michael met and fell in love,' Anna protested.

'They are certainly well matched,' Mrs O'Brien conceded, 'but I think you and James will be very happy together. I know you want to remember the pleasant side of Eugene, but don't forget, Anna, there was another side to him. James would never hurt you as he did.'

'I know that,' Anna said quietly.

Changing the subject, Mrs O'Brien asked how long it would be before her father's return. 'I asked at the shipping office and they said a month approximately, so it won't be long,' Anna said. 'I can bear with Mama until then.'

'You are very welcome to stay here, Anna, until your father's return or until your wedding,' Mrs O'Brien said. 'You know that, don't you?'

'Thank you. It's very kind of you, but I think Father might be hurt,' Anna said. 'I'll be all right.'

'Well, bear it in mind,' Mrs O'Brien said, smiling.

Soon afterwards Anna and James left to walk to Westbourne Street and Anna told him of Mrs O'Brien's offer. 'She means it too,' she said. 'It's not just a vague suggestion.'

James insisted on coming in with her to see her mother. 'It's only eight o'clock,' he said, 'and she has brought me into it herself,' so Anna agreed.

Her mother and aunt were in the parlour, her mother in her usual seat on the sofa.

Anna introduced James to Nelly in the hall, so that her mother and aunt were forewarned when she and James went into the parlour.

'Mama, this is James Hargreaves,' she announced, and to James, 'My mother, Mrs Furlong.'

James bowed and said, 'How do you do,' but Mrs Furlong only gaped at him, then Anna introduced him to her aunt. Clara shook hands with James and moved papers from a chair so that they could sit down.

Mrs Furlong was still silent and James leaned forward and said pleasantly, 'I've come in to see you to tell you that Anna and I are planning to marry as soon as possible. We became engaged two weeks ago, but we intended to say nothing until I could see Captain Furlong and ask his permission as a matter of courtesy.'

'He won't give it,' Mrs Furlong burst out. 'I can tell you that now. The impudence! Sly, underhand, deceitful.' She fell back, gasping and passing smelling salts under her nose.

James said calmly, 'As I said, it was a matter of courtesy, as we are both legally free to marry whenever we want. I'm sure the Captain would have preferred that arrangement, but as you have had Anna followed to my house our hands have been forced.'

'What do you mean?' Mrs Furlong shrieked.

'I mean that now our engagement must be announced before I have the opportunity of speaking to Anna's father, so that it's not the subject of gossip and innuendo by the sort of people who sneak around following people,' he said.

'I think you're very wise,' Clara said, and her sister-in-law shot her a venomous look.

'Her opinion counts for nothing,' she said. 'She'll chase anyone's leavings, like her niece.'

James looked at her with dislike. 'I can see what Anna has had to bear,' he said. 'When Anna came to tea with me my housekeeper, Frances O'Neill, was always present. I have too much respect for Anna to suggest anything that might compromise her.'

'Why wasn't I told? Because she knew I'd forbid it, that's why,' Mrs Furlong shrieked. 'Disgracing our family. What are you?'

'I gave Dr O'Brien as one of my references when I wrote to your husband, so we've been to see the O'Briens before coming here,' James said. 'Mrs O'Brien has offered to have Anna to stay with her until her father returns or until our wedding, but Anna is reluctant to hurt her father. If you make her life intolerable, though, I'll insist that she accepts Mrs O'Brien's invitation and explain why to Captain Furlong.'

Mrs Furlong seemed unable to speak, spluttering and gasping, but Clara said to James, 'Don't worry, I'll have a lot to tell my brother. Don't think he'd approve of all this creeping about following people. He's an honourable man.'

Mrs Furlong's face was red and she was glaring at Anna and James, but everyone ignored her, and James turned to Anna. 'Will you be all right, love?' he said quietly, and she nodded. They both stood up and James shook hands again with Clara and wished her well, then, saying curtly to Mrs Furlong, 'Goodnight,' he went out of the room, followed by Anna.

'I'd no idea you could be so forceful,' she said as they stood in the hall. 'Mama will never recover.'

'I hope you didn't think I was too rude,' he said, 'but if there's one thing I've learned, Anna, it's that the only way to treat a bully is to stand up to them. Fight fire with fire.'

Anna sighed. 'Mama's learned a great deal tonight, I think,' she said. 'I wish I'd had more courage in the past.'

James put his arms round her and kissed her. 'You were simply too nice to deal with that, but you must tell me, Anna, if your mother makes you unhappy. I'd no idea that you had so much to endure. Dr O'Brien told me about her and the reasons for her behaviour and I can feel sorry for her, but I can't bear to think of you being treated like that.'

'It's not too bad now,' Anna said, wondering what Dr O'Brien had told James. 'Aunt Clara is on my side.'

James left and Anna went up to bed feeling that their relationship had moved on a great deal since the morning.

The next day there was a bulky letter from Dorrie. Often her letters were scanty, but occasionally she wrote to Anna at length, and as soon as her tasks were done Anna took the letter to her room to read it in peace.

Since she moved to Caterham, Dorrie had sometimes grumbled about other women or conditions in married quarters, but never about Michael, and although she had recently made occasional critical comments about him or his family Anna was shocked by what she read. This letter had been written when Dorrie was bitterly angry with her husband and she poured out all her grievances.

'Dear Anna,' she wrote, 'I have just had a furious row with Michael and I'm sure you will agree that I am in the right and have every reason to be angry. I didn't have a chance to tell you, when we came back from Ireland, how annoyed I was by the way he was always having long talks with his mother and she was telling him what to do. His father is always sweet to me, but Michael talked to him too.

'I know now it was about his future, *but it's my life too* and he should have been discussing it with *me*. He has just informed me that he is leaving the Army, his term is up, or something, and he doesn't intend to re-sign. I told him I had no intention of being buried alive on the Irish farm, being bossed about by his mother and he made a nasty remark about Mrs Rafferty, which really made me lose my temper. He knows she's my best friend.

'He didn't take any notice of what I said, only said he has made arrangements to go into partnership with a friend and we will go to live in this place in London where he took me a few months ago. The slyness! He said nothing then. I said I liked the place, but I'd no idea he was planning to dump me there. I was hysterical and told him I was happy as I was, and he said, "Too happy. That's why we're going," so he admits he doesn't want me to be happy. I would leave him, Anna, if I had anywhere to go. At least, thanks to Mrs Rafferty, we haven't any children. Mama would welcome me home, but Father would never allow it. I see now why you went on about women running their own lives. Not being ruled by fathers and husbands. Anna, I'm so unhappy. Your loving sister, Dorrie.'

Anna sat holding the letter, shocked and dismayed by the raw unhappiness it displayed. Dorrie was always dramatic, but in the details and in the abrupt, despairing ending there was real misery and sadness. She could feel only sympathy for Dorrie and anger at the callous way her life had been disrupted.

How could Michael treat her like this? He had seemed so truly in love with Dorrie, and to want only her happiness. How could he have changed so quickly into the overbearing husband Dorrie described?

Anna tried to remember everything that had happened on their last visit. Michael had changed, she had thought, but only to become more mature. She also remembered that he had been worried about Mrs Rafferty's influence over Dorrie. Perhaps he had consulted his mother, but this was too drastic a solution, surely.

She read the letter again, pleased that Dorrie had turned to her for comfort, but realising that it placed her in a dilemma. She had planned to write to tell Dorrie of her engagement, but now Dorrie needed a loving, comforting letter about her own troubles.

Finally she wrote a letter sympathising with Dorrie, but suggesting that as she had dreaded going to married quarters yet been happy there, perhaps the next move would have the same happy ending. She made no criticism of Michael, thinking that she needed to know more before blaming him. As a postscript, she wrote that she had some news, but would save it until the next letter.

Anna found that her mother seemed to avoid her during the next few days, but Clara told her that she approved of the engagement and of James and that she would tell her brother so.

'I haven't seen Mr Hargreaves for some time,' she said. 'Not since I started going to eight o'clock Mass on Sundays. I used to see him with his mother, but he looks more personable now. You seem to have found a man who will look after you. Stand up for you.'

'I was surprised,' Anna admitted, 'because he's usually very diffident.'

'Perhaps he's one of those people who can stand up for others, but not for themselves,' Clara said. 'Anyway, you'll be well out of here, away from her, although I'll miss you.'

'Thank you, Aunt,' Anna said, thinking of the years she and Dorrie had suffered from Clara's sharp tongue. Her mother had certainly made a bitter enemy of her sister-in-law and changed her attitude to her niece too.

There was another letter for Anna from Dorrie, evidently written before she received Anna's letter, but after receiving one from her mother.

'Mama tells me you are to marry James Hargreaves,' she wrote. 'I just can't believe that you would do such a thing. You must know that he is still in love with me. Mrs Rafferty says he will be marrying you for a housekeeper and you will marry him for a home, but I can't believe you would descend so low. Mama says you have been chasing him for months, yet you've said nothing to me. I feel that now I can't trust anybody and I'm only sorry I told you so much of my affairs. Dorrie.'

Anna had opened the letter eagerly and its contents were like a blow. She rushed to the bathroom and locked herself in to weep in private. I might have known, she thought, that Mama would waste no time, but for Dorrie to write like this!

And to discuss us with Mrs Rafferty! She was shaken by anger and felt as though a dirty finger had touched her relationship with James, then she rinsed her face with cold water and crushed the letter in her pocket.

Lifting her head proudly, she walked downstairs, determined that no one would see that she had been hurt. Perhaps Michael has had more to put up with than we know and he's doing the right thing, she thought, in taking Dorrie from that circle.

For the rest of the day she worked in the house, saying as little as possible, although it was necessary for her to speak to her mother as her aunt would still not speak directly to her. She longed as never before for her father's return.

She said nothing to James which would destroy his illusions about Dorrie, but she sent no reply to the letter and received none from Dorrie in reply to her attempt to comfort her.

She wrote to Isabel, telling her of all that had happened and that her engagement to James could not wait until her father's return. 'We have both written to Father, but you know only too well how chancy letters are to men at sea. I don't want to hurt Father, but if necessary I will tell him how my hand was forced. I think Father will like James. Do, please, write quite freely to me, Isabel. Mama is very subdued at present. Much love to all the family, Anna.'

It was true that Mrs Furlong had been very quiet since her encounter with James, and she and Anna spoke to each other only when necessary. Two of her cronies came to visit one afternoon and Nelly served tea and cakes to them, but Anna took the opportunity to go to the Deagan house.

She knew that the cronies would be fully primed with gossip which would spread round the parish like wildfire, so she wanted her friends to hear her news from her.

Maggie was out, but Jim opened the door and they went

287

into the kitchen, where he made tea. 'I'm off today. Been signing papers for the new premises and making various arrangements,' he said. 'How are you, Anna?'

Anna always found it easy to talk to Jim and he listened approvingly as she told him of her proposed wedding.

'I'm very pleased and relieved to hear it, Anna,' he said. 'I've always liked and respected James Hargreaves. He's survived a rotten childhood and he deserves some happiness if anyone does. You both do, and I know you'll make each other happy.'

'But, Jim, it won't be an ordinary marriage,' Anna said. 'Not romantic. It's for companionship, but we wouldn't marry if we didn't like and respect each other. You see, we both love other people in that romantic way, but marriage to them is impossible.'

'People come to marriage in various ways, Anna,' Jim said gently. 'There are very few like Dorrie and Michael, but most people are happy. Liking and respect is the best basis for a good marriage, I think.'

Anna looked down at her clasped hands and said in a low voice, 'Dorrie's friend said James was marrying for a housekeeper and I was marrying for a home, but that's not true, honestly, Jim.'

'That was a nasty remark!' Jim exclaimed. 'Which friend was this?'

'Nobody here,' Anna said. 'A friend in the married quarters, and Dorrie told me in her letter.'

'I'm surprised at Dorrie,' Jim said indignantly, 'and I think she should be more selective in her friends.'

'She might have been angry because James was in love with her. Still is,' Anna said, 'and I am with Eugene, but we both know they are just impossible dreams.'

'You'll probably both forget them when you're married.

Perhaps you needed someone to dream about while you were so unhappy,' Jim said, smiling at her.

'That's what Dr O'Brien said!' Anna exclaimed.

'He always hits the nail on the head,' Jim laughed. 'I don't think I'd mention them to anyone else if I were you, Anna. Just concentrate on being happy with James.'

There was a sound at the door and Maggie came into the kitchen. Jim said immediately, 'Anna came to give us some good news, Mag. She's going to marry James Hargreaves.'

Maggie dropped her basket on the table and flung her arms round Anna. 'I'm made up,' she said, 'and Ma would have been too. He's a real good man. He carried my basket for me one day and I was upset about Ma so I couldn't speak, but I didn't feel a bit awkward with him.'

'He's very well regarded in the parish, Anna, and everyone will be pleased that he's getting such a good wife in you,' Jim said. 'And all your friends will be delighted with James too. I'm sure you'll both be very happy.'

'Have you fixed the date?' Maggie asked, but Anna explained about waiting until her father came home.

When she returned next door she felt pleased and encouraged by the way her news had been received, but she reflected sadly that, though friends might rejoice, her mother and her sister did not wish her and James well.

On the following Sunday, which was cold but bright, James asked Anna to look at a house he had seen. Many wealthy merchants had built houses on the brow of the hill, and many smaller houses had also been built when Everton had been regarded as a healthy place to live because of the fresh breezes from the River Mersey.

Many of the mansions had been demolished and cottage property built on the site, but several houses had survived. The one James had found was a Georgian-type house set in large gardens and Anna loved it immediately.

'I only rented the present house, but I thought when I married I would buy a house so that my wife could choose it and could furnish it as she wished,' he said, but then he added honestly, 'I've got to tell you the truth, Anna. It was Frances who advised me. I'd still be stuck in that mausoleum if it wasn't for her.'

James had the keys and they looked over the house, which was named Rosemount, delighting in the size and lightness of the rooms. There was dark paint everywhere, but they decided that it would be replaced with white and made many plans, the most important being a bedroom for Frances. It was more and more difficult for her to climb stairs, but there was a bright morning room looking out on to a secluded part of the garden which Anna decided would be perfect for her bedroom.

'We'll keep it as a surprise until it's all ready for her,' James suggested, but Anna shook her head.

'She may be worrying about the stairs in a new house and how she'll manage them. I think we should tell her, James, so she can look forward to the move.'

'Whatever you think best,' he agreed.

Anna said eagerly, 'I do hope we can get this house. I'll be really disappointed if we don't. I like it so much.'

'Don't worry,' James said. 'I can pay cash for it if necessary. You know, with the money my mother saved and the sale of the house and furniture and my own savings, I now have thirteen hundred pounds in the bank, Anna. I've got all these details ready for your father, but really you're the one most affected and I should be telling you.'

'Thank you. That's an unusual point of view. Most men seem to think women are too stupid to understand money, even those who do wonders with their housekeeping.'

'Do I hear the voice of a suffragette?' James teased her, but she retorted, 'No, a suffragist. I don't believe in violence. Kate tried to recruit me years ago. I agreed with her arguments, but I couldn't join at the time. Oh, look at that bird. What is it?'

'I don't know,' James said, 'but I'm sure we'll see many we don't know in these gardens.'

Twilight was falling, so they went home to tell Frances about the house and the wildlife. She wept when Anna described the room they had earmarked for her bedroom.

'I was worried,' she admitted. 'I can just about manage these stairs, but bigger ones in a new house! It's been on my mind.'

'I'm going to see the lawyer in my lunch hour,' James said. 'Get things moving. I don't see any difficulty.'

The next day, when he told Henry Mortimer of his plans, his friend warned him not to be too enthusiastic about the house. 'Get a survey done and be doubtful about a few things,' he said. 'That's only the asking price. You make an offer below that.'

'Who's the vendor? Who owns it?' asked another man.

'An old lady lived alone there for many years,' James said. 'A clerk in the agent's office told me she died without making a will and she had no relatives, so the money will go to the Crown, he said.'

'That was a bit indiscreet of him,' Henry said, laughing. 'Well, you need have no qualms about beating them down and they won't be pushing for a higher price as they would for a client. Say you think you saw dry rot and other signs of neglect.'

James took their advice and was more cautious in his approach than he would have been. A survey was arranged and the surveyor found dry rot round the kitchen door, some defects in the guttering, and other small items, but basically a sound, well-built house.

The price was reduced by one hundred and fifty pounds and work began to correct these faults and decorate the house to make it as light and pleasant as the one in Eastbourne Street.

Chapter Eighteen

In the midst of all this activity about the house, Captain Furlong arrived home. Anna had been sent by her mother to match some embroidery silk in Bold Street, which meant that she was away for nearly an hour and missed her father's arrival.

When she returned, Nelly detained her in the kitchen. 'What a carry on,' she whispered. 'Your ma fell dead asleep, no wonder after the lunch she ate, and she was asleep when he come. Miss Clara took him in the dining room and told him her side, then your ma woke up and carried on sumpn shocking. Crying and saying how she was treated. Called you and your fella for everything.'

'My poor father,' Anna murmured, and Nelly said, 'He doesn't know whether he's coming or going with the pair of them.'

Anna went into the parlour, where her father was sitting beside his wife's sofa. He rose to his feet and Anna went to him and kissed him, saying as she always did, 'Welcome home, Father,' and he said, 'Thank you, Annabel.'

'I've told your father the way you've treated me,' her mother shrieked, 'the unkindness, the impudence,' but Captain Furlong said firmly, 'Don't upset yourself, my dear. Lie down and compose yourself. I have to speak to Annabel. Come, Annabel.' He led the way to his study, followed by Anna.

Her father told her immediately that he had received the letters from James and herself, but they left many questions unanswered and her mother appeared to think James was unsuitable.

'I've known James for many years through the church, Father, and since he moved to live in Eastbourne Street we often meet on our way to ten o'clock Mass. Dr O'Brien knows him well,' Anna said. 'I've been to tea at his house, but his housekeeper was always there as a chaperone. When we decided to marry we said nothing to anyone, because we wanted to wait and ask your permission, but one of Mama's friends followed me to James's home. James thought it was better to announce our engagement to stop any gossip.'

Her father lifted his head and smiled. 'Admirably explained, Annabel,' he said. 'You would have been a good advocate, had you been a man.'

A few bitter replies rose to Anna's lips, but she said nothing and her father said he would like to see James as soon as possible.

'Could he come this evening?' Anna asked eagerly.

'Yes, but it must be later. I must see Dr O'Brien first. I'm worried about your mama. I'll send down to O'Brien then I'll speak to you again, Annabel.'

He went back to his wife and Anna went to help her aunt with the meal. While they were eating a reply came from Dr O'Brien, suggesting that he came to see Captain Furlong within the hour.

He also suggested that James Hargreaves be asked to come at nine o'clock. 'If we overrun,' he wrote, 'James can wait with Anna until you are ready to see him.'

Another small boy was sent with a note to James from Anna, telling him that she would meet him on the corner at a quarter to nine.

She met him and told him what had transpired since her father's return. 'He's still in his study with Dr O'Brien. I think it's mostly about Mama. Father's worried about her,' she said. Nelly was still at church and they sat by the kitchen fire,

294

waiting until Captain Furlong was free.

Eventually, Dr O'Brien came to them. 'Your father needs a spell on his own,' he said. 'I've just had to give him some bad news about your Mama, Anna.'

'Is she really ill, then?' Anna exclaimed. 'I thought it was all imagination.'

'Yes, well, not in the way you mean,' the doctor said. 'This is a recognised condition and she has all the symptoms. She has always lived in a fantasy world to some extent, been highly strung and neurotic, so she was always vulnerable to this.'

'What are the symptoms?' asked Anna.

'A pathological dislike of one person, usually someone close to them, a voracious appetite, because food seems to bring comfort, resentment of any attempts to help, which are seen as criticism, and a feeling that they are misunderstood and disliked by everyone.'

'That does sound like Mama in many ways,' Anna said doubtfully.

'Yes. Something has to be done and quickly and your father and I have been discussing that,' the doctor said. 'So don't be insulted if he can't give his full attention to your plans. I've told him I think you're very well matched and you'll do well together.'

He omitted to tell them that Captain Furlong had told him that his wife said James was really Dorrie's admirer and was marrying Anna for a housekeeper. 'Rubbish,' the doctor had said. 'He's got a housekeeper, and when she's past it he can easily pay for another. I know a dozen girls who'd jump at the job. He doesn't have to marry to get a housekeeper. And that with Dorrie was just calf love. Haven't we all gone through that? Dorrie had hordes of admirers, but you were lucky she met the right man at the right time, though he is my own nephew. They're as happy as the day is long.'

Captain Furlong was convinced, although he said quietly, 'I have to tell you. That other nephew. I'd never have given my consent to marriage with Annabel.'

'That blackguard! I should hope not,' the doctor exclaimed. 'He's travelling abroad and long may he stay there. If I never see him again it'll be too soon. What turned you off him?'

'Dorrie's wedding. A matter of my young cabin boy. I hope he never crosses my path again.'

'Nor mine,' said the doctor grimly and said no more.

Now he told the couple that he was pleased they had suggested a quiet wedding. 'Better all round in the circumstances,' he said, and the next moment Captain Furlong appeared to call them into the study.

Anna introduced James, and her father said, 'Of course. I've seen you at church.' James began to apologise for not waiting for his permission, but the older man waved him down. 'Annabel has explained all that,' he said.

'I hope we have your approval, sir,' James said. 'I'll do my best to make Anna happy, and I can keep her in reasonable comfort.'

He began to pull out papers from his pocket, but Captain Furlong told him that the doctor had assured him on that point, and also that James was of good character. 'That's more important to me,' he said. 'That you treat my daughter well. She's very dear to me and I find she's had a lot to endure lately.'

He turned to Anna, who was dumbfounded at hearing her father, usually so formal and correct, speaking so freely. To say that she was dear to him! She was near to tears.

'Annabel,' her father said gently, 'I hope you haven't been influenced by what has been happening in this house. The need to escape.'

Anna moved closer to James. 'No, Father,' she said proudly.

'I wouldn't consider the sacrament of marriage unless it was with someone I could respect and admire.'

'Forgive me, my dear,' her father said. 'I shouldn't have expected anything less from you. It's just . . .'

He turned away and poked furiously at the fire. 'I think we'll have Dr O'Brien in,' he said. 'There's so much to discuss and he's always helpful.'

Anna called Dr O'Brien, who was talking to Nelly in the kitchen, and he joined them.

'I think you can help us, doctor,' Captain Furlong said. He looked at Anna and James. 'Is it true you prefer a quiet wedding?' he asked.

'Yes, we've already spoken to Father Kavanagh. He says we could have a Nuptial Mass at the eight o'clock Mass at the side altar, and I've enquired about a special licence. We'd like to marry while you are still at home sir,' James said.

Anna added, 'We only want a few people there. No fuss.'

The two older men looked at each other. 'That would be perfect,' Dr O'Brien said, 'In view of Mrs Furlong's health. Have you fixed a date? What is it today?'

'Tuesday March the fifth,' James said. 'We thought perhaps Saturday the sixteenth or Monday the eighteenth. If there's no hitch with the special licence.'

The wedding date was fixed for 16 March and James and Anna spoke to her father about the new house and their plan to live in Eastbourne Street until it was ready, but it was plain to both of them that the captain's mind was filled with worry about his wife. They left him with Dr O'Brien and went out to walk along the windy streets, making their plans.

Anna felt that their big moment in seeing her father had fallen flat and she was sure that James felt the same after his careful preparation of the details of his financial state. Still, she knew all about it, she thought, which was more than most wives did of their husband's affairs, she was sure.

When James left her at the door her father came from the parlour as she entered the hall. 'Mama is calmer now,' he said. 'Dr O'Brien is bringing a colleague to see her tomorrow, although we must pretend he's my friend. We'll soon see her much improved, Annabel.'

'I hope so, Father,' she said. 'Dr O'Brien is very clever.'

'He is indeed,' he said. 'I'm very pleased about your marriage, Annabel. I like that young man. Your life hasn't been easy, but I'm sure he'll take good care of you.' He had drawn her into his study and he said now, 'Has Mama done anything about your trousseau?'

Anna blushed and shook her head and he opened a drawer in his desk and took out a canvas bag. 'There's thirty pounds in there,' he said. 'That's all I have by me now, but I'll do the same for you as I did for Dorothea.' He smiled. 'Unfortunately, I didn't know in time to bring material for your wedding dress and so forth.'

Anna was speechless for a few moments, then she gasped, 'But Father, thirty pounds.'

He came round the desk and kissed her goodnight. 'Spend it wisely,' he said.

'I will. Thank you, Father. Goodnight.'

She kissed him and turned away and he said quickly, 'Mama is sleeping. Don't disturb her, Annabel.'

'No, Father,' she assured him, thinking bitterly, That suits me. She went upstairs with a light step, carrying the bag of sovereigns, and tipped it out on her bed. What a difference it would make. Although she and James would have separate bedrooms, she had worried about her shabby underwear being seen on the washing line.

She had been unable to buy any clothes since the trip to Dublin and the fact that her clothes were so few and shabby had been a worry since the wedding was planned. How kind of her father to think of giving her this money now, especially while he was so worried about her mother, she thought.

She put the money back into the canvas bag and put it in a drawer, then stood looking out of the window at the trees tossing their branches in the park.

I wonder if it's true that Mama is really ill, she thought. I think she's just an evil, spiteful woman. I shouldn't have told Mrs O'Brien so much of the way she treated me. I suppose she told the doctor and he came up with the idea it was Mama's nerves. And this so-called craving for food. She's always been greedy. What about the trays Dorrie and I had to take in to her, the plates piled high with food?

Dorrie! Anna thought. I must write to her. I was hurt by her letters, but I don't want to fall out with her for ever.

The letter was difficult to write and in the end she wrote briefly that their father had arrived home, Dr O'Brien said that Mama was suffering from a nervous disease, and she and James were to be married quietly by special licence on 16 March. She said she hoped that all was well with Dorrie and Michael and signed it, 'Your loving sister, Anna.'

She received no reply, but her father told her that he had written to Dorothea and she had replied that she was grieved that she was unable to come home at present, as her life was in turmoil. Michael had left the Army and she had had to leave all her friends and was living in a horrid house in London and Michael was hardly ever at home.

'I had no idea that things were going so badly wrong at home, Annabel,' he said wearily, and Anna thought how old and haggard he suddenly seemed. Her father went on, 'I'm sorry to hear that you don't correspond with your sister now. That seems another cause of grief to her.'

'I write to her, but I don't receive a reply,' Anna said,

thinking that she would challenge any lies about her in future.

'Your letters must go astray,' her father said. 'Mine had to be forwarded to her. Ask James to make enquiries.' Anna smiled and said nothing.

The wedding plans were quickly made. James asked Jim Deagan to be his best man, and Kate was Anna's bridesmaid. Dr O'Brien spread the news that Anna's mother was ill with a nervous collapse and she was unable to attend, so they had decided on a quiet wedding. Captain Furlong gave Anna away and Clara came with him.

James brought Frances in a cab, and a few close friends came, Luke, Maggie and Walter, and Norah from the Deagans, and Isabel Jenson and her mother, whose brother had brought them to Liverpool and booked them into a hotel overnight.

Anna wore a brown tussore suit and a large brown hat with a cream silk rose at the brim, and Kate looked more bridelike in her pale blue outfit and a large blue hat trimmed with pink roses. 'I tried to persuade Anna to have cream silk, but she's very stubborn. Be warned, James,' Kate laughed.

Mrs O'Brien had asked to be allowed to provide a simple wedding breakfast for the friends. There were no speeches, but Captain Furlong proposed a toast. 'To Annabel and James. May they enjoy long lives, health and happiness, which they both deserve.' Shortly afterwards Anna's father and aunt left, as they were uneasy about her mother, and it was surgery time for Dr O'Brien.

Anna had been able to spend a few hours with Isabel the previous evening, and with promises to meet again soon they parted. There were kisses and good wishes from all the other guests and the O'Briens.

A cab was called and Anna and James drove with Frances to the house in Eastbourne Street, leaving her with a niece who had come to stay, while they set off for a few days' honeymoon in a hotel near Kendal in the Lake District.

'That all went very well, didn't it,' James said, smiling at her, as they finally sat in the train.

'Yes, people have been very kind, haven't they?' Anna said. 'Kate said my wedding suit was her wedding present to me. It was good of her, when I wouldn't have what she wanted.'

'Why wouldn't you have a cream suit?' James said.

Anna blushed and looked out of the window. 'I thought the brown was more appropriate,' she said in a muffled voice. 'I – I didn't want to give a false impression. Do you understand? I felt ours was a different sort of marriage.'

'You must do as you think fit, Anna. It's all right by me,' James said. 'I like your father.'

'Poor Father,' Anna sighed. 'It was a sad homecoming for him, but he's been so good to me. I was always rather afraid of him because he seemed so remote, but now I just wish I could make him happy.'

'This bad time will pass for him,' James consoled her. 'If your mother has treatment, and Dr O'Brien is always a tower of strength, isn't he?'

Anna felt unable to tell him that Dorrie's behaviour had added to her father's troubles.

The shipping company had proved sympathetic to his situation and it had been arranged that Captain Furlong would spend three months ashore. Mrs Furlong had been booked into a nursing home in Southport, where Dr O'Brien assured her husband she would soon be well again.

'They'll cosset her there,' he said. 'Give her plenty of attention, and she'll have peace and calm, good food and fresh air. They're very good with nervous cases. Endless patience. She was on the verge of nervous collapse, but you came home at just the right time.'

Captain Furlong visited her several times a week and spent

the rest of his time with an easy mind, seeing seafaring friends.

Anna and James enjoyed their time in the Lake District. Anna had bought herself a suitable pair of walking boots and they spent the days walking round the lake or scrambling up the hills, delighted with the signs of spring. There were leaves unfolding on the honeysuckle in the hedgerows and on the trees in sheltered places, and Anna was enchanted to see some tiny lambs in a field one day.

'I didn't realise I knew so little about the countryside,' she said to James, and he promised that they would spend many days out in the summer to come.

'Isabel thought you looked a lot better at the wedding than when she had last seen you,' James said, 'but she should see you now. You look a picture of health.'

'I feel it,' said Anna, but she reflected that she had looked better for her wedding day because of the happy days she had spent before then, thanks to her father. She had spent hours shopping and sewing and had quickly laid in a stock of underwear and nightdresses, stockings and corsets, and bought several pairs of boots and a pair of low shoes.

She had also ordered two shantung suits from a Chinese tailor and two day dresses and hats and gloves. Anna felt she had not realised how worried she was by her shabby state until she had the chance to rectify it, but she felt immensely happy and confident now.

Even the prospect of staying with Isabel, although so welcome, had been spoiled by this underlying worry. She felt fresh anger towards her mother at the thought of all the petty humiliations she had endured, but as though he read her thoughts James said, 'I'm glad Isabel was able to come to the wedding.'

'Yes, I'd have asked her to be bridesmaid if I'd known,' Anna said. 'Although all the Deagans have been so good to me.'

'You must have Isabel to stay,' James said, 'or you can go and see her now. The Jensons all seem to have settled well into their new home, although they must still miss Captain Jenson.'

'Yes indeed,' Anna agreed, but her mind was still on the difference the money her father had given her had made.

She had shopped carefully and still had much of the thirty pounds left when he gave her a further twenty pounds, so she had spent a morning at Hawkins in Liverpool, buying sheets and pillowcases, table cloths and napkins. It was traditional for a bride to provide household linen, so Anna thought happily that at least in that way she would be a traditional bride.

On the day before the wedding her father had called her into his study and given her a bank book. 'I have deposited fifty pounds in your name, Annabel,' he said, 'as I did for Dorothea. James will advise you what to do if you need to draw on it, although I understand that these days a wife controls her own money.'

'Yes, that's so, Father,' she said, 'but you've already given me so much. I'm very grateful, but you'll have a lot of expense now, won't you, with Mama's illness.'

Her father looked astounded, 'as though I'd grown two heads' she afterwards told James, then he patted her shoulder. 'Don't bother your head about that, my dear, although I'm touched that you thought of it. The wolf is not at the door yet.' He smiled and patted her shoulder again, so Anna simply thanked him again and carried the bank book away.

While they were in Coniston she told James about the bank book and also about the balance of the money her father had given her.

'Thanks for telling me,' he said, 'but that's your money, Anna.'

'I wanted you to know about it, as you've been so open with me,' Anna said.

James replied, 'While we are on the subject, I think we should decide about our arrangements. Henry Mortimer told me once that his wife has a personal allowance as well as the housekeeping money, so she has some independence. I thought it was a good idea.'

'I think so too,' said Anna. She had always been too ashamed of her penniless state to speak of it to anyone, but now she told James of the humiliations she had endured. 'It affected everything,' she said. 'I helped with free dinners for destitute children, but the ladies put money together sometimes for treats for the children. Only a shilling or so, but quite beyond me, so I dropped out. I couldn't join the suffragists with Kate for the same reason – lack of money.'

'I understand,' said James. 'My mother demanded all my salary. I think I acquired a reputation for meanness in the office, but I simply had nothing. Only those who have never been without money think it's not important.'

Later, Anna reflected that she and James could speak freely to each other on subjects that were taboo to others, but they could never speak about emotional matters.

The last day of their holiday arrived and she looked forward to their return home with a mixture of hope and dread. Could this marriage work? She would soon know.

Chapter Nineteen

As the cab drew up to the house in Eastbourne Street the windows sparkled in the thin March sunlight, and there were gleams from the brass fittings on the door. 'Someone's been busy,' James remarked as they alighted from the cab, and Frances's niece opened the door to them.

James went straight in to greet Frances, but Anna lingered in the hall to take off her coat and hat and give them time alone. Bridie, the niece, looked surly as she helped Anna and grumbled that she had never worked so hard in her life. 'Me aunt's a proper slave driver,' she said.

'Everywhere looks beautiful,' Anna said, glancing through the open doors of the parlour and dining room. She took a sovereign from her purse and pressed it into Bridie's hand. 'That's for all the extra work,' she said.

The girl stammered, 'But, missis, me aunt,' glancing fearfully at the kitchen door.

Anna smiled and put her finger to her lips. 'Just between us,' she said, and followed James into the kitchen.

She found him sitting by Frances's chair, holding her hand, but he stood up when Anna appeared. 'The house looks beautiful,' Anna said when she had greeted Frances.

Frances smiled complacently. 'I was determined it was going to be spotless when you came home,' she said. 'It was a good chance to spring clean while you were away.'

Later, when she was sitting in the parlour with them after their meal, she dropped a bombshell. 'You know your sister's been home,' she said casually.

Anna felt James, who was sitting beside her, jerk with surprise and she said coolly, 'No, I didn't know, Frances. We're going to see them later.'

'She's gone again now,' said Frances, 'but I met May Beddoes and she said Dorrie told her that her life's upside down since her husband left the Army and went into business, and she's had to leave all her friends. And then all the worry about your Mama. She couldn't understand why you suddenly decided to get married by special licence in the middle of all their troubles, when you knew she couldn't get home for the wedding.'

Anna and James stared at her, too surprised to speak, and she said hurriedly, 'Don't worry, I gave her a flea in her ear. She won't come to me with no more gossip. I thought I'd tell you, though. Forewarned is forearmed, as they say.'

Anna said nothing, but later, when she was in her bedroom preparing to go out, she took out the photograph of Eugene and looked at it. She still felt the pain of love and loss, though not strongly, and she reflected that he could become a memory, but Dorrie was still a living, breathing person whom they were bound to see, so James's love for her would always be kept alive. Unbidden tears filled her eyes, but she swallowed and blinked them away. She had no right to shed them, she felt.

When they went to Westbourne Street they found Captain Furlong quite cheerful and being well looked after by Clara. He told them that Dorothea had paid a flying visit, alone, as Michael was tied up with business. 'He put her on the train and I met her at Lime Street,' he said. 'She was so sorry to miss your wedding, but she said her life is upside down at present. She spent a lot of time in Southport with Mama.'

After visiting her father, Anna and James walked up to the new house and were dismayed to find that little progress had been made with the repairs.

As the days passed, Anna became more and more impatient for the move to the new house. She often felt like an interloper in Eastbourne Street. On their first day home Frances had made several remarks which suggested that she expected to continue running the household and planning the meals, and Anna wondered how she could assert herself without giving offence.

In the evening James produced money he had drawn from the bank and handed Anna the housekeeping budget and the allowance they had agreed on. 'I hope Frances doesn't mind,' Anna said. 'I think she might still expect to do the shopping.'

'No. She'll be glad to be rid of it,' James said. 'Walking is such an effort for her. I've always paid her wages separately from the housekeeping, so there'll be no problem.' Anna was not so sure, but she was determined to try to please Frances and hoped she would succeed.

Bridie had returned to her job in the doll factory, declaring that she'd starve before she went into service, and Anna did the housework herself, with some help from Frances.

She was conscious of unspoken criticism from Frances, but she felt she was bound to resent her and tried to ignore it, until one day she looked disparagingly at some steak Anna had bought. 'He wouldn't have palmed that off on me,' she said, and Anna's temper flared.

'Are you implying I don't know how to shop?' she demanded angrily.

Frances said quickly, 'No, no. Just he knows me and you're new to it.'

'To this butcher, but I've shopped for years for Mama. I'll go back to her butcher if you think this man's dishonest, but you recommended him,' said Anna.

'I didn't mean no harm,' Frances said, so obviously upset that Anna's anger died away.

'I'll stay with him then,' she said.

Later, Frances said to her, 'I *must* have annoyed you. You're always so reserved, just like James,' and Anna wondered if perhaps they were too reserved.

Mrs Furlong returned from Southport, apparently cured, and her husband returned to sea, but only for a short voyage.

Anna and James paid a duty visit to her mother and aunt every week, but it was short and formal. Dorrie was never mentioned, but one day Clara said, 'Have you heard from your sister, Anna?'

'No, but I think she's very busy,' Anna said.

Clara seemed about to say more, but Mrs Furlong said plaintively, 'She's coming to see me soon. She's very worried about me,' and Clara snorted and turned away. Anna wondered what she had intended to say, but Mrs Furlong dominated the conversation until they left.

If Dorrie was coming for a visit Anna would have to decide what to do. So far, Dorrie's changed circumstances had meant that the rift between the sisters could be concealed, but now they must either pretend to be friends or be open enemies.

Anna lay awake for a long time, thinking about her sister and James's feelings for her. It was one thing to think of her as a dream figure beyond his reach, but another to meet her, not even as just an acquaintance, but as her brother-in-law. Could he subconsciously have thought of that when he proposed to me? Anna wondered at the time of night when her spirits were at their lowest ebb.

In the morning light, commonsense reasserted itself. James was an honourable man, and had probably not thought of having to see Dorrie any more than she had.

By the terms of their arrangement, their marriage was working well. They had married for companionship and to improve life for both of them, and in that they had been very successful. They enjoyed each other's company and could discuss most subjects, although not emotional ones, and Anna found that James could be very sensitive to her feelings.

She had felt excluded when Frances talked knowledgeably to James about the men in his office, and thought that James was unaware of it, but he had made a point of telling her about his colleagues and their families. She was sure that such a sensitive man would never do anything to hurt her and she would not let unfounded fears spoil their happiness.

Anna decided that she would write a short letter to Dorrie so that the outward form could be preserved, although she would never feel the same about her after the nasty letter, but before she had time to write, a parcel was delivered.

It was a belated wedding present, a large damask table cloth and twelve napkins, and a note apologising for the delay due to circumstances and wishing them well.

'I'll write to Dorrie and Michael right away,' Anna told James, and later she wrote a short, stilted letter, thanking them for the gift and good wishes. She addressed it to Dorrie and Michael and signed it Anna and James.

She told her mother and aunt of the gift and mentioned it to several friends so that the illusion of harmony between herself and Dorrie was maintained.

Dorrie and Michael arrived a week later, on a day when Anna and James had tickets for an evening concert. They were going with Jim and Luke Deagan so it was an excuse for a short visit to Anna's mother's house.

Michael looked older and tired, although as handsome as ever, even in civilian clothes. He kissed and hugged Anna and shook James's hand firmly. 'Congratulations to you both and all good wishes for a happy future,' he said in his soft brogue, smiling at them.

Dorrie was sitting beside her mother, who was holding her

hand, and she held out her other hand to James with a coquettish look from under her eyelashes. She evidently expected him to kiss it, but he shook it and said, 'Good evening,' then bowed to her mother.

Anna bent and gave Dorrie a peck on her cheek and asked if they had a good journey.

'They can only stay five days,' her mother complained. 'It's ridiculous.'

'I have to be back to pay the men's wages,' Michael said. 'You wouldn't want me to leave them hungry.' He laughed, but there was no answering smile from Dorrie or her mother.

Anna thanked Dorrie and Michael again for their wedding present and James asked Michael how his business was going.

'Grand,' Michael said cheerfully. 'We have a contract for twenty-eight houses. Just the right size to start off.'

Dorrie and Mrs Furlong made no contribution to the conversation, and Anna was relieved when James took out his watch and said to her that he thought it was time to meet the Deagans, and they made their goodbyes.

Dorrie had looked at James with a sneering expression as they left, and Anna hoped he had not seen it. She was furious on his behalf, but the music calmed her and she firmly rejected any more thoughts of Dorrie.

At last the new house was ready. Curtains had been hung, carpets laid and the new furniture chosen and put in place. Most of the furniture from Eastbourne Street had been suitable, but more had been needed for the larger house. The light paint and wallpaper gave the same feeling of brightness to all the rooms, and the large, airy kitchen had been fitted with a gas cooker as well as a modern coal range.

From Anna's point of view the greatest advantage was that Frances had her own pleasant room on the ground floor. It was large enough to be both bedroom and sitting room, with French windows opening on to the garden. In Eastbourne Street Anna had never been alone in the kitchen and the large fire which Frances needed made it like an oven. Now a large fire burned in Frances's room, with her chair drawn close to it, and Anna had the airy kitchen to herself.

Frances sometimes hobbled in to help, but it was clear that her arthritis was much worse, even though it was now high summer. Dr O'Brien had been to see her, leaving aspirin and sleeping tablets to dull the pain, but with Anna's connivance the gypsy medicine had travelled with Frances and she was perfectly happy.

A few weeks later the gypsy came to the kitchen door with a toddler clinging to her skirts and Anna took them through to Frances's room. She brought them a pot of tea and some sandwiches and cakes and told Frances that she was going to work in the garden. 'Take anything you want from the kitchen, won't you, Frances?' she said, smiling at the toddler.

Rosa rose to her feet and stretched out her hand for Anna's hand, then studied her palm. 'You have known unhappiness,' she said, 'but if you believe in yourself there are happy days ahead. You must fight evil, but have faith in yourself and your husband and all will be well.'

She still held Anna's hand, but her eyes were closed and she was swaying. 'You will have a long and happy life and three children to cherish you in your old age, but you must believe in yourself and in your husband's love.'

She opened her eyes and Anna said quietly, 'Thank you,' and gently withdrew her hand.

She went into the garden with the gypsy's words running through her mind. Believe in yourself. She seemed to understand and yet – three children! Anna's ignorance of childbirth and procreation would be unbelievable to later generations, but she knew that husband and wife must sleep together before

311

babies appeared. Rosa had seemed convincing, but Anna doubted her words.

Later, Frances thanked her for the welcome and the gifts she had given Rosa. 'She took the rest of the food you brought in and I gave her some sugar and tea from the kitchen, and a loaf and a pot of jam. I'll make it up to you,' she said.

'Don't be daft,' said Anna. 'Can she really tell fortunes?'

'She's told me things I couldn't believe would happen, but they have,' Frances said. 'Mind you, she'll only do it if she likes you. She says it's only with certain people that the gift comes to her. You'll find out she's right.'

Anna smiled and hid her doubts.

The long grass in the garden had been scythed and the borders dug over before they moved in and James engaged a jobbing gardener to come three days a week. He wanted help for Anna in the house too, but she was unwilling to take any more of Frances's relations, then Dr O'Brien told them of a girl who needed a place.

'She'll suit you, Anna, a nice quiet girl. She's from the west of Ireland, County Mayo, and she's been working as an undercook in Powerscourt, the big demesne in Wicklow. She was coming over to marry a blacksmith, but he was killed by a kick from a horse before she arrived.'

'Poor girl. What a shock!' Anna exclaimed.

'She's staying with friends in Soho Street, but I'll send her up to see you, if you like,' the doctor said. 'Her name's Julia O'Boyle.'

Two days later Anna saw the girl hovering timidly by the gate and brought her into the kitchen. At first glance she looked more Spanish than Irish, with straight jet-black hair, brown eyes and an olive complexion, but she explained in her soft brogue that Spanish sailors who were washed ashore after the *Armada* was wrecked settled in Mayo and married Irish girls.

'But that was in fifteen hundred and something,' Anna said, and Julia said softly, 'Was it so?'

Anna liked her immediately and Julia settled in quickly. Her cooking was a revelation to Anna. 'The potatoes are like balls of flour, and whatever the meat it just melts in the mouth,' she told Mrs O'Brien. 'She's shown me what to do, but it never turns out the same. I think it's a gift you're born with.'

Julia was gentle and deferential with Frances, addressing her as Miss O'Neill, and offering to rub embrocation into her limbs.

'No thanks, girl,' Frances said, 'but you can do something else for me.' She showed her the black bottle Rosa had brought and the bag of medicine bottles. 'Will you fill these outa the black bottle? They're handier to keep by me. Mrs Hargreaves knows about them, but I don't let on to the doctor or Mr James. Least said soonest mended, eh?'

'Indeed,' Julia said, and filled the bottles neatly and without further comment. After that, Frances regarded her as a friend, and everything went smoothly in Rosemount.

Anna and James invited her mother and aunt to see the new house, but Mrs Furlong said it would be too much for her. Clara, however, accepted and Anna's only worry was how to explain her sleeping arrangements.

She told James she wondered what Clara would make of the separate bedrooms, and he said, 'Need she know? If the bedroom doors are closed you can just wave at them and say that these are bedrooms, then show her the bathroom.'

Anna looked at him with respect. 'Why didn't I think of that?' she wondered.

'Because you were too close to the problem,' he said promptly, and they laughed together.

Every night they kissed goodnight on the landing and went into their separate rooms without any self-consciousness, but

Anna had worried about visitors' opinions of their arrangement. Now she knew what to do.

There had been a constant stream of visitors since they moved in. Norah Sutton, née Deagan, who advised Anna about plants for her garden, other members of the Deagan family, although Kate had left for London, the O'Briens, and school friends of Anna's with whom she had lost touch. Frances also had her friends to visit her in her room.

The most eagerly awaited friend came when Isabel arrived for her long-promised visit. She was delighted to see Anna so happy and living in such a lovely house and was greatly impressed by the change in James. Although she'd seen him briefly at the wedding, she remembered him chiefly as a plump, stolid young man, dominated by his mother.

'I wouldn't have known him,' she said frankly. 'He's really smart and handsome. And so confident and easy to talk to.'

'I think he began to look better soon after his mother died,' Anna said. 'More healthy, because he had better food and did a lot of walking and bicycling. I'm glad you think he's more confident. That old witch nearly destroyed him.'

As Isabel knew so much about Eugene, and Anna's feelings for him, she had told her about James's proposal. 'I had my romantic notions about Eugene, and James had his about Dorrie,' she said lightly, 'but we knew they were impossible and we decided that as we'd got the romantic stuff out of the way and we were good friends it was a good basis for marriage.'

Isabel agreed rather doubtfully and said that when Anna had described the proposal she liked the bit where James had poured sherry and spoken about plighting their troth. 'Shows he has a sense of humour,' she said. 'I think there's a lively man under that quiet exterior.'

'We often have a laugh together,' Anna said defensively,

and Isabel said soothingly, 'I'm sure you do.'

She asked about Dorrie, and Anna told her that she had only seen her once, briefly, since her wedding. 'She and Michael came for five days,' she said. 'We went to see them, but we were going on to a concert, and we invited them here but they made an excuse. She's changed, Isabel.'

'Your aunt said that,' Isabel said. 'She said her letters were full of complaints about Michael. Whatever went wrong with that fairytale love affair?'

'Michael is still as much in love with her,' Anna said. 'He's made sacrifices for her. Left the Army which he loved to get her away from bad influences. I'm not so sure about Dorrie.'

'To love anyone is to want what's best for them, even if it's not for you,' Isabel said shrewdly. 'She doesn't seem concerned about his happiness, does she? Your aunt told me he's working hard to set up in business, but Dorrie won't settle and join anything in the parish. Just sits at home crying because he has to be out a lot.'

'I can't understand how she can have changed so much,' Anna said, looking troubled. 'She was so sweet-natured when she was at home.'

'Yes, but everything was going her way then, wasn't it?' Isabel said. 'She thinks that should last for ever, but it doesn't for anyone. She'll get over it.' They were in the garden and she began to ask about the plants and talk about her own garden and about her brothers and baby sister.

'My uncles are so good to us,' she told Anna. 'It seems strange to see Mama being treated like an indulged baby sister, but it's what she needs now. It has suddenly hit her that Papa won't ever be coming home. At first it seemed as though he was just at sea.' She wiped away a tear. 'Mama's been very brave, though, and we all love the life in the country.'

She also told Anna shyly that there was a new headmaster

at the village school and they had become friends. 'His name's John Holland and he's a really good teacher,' she said. 'Our boys think he's wonderful.'

'And so do you,' Anna teased her.

Isabel blushed. 'He's had a hard job pulling the school round, but he's doing it so well,' she said. 'The previous headmaster took to the bottle after his wife died. Everyone was sorry for him, but he got worse and worse and the children, especially the big boys, were right out of control, but John's made them respect him.'

Anna thoroughly enjoyed Isabel's visit and was sorry when it was over, but she was happy to know that the family had recovered from their loss, and were leading such a contented life in the country, with the prospect of a happy future for Isabel and the headmaster.

She had always confided in her friend, especially since Dorrie's marriage, and she had enjoyed discussions with her, but there were things she could not say even to Isabel.

She could discuss Dorrie's marital problems, but not her feelings towards her, or James. On their one brief meeting Anna had missed nothing of what happened, of Dorrie's flirtatious glance at James, or his stiff reaction to it. She felt that it was for Michael's benefit more than James's, although Michael had ignored it, but what had James really thought? Had he seen her sneering glance as they left?

She and James had not discussed her sister's brief visit, either immediately afterwards, or since. They had discussed the concert that followed it and James had told her that he knew nothing of music, but had enjoyed it and would like to hear others. 'Another way you have improved my life, Anna,' he had joked.

They talked about his colleagues and his work in the office, items in the newspaper or local gossip, but Dorrie was never mentioned. Even if she was spoken of by other people they never discussed it as they discussed other parts of the conversation as they walked home.

On the last evening of Isabel's visit the two girls sat in the garden. It had been a mild and sunny day, without any nip of autumn in the air, and a full moon made the garden almost as bright as day. The scent from night-scented stock and tobacco plants filled the air and Isabel leaned back on the seat and said dreamily, 'On such a night.'

'It's beautiful, isn't it?' Anna said as softly.

Isabel sighed. 'A night for love,' she said and smiled. 'I have immortal longings in me.'

'For John?' Anna murmured, and Isabel looked at her and smiled, then whispered, 'Yes.' She longed to ask Anna who she was thinking of, but she said nothing and they sat in silence for a while, busy with their own thoughts. Anna was trying to recall details of Eugene's face and recapture the feelings of love and longing for him that the memories of their happy times together could evoke, but she was dismayed to find that even the scented beauty of the night could not arouse these feelings.

Instead, she thought of James, who had gone to the front garden to leave her and Isabel to talk. Was he affected by the beauty of the night? she wondered. Was he suffering, thinking of Dorrie, so beloved and so unattainable? She felt pain herself at the thought.

As though on cue, Isabel stirred and turned to her. 'Do you ever think, Anna, that you and James were a bit hasty? I know you're happy but – but weren't you both a bit young to put love so firmly behind you? You know, on a night like this . . .'

'No, but I see what you mean,' Anna said. 'I can only say I enjoy a night like this, but it doesn't arouse longings in me, immortal or otherwise.'

They both laughed and Isabel said, 'I had a cheek to ask. It's just that I care about you, Anna, and I want so much for you to be happy.'

Anna moved along the bench and kissed her friend. 'That's exactly how I feel about you,' she said, 'and I'm quite sure you are going to have a truly happy life. You deserve it.'

They heard footsteps on gravel, then James came across the grass to them. 'Julia has some supper ready,' he said. 'What a lovely night! I suppose you countrywomen call this a harvest moon, Isabel?'

'I'm not the complete countrywoman yet,' Isabel laughed. 'Although I do love living there.'

'I think your knowledge of Shakespeare might come in more useful,' Anna teased her as they went into the house. 'Isabel has been quoting Shakespeare,' she said to James.

'I'll have to introduce you to Henry Mortimer from the office,' James said. 'He's always quoting poetry, especially Shakespeare. I've had to begin reading it so that I don't look a complete ignoramus.'

'But do you enjoy it?' Isabel said.

'I do, and Anna does too, don't you? We're discovering books we want to read, getting to know all the secondhand bookshops,' he said, smiling at Anna.

'Yes, Mama didn't like me to read,' she said simply. 'It's lovely to be able to buy books and read whenever I want to.'

James felt a surge of anger against her mother and said to Isabel, 'Anna's introduced me to music too, and I enjoy that. Another dimension to my life.'

'You've broadened my mind too,' Anna said. 'I know a lot more about politics now.'

When the two girls said goodnight Isabel whispered, 'I take back what I said about the romance, Anna. You've got a perfect marriage, perfect. You're so good for each other.'

'I think so. I'm glad you do,' Anna said.

Isabel hugged her. 'Think back,' she said. 'Could either of you have spoken as you did tonight before you were married? James especially. It took courage to say what he did and you've given him that. You've given each other confidence because you really care for each other.'

'We wouldn't have married each other if we didn't,' Anna said. 'We said from the start we felt respect and affection for each other.'

Isabel smiled. 'I know,' she said, 'but I think it's much more than that now,' and she kissed Anna warmly before going into her own bedroom.

Chapter Twenty

Captain Furlong was due to arrive home shortly after Isabel left, and Dorrie and Michael were coming to Liverpool at some point while her father was home. Anna dreaded the meeting, although she reflected that Dorrie would have to behave herself while under her father's eye.

James had mixed feelings about seeing Dorrie again. He had been shaken by her behaviour at their last brief meeting, at the hand languidly extended, obviously meant to be kissed, and the flirtatious glance she had given him.

He was too aware of his own shortcomings to believe that it was anything but an attempt to annoy Michael, but he worried that Anna might feel humiliated by it.

Since his marriage his life had been transformed and now he thought humbly that Anna had been so good to him he must be careful that nothing occurred during the visit that might hurt or upset her in any way.

Captain Furlong arrived home on a Wednesday in late October and Dorrie and Michael were due to come on the following Saturday, but instead a telegram arrived stating that the visit must be postponed and a letter would follow.

The letter, when it came, was from Michael and he told them that Dorrie was ill and unable to travel. 'The doctor says she has suffered a miscarriage, which was a great shock to me. It was very early days and Dorrie had said nothing to me until she was sure. She is being very brave, but it is a great disappointment. The doctor says we are young yet, and please God things will go better next time. I will make sure I spend more time with her and the worst is over now with the setting up of the business.'

He had written a similar letter to his aunt and uncle, but it was received with less sympathy by Dr O'Brien. 'She hadn't told her husband!' he said. 'Why not? Did she hope she wouldn't need to?'

'What do you mean, Paddy?' asked Mrs O'Brien.

'I mean I think that girl's been well tutored by someone,' he said grimly. 'I'd like to have a word with the doctor who attended her.'

Mrs O'Brien looked alarmed. 'Don't be reading too much into her not telling him,' she said. 'He says himself it was early days and you know what she is for romantic notions. She might have been wanting to set the scene, a candlelit dinner or something.'

So the doctor said no more and Mrs O'Brien sent a lacy bedjacket and a sympathetic letter to Dorrie and Michael.

Anna was unsure how she felt when she heard the news. There was a sense of reprieve, but then she thought that she wanted to meet Dorrie again while her father was at home. The nature of her illness was a shock too and she wondered how James would feel about Dorrie as a mother.

James himself was also ambivalent about his feelings. In one way he longed to see Dorrie and in another he dreaded it, so he was not sure whether or not he was disappointed. As usual, he and Anna said nothing directly about Dorrie or her illness. They had been told about the letter when visiting her parents.

The following day, when James had returned from the office and they were eating dinner, Anna said suddenly, 'Father and Mama and Aunt Clara are very disappointed after all the preparations for the visit. What do you think of asking them here for a meal to cheer them up?'

James was taken aback for a moment, then he said, 'Yes, of course. That's a good idea. Let them taste Julia's cooking. When?'

'I hadn't really thought,' Anna said.

They discussed the idea more fully later when they sat in the garden and decided to make it the traditional Sunday midday roast dinner, and to ask Dr and Mrs O'Brien and a doctor friend who was staying with them.

'Did you want to ask anyone else? Henry Mortimer perhaps?' Anna said, but James shook his head.

'Six people. I think that's enough for our first attempt, don't you?' he said, and Anna agreed.

'It won't matter with them if anything goes wrong,' she said. They were both secretly nervous, and each wondered if their new confidence would stand the strain.

Frances and Julia were delighted with the prospect of the dinner party, and plans were made for a conventional dinner of soup, roast beef for the main course, followed by Julia's speciality, charlotte russe.

'I don't want to seem to be showing off,' Anna said, but she knew that any food cooked by Julia would be superlative.

Frances told them the tale of the overlarge joint of beef she had bought to show off before her sister-in-law, and James's remedy for it.

'I was that upset when I seen the size of it when it was delivered. I knew the two of us would never eat it before it went off, but he was that good. Told me I was daft to get upset over a bit of meat and I could easily give away what we couldn't eat. Me niece's family were very near starving and they made good use of it, I can tell you, but how many men would have taken it like that? He's one in a million.'

'Ah, he's a grand man altogether,' Julia said, and Anna felt a glow of pride in James.

Julia came with her to the butcher's to choose the beef for the dinner party. The shop was full, but the butcher himself came to serve Anna. She told him what she wanted and said firmly, 'I need enough for ten people and I don't want to stint.'

'Ten people?' Julia queried when the butcher went away.

'Yes. Six guests, my husband and I, and you and Frances,' Anna said. She had noticed a sharp-featured woman edging through the crowd of customers to be near them, and was sure that she was the sister-in-law who had been so unkind to Frances.

They chose a massive sirloin and Julia whispered, 'That's grand. The meat and the fat are just the right colour. It'll cook beautiful, sure it will.'

'The very best, Mrs Hargreaves,' the butcher said.

Anna had seen the sharp-featured woman staring with round eyes at the magnificent sirloin, and as she was close enough to eavesdrop Anna said, 'We had our instructions from Miss O'Neill, didn't we, Julia? I warn you, she'll be scrutinising the meat when it's delivered.'

She was smiling, but she was pleased to see a sour expression on the woman's face, especially when the butcher asked, 'How is Miss O'Neill?'

'She can't walk as far as she used to, but she's fine in the house. She and Julia are great friends,' said Anna.

'She's a grand lady,' Julia said. 'Very brave. We have a great crack together when she doesn't be having visitors.'

Frances was delighted when Anna told her about the eavesdropper. 'That's her! That's her!' she exclaimed when Anna described her, and Anna had to tell her every word that had been said, over and over again.

James laughed when she told him about it. 'You seem to have made Frances very happy,' he said.

'I think I did,' said Anna.

'You can't blame her for feeling bitter towards the woman, though,' said James. 'How did you know it was her?'

'I didn't really,' Anna admitted. 'It was just the way she was worming close to eavesdrop, and Frances has often told me about her. I'm always ready to strike a blow for any woman who's bullied and unable to strike back.'

James said nothing, but laid his hand on hers, which was gripping the arm of her chair, and she relaxed and smiled.

Anna had no worries about the dinner, but the familiar one about the separate rooms reared its head again and she spoke to James about it.

'The ladies' coats will have to go on my bed,' she said. 'That's what's usual at parties, and ladies want to do their hair after taking their hats off. I'm not worried about Mrs O'Brien, but Mama and Aunt Clara!'

'Don't worry about it,' he said, and on the Saturday night she found that he had pushed his wardrobe into her room, and placed two silver-backed hairbrushes that she had given him for his birthday on top of the tallboy. There were double beds in both rooms and the two wardrobes were part of a bedroom suite.

They were both nervous and half regretting the invitations, but James said as they said goodnight, 'Even if something goes wrong, they're all family or old friends, so it won't matter,' and Anna went into her room smiling.

On Sunday the preparations went smoothly and the dinner was a great success.

The guests all arrived together and Anna led the three ladies upstairs to shed their hats and coats and visit the bathroom. James took the men into the small room they called the study for pre-dinner drinks.

The O'Briens' visitor, Dr Hugh Parr, was impressed with

the house and when they were seated round the table he asked James about it. 'It's a little gem,' he said. 'Especially with so much new property around it. I'm surprised it wasn't knocked down for building land.'

'We were lucky,' said James. 'An old lady lived here for about fifty years, almost a recluse, so the house was not available.'

'But surely the speculators were waiting,' Dr Parr said. 'I believe mansions have been knocked down for building land all around here.'

'Two things helped,' James said. 'The garden is large, but there's not enough ground to interest a builder, and I made an offer as soon as it came on the market.'

Anna and Julia had brought in soup tureens and begun to serve it. 'Asparagus soup, not too heavy to take the edge off their appetites,' Julia had suggested, but the soup was so delicious that the guests, led by Dr O'Brien, had second servings of it.

James carved the sirloin and Julia carried round dishes of potatoes, followed by Anna with cauliflower and carrots, then Anna slipped into her place at the table while Julia served horseradish sauce and gravy.

They had placed the serving dishes with some food remaining in them on the table and Dr O'Brien said heartily, 'That's good. If these are up to your usual standard, Julia, I'll be back for more.'

He laughed, but Anna thought Mrs O'Brien seemed embarrassed and she said quickly, 'We'll be disappointed if second helpings aren't needed. Frances is keeping more of everything warm in the kitchen.'

Julia was pouring wine, but at that moment there was a diversion when Frances appeared in the doorway. 'The roast potatoes,' she said tragically.

'Holy Mother!' Julia exclaimed, ready to abandon the wine, but Anna said, 'No, carry on Julia. I'll get them.' She brought in a dish of roast potatoes and went round the table with them, thinking bitterly, Just when everything seemed to be going well. How could we all have forgotten them?

When she came to James he looked at her and winked, then whispered, 'Remember, only family and friends,' and she immediately felt better.

Dr Hugh Parr was fascinated by the high standard of the meal and the informality of the serving, and studied his host and hostess with interest. He wondered who was responsible for the tasteful decoration of this little gem of a house. Everything was light and modern, yet nothing jarred. The wife he thought, looking at her graceful movements and intelligent face, yet Hargreaves himself had run his hand lovingly over an antique desk in the study. Perhaps they had chosen the furnishings together.

They seemed to be in accord and he decided that both must be responsible for the air of peace and harmony in the house. No servant problems here, evidently. He turned to Clara, who sat next to him, and said, 'I've never before tasted such food. Truly food for the gods, isn't it?'

'Yes, Julia is a trained cook, but my niece grew the vegetables,' Clara said proudly.

'Did she indeed,' he said. 'A very talented lady.'

Captain Furlong was sitting opposite them and heard the conversation, and he said to Anna, 'You never showed any interest in gardening before you were married, Annabel.'

'We didn't have a garden, Father, did we?' she said. 'But I always loved flowers.'

'The garden had been neglected for some years,' James said. 'Before we moved in we had it tidied up a bit and dug over, borders and lawns laid out, and we had a jobbing gardener for three days a week at first. Now he can only come for one day a week, but Anna discovered she had green fingers.'

He smiled at her. 'She only has to stick a twig in the ground and it grows.'

Anna laughed. 'James does all the dull, heavy part of gardening. I have the easy side, planting and weeding. Norah helped me to choose plants.'

'Norah used to own a florist's shop,' Mrs O'Brien said to Dr Parr. 'She made the loveliest bouquets and wreaths.'

'She did all the flowers for the church for Dorrie's wedding,' Mrs Furlong said, and explained to Dr Parr, 'Our younger daughter.'

'She and her husband hoped to be here while I was ashore,' Captain Furlong said, 'but she was too ill to travel from London.'

'They've missed a feast. Michael would have enjoyed this,' Dr O'Brien exclaimed. He seemed about to say more, but a look from his wife seemed to silence him.

The main course was cleared away and the charlotte russe and a cheeseboard brought in. The charlotte russe was a great success and Anna told everyone that Julia had been making it for years before she ever tasted it.

'None ever came down from the dining room in the mansion where she worked, but she made one here just for the four of us. We thought it was delicious, didn't we, James?'

'Yes, I could have eaten it all myself, but I didn't dare, not outnumbered three to one the way I was,' he said with a grin.

Relief at the success of the dinner made him feel confident and light-hearted. He asked Captain Furlong about his voyages to China, telling him that he often wondered about foreign lands when he was dealing with ships' manifests.

This led Dr Parr to say how much he was enjoying his stay in Liverpool. 'I'm a land-lubber,' he said, laughing, 'but I'm fascinated by the River Mersey and all the shipping. I felt privileged to see the Cunard ship *Lusitania* setting off on her maiden voyage to New York.'

'Yes, a wonderful sight, Wonderful!' Dr O'Brien exclaimed. 'I was as excited as Parr. And she did it in under five days – Liverpool to New York. Amazing!'

'She did it in four days, nineteen hours, fifty-two minutes,' said Captain Furlong. 'A record, but soon someone will beat even that.'

'As long as they don't take risks to do it,' Mrs Furlong said. 'Human life is more important.'

Anna looked at her mother with a new respect. Perhaps Mama really was ill before, she thought. She certainly speaks more sensibly now. Mrs Furlong also spoke prophetically, although no one around the table realised it at the time.

Later, Anna and James showed their guests round the rest of the house and Frances invited them to see her room. Everyone admired it and Dr O'Brien said, 'Perfect for you, Frances. I don't know how you managed those stairs for as long as you did.'

'Yes, I dreaded leaving the kitchen, although James always lit a fire in my bedroom and put a hot water bottle in my bed,' Frances said.

'That was very kind of you,' Dr Parr said, looking at James with respect.

His face had grown red and he said gruffly, 'Only trying to repay Frances for all she's done for me since I was a child.'

Later, the whole party walked round the garden, although Mrs Furlong went no further than the flower garden at the back of the house, where she sat on the seat where Anna and Isabel had often sat.

'I'll stay here, if you don't mind,' she said. 'It's so lovely and such beautiful scents. The roses are beautiful.'

'They were here when we came,' Anna said. 'I like scented

plants. I've got mignonette and musk, and stocks, and of course night-scented stock and tobacco plants.'

Her father stayed with her mother and James joined them on the seat while the rest of the party walked round to the kitchen garden. They admired the neat rows of cauliflowers and cabbages and onions, and the neatly staked peas.

'I had broad beans as well, but they got black fly so we had to destroy them,' Anna said.

Dr Parr was interested in the wagon wheel buried near the kitchen door, with different herbs growing in the sections of the wheel. Sage, parsley, mint, rosemary, coriander, chives and fennel were all flourishing, but the bay tree in the centre was not.

'It's too cramped, I think. We'll have to move it,' Anna said. 'Julia uses bay leaves often.'

'Does she use the other herbs?' Dr Parr asked, and Anna said, smiling, 'Yes, all of them, but don't ask me for which dishes. I can never remember.'

Meanwhile, Captain Furlong was saying to James, 'You have a very good house here. When you were trying to tell me the state of your affairs I'm afraid I was unable to listen, but I had many worries at the time.'

It was clear that he was ready to listen now and James said readily, 'I haven't got the figures by me now, but I wanted you to know that I could look after Anna. I inherited money and I have a good position in an old, established firm of importers in Hackins Hey.'

'You've certainly done well with this house,' Captain Furlong said.

'Yes. I intended to buy it for cash, but a colleague at the office advised me to take out a mortgage. He said my money was earning more than the mortgage would cost, so I took his advice.'

'But you have to make mortgage repayments from current income,' the captain said.

'Yes, but it's well within our means. My salary is very generous, and we have a bonus at Christmas and an increment every year, and Anna is an excellent housekeeper.' He saw Mrs Furlong's head jerk round and he added hastily, 'I mean, she never stints on food, but she spends the housekeeping money very wisely.'

'Yes, I'm very impressed with Annabel,' her father said, 'and she seems very happy.'

Later, when the guests had gone, James told Anna that her father had enquired about his finances. 'He told me he was sorry he didn't allow me to tell him before we were married, because of his worries, but he seemed to want to know now.'

'Did you tell him?' Anna asked.

'Yes, he had a right to know, and we've got nothing to hide, have we?' James said.

They were sitting on the garden seat, both happy and relaxed, now that the visit was successfully over, and able to admit how nervous they had been.

'I was terrified of carving that joint. Pictured it skittering away from me down the table,' James said.

'Fancy us all forgetting the roast potatoes,' Anna said, 'but it didn't matter and everyone enjoyed the food. Dr Parr is a nice man, isn't he? He gave Julia two sovereigns and told her what a wonderful meal he'd had. She gave one to Frances.'

'She's a good girl,' James said. 'He admired the house too. Said that some people in London had all these light colours, but he didn't expect to see it in the provinces.'

'Provinces!' Anna exclaimed indignantly, but James laughed.

'It's how they see anywhere but London. I told him about Eastbourne Street and said we liked the style, so we recaptured it here and I told him we bought the furniture in salerooms. He was asking about the desk in the study and I told him the state it was in, and the same with the dining table and chairs, and how you recovered the seats of the chairs.'

'You seem to have told him a lot,' Anna said.

'I do, don't I?' James said. 'I suppose that's why he's so successful. He's so easy to talk to. He's very impressed with you, Anna. Thinks you are very talented.'

Anna stood up and walked over to a rose bush. 'I wish I was,' she said, bending over a rose to smell the perfume.

James looked at her tall, graceful figure and smiling face, and felt a rush of feeling which made him grip the seat. It took an effort of will not to go to her, but he quickly recalled an incident in the garden earlier and that helped.

Anna had been with her aunt and Mrs O'Brien, who were looking at a flower border. The two doctors were strolling to join them, followed by James, when Dr Parr remarked, 'I didn't realise you were related to the Captain, O'Brien.'

'By marriage,' Dr O'Brien said. 'His daughter and my nephew.'

James had paused and missed some of the conversation, but he suddenly heard the word D'Arcy. Anna's head had jerked round, and she broke off a twig. She turned back to the other ladies, bending her head to hide the blush which covered her face, but James had seen it.

Now he thought bitterly, She still cares for that swine, and said abruptly, 'I must have a pipe,' and went back into the house. He sat for a while in the study, smoking and trying to recapture the happiness he had felt, but he felt both sad and confused and tried to understand why.

The day had been a success, and everyone had admired Anna's talents. I'm a very lucky man, he thought. A wonderful wife, a happy home, good health and enough money, and yet suddenly it all seems empty. I should be perfectly happy, but I feel miserable. Why?

His mind knew the reason, but shied away from it. They had married for companionship and Anna had done enough and more than enough to make the marriage work. Whatever she felt for D'Arcy she had concealed, and she had done everything she could to help him and enrich his life. Their marriage was a success, Anna was happy and satisfied with the arrangement, and he must keep to his side of it.

He jumped to his feet and went upstairs, opening the door of his bedroom then going into Anna's room. He began to move his wardrobe and paused. The room was fresh and sweet-smelling, the scent of the lavender water that Anna used filling the air.

James leaned against the wardrobe, trembling, with perspiration rolling down his face, and not from the effort of moving the wardrobe. He leaned his face against the wood, then suddenly, savagely, pushed the wardrobe into his own room. He mopped his face and unbuttoned his collar, then shut the doors of both rooms, unable to face going into Anna's room again for his hairbrushes.

Twilight was falling and Anna had come in from the garden to the drawing room when he came downstairs. She turned to him, smiling, but he snatched his hat from the stand, and said brusquely, 'I'm going for a walk. Don't wait up for me. I may be late.' He escaped through the hall door, feeling that tonight the usual brotherly goodnight kiss was more than he could bear.

He walked for miles, his mind a jumble of thoughts about Anna, about Dorrie, about D'Arcy and about himself. He was exhausted when he returned home, but except for the gaslight in the hall the house was in darkness, and everyone apparently in bed.

James lay awake for a long time, wondering whether he had hurt Anna by his abrupt plunge away from her, but at breakfast the next morning she seemed unperturbed.

'Did the walk make you feel better?' she said. 'I had some indigestion myself. I think we were too keyed up and nervous to digest the food properly.'

'You're probably right,' James agreed thankfully. 'We'll be better for the next one.'

At lunchtime he told Henry Mortimer about the success of the meal and Henry said, 'Splendid. You're a lucky man, James.'

Since Henry had advised him about buying the house they had become close friends and now lunched together every day. Now Henry told him that he would be unable to lunch with him on the following Thursday as his wife was coming into Liverpool and he was meeting her for lunch. 'She likes to do her Christmas shopping early,' he explained.

'That sounds a good idea,' James exclaimed. 'I might suggest Anna does it one day.'

'Perhaps the same day and we could make a foursome for lunch,' Henry suggested, but James thought Henry should consult his wife before he said anything to Anna. 'She'll love the idea,' Henry said confidently, but James still thought they should be sure before he spoke to Anna about it.

Mrs Mortimer was enthusiastic about the plan and so was Anna. 'I'd love to meet Henry Mortimer and his wife,' she said. 'I've heard so much about him.'

It was arranged that the two ladies would shop separately, but all would meet outside Lewis's and a friendship began that day that lasted throughout their lives.

Anna and James were busy and happy visiting salerooms and working together on various ideas to improve the house.

James had taken a firm grip on his feelings and decided

not to explore them too deeply. He had retrieved his hair-brushes from Anna's room, but had not lingered there.

Soon after Julia had arrived at Rosemount Frances had said to her, 'Mr and Mrs Hargreaves have separate bedrooms, but I don't want it talked about to anyone.'

'Sure there's nothing strange in that,' Julia said. 'A lot of the quality who came to stay had separate bedrooms, or the gentlemen had beds in their dressing room for when it suited.'

'There's some who'd like to know about it, but it's not their business or ours, so don't forget, Julia, no talk.'

'Indeed, and why would I?' Julia said calmly. 'As you say, it's their business entirely, Miss O'Neill.'

The weeks before Christmas seemed to fly past. Julia had made several Christmas puddings and cakes, and all the other cooking preparations were well in hand.

Captain Furlong had returned to sea for a brief trip, and in London Dorrie had recovered her health, though not her spirits. She had not been pleased by the glowing accounts of the dinner party at Anna and James's house which her aunt had sent, and the O'Briens had written to them as well. Even her mother had said that the food was delicious, but she added that James had said that Anna was a good housekeeper, which consoled Dorrie slightly.

Michael and his partner had set up the framework of their business, and with the winter weather work outside was impossible, so he was able to keep his promise to spend more time with Dorrie. She found this was a mixed blessing. She had been used to having a day in town when Michael was safely tied up with business, when she could meet Mrs Rafferty and spend some happy hours gossiping and being advised by her friend. She also relied on seeing Mrs Rafferty so she could receive supplies unobtainable elsewhere.

Dorrie was still determined to delay any pregnancy, and

Mrs Rafferty not only helped her with this, but also supplied her with some evil smelling liquid to take if the preventative methods failed. It's only until I'm happier and stronger, Dorrie excused these measures to herself, but she had been alarmed by the result of taking the liquid.

She thought the doctor's manner had been odd, and worried that he might say something to Michael, but Michael blamed himself for neglecting her, and believed her story of waiting to be sure before telling him about the baby.

The doctor told him he should wait three months before resuming marital relations with Dorrie, to allow her to regain her strength before the next pregnancy, and Dorrie was sure that before that time was up she would be able to see Mrs Rafferty again.

Two of the ladies of the parish came to visit her when she was recovering and gave her food for thought. 'What a shame you've been ill practically since you moved into the parish,' one of them said. 'We've scarcely met you.'

The other one, a middle-aged woman with protruding teeth and a roguish manner, said archly, 'We all know your husband. *Such* a handsome man. All the girls thought he was single and fell in love with him.'

'And were disappointed to find my illness wasn't fatal,' Dorrie said angrily.

'No, no, dear Mrs Farrell,' the other woman said hastily, 'Miss Knibbs was only joking,' but Dorrie's manner was cool for the rest of the visit.

When they had gone she stood up and looked in the mirror. Her face was pale, with dark shadows beneath her eyes, and her hair, which had not been washed for a while, hung lank and colourless on her shoulders. She wore a dark housedress, too large now for her thin body.

She sat down again and wept with self-pity, as she pictured

Michael as he looked when he left that morning. He had lost the devil-may-care attitude of the early days and wore a navy suit instead of the uniform, but as that fool had said, he was still a handsome man. She pictured the girls in church eyeing him, perhaps welcoming him to the parish. As one of the Army wives had said, he could charm the birds off the trees. And he's *mine*, she thought savagely.

With sudden decision, she jumped to her feet and went to wash her hair, then, as she sat before the fire brushing it dry, she made her plans.

When she had coiled her hair, already looking brighter and curlier, and changed her dress she went to the kitchen. Since she had been ill, a daily woman had taken care of the cooking and shopping and she usually left when Michael came home, and he took over the serving of the meal and the care of Dorrie. Now Dorrie said brightly, 'You can go now if you like, Mrs Burns, and I'll see to things. I'm feeling better today.'

'You look better, thank God,' Mrs Burns said. 'There's a hotpot in the oven and I've made an apple pie.'

When Michael came in he was surprised and delighted to see Dorrie in the kitchen, and to find that she intended to join him at the table for the meal.

'You look wonderful,' he said, gazing at her adoringly, and she thought briefly of the toothy Miss Knibbs. Aloud she said, 'I've just realised it will soon be Christmas and we'll be travelling to Liverpool. There'll be all sorts of preparations going on there for our visit. I must get really well, because Father will be home too.'

'You must try to eat more,' Michael said anxiously. 'We must build you up.'

'Yes. I'm nearly as skinny as Anna,' Dorrie sighed.

'I wouldn't call Anna *skinny*,' Michael protested. 'She's just not as nicely rounded as you were.'

Dorrie laughed. 'She's certainly not what Mama would call "a fine figure of a woman",' she said, 'but on that subject, Michael, all my clothes are too big for me now.'

'Then get new ones, alannah,' he said fondly. 'The money is there and I want your family to see that I'm looking after you.'

On the following Sunday Dorrie, wearing a blue serge suit with a three-quarter-length coat and a large blue hat, was proudly escorted to church by Michael. She had written to tell her mother that she was quite recovered and would be home for Christmas.

Unless the crossing was too rough, she and Michael would spend some time with his family in Ireland and stay in Liverpool overnight on their way back. It appeared she intended to be a model wife from now on.

Chapter Twenty-One

On the pretext of shopping for clothes for the Christmas visit, Dorrie managed to see Mrs Rafferty again one day. They met in a secluded corner of a small café and Dorrie poured out all the details of her miscarriage. 'The pain was terrible,' she said. 'I thought I was going to die.'

'You must have took too much,' the older woman said, 'but never mind, it done the trick and you'll know better next time.'

'I'm all right for a few weeks,' Dorrie said. 'The doctor told Michael to wait for three months until I'm stronger.'

'And will he?' Mrs Rafferty said cynically, but Dorrie looked surprised.

'Of course,' she said. 'He's very good. Can't do enough for me because he thinks it's because he left me alone so much.'

'And so he should,' Mrs Rafferty said. 'Snatching you away from all your friends and dumping you in the middle of nowhere without a by-your-leave.' She saw that her remarks were not well received and added swiftly, 'And Liverpool? What's happening there?'

Dorrie, easily diverted, launched into a tale of the dinner party and James's lovely house and wonderful cook and Anna's gardening. 'There was a London doctor there who praised everything, my aunt said in her letter.'

'So your sister's fell on her feet,' said Mrs Rafferty. 'Everything going right for her and wrong for you and it's all her fault. If she hadn't covered up for that pervert, pretending he was courting her, he'd have been found out long ago, and your poor husband wouldn't have been driven to leave the Army.'

Dorrie looked at her, round-eyed. 'I never thought of that,' she said, 'but Mrs Rafferty, she did believe him, I'm sure. We used to think he was slow to propose because he'd had a sad love affair.'

'*You* thought that, and she pretended to, but I'll bet she knew the real reason. Her woman's instinct would have told her, but she liked people to think she was courting. She's crafty. She seems to have finished up better off than you, but she's only a housekeeper. That feller married her to save talk, but it's you he's in love with, isn't it?'

Dorrie smiled complacently. 'Yes, I'd only have to crook my little finger,' she said. 'And she is only a housekeeper. He said that to Father, that she was a good housekeeper. Mama said they don't sleep together. They had separate bedrooms in the first house and they probably do in this. She said Anna's got that look anyway, untouched, Mama said.'

They giggled together, then Mrs Rafferty said thoughtfully, 'That's worth knowing. If they haven't slept together the marriage hasn't been consummated and can be annulled. He'd be free to marry again, legally and by the rules of the Catholic Church. That's a shot to keep in your locker, ducky.'

'Oh, I *do* miss you, Mrs Rafferty,' Dorrie cried, leaning close across the table. 'You know so much and you can always advise me. D'you know . . .' She hesitated, then rushed on. 'We were having a row and Michael said he left the Army to get me away from you. He must have been jealous of you.'

'I know, but he didn't manage it, did he?' Mrs Rafferty said triumphantly. 'We still see each other.'

Shortly afterwards they parted, Dorrie saying that she would be in touch after Christmas, then leaving the café first.

Mrs Rafferty lingered for another cup of tea in case they

were seen together, then left, well satisfied with the seeds she had planted in Dorrie's mind.

Dorrie brooded on the remarks and by Christmas almost hated her sister and blamed her for all her misfortunes.

Captain Furlong arrived home ten days before Christmas and came to visit Anna and James. While James worked in the garden, Anna and her father were left alone in the drawing room. He seemed ill at ease, clasping his hands between his knees and staring down at his boots. 'What do you think of your mother's health now, Annabel?' he finally said abruptly.

'I think she's quite recovered, Father,' Anna said. 'Of course, we only visit once a week, but she seems quite well. Perhaps we should go more often, but we've been so busy with the house.'

Her father shook his head. 'No. I think it's magnanimous of you to go at all. I've been hearing more of what you had to bear, but you do understand, Annabel, it was the illness which made your mother behave in that way.'

'Of course, Father,' she said gently, 'but as Mrs O'Brien would say, it's all water under the bridge now, and Mama's well again.'

'You're a good girl,' he said gruffly, patting her hand. 'I'm very happy to see you so well settled and with such a good husband. I wish Dorothea was as happy. Mama has shown me some of her letters and she seems to be finding it hard to settle into civilian life. I would have expected her husband to be the one to find it difficult.'

'She doesn't like change, but I think she's settled down now,' Anna said soothingly. 'Would you like to see the sewing table we've bought Mama for Christmas?' They went to look at it and the subject of Dorrie was forgotten.

Captain Furlong enjoyed walking, after spending so much time aboard ship, but the distance to Anna's house was too great for his wife and sister and they were busy with Christmas preparations, so he came alone several times. Anna felt that she drew much closer to her father and understood him better after these visits.

Christmas Day fell on Wednesday and Dorrie and Michael arrived on the previous Saturday. The family were shocked by Dorrie's fragility, and her mother even vacated her sofa so that Dorrie could rest there. 'You're so *thin*,' she wailed, 'and so pale, my darling. What has been happening to you?' She looked reproachfully at Michael and he shuffled his feet and looked uncomfortable. Dorrie enjoyed the fuss and even Clara joined in the cosseting.

'Anna and James will come to see you this evening,' Aunt Clara said. 'So that you have time to recover from the journey and have your meal.'

Dorrie made no response until she realised that her father was looking at her, then she smiled and said faintly, 'That'll be nice.'

After the evening meal Mrs Furlong resumed her place on the sofa near to the fire, and Dorrie and Michael sat together on another sofa. When Anna and James arrived Michael, who was nearest to the door, jumped to his feet and hugged Anna, then kissed her cheek. 'Lovely to see you, alannah,' he said, anxious to heal the coolness between her and Dorrie.

Dorrie had also risen to her feet. James held out his hand, but she put her arms around him and reached up to kiss his cheek, although she managed to press her lips to his ear. Only Anna saw this, but she moved on to greet Dorrie while James, looking bemused, was shaking hands with Michael.

Dorrie offered her cheek to Anna, but she only touched it with her lips before turning to Clara, who was offering to take her coat. In the general bustle, as Anna's father was arranging chairs near the fire for the newcomers, James was able to recover from the shock of Dorrie's kiss.

Captain Furlong announced that he had asked Dr and Mrs O'Brien to call in and they arrived a little later.

Dorrie was the centre of attention and responded by being the bright and sparkling girl they all remembered. She teased Anna about her wonderful cook and her gardening skills, which she had heard about in every letter, and Anna slipped easily into her role of quiet foil for Dorrie.

'Dr O'Brien should take credit for Julia,' she said. 'He sent her to me.'

'Yes, and I've had many a good meal at your house in gratitude,' he said, 'because Julia's glad to be there.'

'She's a good girl as well as a good cook,' James said. 'She's very good to Frances.'

'Frances who was your housekeeper? Is she still with you?' Dorrie exclaimed.

'Of course,' Anna said.

Dorrie was tempted to make an artless remark about James looking after Anna as well if she was unable to work, but with Dr O'Brien and her father both looking at her she said instead, 'I thought she might have gone to her family.'

'No. We're her family. She did so much for James and she's still a great help to us,' said Anna.

At a quiet moment Dr O'Brien sat down by Dorrie and began to ask searching questions about her illness. She looked to Michael to rescue her, but he was deep in conversation about his business with James. Then help came in another way.

Nelly came into the room, saying, 'I'm sorry, doctor, there's a lad here for you. A man in Aber Street got his arm crushed at work. He made it home, but he's outa his mind with pain, the lad said.' She pulled a note from her apron pocket. 'Your Mary give him this at the surgery.'

Dr O'Brien read it rapidly, then said to Mrs Furlong, 'I'm sorry. I must go. Lucky I've got my bag with me.'

'We'd need a surgical operation to part you from it,' his wife said tartly, but she came into the hall with him to see him warmly wrapped up before he said a general goodbye and left.

The boy was standing by the kitchen fire, drinking a cup of cocoa. 'Finish it, finish it, lad,' the doctor said, before hustling him out with him to Aber Street.

Dorrie was relieved to see him go and told Michael so. 'I was glad he was called away,' she said. 'He was asking all sorts of questions about my illness. How do I know? I was too ill to know what was happening.'

'He's just concerned about you,' Michael soothed her, but she was annoyed that he had not been alert to her distress signals, and looked about for James. He was deep in conversation with Captain Furlong, but glanced over when he felt her eyes on him then looked away quickly, but Dorrie was satisfied.

The evening broke up early as everyone was concerned about Dorrie's health. Captain Furlong escorted Mrs O'Brien home, and Anna and James left at the same time.

Dorrie's father took the opportunity to confide in Mrs O'Brien, sharing his worries concerning his younger daughter. 'She was such a happy child, but she seems so changed since her marriage,' he said.

'She's a good girl, but she's easily led,' Mrs O'Brien said. 'She was all right while she was with Anna, influenced by her. When she went to London I think she had romantic notions of a glittering social life, which she might have had if Michael had been an officer, but it's different for other ranks in the Army.'

'We thought she had settled down well at first,' her father said. 'But Michael tells me that she became too friendly with a bad type of woman, who influenced her.'

Mrs O'Brien waited for him to say more, but she realised that Michael had been deliberately vague to Dorrie's father. He had evidently not told him that he had been called before his Commanding Officer and told to control his wife, who was causing trouble by flirting with married men and upsetting their wives. Michael had blamed Mrs Rafferty's influence for this too.

She said consolingly, 'Things will be better now. She is away from that woman and Michael's business is going to be a great success, so they'll be able to have a wonderful life. Dorrie is the same good girl she always was,' and by the time he left her Captain Furlong felt a much happier man.

James called a cab for the journey back to Rosemount, and as they were both tired they went to bed soon after they arrived home. There was little discussion about the evening, but Dorrie's greeting to James filled both their minds. Anna tried to convince herself that Dorrie was simply copying Michael's greeting for her, but she knew that it was quite different.

James had been shaken by the lover-like embrace and the kiss pressed against his ear, but, like her behaviour to him on her last visit to Liverpool, he saw them as being for Michael's benefit. Either to match his greeting for Anna or to inspire jealousy in him.

He was as much shaken by his own response. Not delight, as he would have expected, but embarrassment and fear that Anna might have seen what happened and been humiliated.

It had been arranged that Anna's parents, Aunt Clara and Dorrie and Michael would come to Rosemount for Christmas dinner and spend Christmas Day there, and Anna and James would spend Boxing Day, or St Stephen's Day as Dr O'Brien called it, with the family in Westbourne Street. The following day Dorrie and Michael would sail for Ireland.

'It'll be a lot of work for you, Julia, so many for dinner,' Anna said, but Julia replied that she was looking forward to it.

'Isn't that the best part of Christmas?' she said. 'Miss O'Neill and myself think it's grand.'

Without discussion James moved his wardrobe and hairbrushes into Anna's room and locked the door to his own room before the family arrived on Christmas Day. The ladies were taken upstairs to leave their coats on the bed, then Anna left them to visit the bathroom while she went down to help Julia. Mrs Furlong immediately opened James's wardrobe and seemed disappointed to see the suits hanging there and the shirts in neat piles on the shelves at the sides.

'What are you doing, Adelaide?' Clara said sharply, but she only giggled, and when Clara went to the bathroom she whispered to Dorrie, 'I thought she might be using it for her own clothes.' Before they went downstairs they discovered that the room next door was locked.

Julia surpassed herself with the dinner and at the end of it Michael voiced the feelings of everyone when he said to her, 'Sure that wasn't just a dinner, Julia. That was an experience.'

Afterwards, the three men went for a walk and the ladies rested in the drawing room. Dorrie and her mother lay on comfortable sofas, covered with rugs, and Clara sat dozing in a deep chair for a while, then wandered out to the kitchen where Anna and Julia were washing and wiping the mounds of dishes and Frances was putting them away.

'I've been falling asleep in the chair,' Clara said. 'I couldn't fall asleep in any chair in our house. Where on earth did you get that furniture, Anna?'

'We got it very old and tattered from salerooms and I recovered the chairs in that chintz. They're not fashionable, but we like comfort.' She laughed. 'James thinks they came from London men's clubs originally.'

'Trust men to find comfort,' Clara said. 'Can I help you?'

'No thanks, Aunt. We're nearly finished,' Anna said.

Clara looked around the kitchen. 'You've got a lovely big kitchen too,' she said enviously. 'In fact, it is a lovely house altogether.'

Anna dried her hands on a roller towel. 'Come and see my little room where I've got my sewing machine,' she said. 'This is what I like most about this house. The main rooms are lovely, but there are all these little extra rooms, like the one we made into a bedroom for Frances.'

'That's not so little,' Clara said. 'She showed it to us last time I was here and I thought it was a fine, big room.'

Anna turned down a short passage and opened the door to another room. 'This is where I keep my bits and pieces,' she said.

The room was small but bright, with Anna's sewing machine in the window, and a long table along the other wall with a bolt of material on it. There was a chair and a table by the fireplace and gardening books and magazines were scattered about. There were also several unfinished pieces of embroidery and various papers and Anna said, laughing, 'I don't have to tidy anything away. Just shut the door on it and come back to it when I can.'

Clara sighed. 'I wish I had my own place. I should never have come to live with your mother, Anna, but it seemed the best solution at the time for my poor brother.'

'But you're speaking to each other again now, aren't you?' Anna said.

Clara replied grimly, 'We had to when we hadn't got you as a go-between, but I haven't changed my mind about her. I'm sorry to see Dorrie seems to be going the same way. Playing the invalid.'

'She has been genuinely ill, Aunt,' Anna said. 'I'm sure

she'll get over it and be back to her old self soon.'

She showed her aunt a butler's pantry, which she used for her gardening impedimenta, and a few storerooms then they went back to the drawing room, where Dorrie and her mother were awake, sitting together on one of the sofas, their heads close together.

Anna began to make up the fire and Clara said, 'I've been looking at Anna's sewing room. She reupholstered this furniture. No wonder it's so comfortable,' but Mrs Furlong said nothing and Dorrie only smiled vaguely.

The men returned a little later and they sat about chatting until Dorrie said, as though idly, 'What's that locked room next to Anna's bedroom? I'm intrigued by locked rooms.'

Anna sat frozen, but James, who was more confident in his own home, said smoothly, 'Sorry to disappoint you. No Chinamen or dead bodies there, only dust sheets and the decorators' pots of paint and trestles.' He smiled. 'The room across from our bedroom is the guest room, where Isabel stayed, and the empty room next to that will be the next to be decorated and furnished as another bedroom.'

'You're wise to do things by degrees,' the captain said and the talk turned to other matters, but Anna sat thinking, Dorrie knows about the separate rooms and so does Mama. She knew by the gloating expression on her mother's face when Dorrie spoke.

How do they know? Not from anyone in this house. She knew that Frances and Julia were completely loyal to her and James.

It had been a relation of Frances, a young girl doing daily work for one of Mrs Furlong's friends, who had innocently spoken of it. She had been saying how good Mr Hargreaves was to her Great-Aunt Frances, lighting a fire in her bedroom at Eastbourne Street every night. 'I don't think him or his wife have fires in their bedrooms, but he does it for my Aunt Frances,' she said.

The woman had pounced on the information and relayed it to her friend as soon as possible. Mrs Furlong had then written about it to Dorrie, but it was several years before Anna realised how the information was obtained.

Now she showed no sign of her dismay as she organised another lavish meal. Afterwards, she played the piano in the drawing room and they all sang Christmas carols and hymns, several of which they had sung at church in the morning. Anna buried her shock and enjoyed the evening as much as anybody, particularly happy to see how much her father was enjoying himself.

He had a fine baritone voice and was easily persuaded to follow the carols with some old favourites like 'Greensleeves' and some popular ballads from musical comedies.

By the time the thirsty work of singing was over everyone gladly welcomed the punch James had made, what he called 'a stirrup cup,' before hansom cabs bore the party home.

When they had gone Anna said quietly, 'You did that very well about the locked room, James. Mama knew as well, but I can't imagine how.' She felt unable to even speak Dorrie's name.

'Perhaps it was just curiosity about a locked room. Perhaps we read too much into it,' James said.

'Perhaps,' Anna said, but they both knew that it was not.

As they were to spend Boxing Day at Westbourne Street they had told Frances and Julia that they could do as they liked in the house. 'You could both ask your friends and relations over and have your own Christmas party,' Anna had said. 'Christmas Day will be all hard work for you.'

There was little left of the goose and pork after the two meals on Christmas Day, but Anna had ordered another large leg of pork and there was a boiled ham which she urged Julia to use.

As always, there were plenty of vegetables and as Julia had made several Christmas puddings and cakes she decided to have a Christmas dinner for their guests.

'They'll all fit round the kitchen table and we can add another little table to make it longer if need be,' said Frances.

Julia had asked the friends she had stayed with in Soho Street and the two sisters of the man she had intended to marry. 'They were very good. Only concerned about me in the midst of their own grief at Matthew's sudden death,' she said.

'You never speak about it, but it must have been a terrible blow to you, Julia,' Anna said. 'To come all this way to marry, then to be told he's died.'

'I didn't really know him all that well,' Julia said frankly, 'and he was a lot older than me. It was my da and him that arranged it and I always did what my da said.' She smiled. 'Sure I wouldn't now. I've taken charge of meself, me own life, since I came here.'

'I know exactly how you feel,' Anna told her.

Frances invited some of her relations, including her brother and his wife. 'It's Christmas, after all,' she said piously, but Anna and Julia knew that there was little goodwill in the invitation, although they hid their smiles and gravely agreed with Frances.

'Is it all right if Eamonn brings his fiddle?' Julia asked and Anna replied, 'Of course. Do as you like. Use any food you want, Julia. This is your home as well as ours.'

Their guests were loud in their admiration of the dinner cooked by Julia and the excellence of their employers. Eamonn brought his fiddle and his wife, Annie, the box accordion which she played and they had a few dances in the kitchen with the table pushed back, then a sing-song in Frances's room.

'Thanks be to God, Julia, after the unhappy start in Liverpool sure ye've found yourself a good home here,' Eamonn said, 'and Miss O'Neill to look after you as well.'

'It's the boot on the other foot,' Frances declared. 'I don't know what I'd do without Julia. And Mr Hargreaves. I think God broke the mould when He made him and she's as good.'

'There's nothing like working in a happy home,' Annie said. 'When I was a young girl just over from Cork I was in a terrible place. The whole family was fighting and rowing the whole time. I cried myself to sleep many a time, listening to them.'

When their guests had gone, Frances and Julia decided that it was the happiest day they could ever remember. 'The dancing,' Frances said. 'I tell you, Julia, I was that happy I could have danced a four-hand reel myself, twisted legs and all.'

'It was grand,' Julia sighed. 'Sure I'll remember it all my life.'

They both knew that for Frances the chief joy had been watching her sister-in-law's face as Frances demonstrated how comfortable and highly regarded she was, but Julia felt she was entitled to gloat over the woman, after hearing how she had been treated by her.

Meanwhile, Anna and James were enjoying the day in Westbourne Street. Everyone was languid after all the excitement of Christmas and only simple meals were required. 'Our stomachs need a rest after yesterday,' Clara declared, and although Mrs Furlong evidently considered the remark coarse, everyone else agreed with Clara.

In the late afternoon Jim Deagan and Norah came to ask if they could borrow Anna and Dorrie for half an hour. 'All the

351

family are gathered next door and Winnie and Gerald have arrived with Susan,' said Jim.

'Ask Winnie to bring the baby in here,' Clara said. 'We'd all like to see her.'

Jim went back next door and Norah said quietly to Dorrie, 'It won't upset you, love, seeing the baby?'

'No, I'd love to see her,' Dorrie said, but her eyes filled with tears as Norah turned away. Michael, ever watchful, came beside Dorrie, but she whispered, 'I'm all right. It's just – I'd forgotten how nice people are.'

Jim Deagan came back with Winnie and Gerald and the one-year-old Susan. She was a friendly child, smiling at everyone as she was passed around.

'She's just taken her first steps,' Gerald said proudly. 'Three clear steps from Winnie's knee to Maggie's. See if she'll do it again, Win.'

Winnie shook her head. 'I think we frightened her a bit. We were all so excited because we didn't expect it. It might be a while before she does it again, Ger.'

Anna was amused to see the timid Winnie now so firmly in control, and later Winnie confided in her that she was expecting another child in August. 'Gerald would like a boy, but I told him, I just want a healthy child, girl or boy.'

Dorrie, who always responded to an audience, was in sparkling form and the baby seemed fascinated by her, gazing into her face.

'Pity she's a girl. You could count another admirer, Dorrie,' Jim Deagan said, laughing, but Anna glanced at James who seemed as fascinated as the baby.

'It's strange, Susan has Winnie's features and colouring, but she's got a look of your ma,' she said, and Clara agreed.

'I was just thinking that, Anna. The way she holds her head like Mrs Deagan did.'

'We often say that, don't we, Win?' Gerald said eagerly. 'And she's like Ma in other ways too. Very determined for all she's only a baby.'

The baby, who was in Clara's arms, turned her head and looked at him and Winnie exclaimed, 'There! You see? It gives me a shock sometimes, but if she grows up like Ma we'll be well blessed.'

Anna and Dorrie accompanied the Deagans back to their house and Anna was delighted to find that Kate was home for Christmas. They saw changes in each other, but for the better, as Kate declared. She was successful and happy in her job and said it was obvious that Anna's marriage was a success too. 'Dorrie's changed as well, but I wouldn't say that was for the better,' she said.

'I thought she was more like her old self today,' Anna said in surprise. 'She's had a bad time, a miscarriage, but she's recovering.'

Kate spoke instead about baby Susan. 'I think we've got another Susan Deagan in the making, just like Ma,' she said, and Anna agreed.

Soon after Anna and Dorrie returned, the O'Briens arrived to spend the evening with them. 'Hogan's taking the calls,' the doctor announced, rubbing his hands, 'so we can have a hand of cards without interruption if you like.' He seemed to have forgotten his curiosity about Dorrie's illness, and she began to be sorry that she had complained of Michael ignoring her distress signals on the previous occasion as he watched her so closely.

A telegram arrived from Michael's mother, saying, 'Longing to see you both. A hundred thousand welcomes and Happy Christmas. Mammy, Dad and Dermot.'

'I hope we don't have to disappoint her,' Dorrie said in a faint voice. 'I couldn't stand a bad crossing.'

'Nonsense. Smooth as a millpond,' Dr O'Brien said robustly and Captain Furlong gave details about tides and winds which meant the Irish Sea could be crossed without fear of seasickness.

Michael still looked anxious, but Dorrie decided to accept the inevitable and was lively and charming. She scarcely spoke to James, however, and when they left bade Anna and her husband a cool and sisterly goodbye.

Michael had said that they could only spend a week in Ireland. 'We'll cross tomorrow, Friday, but we'll have to cross back on the following Friday's night crossing. Then we'll have to leave here first thing Sunday morning. I have to be back at work by Monday the sixth, no matter what. I can't leave Eddy on his own any longer. He's my partner,' he explained.

'You'll have New Year at Ballinane, anyway,' Mrs O'Brien said.

'Yes, but I'm saying we may not see Anna and James again this visit. Dorrie will just need to sleep after the crossing, although we'll have berths,' Michael said.

Anna was secretly pleased, although she and James made no comment on it and she was unsure how he felt. He had certainly seemed dazzled by Dorrie, but there had been no repetition of her enthusiastic greeting.

She felt that in many ways Dorrie had become a stranger, but at times there were signs of the sister she had known and loved. She had certainly experienced unhappiness and Anna decided that she must make allowances for her and be thankful for her own happy life. It had been the happiest Christmas she could remember.

Chapter Twenty-Two

Isabel's letters to Anna had been full of details about John Holland, the headmaster, so it was no surprise to Anna to hear just after Christmas that Isabel and John intended to become engaged on her birthday, 10 January.

They planned to visit Liverpool the previous weekend to choose the ring, and it was quickly arranged that they would spend the weekend with Anna and James. It was the weekend when Dorrie and Michael would arrive from Ireland, en route to London, but on the Saturday morning Michael came alone to see them.

'We crossed last night, but it was very rough,' he said. 'It was terrible for Dorrie. She went straight to bed when we got here and my uncle gave her a sleeping draught, but I think she'd have slept anyway. She's exhausted, so I don't think she'll be able to see you this time, Anna. We leave tomorrow morning.'

'Never mind,' Anna said. 'I'll see her again when she'll be in better health, please God.'

Michael was delighted to see Isabel and hear her news and they talked of old times. 'Will you ever forget that bazaar?' he said, laughing. 'Young and foolish we were, without a care in the world.'

His face darkened, but Anna was glancing at James, thinking that that was the day his hopes of Dorrie died, and it was Isabel who said cheerfully, 'I suppose we have to have the bad times to make us appreciate the good times.'

They all smiled and the moment passed, but after Michael

had gone Isabel said thoughtfully, 'He's not the happy-go-lucky lad he was, is he? Doesn't seem that his life has been easy.'

'I think it was a wrench for him to leave the Army,' Anna said. 'But he seems to be doing well in civilian life.'

'He's doing very well,' James said. 'His business is really successful already and he has a good partner. They've both worked very hard and I think he'll go far.'

Anna and James both liked John. He was a pleasant young man, as dark as Isabel was fair, with an air of quiet authority which had made him a success as the village school headmaster. It was obvious that he and Isabel were deeply in love.

Isabel and John went home on Sunday night, but the visit had been a very happy one. Anna was delighted to see her old friend so happy and told her so when they were alone.

'I didn't think it was possible to feel like this about anyone,' Isabel confessed, 'and the lovely thing is, John says he feels the same about me.'

'It will be a real "marriage of true minds",' Anna said.

Isabel smiled. 'We do think alike about everything,' she said, 'and he gets on so well with Mama and the boys. They all like him.'

The engagement was to last for eighteen months and Anna promised to help Isabel with the sewing for her bottom drawer.

There were many other visitors to Rosemount and one of the most frequent was Mrs Mortimer. She enjoyed helping Anna in the garden and they were soon on first-name terms.

The two men had also grown closer. At Christmas Mr Duggan and Mr Reade, the senior clerks, both retired and James and Henry were promoted. They enjoyed the increased responsibility and also the increase in status and salary. Often the two couples spent the evening together at the theatre or a concert.

The Mortimers had two sons, Richard, an officer in the Royal Navy, and Robert, who was in France training to be a confectioner. 'It hasn't been easy for either of them since they left home,' Margaret Mortimer told Anna, 'but they're doing what they want to do.'

'That's important, isn't it?' Anna said. 'But it's unusual for parents to allow it.'

'We couldn't stop Richard,' Margaret said, laughing. 'He was so determined. There was a bursary offered by a Liverpool man for a boy to go to naval college, everything paid for, uniform and everything. He said in his will the Navy needed people with brains, not just from the right families. I could see what he meant when we went for an interview.'

'You went too?' Anna said.

'Yes. Richard came top in the exam, but he still had to pass a board and I went with him. I suppose they wanted to see if I wore clogs and a shawl,' she said bitterly. 'Such a collection of snobs. They didn't want him there. One of them even said it was ridiculous. Why should their boys have to mix with the lower orders at an important time in their lives.'

'The impudence!' Anna exclaimed. 'While you were sitting there. As though they would be defiled.'

'They told him the boys all knew each other and so did their families, but he would be an outsider. I can't remember the rest, but all things like that. I was ready to fly at them, but Richard was quite cool. A nice man leaned forward and said to him, "Wouldn't that upset you? If you were one among thirty boys and they jeered at your accent or your manners. Said you were uncouth?" '

Anna looked horrified, but Margaret said, 'I was proud of Richard. He said, "My parents wouldn't allow me to behave like that and if those boys didn't know any better I'd despise them." ' The man asked if he'd tell the boys that and Richard

said only if he was asked, so the man said the boys wouldn't
know how Richard felt. He just lifted his head up and said
loudly, "No, sir, but I'd know." The others just sat there with
their mouths open, but the nice man said, "You'll do," and we
came out, but, Anna, I was so proud. The proudest day of my
life.'

'Robert's doing well too,' Anna said.

'Yes. He wasn't clever like Richard, but he had a flair for
making cakes. He went to London first to work in an hotel,
and then went to train in France. He had to learn to speak
French and he said that was the hardest part. He's coming
home again now,' Margaret said.

She glanced uncertainly at Anna and Anna said quickly, 'I
know he's starting up on his own and James is backing him.'
She laughed at Margaret's relieved expression and said, 'It's
all right. James and I have no secrets from each other.'

Later, when she was alone in her bedroom, she thought that
that was not really true. Although there were no actual secrets
there were areas which were taboo, topics and situations that
they both avoided. Neither of them ever spoke of Dorrie, and
Anna could only guess at James's feelings about her from
quick glances at his face when he saw her or someone spoke
of her.

A priest who had left Liverpool a few years ago and was
returning for a visit had seen Michael in civilian clothes, and
innocently asked Dr O'Brien, 'Is your other nephew still in
the Army?'

'No. Stravaiging about the Continent,' the doctor said
shortly and the priest smoothly changed the subject.

Anna knew that James was looking at her and was annoyed
to find herself blushing. It's not even as if I care about him,
she thought. It's only because James was watching me.

Although this was a happy time, with everything going

well for them, she often felt unsettled, as though something was missing in her life. It must be seeing Isabel and John so completely happy, so truly in love, she thought. Some of those immortal longings Isabel once spoke about.

She told herself firmly to count her blessings and enjoy her happy life. Their first wedding anniversary fell on 16 March and James had taken tickets for a concert for them. 'Just the two of us, unless you'd like to do something different,' he said, but she said it was a perfect plan.

Soon after he left for the office a huge bouquet of flowers arrived with a card attached. 'Thank you for a very happy year. Love, James.'

Her eyes filled with tears and Julia, who had carried the flowers in to her, wept too and blurted out, 'Isn't he the grand man entirely? Sure I'm storming heaven every night with prayers ye'll be soon blessed with little ones.'

It was an awkward moment and Julia blushed at her lapse in her usual discretion, but fortunately Frances came limping in to investigate. Julia hastily retreated and Frances said to Anna, 'You've made a big difference in James, y'know. Twelve months ago he wouldn't have had the nerve to do this. That old bitch had knocked the stuffing outa him.'

'I don't know how she ever had a son like him!' Anna exclaimed, but Frances said swiftly, 'Because he's all his father. There's nothing of her in him. That's why she hated him, but never mind, he's beat her. He's happy now.'

Anna was glad to take her flowers away to arrange them and be alone to think of the comments by Julia and Frances. Poor Julia. Shall I tell her she's wasting her time praying for children for us? Yet she knows about the separate rooms. Anna found that people spoke more freely before her as a married woman, so now she knew more about the facts of life, but she wondered if Julia was still unaware of them. Or perhaps she thinks James visits my bedroom, she thought, then firmly concentrated on arranging the flowers.

Dr and Mrs O'Brien called with a gift of wine glasses. 'We can't stay, but I believe you're going out tonight,' the doctor said, 'so I won't see my favourite patient, but I came to congratulate you, Anna. James is a different man.'

Anna blushed. 'The credit must go to Frances,' she said, 'and even more to James. He's fought his own devils.'

'Indeed, but you've done most to make him whole again. Not just to bury his past, but to be happy,' the doctor said.

'He's done a lot for me too,' Anna said. 'I was a wreck when he married me last year.'

'So you've been good for each other, and that's grand,' Mrs O'Brien said briskly. 'Come along, Paddy. Have a fine time tonight, Anna, you and James.'

Anna smiled as the doctor was marched firmly away. His wife evidently thought his remarks intruded on their privacy, but Anna was not offended. She knew that they were made as a result of a genuine concern and love for his patients.

Only Dr O'Brien and Frances knew of the details of James's unhappy childhood and young manhood. He never spoke of it except in general terms, but Anna knew that before their marriage he had often walked all night to escape his memories. At least he hasn't done that since we were married, except for that night after our first dinner party, she thought now, quite unaware that James's problems were different on that night.

She said nothing to James about the various comments when she showed him the wine glasses and they spent a happy evening at the concert. Both thought with wonder at their former feelings for Dorrie and Eugene when they returned home and parted with a friendly goodnight kiss, after their happy anniversary.

The gardener, Mr Cleary, was a taciturn man who worked hard on his one day a week and never failed to arrive. One evening in April a young man came to the kitchen door with a note from him, stating that a cut on his hand was septic and he was sending the bearer of the message, Gerry Byrne, in his place for the next few weeks. Julia invited him in and called James who stepped into the kitchen and stopped short in shock.

The young man who stood near the door, cap in hand, was a replica of Eugene at first sight. He was the same build, with a straight nose, a cleft chin, and fair curls clustering round his forehead. Anna had followed James and he heard her gasp as she saw the young man.

Gerry Byrne moved forward, smiling, and said in a thick Liverpool accent, 'Good evening, sir. I've worked with Mr Cleary.' At closer range he was not like Eugene at all. His features were much coarser and his skin was pitted with scars from acne or chicken pox, but at first glance the resemblance was striking.

With an effort, James said in a steady voice, 'Good evening. If Mr Cleary recommends you that's good enough for us. Can you come this week?'

'Yis, sir,' he replied.

Anna said quietly, 'How is Mr Cleary? Is his hand very bad?' James glanced at her and she was pale, but seemed quite composed.

'Bad enough like,' Gerry Byrne said. 'He'd poulticed it himself, but it took bad ways like and the doctor at the dispensary had to cut it open. He says it's not so sore now.'

'That's good,' James said. 'My wife is the gardener. She'll tell you what needs doing.'

Before they left the room Anna added, 'Have a hot drink before you go and I'll see you on Wednesday at eight o'clock.'

'Thank you, ma'am,' he said, smiling at Julia, who already

had the kettle boiling, and at Frances, who had arrived to investigate.

'Poor Mr Cleary,' Anna said as she and James went back to their books in the drawing room. Neither mentioned the new gardener's resemblance to Eugene.

On Wednesday morning he arrived promptly and Anna gave him the key of the toolshed and set him to clearing a shrubbery. 'Mr Cleary intends to plant potatoes here,' she said. 'You can throw the laurels away, but the buddleia will go at the end of the borders. They attract butterflies.'

She found it quite easy to ignore the resemblance to Eugene, partly because she was closer to him, but also, she was pleased to realise, because she now felt nothing for Eugene except a vague pity.

She went back to the house, where James was preparing to leave for the office. He looked apprehensive, but she said cheerfully, 'I've set him clearing that shrubbery of the laurels. I want to grow potatoes on that ground.'

'You're determined we'll be self-sufficient,' he said, smiling at her.

Gerry worked hard, but he was inclined to linger to talk to Julia when he was called for his break or his lunch. Frances told him bluntly that Mr Cleary never hung about after he'd finished his food, and she made sure that she was in the kitchen whenever he was.

'You don't know nothing about him, girl,' she told Julia. 'Don't go falling for him, now, no matter how he makes sheep's eyes at you.'

'Don't worry, Frances, the same feller will never love anyone but himself,' Julia said. 'Anyhow, he's not straight.'

'What do you mean, girl?' asked Frances.

'Those bushes he's supposed to be throwing away. When I went out for a cabbage there was a little wooden cart there,

362

full of bushes with the roots wrapped in sacking.'

'Have you told the missus?' Frances demanded.

'No. I didn't know what to do, but the cart *was* kind of hid.'

'I'll tell her,' Frances declared and did so right away. 'They're not going on no dump wrapped in sacking,' she said. 'He'll be selling them to his other people.'

'Well, I only told him to get rid of them,' Anna said. 'They're no use to me, Frances.' But it made her watch her new gardener more carefully. It must go with the type, she thought grimly.

She and James had still not mentioned the gardener's resemblance to Eugene, but as Anna went about her tasks that day she thought how ridiculous it was when it meant so little to her.

She told James that evening about Julia's discovery. 'It doesn't matter, because I told him to get rid of them,' she said. 'But it's sly. He said nothing to me.'

'Mr Cleary wouldn't have done it,' said James.

'No, he wouldn't,' Anna said, and she laughed. 'I was thinking perhaps it goes with the type. Did you notice how like Eugene he was at first glance? And just as untrustworthy.'

James was silent with shock for several minutes, stealing glances at Anna, but she continued sewing placidly. Finally he said, 'I did notice it. Gave me quite a shock, but it's only at first glance. He's quite rough really.'

Anna bit off a thread and looked at him, smiling. 'I was thinking earlier about those snobbish relations of his in Dublin with their social aspirations. How affronted they'd be if they knew we thought Gerry looked like their precious son.'

After that, although they said little more about Eugene, their relationship was even easier and they could speak more freely about anything concerning him. James, especially, felt it as a lightening of a load he had not realised he carried.

They were still unable to speak as freely about Dorrie. She had written to them after her return to London, apologising for being unable to see them. 'I was prostrated after that dreadful journey from Ireland,' she wrote, 'but I am better now and very excited at the plan to move to a larger house in a better district. Everything is going very well with Michael's business and we have a wonderful social life.'

Mrs O'Brien had accompanied the doctor to London for a visit with Dr Parr, and they visited Dorrie and Michael in their new home. Afterwards she told Anna that it was true that all was well with them. 'The business is making money hand over fist,' she said. 'It's a real mansion and Dorrie queening it there to the manner born. She looks well, though, and she has beautiful clothes, but of course they have to do a lot of entertaining.'

'She said that in her letter,' said Anna.

'Yes, well, Michael does that side of the business. He has the contacts and he gets the jobs and he's very good at it. His partner Eddy, is more rough and ready. He's been in the building trade all his working life and he knows all the tricks, so he's good at that side of it. They've just taken on a foreman, Jeremiah Busteed. He's a Wicklow man married to a Liverpool girl so that's another friend for Dorrie.'

After Mrs O'Brien had gone, Anna and James only spoke obliquely of Dorrie. 'I'm glad Michael is making such a success of his building business,' Anna said. 'It'll compensate him for leaving the Army.'

'Yes, I admire anyone who has the nerve to strike out on his own,' James said. 'I'm afraid I haven't the courage.'

'You have the courage to back those who do,' Anna said. 'And you seem able to pick winners.' They both laughed. James had originally lent money to Robert Mortimer, to enable him to fit out a kitchen in London to make confectionery for a firm of caterers which supplied weddings and various other functions.

Robert soon realised that the caterers were the ones profiting financially and he asked James if he was prepared to increase his stake. 'Dad and I have used all our savings,' he said frankly, 'but if I had another two hundred pounds I could open a tearoom. I know I can make a lot of money and it would be done on a proper basis so you shared in the success.'

Henry and Margaret Mortimer were not as confident, and worried that James might lose his money. 'We don't think so,' James said, 'but if we do it's money we can afford to lose, so don't worry. Anna agrees with me.'

They had been proved right. The first tearoom, named La Patisserie, had been discreetly advertised with the magic words, 'Booking Advisable', and had become the fashionable place to take afternoon tea.

Everyone talked of the delicious confectionery and the quiet luxury of the surroundings, and the fact that it was impossible to get a table there without booking well in advance. Robert was already negotiating to open other tearooms, and orders for wedding and special-occasion cakes were pouring in.

James and Anna had also lent money from the 'nest egg' to Jim and Luke Deagan, to enable them to expand their successful printing business, and to the owner of the shop where they had bought their bicycles. He wanted to start dealing in motor cars, but had insufficient capital and James offered to invest in the business. 'They might be a nine-day wonder, I must warn you,' the man said, 'but I don't think so,' and neither did James or Anna.

They decided they must keep the rest of the nest egg as a rainy-day fund, but with Anna's careful budgeting they were living well within their means, and as the months passed they enjoyed life and the company of their many friends.

Isabel and John had spent a week with them during the school holidays and Anna and James had been to the cottage for a long weekend. Anna shared Isabel's bed, 'So we can talk all night,' Isabel told her mother gaily, 'and James won't mind that little boxroom for a couple of nights.' Anna enjoyed these meetings, but afterwards felt restless and vaguely unhappy.

Gerry Byrne had offered to work two days a week and Anna had agreed so that most of the heavy work could be done before Mr Cleary returned.

She was well aware that Byrne pilfered vegetables from the garden and would have pilfered from the kitchen if Frances had not watched him so closely. This seemed particularly mean, as Julia made him a large meaty pasty for his dinner, and another the same to take home, as she had done for Mr Cleary.

Fortunately, Mr Cleary returned within a month and within minutes of his return he came to Anna. 'Some of the tools are missing from the shed,' he said, 'and a sack of bonemeal and a sack of dried blood. Have you used them, Mrs H?'

'No, but Gerry might have used them on the garden,' Anna said.

After Mr Cleary had been in for his break and heard what Frances had to say, he came to Anna in great distress. 'I'm sorry, Mrs H,' he said. 'I sent a thief here. I'd no idea, he was so plausible. I'll make it good. I'll replace the tools and the sacks and anything else you've missed.'

'Indeed you won't, Mr Cleary,' Anna said. 'You sent him in good faith and he was a good gardener. I knew he was taking vegetables, but I didn't need them, and he didn't get much chance for anything else with Frances after him like Sherlock Holmes.' She laughed, but the man was upset and she said gently, 'Don't worry, Mr Cleary. It didn't worry us and I think Frances enjoyed outwitting him.'

'He picked the wrong one with me. I'll make sure my people know about him and my nephew's a policeman. He'll give him a fright that'll cure him once and for all,' the gardener said grimly.

'Restores your faith in people, doesn't it?' James said when Anna told him of the gardener's offer to replace the stolen items.

'Yes, and at least I got all the heavy work done before Mr Cleary came back. He still looks far from well,' said Anna. 'I'm glad to see the back of Byrne, though. I hate deceit.'

Mrs Furlong had resented the fact that Anna seemed more prosperous than Dorrie, and said she was forgetting herself and giving herself airs above her station in life. To Dorrie she wrote that *they* knew Anna was only a housekeeper, but she was accepted by everyone else as James's wife. She was delighted at the sudden rise in Dorrie's fortunes and bragged to all her cronies about Dorrie and Michael's rich friends, their mansion, the three indoor servants and the gardener–handyman.

It troubled Anna's sensitive conscience that although on the surface she accepted the explanations and excuses for her mother and Dorrie's behaviour, she found it impossible to forgive them. The sisters corresponded, but infrequently, and on Anna's part briefly. Dorrie wrote of her busy social life, her fashionable friends and clothes. She always mentioned her house and servants, and several times wrote that she and Michael were like newly-weds again.

If she hoped to make Anna jealous, she failed. The only thing Anna envied was the whole-hearted love between Dorrie and Michael. She told herself that she and James had married on a basis of respect and liking and she must be satisfied with that.

She now knew that her love for Eugene had been false, although it seemed so real at the time, but James was still in love with Dorrie and she must accept that, but sometimes she found it very hard.

It was true that Michael was even more in love with Dorrie now that he could be proud of her instead of worrying about her. All he needed to complete his happiness was a family, but there was still no sign of one.

Only Dorrie knew the reason for this. In spite of her full life she still managed to meet Mrs Rafferty. 'You seem to be having the life you were born for,' the woman flattered her. 'You don't want to start childbearing now and spoil everything.'

'I do intend to have children,' Dorrie said, 'but perhaps we could wait a bit longer. Just until we've had time to enjoy this life for a while.'

'Yes, indeed,' Mrs Rafferty said. 'He couldn't begrudge you that.' Before they parted she passed a parcel of supplies to Dorrie, and a small bottle of dark fluid. 'If you're careful you won't need this, but if you get caught use it as soon as you fall late, just don't take as much as you did last time. I've fixed up a few women, but they've took it as soon as their monthlies were late and there's been no questions asked.'

Dorrie passed over a small packet of sovereigns in return, and as usual left before Mrs Rafferty.

Michael, unsuspecting and trusting Dorrie, still hoped that they would soon be blessed with a family. Dorrie had not confided in anyone and her mother wrote commiserating with her, adding, 'At least you don't have to worry about your sister being the first.'

Dorrie handed the letter to Michael and he said, 'What does she mean – about Anna?' but she only smiled secretly and slipped her arms around his neck.

'Women's secrets, Michael,' she said gaily, and kissed him.

Chapter Twenty-Three

It was a supremely happy time for Michael, free from all the distress and worry about Dorrie's health. She seemed to blossom in this new environment, helping Michael by entertaining people who could put business his way, and charming everyone in their new circle of friends.

Most of these people were as newly rich as they were and they welcomed the young couple, the pretty wife and handsome husband, both obviously devoted to each other.

Dorrie was careful not to repeat her mistake of flirting with the husbands and antagonising the wives, and was regarded as a model wife.

There was only one small flaw in Michael's happiness, the fact that there was still no sign of a family. He was an innocent young man in many ways and like many of his type and class had no sexual experience before marriage, in spite of his years in the Army.

He had gone into the Army at eighteen years old, straight from his sheltered home, and his first sergeant had terrified the recruits with graphic details of the diseases which could result from casual sex. A natural fastidiousness, combined with his strict upbringing and the restrictions imposed by his religion, made it easy for him to resist temptation. This meant that on his wedding night he was as inexperienced as Dorrie.

Although Michael would never have admitted it, at heart he was as much of a romantic as his wife, and was proud that Dorrie was his first, as he was with her.

There was little time to brood in his busy life, but

sometimes he wondered if there was something not quite right with Dorrie 'down below', as he put it to himself. He was a gentle and considerate lover, but sometimes, even at the height of his passion, he had to restrain himself with a great effort of will in case he damaged Dorrie. He knew there was some obstruction, but he was too inexperienced and too trusting to suspect the reason.

He tentatively suggested to Dorrie that she should see a doctor, but this provoked such a storm of hysterical weeping that he was afraid to suggest it again. The thought of the miscarriage seemed to have been dismissed from Dorrie's mind, but it was often in his.

He had been sitting with Dorrie, and the doctor and the nurse had gone into the other bedroom. When Dorrie fell asleep Michael followed them and found them bending over a small object on a piece of blotting paper. 'About eight weeks,' the doctor was saying.

'What is it?' Michael asked.

'The foetus. Your son or daughter – or would have been,' the doctor said bluntly.

The blood drained from Michael's face as he looked at the tiny form, and the nurse pushed him gently into a chair and gave him a glass of brandy. The doctor nodded to the nurse, who folded the blotting paper over and picked it up, but Michael said weakly, 'Please,' and with a glance at the doctor she replaced it. Dorrie called and they went to her.

Michael remembered every detail of that day and particularly of his son. He was sure the child was a boy. He had turned back the blotting paper and looked at him.

The tiny figure, about an inch long, lay curled up in the shape of a new moon. The head was pointed and the shape of an arm and a leg had been formed, and the outline of a face, but it was a spot of bright blue which would become an eye which made the baby real to Michael. He remembered his grief and his determination that this must be hidden from Dorrie. It would break her heart.

Later, he had lined a matchbox with cotton wool and reverently laid the tiny figure in it, then sprinkled it with holy water and said, 'I baptise thee Michael John.' After dark he had slipped out with the matchbox, a torch and a bottle of holy water, and gone to the old churchyard. He chose a secluded corner where a small headstone was almost buried, and cleared the moss and soil from it.

'Mary Ann Pearson. Laid to rest 10 October 1849,' he read, and he dug a small hole near the stone, laid the matchbox in it and sprinkled it with holy water. As he covered it with soil he said, 'Into Thy care, O Lord, I commend his spirit.'

Before he left he scratched MJF on an inconspicuous part of the headstone, and said a prayer for Mary Ann Pearson. He was sure she would not mind sharing her grave with his son. He said nothing of any of this to Dorrie, thinking that she would find it too hard to bear.

As a child in the Ballinane farmhouse kitchen he had overheard a woman say, 'They said her womb was tilted,' and he told Dorrie of this, hoping it might induce her to see a doctor, but she only said lightly, 'What a place for gossip and old wives' tales it is. No wonder you couldn't wait to get away.'

The business was flourishing, with more contracts obtained and more men employed all the time, 'Begod, Michael, it's true that money breeds money,' his partner, Eddy, told him. 'We're making so much it frightens me.'

'It doesn't frighten *me*,' Michael said, laughing. 'I'm enjoying every minute of it.'

Letters went back and forth between them and their families in Liverpool and Ireland, but there never seemed to be time for visits. The rapid growth of the business was an excuse readily accepted, but it was their full social life which really made it impossible to go home.

Anna felt it as a reprieve. She dreaded that Dorrie could cause a disruption in their happy, peaceful lives, although even in her absence she still felt her sister like a cloud hovering above her, the one topic which could never be discussed between herself and James.

Michael's parents were equally relieved. Dermot was still active in the Irish Republican Brotherhood in different parts of the country, and while he was in Kerry he had fallen foul of the authorities. The farmhouse at Ballinane had been searched by English soldiers and Dermot had been furious when he returned.

'Thank God Michael has stopped taking their dirty money,' he told his mother. 'He could have been one of the scum upsetting you here.'

'Never!' his mother exclaimed, but John Farrell had stepped in as peacemaker.

Dr O'Brien went to London for medical conferences during this time and paid brief visits to Dorrie and Michael. He always carried home glowing accounts of their prosperity and popularity, saying that they were entertaining at home or invited out nearly every night.

In May 1910 the whole nation was saddened by the death from bronchitis of King Edward VII. He had been a popular King. His reign had coincided with a period of increased prosperity and treaties with other countries, and with the introduction of reforms such as the Old Age Pension in 1909, which had made him popular at every level of society. He had also presided at the throwing off of Victorian restrictions, by no one more enthusiastically than himself, and the people loved him for it.

Dorrie and Michael were at a dinner party where the news of his death was being discussed, and one man said, 'We must admit, though, King Eddy was a bad lad.'

'A bad husband,' a woman said. 'Poor Queen Alexandra had a lot to bear.'

'I don't know. They don't have marriages like ours,' Michael said. 'Take the new King and Queen, George and Mary. She was engaged to his elder brother and when he died she just transferred to George. It was the job that mattered, not the man.'

'You're a cynic, Michael,' another man said, but Michael replied light-heartedly, 'Not at all. Sure if I died you wouldn't have taken on Dermot, would you Dorrie?'

'I wouldn't have taken on *anybody* else,' she said, looking at him adoringly, and several people felt a twinge of envy.

Michael was extra-loving for the rest of the evening and when they went to bed Dorrie slipped into the bathroom before lovemaking began. She always did this, Michael believed to make herself fresh and sweet for him, but it was to use one of Mrs Rafferty's supplies, a tiny impregnated sponge. Afterwards, she paid another visit to remove it and use the rest of her preventative.

Dorrie always enjoyed the kissing and cuddling which preceded intercourse, although she resisted if his hands wandered too far. Tonight, however, Michael was determined to try to bring Dorrie to the same pitch of arousal as himself, and at the same time.

He kissed and caressed her fiercely, with his hands moving freely about her body, then suddenly he stiffened and drew back. '*Dorrie!*' he exclaimed incredulously, then seeing the guilty expression on her face he threw back the bedclothes. 'Dorrie,' he said again, then shouted angrily, 'You lying, deceitful cheat. All this time!'

She tried to move closer to him and put her arms around him, but he thrust her away. 'Don't touch me. What a fool you've made of me.'

She burst into tears, crying, 'Oh, Michael,' but for once her tears failed to move him.

'How long?' he demanded. 'And how did you know? Where did you get this?'

She sobbed without answering and like a blinding flash he realised and gasped, 'Mrs Rafferty. But it's been years.' Then he said accusingly, 'You've been seeing her. Deceiving me.' He jumped out of bed and dragged her after him. 'Show me,' he ordered, and she opened her wardrobe and took out the packet. He opened it and saw the sponges and various phials and a small bottle of black fluid.

As he picked up the bottle he suddenly remembered. He had seen something like this before. In the other house. Only a fleeting glimpse, and he had thought nothing of it at the time. Now, seeing it in this package, he remembered it was just before Dorrie's miscarriage and he stood as though turned to stone, thinking, then he shook Dorrie. 'What's this for? Answer me.'

She had seen Michael angry before, quick rages, soon over, but she had never seen anything like the ferocious, bitter anger she had roused now. 'In case – in case I was late,' she whimpered.

'You used it – in the other house,' he said implacably.

Too terrified to lie, she nodded. 'I took too much,' she faltered, and he thrust her away, his face congested and his eyes wild.

'And you murdered my son. God stiffen you,' he said, with such venom that Dorrie screamed in terror.

'I saw him,' he said. 'Tiny he was, with blue eyes. Eight weeks, the doctor said. I've thought of him as a baby in my

374

arms, staring at me with those blue eyes, or a little lad beside me, looking up at me with the same blue eyes.'

He turned and laid his arm against the bedroom wall and pressed his head against it, his body shaking with grief. Dorrie stood, afraid to touch him or speak to him, then she whimpered, 'Michael, I didn't know.'

He lifted his head. 'No, you didn't know. I wouldn't let you see him in case it broke your heart.' His bitter laughter was a sound that Dorrie would never forget.

'I christened him Michael John and buried him in the churchyard in the grave of Mary Ann Pearson. My son. In a matchbox. I said the prayer for the dead over him, and what was his mother doing? Lying in bed, pleased with herself, or writing to her crony to tell her that she had got rid of him and no one suspected, especially not her gullible fool of a husband.'

'I wasn't. I didn't,' Dorrie tried to protest, but Michael stormed on, 'You must have been laughing up your sleeves at me, you and that one. What a fool, a gullible fool I've been, but never again. I'm finished with you. Go to her. You're two of a kind. Do as you like, but never ever come near me or I'll kill both of you.'

He snatched up the package. 'I'll see she gets what she deserves,' he said and turned and walked out of the room without a backward glance. Dorrie stumbled to the bed and lay there weeping for the rest of the night.

Michael was too restless even to sit down. He drank a glass of whisky and, putting the package in his overcoat pocket, he went out and walked about the streets for hours. Eventually, he took a cab to the site office.

Eddy was always the first there and he greeted Michael, at first with pleasure, and then with dismay. 'Michael, lad, what's happened?' he exclaimed.

'I've been had for a mug, Eddy,' Michael said.

The other man said calmly, 'Well, you're not the first and you won't be the last. Sure she was always too pretty for her own good and there's always fellas ready to take advantage.' He was pouring hot strong tea as he spoke, then ladled sugar into it.

'Get that down you,' he said. 'There's a drop of rum in it as well. It's just the first shock, lad. Everything will look better in a couple of days.'

Michael drank the scalding tea, deciding to stay with Eddy's version of events. He felt too ashamed to tell anyone but one man the real story. During his solitary walking he had decided to go to the chaplain of the regiment and ask his advice about Mrs Rafferty.

Now he said to Eddy, 'I'll need a few days to myself, Eddy. Can you manage?'

'Indeed we will. The manager in your office is a good lad and he'll deal with day-to-day stuff. Anything else can wait until you're better. I'll give out you're sick. What are you going to do?'

'I'm going to see the padre, ask his advice,' Michael said. He stood up. 'Thanks, Eddy. I'll get away now. I don't want to see the lads.'

'The Army, you mean?' Eddy said, and when Michael nodded he said, 'Go to a barber's, lad, get yourself tidied up like.'

Michael ran his hand over his face. 'God, yes. Thanks again, Eddy.'

His friend escorted him to the door. 'Don't do anything rash now, lad, and remember, me and Mary are always there. Come any time. Stay the night or stay the month. You're always welcome.'

Michael took Eddy's advice and went to a barber's for a shave, realising how necessary it was when he confronted his image in the mirror. I'm not going to let those two destroy me, he thought with a spurt of anger, and when he left the barber's he bought a new shirt, then went to another establishment where he could have a bath and have his suit pressed. He marched into the barracks to ask to see the chaplain looking as smart as the man who had left there.

Fortunately, he saw no one he knew except the chaplain, who took him to his room. 'I don't know where to start, Father,' Michael said.

'Take your time, my son. Start with your real reason for leaving the regiment,' said the priest. 'You know you can say anything to me and it will go no further.'

Once he started, words poured from Michael's lips and the priest listened in silence, merely nodding encouragingly from time to time. When Michael spoke of the baby he had buried he was suddenly overcome with grief for what might have been and wept, covering his face with his hands. The priest stood up and placed a glass of brandy beside him and Michael wiped his face and said thickly, 'Sorry, Father.'

'Not at all, you needed it,' the priest said. 'I'll tell you now that your wife is not the only victim of that lady. The doctor has been worried, but there's no proof.'

Michael hesitantly withdrew the package from his coat pocket. 'This is proof, Father, but I don't want my wife's name drawn into it.'

He felt embarrassed when the celibate priest opened the package, but Fr Doyle only said quietly, 'This is what the doctor needed, Michael, but I won't tell him without your permission.'

'But wouldn't you need to say where you got it?' Michael said.

'No. I would like the Commanding Officer to be involved too, but I promise you, you and your wife would never be mentioned. I would say it was given to me and I was told about Mrs Rafferty, but in confidence. Neither of them would ask me further questions.'

'They'd think you were told in Confession,' Michael suggested.

Fr Doyle shrugged. 'That might be the conclusion they might draw,' he said. 'Several women have had unexplained illnesses which left them very weak, but they would never admit why. One bonny young woman nearly died and will never regain her strength. We can root out evil with this, Michael.'

'Very well, Father. I'll leave it with you,' Michael said, and the talk turned again to his relationship with Dorrie and the bitter quarrel of the night before. 'I never want to see her or speak to her again,' Michael said angrily. 'She's not the girl I married, or perhaps this is her true nature. Anyway, I'm finished with her.'

'You think it is all Dorrie's fault. You are not to blame in any way,' Fr Doyle said.

'I'm to blame for being too gullible, that's all,' Michael said.

The priest said quietly, 'I remember her when she came here newly married. Tell me about the home she came from.'

Michael described Dorrie's family and her lifestyle in Liverpool, and in spite of himself his voice softened when he spoke about those days.

'So she came from a sheltered home, where she was loved and cherished, especially by her protective elder sister,' Fr Doyle said. 'An innocent young girl to come as a stranger among strangers with whom she had little in common. Did you cherish her as carefully, Michael?'

'I did what I could,' Michael protested. 'I *wanted* to be with her. She knew that, but I'd been detailed for the entertainments committee, quite apart from my Army duties. We were all shaking down together at that time.'

'The fact remains that she was alone quite a lot,' the priest said.

'I thought she'd make friends easily,' Michael said. 'She was so popular at home, so many friends and admirers. She didn't sit at home like a mouse. They were involved in so much at the church, and socials and dances and wagonette trips and bicycling in the summer.'

'They! You mean she was always with her sister?' Fr Doyle said.

'Yes, but Anna was the quiet, reserved one. Dorrie was always popular,' said Michael.

'Think, Michael, of the change in her life here. Wouldn't she be glad to clutch at any friendly hand?'

Michael was silent for a moment, then he said, 'I must admit, Father, I was glad at first when Mrs Rafferty looked after her. Showed her the ropes and that. I didn't know what she was then.'

'And neither did Dorrie,' the priest said. 'She was too innocent to realise that she was being manipulated, but you should have been watching more closely, to protect her.'

'I was just pleased that she was making friends,' Michael admitted. 'And we were together a lot of the time, and she was happy.'

'But she changed?' the priest suggested.

'Yes, even her sister thought she'd changed when we went to Liverpool, and my mother when we went to Wicklow. I knew by then she was completely under that woman's spell. Dorrie was upset about the gossip about my cousin, D'Arcy, but how would she know unless that one told her? No one would say it to her face.'

They sat in silence while Michael thought, then he said, 'I

379

did what I could, Father. I suppose you know there was gossip about Dorrie too. I didn't until the CO told me to control her. She was causing trouble, flirting with married men, but that one was manipulating her.'

'And that was why you left the regiment?' Fr Doyle said.

'You know how hard it was for me, Father. How much the regiment meant to me, but I knew I had to get her away from that woman. My mother said the same. She said marriage was for life and my first duty was to my wife. Fine thanks I got for it,' he added bitterly.

'You didn't do it for thanks,' the priest said. 'You did it to protect your wife, but that evil woman had a stronger hold over her than you realised. Did you tell your wife why you left?'

'No. I said I had a good business opportunity, which was true. We have a good life now, Father – or had. Dorrie's health is better and she's happier and I'm making money hand over fist, but it was rotten inside.'

'Nonsense. Think of Dorrie before she met Mrs Rafferty and think of your marriage vows. For better, for worse, for richer, for poorer, in sickness and in health. Think of this as a sickness in Dorrie which can be cured so she can become her old self again.'

Michael shook his head. 'I can't, Father. I can't forgive her for my son. And she deceived me, went on seeing that woman. I suppose, for her supplies.'

'That's what really irks you, isn't it? The fact that you were taken for a mug. Your pride is what's hurt, and you don't want to admit that you're to blame in any way. You want to be the victim, the injured party,' the priest said.

Michael flushed. 'I admit I should have taken better care of Dorrie and I should have realised what Mrs Rafferty was,' he said, then he hesitated and said grudgingly, 'And I suppose it is my pride that's hurt, but it's such a fundamental thing to be deceived about, Father.'

'I know, my son. I sound hard on you, but I just want you to face facts. To see that your marriage can be saved.'

Michael said nothing and the priest said gently, 'You must show your wife respect as a person. Tell her what you are planning. If you'd told her why you were leaving the regiment and how hard it was then she might not have been cajoled into meeting Mrs Rafferty again.'

'Oh, no. She'd have hated me for separating them,' Michael said.

The priest sighed. 'You're too hurt and angry now to see things straight, my son,' he said. 'But think about it. You have a good marriage. You love your wife. It wasn't hurt pride that brought you here to find a solution without hurting her, and you know that she loves you. The good, innocent girl who lived among good people for twenty-one years, that's the real Dorrie.'

'But she's changed, Father,' Michael said.

'Yes, and she can change again, back to her real character. Remember, the Jesuits say, "Give me the child for the first seven years and I will give you the man." But you must be very patient and considerate. Think of this as an illness and remember your marriage vows.'

He stood up and laid his hand on Michael's head, then blessed him. 'I will pray that God will give you strength,' he said, 'but now I must take this package to the CO. Normally I would ask you to stay to lunch, but I don't want to alert that woman.'

'Thanks all the same, Father. I'd rather go before I see anyone I know,' Michael said, and the priest agreed.

'Let me know how things go. God bless and guide you.'

Michael managed to leave without being seen by anyone

he knew and walked for a while, thinking deeply. His rage against Dorrie had died as he turned the priest's words over in his mind. Perhaps he was to blame. Perhaps he had made it easy for that one to get her claws into Dorrie, and Dorrie did love him, he was sure, and she needed him.

She should have been able to tell him she wanted to delay a family until they were away from married quarters. There were ways and means acceptable to the Church, Fr Doyle had told him. It was true they hadn't talked about the things that mattered and it was his fault. Dorrie was afraid of him. He groaned aloud at the thought, and a passing man glanced at him then walked quickly away.

His mind turned to Mrs Rafferty. The CO and the doctor would know how to deal with her after the padre had given them the evidence. They'd soon fix her without bringing Dorrie's name into it, or any scandal to affect the regiment.

A savoury smell drifted from an open doorway and he realised that he had eaten nothing since the dinner party last night. Last night! It seemed a lifetime ago. He looked up at a sign for Charlie's Chop House and went inside.

Later, fortified by a good meal, he walked on, thinking of Fr Doyle's words about his marriage vows and remembering the day he was told that Dorrie was flirting with married men and causing trouble. He knew she was only giving her flirty little looks as she always had. They meant nothing, but that one had manipulated her and used her to pay off old scores.

He dwelt on the picture the priest had drawn of Dorrie, innocent and vulnerable among strangers. My poor little love, he thought fondly. She didn't have a chance between that faggot and me bumbling along, not looking after her or seeing what was under my nose.

Even with the baby, she hadn't realised what she was doing. He recalled Fr Doyle saying to him, 'It would just have been a word, miscarriage, to you if you hadn't seen the foetus. The doctor probably suspected you and meant to shock you, but he was wrong to do it.'

I must put it all out of my head, Michael thought now, and we must start afresh. He took a cab the rest of the way home, wondering what had been happening since he left, and feeling guilty and ashamed that he had left Dorrie in such distress.

The house seemed quiet when he let himself in, but the head housemaid came into the hall. 'My wife . . .' Michael began, but the woman said nervously, 'The mistress left this morning, sir. I heard her tell the cabby to take her to the train station for Liverpool.'

For a moment Michael was silent with shock then, as he saw the curiosity on the woman's face, he made an impatient gesture. 'So she went ahead alone. Is there a message?'

'No, sir. She wore a veil and I think she'd been crying. She hardly spoke.'

'Of course. Upset about her mother,' Michael said. 'I meant a telegram.'

'No, sir,' she said again.

He picked up his hat. 'They'll have sent it to my office. I've been at the site office all day, arranging time off. Call me a cab, Jessie.'

He went to the post office and sent a telegram to Dr O'Brien, asking about Dorrie and requesting a speedy reply. He also sent a wire to the couple he had remembered they were due to dine with, regretting their absence due to family illness.

He went back to the house, suddenly exhausted, but feeling that he had done all he could to explain away Dorrie's flight. He felt it was important if they were to make a fresh start. The housemaid came to take his coat and he said, 'As I thought. Matters are not as bad as we feared.' He smiled. 'Mrs Farrell could have waited for me. I'm going to lie down. Call me if another wire comes.'

'Yes, sir. Please, sir, Cook wants to know about dinner.'

'I'll be in, but anything will do, tell her. I may travel tonight or it may be tomorrow morning,' he said, then went upstairs. He had time only to notice that the bed was made and everything in the bedroom and bathroom neat and orderly before sleep overcame him.

He was wakened for the telegram from Dr O'Brien, which said briefly, 'Dorrie at my house. Will expect you tomorrow. Love from us both.'

Michael decided to travel on the morning train and after a meal returned to bed and slept all night. Very early the next morning, after he had bathed and dressed, he packed a case with overnight necessities and left for Liverpool, telling the servants that he and his wife would return in a day or two.

He also left his uncle's address in case anyone needed to contact him. 'We're not entertaining anyone, are we, Cook?' he asked.

The cook, a large, gloomy woman, said, 'No, not till next week, sir, but a lot of things are being cancelled because of the King's death. Out of respect,' she added accusingly. She wore a picture of King Edward, framed in black, pinned to the white apron covering her ample bosom.

Michael left feeling rested and refreshed and ready to use any amount of loving patience to persuade Dorrie to make a fresh start, and to put their marriage on a different footing.

Chapter Twenty-Four

After Michael left, Dorrie crept under the bedclothes and drew them around her. She was shaking with cold and fright, unable to forget Michael's rage or the way he had looked at her. He hates me, she thought. I don't think he ever really loved me.

Mrs Rafferty was right. She said he only cared about himself. When it suited him he could become a civilian, but when we married he dragged me halfway across the country, away from everyone I knew, so he could play at soldiers.

And all that wild talk about his son. I was only a few weeks late. He must be mad. She sobbed afresh as she thought of him storming out with her supplies, determined to make trouble for Mrs Rafferty. She could even go to gaol and she's been my one true friend since I left Liverpool, Dorrie thought.

If only I'd stayed there, among people who loved and admired me. I could have married anyone I chose if Michael hadn't swept me off my feet. James Hargreaves, for instance. How changed he was from the plump, spotty youth dominated by his mother. The last time she saw him he looked entirely different. Slim and well dressed, with handsome features and a pleasant manner.

He was unchanged in one way though, she thought, feeling happier. He was still fathoms deep in love with her and always would be, even though he had gone through a form of marriage to have a live-in housekeeper. How he would have loved and cherished me, and how happy I could have been if only I'd married James and stayed in Liverpool, instead of throwing it all away for Michael.

She lay crying and brooding on her wrongs until she heard sounds downstairs and thought in alarm that Michael had returned, but then she realised it was only the maids doing the fires.

One of the maids tapped on the door. 'Are you ready for tea, madam, or do you wish for breakfast?' she asked. She was a new girl and Dorrie said brusquely, 'Just tea.' When it came she stopped the girl from drawing up the blinds and from pouring the tea, keeping her face hidden and saying, 'That will be all.'

After drinking a cup of tea, Dorrie went to the bathroom and was alarmed to see how red and blotched her skin was and how swollen her eyes with crying. She bathed her face repeatedly in cold water, but it made little difference so she washed and dressed, then dressed her hair with an Alexandra fringe and tied a heavy motoring veil over her face.

She hastily packed a case, then opened a locked drawer and swept some sovereigns into her purse before ringing for the maid to take her case down and call a cab.

When she went downstairs Jessie met her, looking anxious. 'Are you all right, ma'am?' she asked.

Dorrie nodded. 'Is the cab here? I must go right away,' she said, and Jessie carried her case out to the street.

At the station a well-tipped porter purchased her ticket and installed her in a first-class carriage. She was wearing a black coat and hat, fashionable mourning for King Edward, and her veil, but it could have been for personal reasons so she was left undisturbed on the journey.

She spent it brooding and indulging in fantasies and by the time the train reached Lime Street she had almost lost her grip on reality. She gave the cab driver the address of James's house and was almost hysterical when she reached it.

It was now nearly two o'clock on Saturday afternoon, and Anna and James had just finished a leisurely lunch. They had heard the cab drive up and walked into the hall.

Dorrie thrust a sovereign at the cabby, who hastily dumped her suitcase on the steps and drove rapidly away, while Dorrie stumbled weeping up the steps.

Anna opened the door, but Dorrie ignored her and rushed down the hall to fling herself into James's arms. 'Oh, James, James, I'm so unhappy,' she wailed. Instinctively his arms had closed around her and she dragged his head down and kissed him long and passionately.

He pulled away and looked about wildly for Anna. She was still holding the front door wide, stunned with shock.

'Anna,' he mouthed frantically over Dorrie's head, but Anna closed the front door and walked into the drawing room.

'James,' Dorrie was moaning. 'You won't be cruel to me like Michael. You'll love me and care for me, won't you, James?'

Stunned and embarrassed by the onslaught, he could only say helplessly, 'Dorrie, Anna,' thinking of nothing but the effect the scene had had on his wife.

Dorrie still clung to him like a limpet, babbling words of endearment and visions of the future, and he managed to half drag and half carry her into the drawing room. Anna stood by the window, her face stony, and he begged, 'Anna, help me,' then he tried to pull Dorrie's arms from around his neck and said to her, 'Dorrie, you're ill. I'm married to Anna.'

'Not really,' she screamed, 'she's only a housekeeper. Your marriage hasn't been consummated. You're free, James, free to love like you've always done,' and she clung closer to him.

A variety of emotions had gone through Anna's mind since she opened the door, but now she was consumed with hurt, anger and outrage. At the look on her face, James suddenly pulled himself together.

'Anna, will you call a doctor? She's not responsible for her actions. We'll have to deal with this together. Please, darling.'

She smiled at the unaccustomed word, 'darling,' and without a glance at Dorrie went into the kitchen.

Julia stood by the table, her fingers over her lips and her eyes wide. It was clear she had heard something, but Anna hoped not what Dorrie had said in the drawing room. She said calmly, 'Julia, my sister's having a brainstorm. Take a cab and go for Dr O'Brien. If he's not in, ask Mrs O'Brien to come and leave a message for the doctor. Don't bring Dr Hogan. Hurry, there's a good girl.' Julia seized her shawl and ran out of the back door.

Anna found that James had managed to disentangle himself from Dorrie and she was sitting on a sofa, silent now. James had also taken the pins from her large hat and he looked hopefully at Anna, but she shook her head and turned away. She felt unable to touch her sister, so James took off Dorrie's hat and she lay down and closed her eyes, as though exhausted.

With the veil removed, it was possible to see that the blotchiness of her skin had faded and been replaced by a waxen pallor and there were dark shadows beneath her eyes. Anna still kept her face averted from her sister, but James went to her and put his arms around her.

'Don't let this upset you, Anna,' he said tenderly. 'Something has happened and she's not responsible for her actions. This is some sort of nerve storm.' She laid her head on his shoulder and he gently stroked her hair with one hand while with the other he held her close. Dorrie lay as though dead on the sofa and soon they heard the noise of the cab bringing Dr O'Brien with Julia.

He bustled in. 'What's this? What's happening?' Then he

saw Dorrie on the sofa. 'God bless my soul!' he exclaimed. He bent over her, but her eyes remained closed and James put a chair for the doctor beside her, then pointed to the door and he and Anna went out quietly, leaving Dr O'Brien and Dorrie alone.

He took her pulse, then said loudly, 'Dorrie,' and she lifted her eyelids as though with a great effort. 'Why are you here? What's happened, girl?'

Tears filled her eyes and poured down her cheeks. 'Where's James?' she asked.

'What do you want James for?' he asked. 'More to the point, where's Michael? Have you travelled here on your own?'

She nodded. 'Michael hates me,' she said, with fresh tears. 'I came home to people who love me. To James.'

The doctor smothered an exclamation. 'Dorrie, you're living in the past, girl. That was all years ago. James is married to Anna now,' he said gently, but she shook her head.

'Not really. He only married her for a housekeeper. Mama said the marriage has never been consummated. He's still free.'

Dr O'Brien sprang to his feet, uttering an oath and his opinion of her mother. 'And for this rubbish you've left your husband and come rushing here on a wild-goose chase after a happily married man. I gave you credit for more sense, Dorrie,' he said.

At these forthright words she screamed, 'No! No!' and began to thrash about on the sofa.

The doctor gripped her wrists. 'Stop this,' he said firmly. 'Tell me, where's Michael and why did you leave him?'

She lay back limply, with tears again sliding down her cheeks. 'Michael hates me,' she said, 'and I hate him. He never wants to see me again.'

Dr O'Brien studied her, then said suddenly, 'How long is it

since you've eaten?' and he passed her a handkerchief.

'I – I don't know,' Dorrie stammered, taken by surprise. 'I suppose last night. The dinner party.'

'Did you have any breakfast? Or lunch?' the doctor demanded and she shook her head. 'Just lie there quietly,' he said, and went out of the room. He met his wife, who had travelled up in the cab with him and gone into the kitchen with Julia, as he entered the hall.

She drew him away from the door, her finger on her lips. 'I'm going to arrange for food for her. She's in a state of collapse,' he whispered, but she shook her head.

'Not here,' she said. 'Anna doesn't want anything to do with her, and I don't blame her after what I've heard. We'll take her back to stay with us, Paddy, until Michael gets here.'

'*If* he gets here,' he muttered dubiously, but she said, 'He will. He will. I'll tell them you want her at our house, under your eye,' and went back to Anna and James.

The doctor went back to Dorrie, who lay apparently limp and exhausted on the sofa, but Dr O'Brien was experienced enough to know that her nerves were like a coiled spring.

He opened his bag and poured a small amount of liquid into a medicine glass. 'Drink this,' he said authoritatively, putting his hand behind her head and holding the glass to her mouth. She drank meekly and as meekly allowed herself to be assisted to her feet when Mrs O'Brien appeared.

'You're coming home with us, love,' Mrs O'Brien said gently, shedding her own ready tears at the change in the pretty, happy girl she remembered. 'Doctor wants you where he can look after you.' Yet another cab was outside and Julia opened the front door and helped to put Dorrie in it. Anna and James did not appear, on the doctor's advice.

The doctor's potion made Dorrie languid and amenable, as Mrs O'Brien and Mary undressed her and put her to bed. They fed her with broth then she lay down and slept immediately.

A little later the telegram arrived from Michael and Dr O'Brien immediately sent an answer saying, 'Dorrie at my house. Will expect you tomorrow. Love from us both.'

'That should bring him,' he told his wife, but she said serenely, 'I'm sure he intended to come anyway, otherwise he wouldn't have sent the wire.'

When Michael arrived the next day Dorrie was still in bed, and before he saw her Dr O'Brien had a long talk with him. 'I can't get any sense out of Dorrie about what's gone wrong between you, so I hope you can tell me,' he said bluntly.

Michael gave him an edited version of the quarrel, omitting any mention of the embryo he had christened and buried. 'I was angry because she'd made a fool of me,' he said. 'I told her I never wanted to see her again, but I didn't mean it. I went to see the padre about that Rafferty one and he made me see it was as much my fault as Dorrie's.'

'In what way?' his uncle asked.

'Well, he made me see what her life had been here, with Anna always with her, and then I'd taken her among strangers and not looked after her properly. That's how that one got her claws into her.'

'She won't be able to rely on Anna now,' the doctor said with a sigh. 'I think her and James have got too much good sense to let it affect their marriage, but Anna's going to feel bitter towards Dorrie for a long time. You know what happened there?'

'Yes, my aunt told me,' Michael said. 'She blamed Dorrie's mother.'

The doctor gave his opinion of Mrs Furlong, and concluded, 'She's half mad and half bad. Can tell herself a lie and make herself believe it. She's another one to keep Dorrie away from.'

Michael groaned and hung his head. 'My poor little love.

What chance did she have? And me that should have looked after her blind to it all. Just pleased with myself making money, and what good is it to us now? I couldn't see what was staring me in the face.'

'Don't be blaming yourself too much,' Dr O'Brien said. 'Dorrie's a grown woman. She's got to take her share, but this should be a lesson for both of you. You did your best, Michael, even to leaving the regiment and I know how hard that was for you.'

'Maybe as well I did,' Michael said, 'with the way things are at Ballinane and Dermot's carry-on. He won't accept Home Rule, Mammy says. It's all or nothing with Dermot.'

'He's a hot head and an idealist, burning to right Ireland's wrongs, and it's a dangerous mixture. Our poor country, Michael, the land of saints and scholars. What's to become of it at all, at all?' The doctor sighed. They were silent for a moment, their thoughts far away, then the doctor said briskly, 'Now, will you take a word of advice, Michael?'

'I thought I'd had some,' Michael said with the ghost of a smile, but Dr O'Brien went on, 'Dorrie's a good girl, a gentle girl, without much belief in herself. She'll always believe that other people know better than her, so she's easily led. She'll always need a best friend. You must be that best friend, Michael.'

'How do you mean, Uncle?' Michael asked.

'I mean talk to her. Get her involved in what you're doing and planning. Don't decide something and then tell her. See what she thinks about the idea, and ask about her day, what she's been doing.'

'I don't think she'd be interested in the business,' Michael said doubtfully.

'How do you know? She might have some bright ideas that could help you. She's not a fool, y'know.'

'I know,' Michael said indignantly. 'Don't worry, Uncle. I've learnt my lesson. We'll make a fresh start when we go back and I'll make sure I talk to Dorrie about everything.'

'And keep her away from Liverpool for as long as you can. Although she won't be anxious to come back here. She'll want to forget this little episode as soon as possible,' the doctor said.

Dorrie was still in bed, but Michael sat beside her and they talked for hours, discussing the mistakes of the past and making plans for the future. Michael found Dorrie subdued but sensible. 'I can't believe I behaved like that,' she told him. 'I must have been mad.'

'Not at all, sweetheart,' he consoled her. 'Your nerves were overstretched and I was to blame, but it came to a crisis and you're over it now. Put it out of your head.' And she gladly agreed.

They stayed overnight and travelled back to London on Monday morning, after telling the O'Briens how grateful they both were.

'We'll come often to see you, but give Liverpool a wide berth for a while,' the doctor said, and his wife said hastily, 'And take care of yourselves, now.'

Michael had wired the time of their return to the servants, and warned Dorrie of her mother's fictional illness, so she was prepared for Jessie's sympathy. Michael told Eddy that he had been misinformed about Dorrie's affair and had 'flown off the handle' too soon, and everyone else seemed to have accepted the story of Dorrie's mother's illness so they were able to resume normal life without any scandal or gossip.

They both made a determined effort to make a fresh start. Dorrie had an enviable capacity for closing her mind to anything she wished to forget, and Michael, always extreme in his emotions, saw himself as the villain and Dorrie as an innocent victim and watched over her with loving care.

He took his uncle's advice and told her more about the business and he was surprised at how quickly she grasped the details. He was even more surprised when she said after looking at some plans, 'I think the kitchen should be bigger and the other rooms smaller. In these houses the woman would only have a daily help, if that, so she'd spend most of her time in the kitchen.'

Michael looked at her with respect and realised that there was a new maturity about Dorrie, as though she had passed through a crisis and had at last become a woman rather than a girl. Their relationship was on a different and firmer footing after this and Michael felt able to tell Dorrie what had happened to Mrs Rafferty.

He had been to see the padre again and had learned that the evidence he had taken there had justified a search of Mrs Rafferty's house. They had found a large cache of her supplies and an amazing amount of money. Some of this she had admitted was the result of blackmail.

Her husband, newly promoted to sergeant-major, was informed of his wife's activities and also told that he was being transferred to a small unit in Scotland. He was furious at what was, in effect, demotion. As the padre told Michael, 'The civilian police have not been informed. It was felt that it was an Army matter and her husband's anger and the move to Scotland would be sufficient punishment for Mrs Rafferty.'

'It all seems like another world,' was Dorrie's only response.

Mrs Furlong, absorbed in her own health, knew nothing of the visit to Liverpool and Dorrie said nothing of it in her letters. She had not written to Anna or received any letters from her, and she and Michael made no plans to visit Liverpool.

Chapter Twenty-Five

When the cab had driven away with the O'Briens and Dorrie, Anna and James went into the garden and sat on a secluded seat. Anna's face was white and she was obviously upset, but James put his arms around her and held her close.

'Don't let it distress you, love,' he said tenderly. 'She's ill. No one in their right mind would behave like that. Perhaps she's inherited it from your mother.'

'My mother!' Anna said bitterly. 'I feel dirty, James,' she wept. 'The thought of them discussing our most private affairs. I hate it.'

'Never mind,' he soothed her. '*We* know they're wrong and that's all that matters.'

'But she's right, not about the housekeeper part, but she is your real love,' Anna said. 'Ours is just a – a friendly marriage.'

'Not as far as I'm concerned,' James said. 'Oh, Anna, surely you've realised that it's you I love. When I've seen Dorrie I've only been concerned in case you were hurt. She means nothing to me.'

He bent his head and kissed her long and passionately, and Anna responded as ardently. 'And I love you, James,' she murmured. They kissed again, and when they drew apart Anna said, 'I was feeling so hurt and miserable and now I feel so happy. I was so sure that you still loved Dorrie. And so was she, evidently,' she added.

'God Almighty, I never got such a shock in my life,' James exclaimed. 'But I'm sure it wasn't really anything to do with me personally. I think she'd had a row with Michael and rushed

395

off to Liverpool, then realised she didn't want to go to your mother and she'd lost touch with all her old admirers. Then she thought, James Hargreaves, I know where he is, and by that time she was in such a state she came storming up here.'

Anna shook her head, smiling now. 'I don't think that was it, but I wish I'd known how you felt about her.'

'I never felt I could speak about it because I thought you were still in love with Eugene and I had to keep my side of our arrangement. I was fairly sure you'd got over him when you spoke like that about that gardener, but then I didn't know how to broach the subject of Dorrie,' James said.

Anna smiled. 'We've both been very foolish, pussy-footing around, afraid to mention Eugene or Dorrie in case we upset each other,' she said.

James kissed her again. 'Isn't that proof that we loved one another from the start, but we were too blind to see it?' he said. 'I think Dr O'Brien was right. We both needed our fantasies while we were so unhappy, but after we married, at least as far as I was concerned, I was too happy to need them.'

'And so was I,' Anna said. 'I was worried because I couldn't remember Eugene's face or feel anything when I thought of him. I suppose I was ashamed that I tipped him overboard so quickly, as though I was very fickle.'

'You won't be fickle with me, will you?' James asked, and they kissed again.

'I'll never forgive Mama or Dorrie though,' Anna said. 'Prying into our affairs and discussing us.'

'Neither will I,' James said. 'All that shunting my wardrobe back and forth and all for nothing.'

Anna laughed, as he had intended, and said fondly, 'Oh, James, you are a fool.'

'I know,' he said, 'but if I put it in your room again can it stay there?' Anna blushed and turned to kiss him, which was answer enough. They sat for a while, Anna's head on his shoulder and their arms around each other, savouring the bliss of having all barriers removed and being able to be truly husband and wife.

The May day had been sunny and pleasant, but as the sun sank a cool wind sprang up and after another lingering kiss they went back into the house.

Julia came back to the kitchen from Frances's room. 'I didn't know what to do about the meal, so I'm after putting a hotpot in the oven,' she said. 'It'll be nearly ready now.'

'That's a good idea, Julia,' Anna said. 'What an afternoon. We never know what'll happen next, do we?'

'We don't,' agreed Julia, 'but she'll be grand with the doctor and Mrs O'Brien, poor lady.'

Anna went to see Frances, who was now completely bedridden. 'Is the pain bad?' she asked, but Frances told her that Julia had given her her medicine and she was fine.

'Rosa's medicine?' Anna asked, but made no comment when Frances nodded.

'I could hear all the coming and going,' she said. 'Julia said your sister was having a brainstorm. What happened to her?'

'She quarrelled with her husband and took off for Liverpool, then realised she couldn't upset Mama, so she came here. Dr and Mrs O'Brien have taken her to their house. Her husband *is* the doctor's nephew, after all.'

'And is he coming after her?' Frances said.

'Yes. He'll be upset about her travelling all this way on her own. She was in a state when she got here, but Dr O'Brien knew what to do.'

'Good job she came here,' Frances said. 'If she'd gone to your ma he'd have had two of them on his hands.'

'We'll keep quiet about it, Frances. Better if Mama doesn't know she's even been,' Anna said, and Frances agreed.

Anna left her a little later, knowing that she had given the sick woman plenty to mull over during her pain-filled hours.

After their meal, Anna and James sat close together on a sofa, talking endlessly about the occasions when they had avoided comments about Dorrie or Eugene, and realising how mistaken they had been. 'It's a wonder we aren't still doing it, even after what happened today,' Anna said. 'You know, pretending it hadn't happened and talking about the price of fish.'

They laughed heartily, then James said, 'We've wasted an awful lot of time just being afraid to hurt each other, but we've always been good friends, haven't we?'

'Yes, and these have been happy years for me, James,' Anna said. 'We said when we married that we liked and respected each other and that has just grown stronger with me. It's a good foundation for marriage, isn't it?'

'I agree, love, but I think almost right away it was more than that for me. I think I loved you from the beginning, although I didn't realise it, or didn't want to because of those barmy ideas of romance.'

'It was the same for me,' Anna said. 'What fools we were, James.'

'I know, but never mind, we know now,' he said, kissing her fervently.

Later, when they went to bed, it seemed quite natural for James to follow Anna into her bedroom, then as they lay in bed she went as naturally into his arms. The tide of passion long-denied rose fiercely in both of them and when it was over and they lay spent and happy Anna said wonderingly, 'I thought I wouldn't know what to do, but it was so easy.'

James covered her face with kisses again. 'Anna, I love you. I'm the luckiest man alive,' he said, and she realised that tears were sliding down his face. She said nothing though, only kissed him tenderly and held him close to her. O God, let me make him happy, she prayed silently. Let me make it up to him for that awful childhood.

They slept, then woke to make love again, then slept again. They rose early and bathed and dressed, but over breakfast they were unable to stop smiling at each other.

Every touch of their fingers as they passed the breakfast things to each other sent a tingle through them, and Julia watched them indulgently. 'Sure they're terrible happy this morning,' she told Frances. 'They must be glad the doctor took that madwoman away.'

'Dorrie was a lovely girl, Julia,' Frances said. 'Real beautiful and a lovely nature. Always the pleasant word and a nice smile.'

'She didn't look beautiful yesterday,' Julia said. 'Far from it, and screeching like a fishwife. The poor missis was properly upset.'

'She must have taken strange ways living down in London,' Frances said. 'Or else she's taken after her mother. God forbid. Still, the main thing is Anna and James are happy. God knows they deserve to be.'

'Indeed, aren't they kindness itself to everyone,' Julia said. 'I say a prayer every night for Dr O'Brien for finding me this place. I'm so happy here.'

'And *I* pray every night that they'll be blessed with a baby. It's the one thing needed to make life perfect for all of us,' said Frances. 'You know, girl, I never thought I could care about anyone the way I care about James, because he's like a son to me, but I love Anna just as much. If I could have picked anyone in the whole world for him it would have been her.'

'Indeed, as God made them He matched them,' Julia said, then she said practically, 'Are you all right, Miss O'Neill, or will I pour out some medicine for you?'

'No, I'm fine. A good talk does me as much good as a bottle of medicine,' Frances laughed.

The following weeks were like a honeymoon for Anna and James. Their nights were filled with passion and they drifted through the days in a state of bliss, although they managed to appear normal.

'I feel as though I'm living on two levels,' James told Anna. 'On one, I'm the sober chief clerk chasing an insurance claim for crates damaged in transit, and on the other, your husband in a permanent state of bliss. What was that Shakespeare play where stardust was thrown in their eyes?'

'*A Midsummer Night's Dream*,' Anna said, laughing. 'It's the same with me, except I mix up the two levels. I'm altering clothes for the poor children, or helping in the kitchens, and all the time I'm smiling like an idiot.'

Even when the first joy died down, they were still blissfully happy, enjoying every day. They did a great deal of entertaining and visiting, but Anna felt unable to face visiting her mother. She saw her aunt at church and Clara asked why they had not been to the house in Westbourne Street.

'I found that Mama was spreading lies about our marriage,' Anna said. 'I don't feel I can visit her, at least not yet, but you are always welcome at our house. You know that, Aunt Clara.'

'Yes, I know. I don't blame you, Anna. She'll never learn and she'll finish up with nobody,' Clara said. 'Even Dorrie hasn't been to see her for ages, too busy with her new friends, and she only writes scrappy letters now.'

Anna looked troubled, but she said defensively, 'She hurt me very much, Aunt Clara. If I went to see her now I'd feel a hypocrite.'

'I understand, Anna. I know your mother's pretended to be ill for years, but she really is ill now. Brought most of it on herself of course. More worry for my poor brother.'

Anna repeated the conversation to James and told him she was uncertain what she should do. 'With Father away it doesn't seem fair to leave it all to Aunt Clara,' she said. 'As the elder daughter I should take the responsibility, but I don't know how I could speak to her, let alone kiss her.'

James considered for a moment, then said, 'If you don't go, Anna, you'll be worrying about it all the time. We could go for a brief formal call. I'll do most of the talking and if Clara's there she'll help.'

'Why should you, James?' Anna said. 'It's not your problem.'

'Of course it is, if it's worrying you,' he said. 'And she *is* my mother-in-law, no matter how unwillingly.' He grinned, then said, 'On a practical level, she won't dare to be rude to you if I'm there, and you can just talk about – what is it you say – the price of fish.'

They went and the visit passed off easily. Anna could see that her aunt was right. Her mother looked shrunken and coughed constantly although the weather was mild. Anna spoke to her aunt in the kitchen. 'Has the doctor seen her?' she asked and Clara shrugged.

'She won't have Dr O'Brien because he's been right about her for years, and I think the other fellow, Dr Hogan, is useless. Just tells her what she wants to hear. That she must rest and take care of herself. When has she ever done anything else? Light, nourishing food, no exertion and no excitement.'

'Is it too much for you, Aunt Clara?' Anna asked. 'I feel I should take some responsibility.'

'No, I do what's necessary and no more,' said Clara. 'She's got Nelly waiting on her hand and foot. Why should you, anyway? She's never given tuppence for you, it's always been Dorrie this and Dorrie that. Well, let her come and take responsibility for her mother. Anyway, my brother'll be home in a couple of months. Put it out of your head, Anna.'

Anna took her advice and found little time to dwell on it since her life was so full. In addition to their many friends and the garden, she was becoming more and more involved in working for the poor. When she was single she had gone with Kate Deagan to help to prepare dinners for destitute children, and it had been a sad day for her when she had had to withdraw, no longer able to face the shame of being unable to donate money, as the other women did. As soon as she had her own money after her marriage she returned enthusiastically to the scheme and also altered the unwanted clothes donated for the children.

'I don't know why you bother, Mrs Hargreaves,' one lady said. 'You know they usually finish up in the pawnshop anyway.'

'Yes, but the children should enjoy wearing them while they can,' Anna said hotly.

One of the organisers, a Miss Bentley, a friend of Eleanor Rathbone, was nearby and she said, 'I do agree, Mrs Hargreaves. All little girls like to look nice, it makes no difference that they're poor.'

'They're only used to rags. These clothes are sent to cover their nakedness,' the first woman said. Miss Bentley and Anna exchanged a glance and from then on were firm friends. Anna attended a meeting held by Eleanor Rathbone, who was now the first woman to be a Liverpool City Councillor, and agreed with her aims and ideals, although Anna was less concerned with wider issues, such as women's suffrage.

She felt that she was bursting with energy and happiness, and James told her he felt the same. 'I feel as though I could move mountains,' he said. Their nights of passion continued and they were not surprised a few weeks later when Dr O'Brien confirmed that Anna was expecting a baby.

'Due late March, beginning of April, I'd say. It's early days yet,' he said. 'I'm delighted, Anna, and I know you and James are. This baby will have a good start in life. Just be sensible. Don't behave like an invalid, but don't do too much. No lifting or stretching, and eat well.'

'I won't have much choice,' Anna laughed. 'Julia will surpass herself. I still feel guilty that you sent her to me and you could have had all this lovely food yourself.'

'No, no. Mary suits us very well. I enjoy myself at other people's tables, but meals here are chancy affairs. I never know when I'll be called out.'

'I wonder whether it'll be a girl or a boy,' Anna said happily. 'Either will be welcome,' she added hastily.

The doctor sighed. 'Yes, this is one I can be completely happy about,' he said. 'Too often down there round Great Homer Street I know half the babies delivered won't see their first birthday. They don't have a chance.'

'I know. It's not fair,' Anna said. 'But Miss Rathbone says it shouldn't happen in a wealthy country like this.'

'Yes, but what's her solution?' the doctor said and went on before she could answer, 'Rowntree found that young couples marry, rent a room or rooms, and are reasonably comfortable while there's only two of them and even up to two children. With every child after that they become poorer and more desperate and the children have less chance.'

'Miss Rathbone says the country should give them money for each child. She says we could afford it.'

'She doesn't say they should limit their families? That's the usual cant,' Dr O'Brien said. 'How can they, Anna? It's all right talking about a safe period, but how can they work it out? It takes them all their time to survive, to find enough to eat and keep a roof of some kind over them. Someone said complete abstinence is the answer. Rubbish. It's the only free pleasure they've got.'

Anna hid a smile, thinking that Mrs O'Brien would have a fit if she heard him, but she agreed with him.

'But you don't want to think about sad things now, Anna. You want to enjoy this moment,' he said. 'But I suppose you felt fairly sure anyway.'

'I told James I did, but we didn't want to get too excited until I'd seen you. Thank you, doctor,' Anna said.

She stood up and to her surprise the doctor came round and kissed her. 'Congratulations!' he said. 'I'll take care of you, never fear.' As he opened the door for her he whispered, 'This'll put paid to Dorrie and your mother, anyway.'

Anna felt as though she was walking on air as she walked home. She glanced at the watch pinned to her dress. James had said he would try to come home at lunchtime and she hurried her steps. A few minutes after she entered the house he arrived.

'Well?' he asked.

She nodded, smiling. 'Late March or early April,' she said, and he swept her into his arms, murmuring her name and kissing her.

They were still not talking coherently when Julia looked in, 'Will I serve the lunch?' she asked.

'Yes. Nectar and ambrosia, please,' James said, then at Julia's puzzled face he said, 'It's all right. I'm only joking.' As soon as Julia went he said eagerly to Anna, 'Should we tell them? Julia and Frances. They should be the first to know.'

Anna would have liked to hug her secret to herself for a while, but she knew James was bursting to announce the news. I could tell him, she thought, so he should be able to tell someone, so she agreed.

Luckily, Julia had gone to Frances's room, so they followed and James sat down by Frances's bed and took her hand. 'We wanted you to be the first to know, and Julia,' he said.

Before he could say any more Julia gasped, 'You're going to have a baby,' and burst into tears, flinging her arms round Anna. James found that Frances was in his arms, kissing him and crying and he looked round the three weeping women.

'God Almighty, I'll never understand women,' he said. 'I thought you'd all be happy.'

'We are,' Anna told him. 'That's why we're crying.' He shook his head, smiling, and she said suddenly, 'Listen, we won't bother with a proper lunch. You stay and talk to Frances, James, and Julia and I will do some sandwiches to have in here – if that's all right with you, Frances?'

Frances nodded, wiping her eyes, and Anna and Julia rapidly made beef and egg-and-cress sandwiches and a pot of tea. As Anna had looked at Frances and James together she had suddenly remembered how much Frances had helped him to endure and then recover from his awful childhood. Our baby will never experience anything like that, she thought thankfully.

Before he returned to the office James asked if he could tell Henry Mortimer. 'Of course, whoever you like,' Anna said gaily. 'I think I should tell Aunt Clara before she hears it elsewhere, though.'

'We could call into Westbourne Street tonight,' said James. 'Tell Aunt Clara and make a formal announcement to your mother.'

When James returned he told Anna that he had only told Henry his news. 'Plenty of time to tell others,' he said.

He refrained from telling her that Henry had advised this. 'I'm sure everything will be fine, but you never know with the first,' he said. 'We had two false starts and it was embarrassing. The fellows felt awkward. Better to wait, then toast the baby in style.'

James had brought home a bottle of champagne and before

their meal he carried Frances into the dining room to lie on a sofa while they all drank to the good news. Julia and Anna had prepared a special meal and after it neither Anna nor James wanted to go out, especially not to Westbourne Street, but they knew it must be done. 'I wish we hadn't got to go,' Anna groaned. 'I'd love to just sit in the garden.'

But she was glad later that they had. Her mother's face was a study when they made their announcement. Conflicting emotions passed over it and she stammered, 'But I thought . . .'

'Yes. You thought,' James repeated in a challenging voice, but she took refuge in easy tears, which could have been regarded as tears of joy. Clara was genuinely delighted and showered them with questions about when the child was due and their choice of names.

'We haven't had time to discuss that yet, Aunt,' Anna said, laughing. 'I only went to Dr O'Brien this morning.'

'You'll be well looked after with him. I've every confidence in *him*,' Clara said, with a glance at her sister-in-law, but Mrs Furlong said nothing.

Anna wrote to her father and to Isabel with her news, but not to Dorrie. 'I feel mean about Michael,' she said to James, 'but I know Aunt Clara and my mother will write to tell Dorrie.'

She felt well and happy and immediately started to sew and knit a layette for the baby. Everything she made was shown to Frances, who talked constantly of holding the baby in her arms, but it was obvious to all of them that she was sinking fast.

Dr O'Brien gave her morphia to ease her pain. 'It can't matter now,' he told Anna. 'She won't last long enough to become addicted to it, and I've room to increase the dosage if she gets worse. It's wonderful she's lived so long, with the strain on her heart from the pain.'

Anna wept. 'We'll all miss her, but James will be broken-hearted,' she said. 'She's like a mother to him and she's done so much to help him.'

'Yes, and you've both been good to her. She had a rotten start in life, a selfish family, but her life changed for the better when James's mother died.'

'So did his,' Anna said grimly. 'He'd have been lost without Frances.'

'Well, she's been happy for many years, especially since you came to this house. She told me she didn't think she'd ever be as fond of anyone as she was of James, but that was before she met you. Don't cry now, Anna. Think of how happy you've made her, holding court there in that lovely room.'

'And scoring off her sister-in-law,' Anna said, drying her eyes and smiling.

'Have you heard from your sister?' the doctor asked abruptly.

Anna shook her head. 'No, but I haven't written to her,' she said. 'I know Mama or Aunt Clara will give her the news about the baby.'

'I thought she might have written to apologise,' Dr O'Brien said, 'but she's probably trying to pretend it never happened.'

Anna smiled. 'How well you know us all,' she said.

It was true that Dorrie had dismissed the entire episode from her mind, including the quarrel with Michael. He was anxious to make a completely fresh start and never mentioned it, but something had gone from their marriage, never to be replaced.

The letters from her mother and her Aunt Clara were a shock to Dorrie and made her face the fact that she had made a fool of herself. Clara's letter, in particular, made the position clear. 'Anna and James,' she wrote, 'are not people who make a great show, but I have always thought them very well suited and happy together. This will be a crowning joy for them. Your mother seems to dislike the prospect of being a grandmother, but your father will be delighted at the news.'

Mrs Furlong thought Anna and James very vulgar and brazen. 'The sort of news which is whispered by one lady to another was announced by both of them with your brother-in-law ready to bite off my head if I spoke,' she wrote.

In bed that night Michael heard Dorrie sobbing and took her in his arms. 'I'm so unhappy,' she sobbed. 'I don't think I will ever have a baby. It's God's judgement on me for what I did.'

'Nonsense,' Michael said. 'It's early days yet. You've got to give yourself time to get Rafferty's poison out of your system and then who knows? We could have a houseful in no time.'

'Oh, Michael,' Dorrie said, but she thought he was probably right and began to take Epsom salts, 'as much as would lie on a sixpence', in an effort to speed up the process.

Michael told her she should write to congratulate Anna and she made a vague promise, with no intention of keeping it.

Chapter Twenty-Six

Isabel's wedding had been planned for early October. Anna had made Isabel's wedding dress in white satin, and bridesmaids' dresses for herself and Wilma, now a pretty blonde ten year old, in pink silk.

Isabel's first question to Anna when she heard the news was whether she would still be able to be bridesmaid. 'Of course,' Anna laughed. 'I might have to let out a seam or two, but I'll be quite respectable.'

'That was selfish of me,' Isabel said. 'I'm truly happy for you and James, Anna, but I would hate to have anyone but you for my bridesmaid. It's going to be hard enough . . .' Her eyes filled with tears.

'I know,' Anna said sympathetically, 'but try to think of it as though your Papa is held up by storms or something.'

Isabel's brother Willie, now a ship's officer, was in the Mediterranean with his ship and unable to be at the wedding and Isabel said sadly, 'Willie won't be able to take his place either, but my uncle is so proud to be giving me away, having no family of his own, and Mama is being so brave. I must keep my chin up too. Papa would expect nothing less.'

Before the wedding took place, Anna's father arrived home in late August and was appalled by the change in his wife. He came to see Anna, to tell her that he had asked Dr O'Brien to see Mrs Furlong but he had refused.

'Said he couldn't do it, Anna, unless she herself decided she wanted another opinion. Professional etiquette! Poppycock! I've taken matters into my own hands and told Dr Hogan

I'd like a second opinion. It's your mother's life that's in danger here, Anna.'

Dr Hogan had agreed to call in Dr O'Brien, but he could suggest nothing that was not being done. 'The bronchitis is too far advanced,' he said, and after a discussion with the two doctors Captain Furlong decided to ask the shipping company if his wife could accompany him on his next voyage, which was to the West Indies.

'Do you think it will do any good?' Anna asked Dr O'Brien.

He shrugged. 'It will get her away from the winter fogs of Liverpool, which will help the cough, and it will help your father. He'll feel he's done all he can.'

The company readily gave permission to such a long-serving captain, and Mrs Furlong set off with her husband in September. She seemed to blossom in the excitement of preparation and departure and Anna felt able to kiss her and hope that she came back restored to health.

'Yes, and you must take care, Anna. Do nothing that risks your health or your baby's.' Anna was always pleased to remember that they parted on such amicable terms.

She was dismayed to find how quickly she was growing in size, and before the wedding she had to let pieces into the side seams of her bridesmaid's dress. The midwife told her that she was probably carrying a lot of water.

Isabel came to Liverpool again before the wedding and confided in Anna that she dreaded leaving her mother. 'We won't be far away, because the schoolhouse is only a few minutes' walk from our cottage. John and Mama get on so well too, but Mama and I have always been more like sisters,' Isabel said. 'With Papa away so much I shared the responsibility of the boys, so even when I was quite young Mama and I talked almost as equals.'

Anna sighed. 'Dorrie and I envied you your happy home,

Isabel. Mama and Aunt Clara were always quarrelling and Father always seemed stern and unapproachable. He laid down the law and we submitted, sometimes not very willingly in my case.'

'Like when you wanted to train as a teacher or go out to business,' Isabel said. 'Mind you, I always felt it was your mother who made the decisions, although your father didn't realise it.'

Anna was amazed. 'D'you know, I didn't either, but as soon as you said that I realised it was true,' she said. 'Mama has always had this idea of herself as a Society lady, with her daughters at home to wait on her. Dorrie was quite happy to do so, but I hated being so dependent on her whims. I've always blamed Father. I can see how she did it, but I never even suspected, and you did.'

'They say the onlooker sees most of the game,' Isabel said. 'But I might be wrong, Anna. I say too much without thinking.'

'No. I don't think so. I've seen a different side to Father lately. He often walks over to see us when he's ashore and we're really close now, more than I would have believed possible. I'm sure James will be a good father.'

'He will,' Isabel said warmly. 'The more I know James, the more I like him. Your child will have a good father *and* a good mother.'

Anna's size did not continue to increase at the same rate, but on the wedding day she was thankful for her huge bouquet of bronze chrysanthemums, clove carnations, honesty and gypsophilia, with long trails of smilax hanging from it.

Isabel was also pleased with the effect of her sheaf of lilies against her white satin dress, cut on classical lines with a small train. She wore her mother's wedding veil of Brussels lace and Wilma strutted along beaming and waving her posy at the schoolchildren who lined the route from the church.

It was a truly happy occasion. John was a very popular headmaster and the uncle who had given Isabel away lived in the Big House and had provided the cottage for the Jenson family. He had arranged a lunch in the village hall for the women and children of the parish and free drinks at the public house for the men when they returned from work.

There were not very many guests at the lavish reception in Alfred's house, although there seemed more because Mrs Jenson's brothers were all large men with loud voices, and their wives were large too.

They were all gentle and protective towards Mrs Jenson, 'Our baby sister,' one of them boomed to Anna. Isabel had told her that they had all helped with money, and by looking after Jonathan and David, who travelled to Manchester for school. 'They invite them to their houses after school and the boys are free to take any number of friends with them. They all have a feast and tips from the uncles. It helped the boys no end to settle into school.'

'I can imagine it would make them very popular,' Anna had laughed.

Alfred was the brother nearest in age to Mrs Jenson, and the quietest. He rarely left her side, taking his position of being in loco parentis very seriously.

'It's a pity Willie's missing this,' James said to Anna. 'Hard on Isabel, and her mother too.'

'Yes, but giving Isabel away meant such a lot to the uncle,' Anna said. 'And Isabel said he's been like a father to them since they came to live here.' She laughed, looking to where Wilma was dancing to entertain a group of guests. 'Willie can give Wilma away. I don't think he'll have very long to wait. Six years from now she'll be thinking of wedding bells with a selection of young men to choose from.'

She shivered suddenly. 'Are you cold?' James said anxiously.

'No. A goose walked over my grave, as Mrs O'Brien would say. The first ten years of this century have gone by so quickly. I wonder what the next ten will bring.'

'Nothing very dramatic I suppose,' James said. 'More motor cars and bigger ships. If Mr King manages to fly across the Mersey and back in his bi-plane with Mr Compton Patterson in November, we might all have our own bi-planes.'

'Not me,' Anna said, smiling. 'I think if we were meant to fly we'd have been given wings.'

James shrugged. 'More trouble between employers and men, almost certainly,' he said. 'I can see that brewing now, but let's forget all that today.'

As the celebrations continued, Isabel and John departed for a honeymoon in Stratford, fulfilling a long-held wish to visit Shakespeare's birthplace.

After a very happy day, Anna and James stayed overnight with Mrs Jenson, and when they returned home they found a letter from Anna's father. He wrote that her mother seemed much stronger. The sea air and the sunshine were good for her and all the crew made much of her. Under her supervision even the cook was producing good meals, so they were all grateful to her and had rigged up a fan in her cabin.

'That's good!' Anna exclaimed. 'The fact that she's supervising the cook. I thought she'd be too weak to do anything but lie on a deckchair.'

'Shows the sea air and sun have made her stronger,' James said. 'Must be a relief to your father, Anna.'

The midwife came regularly to see Anna, and seemed perturbed about her size, although she maintained it was probably caused by water.

One day in November, after examining Anna, she said she

413

would like Dr O'Brien to see her. 'Nothing to worry about,' she said hastily. 'It's just that I think I can hear two heartbeats. You could be carrying twins, but I'd like the doctor to see you. Any twins in your family or your husband's?'

'Mama spoke once about an aunt who had twins, but she and the twins all died. I don't know of any others,' said Anna.

'Don't be thinking you'll die, or your babies,' the midwife said. 'We've come a long way since then. Ask your husband about his family.'

Dr O'Brien agreed with the diagnosis and was equally reassuring. 'We'll keep a closer eye on you, because they might come a bit early,' he said, 'but you'll be fine.'

'I feel quite well, just tired,' Anna said.

'That's nothing to worry about. You're a strong, healthy girl, with plenty of good food available to you, able to rest when you need to. And don't forget, medicine's very different now to how it was in your aunt's day. How do you like the idea of twins?'

'It was a bit of a shock at first,' Anna admitted. 'But we were both hoping you'd confirm it. I'm really excited about the prospect now, and so is James.'

She asked him to look in on Frances. 'I think she's in a lot of pain, although she tries to hide it,' she said.

'Yes. I'll go and have a cup of tea with her while you get dressed. Does she know about the twins?'

'No, I wanted to be sure first,' Anna said.

The doctor said he would leave it to Anna to tell Frances. 'It'll do her the world of good.'

Frances was delighted with the news and so was Julia, but they and James insisted that Anna should rest more. She found that she tired more quickly because of her bulk and was glad to obey them, but she occupied herself by making a second set of baby clothes. She sat with Frances while she sewed flannel binders and barras and more long dresses and petticoats. She also made more short dresses, for when the babies would be 'shortened' at three months old. Boys wore dresses too, until they went into trousers at three years old, so she made the dresses fairly plain. 'If I have girls I can easily add more lace and embroidery,' she told Frances, who seemed stimulated by watching her.

Anna also talked to Julia about having more help in the house because she could do so little now and Frances needed so much care. 'I'd like to get someone settled in before the babies are born,' she said. 'Poor Frances is going to need more and more care and I don't want her to suffer because we'll be kept busy with the babies.'

'Ah, sure I don't think Miss O'Neill is long for this world. I don't think she'll live to see the babies,' Julia said, wiping away a tear.

'Oh, Julia, I hope you're wrong!' Anna exclaimed. 'Dr O'Brien warned me about this, but Frances is such a fighter.'

'I know, m'm, but sometimes she does be in such awful pain I think it would be a mercy if God would take her for her own sake. I have to give her some of Rosa's medicine as well as the doctor's before she gets any ease.'

Anna's face was white and Julia exclaimed, 'I've upset you, m'm, and I wouldn't do that for the world!'

'No, no. I'm just facing facts, Julia. Better to do it now than later,' Anna said. She asked if Julia could recommend anyone and Julia said she knew of a young girl, Imelda Burns, who lived near her relatives in Stitt Street.

'She's a quiet, clean girl,' she said. 'She was in a place near Breck Park, but her mammy brought her home to look after her grandmother. She died a few weeks ago.'

'If she suits you, Julia,' Anna said. 'You'll be working with her. You wouldn't like an older woman?'

'Ah, no. Sure I'd be nervous with her,' Julia said.

It was arranged that Mrs Burns and Imelda would come to see Anna and she told Frances that she was getting a girl to help with the babies. 'I know why you need more help,' Frances said in her weak voice. 'You're a good girl, Anna.'

Imelda was a quiet, timid girl and Anna liked her immediately and had no hesitation in offering her the job. Before she could answer, her mother said eagerly, 'Isn't it a dream come true for her to be working here? I know well what a grand place it is.'

Anna said firmly to Imelda, 'Before you decide, Imelda, Julia will show you your room, won't you, Julia? I'll be with Frances.'

They came back to Frances's room and were introduced to her, Mrs Burns talking volubly about the party her neighbours would be attending on Boxing Day.

Imelda said nothing, but her eyes were shining and Anna said quietly to her, 'What do you think, Imelda? Will you come?'

'Yes please, miss,' Imelda said and blushed at her mistake, but Anna only said, 'We'll have a very quiet Christmas this year. No parties, but I think you'll be happy working with Julia. Frances approves of you too.'

'Yes. Just be a good girl and do what Julia tells you,' Frances said, but her voice was weak and she closed her eyes.

Anna looked at Julia. 'Will you take Mrs Burns and Imelda into the kitchen for a cup of tea, Julia, and talk to Imelda about the work.' Julia gestured to the woman, nodding at Frances, and they crept quietly from the room.

Imelda learnt quickly and was a great help, so Anna felt less uneasy about leaving so much to Julia. She and James did scarcely any entertaining now, although Aunt Clara came occasionally for a meal.

One evening in late November she came uninvited and told Julia that she wanted to see James, but his wife must not know. 'Just say that a lady has called to see him. Don't say it's me.' Puzzled, but obedient, Julia gave the message quietly to James.

He found Clara looking very agitated. 'It's about Anna's mother,' she said without preamble. 'A man came from the shipping office and he asked for the nearest male relative. I told him that was you, but I didn't want him coming here upsetting Anna. I said I'd tell you.'

'Sit down, Aunt Clara,' James said gently. 'Now what has happened?'

'She's died. Died at sea and been buried at sea. Only ill twenty-four hours. My brother is going ahead with the voyage,' she said. 'I'd not long had a letter from him saying how well she was.'

'Yes, we had one too,' James said. 'It was good of you to come here with the news, Aunt Clara.' He stood up and poured a glass of sherry for her, before going to break the news to his wife.

'Poor Father,' was Anna's first thought. 'Just when he thought she was getting better.'

They tried to persuade Clara to stay the night, but she insisted on going home. 'Nelly's there on her own and she's very upset. She really loved your mother, Anna.'

James took her home and when he returned Anna said, 'I'm glad that Mama and I parted on good terms, but I'd be a hypocrite if I said I felt much grief, James, although I wish I could comfort Father.'

'His work will be his comfort and the thought that he did all he could to make your mother happy,' James consoled her.

A few weeks later a letter arrived from her father. He said that his wife had seemed better than she had for years in the weeks before her death. 'Well and happy, almost like in the first years of our marriage,' he wrote, 'but the fever developed suddenly. I sponged her with cold water and the fever subsided. She became calm and lucid and told me how much she had enjoyed the voyage and how much better she felt, then quite suddenly she passed away.' The letter went on to tell them that he would be home in about two months' time and to urge Anna to think of her unborn child and not allow herself to become upset.

Anna wept when she read the letter, but for her father not her mother.

She was more upset about Frances, who was becoming weaker every day and needing more nursing. James suggested engaging a nurse, but both Julia and Anna felt it would upset Frances to have a stranger doing the intimate tasks that Julia did for her.

'Melda's such a good little girl we can leave Julia free to just look after Frances,' Anna said, but James was concerned about Anna, who looked pale and tired.

Margaret Mortimer and Maggie Doyle, née Deagan, offered to help, but Clara provided the solution. She had been invited for Christmas Day and it was now only two weeks away, so she offered to come to stay at once. Nelly could go to relations and she would close the house. Anna was glad to agree. She felt lethargic and queasy, so she was eating little, and she had a constant pain in her back. She was unable to walk far or to stand for any length of time.

Although Dr O'Brien was always cheerful and reassuring, she knew by the frequency of his visits that all was not as well as he pretended. The midwife came twice a week to see her too, but she told her no more than the doctor.

Anna concealed her misgivings from James. He already worried about her so much, and also he was worried about

Frances. Even the lightest invalid diet, carefully prepared by Julia, seemed more than she could manage and she grew steadily weaker.

Christmas was a very quiet holiday for them. Frances was sleeping a drugged sleep for most of the time now, and during the day Anna lay on the truckle bed beside her. Julia slept there at night, in case the pain woke Frances, and she now spent more time in the kitchen, cooking and talking to Melda and Clara.

'You need a break from the sickroom,' Clara said bluntly, but Julia only said, 'Sure I don't begrudge a minute I'm with her. She's a grand woman.'

Two hours after midnight on the first day of January, Frances died. She rallied briefly, enough to know that James was beside her, holding her hand, then she smiled and gently died. James and Anna and Julia had truly loved the indomitable little woman and their grief was deep and sincere, but James's was overlaid with anxiety about Anna.

He had the funeral to arrange and all the business connected with death to fill his mind too. Anna could only rest and think sad thoughts of Frances and of James's childhood, and was able to fill her mind with little else, although Clara, who was still with them, tried to distract her.

'It's a good thing your mother died at sea,' she said one day. 'Otherwise your sister would have had to come home for her funeral and you'd have had to meet her.' She paused but Anna said nothing, so she went on, 'I don't know what's gone wrong between you, Anna, but I know you don't write to each other. Surely your mother's death should unite you.'

'I don't want to talk about her, or to see her ever again, Aunt,' Anna said in a way that closed the subject.

In London, Michael had a similar conversation with Dorrie as Christmas approached. 'Don't you think we should write to

James and Anna?' he said. 'You know, dearest, the season of goodwill. It will be a sad Christmas for you and for Anna, both grieving for your mother. Surely that should draw you together?'

Dorrie turned her head away without answering, and Michael said more firmly, 'I know you don't like to talk about Liverpool, but we'll be sending presents to my aunt and uncle and to Aunt Clara. Surely it's time to bury the hatchet and send something to your sister.'

For answer Dorrie burst into loud sobs, and Michael took her in his arms. 'Dorrie, Dorrie, don't cry. I'm only trying to help. I think this feud is bad for you and now with Anna expecting . . .'

She sobbed even more, saying that Anna had everybody there in Liverpool, all fussing about her. 'I only have you, Michael. If you turn against me and take her side I'll have nobody. I'd rather be dead.'

Michael, alarmed by the storm he had aroused, promised that he would never write without telling her, and would never again ask her to write to Anna and James.

He was on her side, although he didn't really see any sides, and would always support her in whatever she wanted to do. When she had become calm and reasonable they talked of other things and Michael vowed to himself that that was his last attempt to reconcile the two sisters.

Chapter Twenty-Seven

Anna dreaded the remaining eight weeks or so of her pregnancy, but it was only three weeks later when she was wakened by a severe pain, then another. She woke James as the pain came again and she felt as though she was being split in two.

Within minutes, it seemed to her, the room was full of people. Dr O'Brien leaning over her and pricking her arm with a syringe, then Mrs O'Brien and the midwife on either side of her, moving and lifting her gently as they made up the bed.

She heard Mrs O'Brien saying, 'Yes, I delivered hundreds of babies in my nursing days in Dublin. Twins too,' and she managed to gasp weakly, 'James?'

'Getting the cots ready for your babies. Him and Julia. You'll be fine now, Anna,' Mrs O'Brien said soothingly. The pain came again and now it was Dr O'Brien beside her.

She lost all sense of time and place as she tossed about in anguish, drawn up to a peak of agony, when she could hear someone screaming, then the blessed relief as the pain receded and she slipped down again, only for the agony to return minutes later.

She was briefly aware of the nurses speaking to her, urging her to do something, but she was too tired.

Then Dr O'Brien spoke to her sometimes, and a tall Scotsman, bending over her saying, 'Hang on now, lassie. Nearly there.'

She was unaware of how much time passed before the fiercest pain of all attacked her and she realised that the screaming woman was herself.

The pain receded and Dr O'Brien was bending over her, saying urgently, 'Anna, Anna, open your eyes.' With a great effort she lifted her eyelids and he held a baby up before her. 'Your son,' he said. 'And you've a lovely daughter too.' She tried to speak and he said, 'Yes. Both perfect,' and her eyes closed again. She drifted in and out of consciousness, unaware of all the frantic activity around her.

At one stage she realised that James and Dr O'Brien were lifting the foot of the bed, and it remained tilted because bricks had been placed beneath it, but it was all like a dream to Anna. Free from pain now, she was living in a half-world, hovering on the edge of eternity, and nothing they could do could rouse her.

James was constantly beside her, holding her hand, stroking her face, and talking to her, but she was unable to respond. At one stage he said to her, 'The babies' names, darling. Margaret Frances and John Patrick. Is that right?' and he was delighted when she lightly pressed his hand. She was unaware of the reason for the question, that her babies were also fighting for their lives in the next bedroom and were to be christened in case they lost the fight.

The baby girl was the smaller and weaker of the two and the nurse estimated her weight at three pounds and the boy's at four pounds. As soon as they were born their bodies had been rubbed with warm olive oil and they had been wrapped in flannel and cotton wool, then swathed in shawls before being put into cots warmed by hot water bottles, before a roaring fire.

A nursing mother had been found who expressed breast milk as the babies were so weak, and Mrs O'Brien soaked a boiled rag in it and tried to persuade the tiny boy and girl to suck milk from it.

Dr O'Brien came in to see them. 'How are they doing?' he asked.

'The girl's making better shape than the boy, but she needs it more. I'll try him with a dropper,' his wife said. 'What about Anna?'

He put his hands over his face and groaned. 'I'm going to lose her, Maureen. She's lost too much blood. Even Dr Fraser couldn't help.'

'No, you're not, Paddy,' she said firmly. 'The bleeding's stopped, hasn't it? You're just exhausted, that's all.' Julia came into the room with a bucket of coal and Mrs O'Brien said, 'Would you bring the doctor a glass of brandy, Julia, please? He's tired out.' She brought it within minutes and he drank it as quickly.

A few minutes later Fr Kavanagh arrived, summoned by Clara, and baptised the babies before going in to Anna to administer the last sacrament and recite the prayers for the dying.

'These prayers are not just to help her on her journey to the next world,' he said. 'They are also prayers for her recovery if it is God's will. We will all be praying for that.'

Clara had also despatched a telegram to Dorrie and Michael. 'Twins, boy and girl, arrived prematurely. Anna has been given Last Rites. Clara.' They can't say they weren't warned, she thought grimly. I can do no more and if they come it may rouse Anna, if only to make her angry.

The doctor's brief moment of despair had vanished and he plunged with renewed vigour into trying different remedies. Anna was forced to drink beef tea from a feeding cup and fed with raw lamb's liver, cut into tiny slivers and flavoured with herbs and disguised in cream by Julia. He also gave her so much iron that James was alarmed.

'Doctor, what's happening? Her teeth have turned black!' he exclaimed.

'Only the ferrous sulphate,' the doctor said. 'She must have

423

it. Her teeth will be all right.' He talked to Julia, who sent Melda for fresh liver and beef and marrow-bones, and with endless patience and care concocted food that would strengthen Anna and restore her blood.

They knew that her slow climb back to health had begun when she asked James about the babies, although her voice was still only a thread.

James carried each baby in turn to Anna and held them so that she could see them, although she was too weak to hold them. James lifted her hand so that she could touch the face first of Margaret Frances, then of John Patrick. 'So small,' she whispered, and he replied, 'Yes, but tough,' smiling at her.

He took the babies back to the midwife, then went into another bedroom and collapsed in a storm of tears, overcome by the long days of pent-up emotion and worry and now the relief. He quickly recovered, and went back to Anna.

Dorrie and Michael were away from home when the telegram arrived, visiting a business acquaintance, but they returned home the next day. Meanwhile, Clara had been waiting for a reply and was furious when none came, but fortunately said nothing.

Dorrie was feeling very cheerful and confident as they drove home. She knew she had sparkled and been a success at the house party and she felt that she was an asset to Michael's career.

They were both smiling when they walked into the house, but Jessie met them with a long face.

'A telegram came, sir, and I didn't know what to do. I didn't know whether to open it,' she said. She produced it and Michael and Dorrie read it together. Dorrie said nothing, but without warning she slipped to the floor in a faint.

Michael carried her into the drawing room and held smelling salts to her nose, and she sat up, then immediately sprang to her feet. 'I must go to her, Michael. Anna. Dying!' She began to weep and, still weeping, rushed to her bedroom and began to throw clothes into a suitcase.

'Pack for me too,' Michael said. 'I can't let you go alone. I'll fix up about trains and see Eddy.'

It was all quickly arranged and they set off for Liverpool, fearful of what they would find.

Michael thought it wiser to book into the Adelphi before driving to the house, but Dorrie was trembling so much that he had to support her as they approached Rosemount. 'At least the blinds are not down,' he encouraged her. 'The worst hasn't happened.' But he was as nervous as she was.

Clara opened the door. 'At last,' she said grimly.

'How is she?' Dorrie gasped.

'Still very ill, but while there's life there's hope.'

'And the babies?' Michael asked.

'Holding their own,' Clara said, her grim face softening. 'Nobody knows I sent for you, only Mrs O'Brien,' she said. 'Anna hasn't been fit to be told. Follow me. I'll go and warn James.' She stalked upstairs and they followed, Michael helping Dorrie.

At the door of Anna's room Clara stopped and put a finger to her lips, then went in alone. When she beckoned them in a minute later James, who had been sitting beside Anna, had risen and moved aside. Dorrie and Michael stared in horror at Anna, at the purple smudges beneath her eyes and her almost bloodless lips, her face as white as the pillowcase.

Dorrie ignored James and flung herself on her knees beside the bed and kissed Anna. 'Annie, Annie,' she wept, laying her face beside Anna's on the pillow.

Anna lifted her hand to Dorrie's back. 'Don't cry, Dolsie,' she said in a weak voice, using a long-forgotten pet name from their early childhood.

Dorrie wept even more bitterly and Michael said gently, 'You'll upset Anna, love,' so she lifted her head and dried her eyes.

Michael and James had already shaken hands and James had said quietly that they were more hopeful now. They moved away from the bed, leaving Dorrie holding Anna's hand, her eyes brimming with tears, and Anna smiling at her but too weak to talk.

'But she looks so ill. I never saw anyone so white!' Michael exclaimed.

'I know, but there's a definite change for the better,' James said. 'God knows I've been in despair many a time over the past few days, but now I feel Anna has come back to us. She's been unconscious most of the time, but yesterday, when she managed to ask about the babies for the first time, I felt sure the tide had turned. Dr O'Brien has been wonderful. Everybody has. I can never thank them enough.'

Anna had drifted off to sleep and James took Michael and Dorrie to see the babies. Nothing could be seen of them but their tiny faces, cocooned as they were in shawls, with the shawls even drawn up over their bonnets.

'John Patrick, and Margaret Frances,' James said proudly. 'They've already been christened. Clara was godmother to Margaret and Mrs O'Brien godmother to John Patrick. The Patrick is after your uncle, and Frances, of course, after our Frances, but the first names are just because we like them.'

He had greeted Dorrie stiffly, but avoided looking at her and addressed himself to Michael, but Dorrie, subdued and tearful, seemed scarcely to notice. She asked if she could sit with Anna again and James took Michael downstairs and introduced him to Julia.

'Will I take up some tea and sandwiches for the lady, sir?' Julia asked when she discovered that Dorrie was upstairs.

'Good idea,' James said. 'You don't mind if I go back myself, Michael? Clara and Julia will look after you.' Julia was laying a spotless cloth over a bowl and he paused to ask, 'Is that for my wife, Julia?'

'Yes, sir, it's herring with chopped watercress in cream. Herring is very nourishing and the doctor says there's iron in watercress.'

'Julia has done as much as anyone to help Anna,' James said to Michael. 'The food she's prepared has made all the difference. Even made raw liver palatable.' He smiled at Julia and went upstairs.

'He's uneasy if he's away from her for five minutes,' Clara said. 'But you can't blame him. The fright we've all had.'

'I'm not over the fright I got myself when I saw her,' Michael said. 'Can she really recover?'

'I think she will now. I think she's turned the corner, although we're not out of the woods yet,' said Clara. 'I'm relieved the way things have gone, Michael. I sent that wire without telling them and I expected Anna to refuse to see Dorrie, but even if it just roused her in anger I thought it would be worth it. And James felt the same as her, I know.'

'Yes, I didn't expect him to take it like this,' Michael admitted.

'Of course, I don't know what happened,' Aunt Clara said, looking at him hopefully, but he said nothing. 'I tried to get Anna to make it up,' she went on, 'but she said she never wanted to see Dorrie or talk about her again, so I said no more.'

'I didn't have any better luck with Dorrie,' was all Michael said on the matter, but he added, 'Thank God they both feel differently now.'

Julia brought tea and sandwiches and James appeared a few minutes later. 'Anna has taken some beef tea and some egg custard,' he said. 'I feel like a new man.'

'Good. I've booked into the Adelphi, so we'll leave soon to get a meal there,' Michael said, but Clara protested loudly and James said, 'I can see it would be helpful if you slept there, the way things are, but you must have your meals here.' He smiled. 'Julia will already have planned them.'

'I'll go and see Anna and tell Julia,' Clara said.

When the two men were alone, Michael said awkwardly, 'I don't feel we should accept your hospitality, James. I think you've been magnificent. You'd have been justified in showing us the door, but instead!' He shook his head.

James said quietly, 'After what's happened here you get things in perspective, Michael. To see someone dear to you as close to death as Anna was, well, it brings you up short. I swore if only she lived I'd be a better man, never do any mean action or anything to hurt anyone. I won't be able to keep to it, I suppose, but at least I've realised now what's important and what isn't. Life's too short to quarrel.'

'I wanted them to be friends again,' Michael said, 'and I tried to get Dorrie to write, but I'll admit it was chiefly because I knew it was secretly tearing Dorrie apart.'

'She's your wife. She must be your first concern,' James said, and shrugged, but Michael replied, 'Yes, but I know she was at fault and I was at fault for not seeing what was happening or taking proper care of her. You and Anna were the victims and nothing can alter that, I know. But I also know that, however much Dorrie tried to pretend, deep down she never stopped loving Anna.'

'It's all over now and Anna is willing to be friends again, so I think we can forget it and start afresh,' said James. 'Will you excuse me? I don't like to leave her for long.'

'Would you mind if I came with you?' Michael asked.

'Not at all. You can check on your wife too,' James said

with a grin. 'And we can have another look at the babies.'

Even in the short time since he had seen her Michael thought Anna looked a little better, or perhaps he had recovered from the first shock of her appearance. He could certainly look more attentively at the babies. James braved the midwife's glare to lift their bonnets a little to show that the girl had a fuzz of fair hair while the boy's hair was dark.

'They're not identical then?' Michael said.

'No. What they call fraternal twins,' James said, then in a burst of honesty added, 'I must admit we expected two boys or two girls, but we're delighted with these two. They've turned the corner too, thank God.'

'You've been through the mill, one way and another,' Michael said sympathetically, but Dorrie only burst into tears.

With a resigned look at James, Michael handed her his handkerchief and said firmly, 'Come downstairs with me, Dorrie. James wants to be alone with Anna.'

Dorrie and Michael were amazed to see the difference each day made in Anna's health. She was now able to nurse her babies and they improved as quickly. Michael used the time to explore business possibilities in Liverpool, after sounding James out about how he would feel if he and Dorrie moved back to the city.

'It's your decision, Michael,' James said. 'But what about the London business? Aren't you doing very well there?'

'We are, but the possibilities are good here. Liverpool is bursting at the seams. The city will take in all the little villages close to it, you'll see, and that means houses.'

'I agree, but what about London?' James asked.

'Eddy, my partner, is a grand man. His brother would like to come in with him but he hasn't the money. I can afford to drop my price for my share and maybe arrange a payment over time. I owe Eddy for the friend he's been to me in my troubles.'

'Your wife would settle here?' James said stiffly.

'She'd be delighted, but we wouldn't be on your doorstep,' Michael said. 'Dorrie will be able to shut away the London years. She can divide her life into compartments. No looking back, except perhaps at the pleasant bits,' he laughed.

James had been afraid that when Anna returned to normal she might remember the episode with Dorrie and decide that she wanted nothing to do with her, but, like James, Anna had been altered by her brush with death.

She welcomed Dorrie eagerly and bore with her tears and excuses patiently and lovingly. 'I just wasn't myself, Anna,' she sobbed. 'That woman was like Svengali.'

'She was an evil woman, but she won't do any more harm, will she?' Anna said.

'I can't believe that I let myself be influenced by her so much,' Dorrie sobbed. 'I was only used to good people like you, Anna.'

'It's all over now,' Anna said. 'We'll all make a fresh start.'

Anna closed her eyes and Dorrie exclaimed, 'I'm tiring you. James will kill me. How could I ever have believed that you were only his housekeeper, Anna?'

Anna had no intention of discussing her marriage, so she merely smiled with her eyes closed and Dorrie crept away.

Before Dorrie returned to London she and Anna spent hours talking together and it was clear to both of them that the girls they had been had gone, never to return. Life had altered both of them and they had matured in different ways, but enough of the affection and closeness of their young days remained to form the basis of a strong and enduring friendship.

Both had secrets from the other. Anna would never disclose her original marriage arrangement with James, or how Eugene and Dorrie came into it. And although Dorrie spoke of her fear that she would never have a child she said nothing about the reason for it, or the reason for the quarrel with Michael which caused her flight to Liverpool.

It was a supremely happy time for Anna. Matters of state and unrest in the city which would once have disturbed her passed her by as she sat in dreamy contentment, watching her children flourish.

When Frances died they had offered her room to Julia, but she had refused. 'No thanks, I'm grand where I am,' she had said. 'Especially now with Melda for company. The room will be grand for the babies, though.' And so it proved.

The two cots were placed in there and soon replaced with one large cot so that the babies could lie together. Although so tiny, Margaret was quickly established as the dominant character, her hands exploring John's face or pulling at his clothes while he lay back, smiling placidly.

Anna regained her full strength and the whole household revolved round the two babies, Margaret with blue eyes and straight blonde hair and John with darker eyes and dark curly hair.

Dr and Mrs O'Brien were frequent visitors and Mrs O'Brien told Anna that her illness had done them a good turn. 'The doctor always did too much and we're not getting any younger. He was pleased with the way Dr Hogan and the young locum ran things while he was here day and night, so he's promoted Dr Hogan and taken young Bligh into the practice as junior doctor. He can take things easier now.'

'I'm glad Father's decided to leave the sea,' Anna said. 'He and Clara went to Hull, but they found everything changed so they'll stay in Westbourne Street.'

'They wouldn't want to be far from the babies,' Mrs O'Brien said, looking fondly at them. 'And of course Dorrie and Michael are coming back to Liverpool,' she went on. 'Have you seen the house they've chosen?'

'Not yet, but I believe it's huge,' Anna said.

'A mansion! Not far from the river at Grassendale. Michael must have done very well in London to afford that,' said Mrs O'Brien. 'Quite far away, at the south end of the city, but of course they have that motor car.'

'James says he's laying the ground to do well here too,' said Anna. 'I'm very fond of Michael.'

'And so are we, and of Dorrie. She seems to have grown up at last. Did you hear about Maggie Doyle? She's expecting a baby after all these years.'

Anna smiled. 'Yes. Mrs Deagan would be delighted, wouldn't she? I'll be having another one sometime. Rosa, the gypsy who came to Frances, said I would have three children who would look after me in my old age.'

Mrs O'Brien looked shocked. 'You shouldn't be meddling in that sort of stuff, Anna,' she said.

'Only joking,' Anna said and changed the subject by telling her that she was planning a party to celebrate the twins' birth. 'About the date of King George's coronation, June the twenty-third,' she said. 'Dorrie and Michael will be in their new house by then. It will be to thank all the people who have been so good to us.'

'That's a nice idea,' Mrs O'Brien said approvingly. 'And you have a lot to celebrate, with all three of you so healthy.'

Before that happened, Rosa came to the house again and Anna gave her the clothes and the small sum of money Frances had left her. She added a substantial sum from herself and James.

'Your medicine gave Frances many hours free from pain and I'm grateful for that. My husband didn't know, or he would have been grateful too,' said Anna.

Rosa took her hand and seemed to go into a trance. 'Dark clouds are gathering,' she said in a dreamy voice. 'But you will always know happiness. A generation of young men will die, perhaps by a plague that attacks young men, perhaps by war.'

'When? Where?' Anna gasped.

'All over the world,' Rosa said, 'but you and your husband and three children will be safe.' Then she opened her eyes and sighed. She would say nothing more about her prophecy, but she offered to tell Julia's fortune. She told her she would marry and have two children. Her husband would be a delicate man who died young, but Julia herself would be rich and successful.

She left carrying a basketful of Julia's cooking and James returned a little later. They told him about Rosa's forecasts. 'I nearly laughed in her face,' Julia said. 'Where would I find a man who would give me half as good a life as I have now? I'd be mad to settle for a little house and a child every year and having to do what my husband told me to. Never!'

'But what about love, Julia?' James teased her, and sang, 'There is nothing half so sweet in life as Love's young dream.'

But Julia said scornfully, 'Sure I don't believe in all that. It's all just a con. I'll not be tricked by that into getting married.'

'Oh, Julia, you're too young to be so cynical,' Anna said. 'I'm sure you'll change your mind.'

James looked at Anna and smiled. 'We had odd ideas too, Julia,' he said. 'But we found out we were wrong. Believe me, there's nothing to beat a happy marriage. I hope you'll find that out too – but not just yet,' he added with a grin and Julia smiled at him.

'Ah, sure we none of us know what's in store for us, as Miss O'Neill used to say, Lord rest her.'

Neither Anna nor Julia spoke again about Rosa's other forecast of plague or war, considering it too fanciful.

433

Dorrie and Michael's new house was soon ready and they came to stay at Westbourne Street while the final preparations for moving in were made. Dorrie must have scarcely paused to greet her father and her aunt before she came rushing to see Anna, accompanied by Michael.

'Anna!' she cried, bursting into the room where Anna was just putting Margaret into the cot. 'I couldn't wait to tell you. I want you to be the first to know. I'm going to have a baby!'

'Oh, Dorrie, I'm so thrilled!' Anna exclaimed, flinging her arms round her sister, then as she saw Michael's beaming smile and shining eyes, she included him in the hug. 'Oh, isn't this lovely news? When?'

'January or February. I'm not sure,' Dorrie said. 'Could even be on the twins' birthday. Wouldn't that be lovely?'

'They'll be able to play together!' Anna exclaimed. 'Isn't it wonderful? I can't wait to tell James.'

'I'll be able to tell people now too,' Michael said, laughing. 'I didn't dare say anything before Dorrie told you, or she'd have murdered me.'

Dorrie and Michael had been in their new house for two weeks and most people had heard of the coming baby before Anna's party took place. It was held on a lovely sunny day. Captain Furlong and Clara came early and made a beeline for the twins, and then Dr and Mrs O'Brien arrived with Dorrie and Michael and Michael's parents, who were staying with them.

'You don't mind me bringing Mammy and Daddy?' Michael asked. 'Sure I couldn't keep Mammy away from a look at the twins. I think she's hoping they run in the family!'

'Could happen,' James said, and Anna added quickly, 'And the birth doesn't have to be like mine. That was just unfortunate, but don't let's talk about it. The babies are here and healthy, that's all that matters.'

'And most importantly, *you're* here,' James said, looking at his wife with love.

Henry and Margaret Mortimer arrived, and Anna's midwife and her husband were soon followed by most of the Deagan family. Winnie and Gerald with their little daughter; Luke and Jim with Norah; and Maggie and Walter, who seemed to glow with quiet happiness.

'I was so delighted to hear your news from Mrs O'Brien,' Anna said softly to Maggie as she kissed her. 'How pleased your ma would be. Congratulations, Walter.'

'Thank you,' they both said, and Maggie added shyly, 'We're not saying too much about it yet.'

'I understand,' said Anna. She looked over to where Dorrie was talking excitedly, the centre of a small group. 'Dorrie's telling the world about hers,' she added laughing.

'Everybody's different,' Walter said tolerantly.

More people were arriving and Anna and James went to greet them. Anna had originally planned the party as a thank you for the people who had helped them at the time of the twins' birth, but it had grown to include many friends from the church and then a wider and more mixed group of people, from all walks of life, whom she and James had met through their many interests. Friends, old and new, mingled happily.

Anna took the babies indoors to be fed, then Julia laid them at either end of the large twin pram on the path outside the windows. James arrived beside them immediately, closely followed by Dr and Mrs O'Brien and Isabel and John who had just arrived.

Baby John lay calmly, examining his hands, but Margaret, although so tiny, was twisting about, clutching at the pillow, seeming to try to pull herself up.

'I think she'll be a handful,' Isabel said laughing, 'but John won't give you any trouble.'

'He has his moments,' Anna said. 'He's not placid all the time, is he, James?'

'No, but they're both very advanced for their age,' James said proudly.

Isabel hid a smile. 'It's wonderful to see how their characters are already forming, isn't it?'

' "In our beginning is our end",' Anna said. 'I think that's probably truer than "Give me a child until he is seven". I think the real character shows through eventually.' She linked her arm in James's and said quietly, 'Certainly true of you, love.'

They had drawn back a little as the others hung over the pram, and James said, 'Frances always said there was nothing of my mother or uncle in me. I was just like my father. I hope she was right.'

'She was,' Anna said with conviction. 'Aunt Clara says I inherited nothing from my mother, all from my father. So that's good news for our children, isn't it?'

Before James could answer, Dr O'Brien was asking if he could take a baby and was picking up John Patrick. Mrs O'Brien followed him, shaking her head as he bore the child to a group nearby.

James bent over the pram. 'We can't leave you on your own can we, sweetheart?' he said dotingly to Margaret as he lifted her up. 'Would you like to come and meet the Deagans? They're splendid fellows.' He set off carrying his daughter, and Anna and Isabel were left by the empty pram and moved to sit on a garden seat.

'The proud father,' Isabel said smiling. 'He idolises them, doesn't he? I'll bet he'll spoil them.'

'Yes. I'll have to be the one to be firm with them,' Anna said. 'But I understand why. After the childhood he had, James could never strike a child. I won't either, but I'll set limits, let them know how far they can go. I think children need that.

We'll give them as happy a childhood as we can, but we have to prepare them for anything life throws at them.'

Isabel kissed her impulsively. 'How wise you are, Anna. I understand what you mean about James. He'll want to give them the childhood he never had.'

'Yes, and I'll see that Margaret has the freedom I didn't have,' Anna said.

John Holland returned to ask Isabel to come to meet someone and Anna went into the house to confer with Julia. When she came out she stood for a moment at the French windows, looking at her guests thronging the garden. The ladies in their pretty dresses and the young men mostly wearing light summer suits and straw hats, and all apparently enjoying themselves.

Suddenly she thought of Rosa's words, 'a generation of young men will die', and felt that a cloud came over the sun, but she dismissed the words immediately as nonsense. How could a plague attack only young men? And war was fought between two countries, not all over the world. She shook herself and went out to join her friends.

Isabel was talking to Agnes Carr, with whom Anna had attended Eleanor Rathbone's meetings, and Anna joined them. 'My life has been filled with the babies lately,' she said. 'But I will soon start attending the meetings again.'

'There's so much still to be done,' Agnes Carr said. 'Life is good for people like you who have understanding husbands, but so many women are still dominated by the men in their lives. Their situations haven't changed.'

'Life hasn't altered much for the poor, either,' Anna said. 'And it won't until we get the vote. Get the power to change things for people who can't fight for themselves.'

'I agree,' Isabel said. 'I can see how much of a difference the Old Age Pension, "the Lloyd George" as they call it, has made to the elderly people in the village. It's only a few shillings but it's independence for them.'

A friend claimed Agnes Carr's attention, and Dorrie approached Anna and Isabel, and linked her arms through theirs. 'Isn't this a lovely day and a lovely party?' she said. 'I feel so happy, don't you? It's like old times, the three of us together.'

'A lot has happened to us since then, Dorrie,' Isabel said, winking at Anna, 'but Anna and I have decided we're not to blame for any of it. It was all decided before we were born.'

She laughed, but Dorrie looked at her wide-eyed. 'I don't understand that. I'm not clever like you and Anna, but I think we've all been very lucky.'

Anna smiled down at her. 'We have indeed,' she said fondly. 'Now, where are the babies?'

'Dr O'Brien has John Patrick,' Isabel said. 'And James has just joined him with Margaret.' As she spoke there was a burst of laughter from the group.

'Let's go and join them,' Anna said. They smiled and moved towards the merry group surrounding James and the doctor.

Now you can buy any of these other bestselling books from your bookshop or *direct from the publisher.*

FREE P&P AND UK DELIVERY
(Overseas and Ireland £3.50 per book)

My Sister's Child	Lyn Andrews	£5.99
Liverpool Lies	Anne Baker	£5.99
The Whispering Years	Harry Bowling	£5.99
Ragamuffin Angel	Rita Bradshaw	£5.99
The Stationmaster's Daughter	Maggie Craig	£5.99
Our Kid	Billy Hopkins	£6.99
Dream a Little Dream	Joan Jonker	£5.99
For Love and Glory	Janet MacLeod Trotter	£5.99
In for a Penny	Lynda Page	£5.99
Goodnight Amy	Victor Pemberton	£5.99
My Dark-Eyed Girl	Wendy Robertson	£5.99
For the Love of a Soldier	June Tate	£5.99
Sorrows and Smiles	Dee Williams	£5.99

TO ORDER SIMPLY CALL THIS NUMBER

01235 400 414

or e-mail <u>orders@bookpoint.co.uk</u>

Prices and availability subject to change without notice.